THE LAST ISLAND AT THE END OF THE WORLD

THE LAST MURDER AT THE END OF THE WORLD

The Seven Deaths of Evelyn Hardcastle
The Devil and the Dark Water

STUART TURTON

THE LAST MURDER AT THE END OF THE WORLD

RAVEN BOOKS

LONDON · OXFORD · NEW YORK · NEW DELHI · SYDNEY

RAVEN BOOKS
Bloomsbury Publishing Plc
50 Bedford Square, London, WC1B 3DP, UK
29 Earlsfort Terrace, Dublin 2, Ireland

BLOOMSBURY, RAVEN BOOKS and the Raven Books logo
are trademarks of Bloomsbury Publishing Plc

First published in Great Britain 2024

A catalogue record for this book is available from the British Library

ISBN: HB: 978-1-5266-3495-5; TPB: 978-1-5266-3491-7;
WATERSTONES SIGNED EDITION: 978-1-5266-7399-2;
GOLDSBORO SIGNED EDITION: 978-1-5266-7924-6;
EBOOK: 978-1-5266-3493-1; EPDF: 978-1-5266-6508-9

2 4 6 8 10 9 7 5 3 1

Typeset by Integra Software Services Pvt. Ltd.
Printed and bound in Great Britain by CPI Group (UK) Ltd, Croydon CR0 4YY

To find out more about our authors and books visit www.bloomsbury.com
and sign up for our newsletters.

To Resa,

For having a heart twice the size of anybody else's. For being funny, even when you're grumpy. For listening. And caring. And the cups of tea. For smiling when I walk into a room. For the life that radiates out of you like sunlight. For being with me, even when it's not easy. You're my best friend, and the person I love most in the world. Next time you catch me looking at you, and you ask me what I'm thinking, it's that. It's always that.

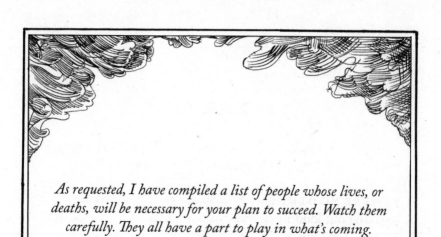

As requested, I have compiled a list of people whose lives, or deaths, will be necessary for your plan to succeed. Watch them carefully. They all have a part to play in what's coming.

THE INVESTIGATORS
Emory
Clara, Emory's daughter

THEIR FAMILY
Matis, Emory's grandfather
Seth, Emory's father
Jack, Emory's husband, deceased
Judith, Emory's mother, deceased

THE SCIENTISTS
Niema Mandripilias
Hephaestus Mandripilias
Thea Sinclair

VILLAGERS OF CONSEQUENCE
Hui, Clara's best friend
Magdalene, Emory's best friend
Ben, newest arrival to the village
Adil, Magdalene's grandfather

PROLOGUE

'Is there no other way?' asks a horrified Niema Mandripilias, speaking out loud in an empty room.

She has olive skin, and a smudge of ink on her small nose. Her grey hair is shoulder length, and her eyes are strikingly blue, with flecks of green. She looks to be around fifty, and has done for the last forty years. She's hunched over her desk, lit by a solitary candle. There's a pen in her trembling hand, and a confession beneath it that she's been trying to finish for the last hour.

'None that I can see,' I reply, in her thoughts. 'Somebody has to die for this plan to work.'

Suddenly short of air, Niema scrapes her chair back and darts across the room, swiping aside the tattered sheet that serves as a makeshift door before stepping into the muggy night air.

It's pitch black outside, the moon mobbed by storm clouds. Rain is pummelling the shrouded village, filling her nostrils with the scent of wet earth and cypress trees. She can just about see the tops of the encircling walls, etched in silver moonlight. Somewhere in the darkness, she can hear the distant squeal of machinery and the synchronised drumbeat of footsteps.

She stands there, letting the warm rain soak her hair and dress. 'I knew there'd be a cost,' she says, her voice numb. 'I didn't realise it would be so high.'

'There's still time to put this plan aside,' I say. 'Leave your secrets buried, and let everybody go about their lives as they've always done. Nobody has to die.'

'And nothing will change,' she shoots back angrily. 'I've spent ninety years trying to rid humanity of its selfishness, greed and its impulse towards violence. Finally, I have a way to do it.'

She touches the tarnished cross hanging around her neck for comfort. 'If this plan works, we'll create a world without suffering. For the first time in our history, there'll be perfect equality. I can't turn my back on that because I don't have the strength to do what's necessary.'

Niema speaks as if her dreams were fish swimming willingly into her net, but these are murky waters, far more dangerous than she can see.

From my vantage in her mind – and the minds of everybody on the island – I can predict the future with a high degree of accuracy. It's a confluence of probability and psychology, which is easy to chart when you have access to everybody's thoughts.

Streaking away from this moment are dozens of possible futures, each waiting to be conjured into existence by a random event, an idle phrase, a miscommunication or an overheard conversation.

Unless a violin performance goes flawlessly, a knife will be rammed into Niema's stomach. If the wrong person steps through a long-closed door, a huge, scarred man will be emptied of every memory, and a young woman who isn't young at all will run willingly to her own death. If these things don't happen, the last island on earth will end up covered in fog, everything dead in the gloom.

'We can avoid those pitfalls if we're cautious,' says Niema, watching lightning tear through the sky.

'You don't have time to be cautious,' I insist. 'Once you commit to this plan, secrets will surface, old grudges will come to light and people you love will realise the extent of your betrayal. If any of these things disrupts your plan, the human race will be rendered extinct in one hundred and seven hours.'

Niema's heart jolts, her pulse quickening. Her thoughts waver, only to harden again as her arrogance takes the reins.

'The greatest achievements have always brought the greatest risk,' she says stubbornly, watching a line of figures walking stiffly in the darkness. 'Start your countdown, Abi. In four days we're either going to change the world, or die trying.'

107 HOURS UNTIL HUMANITY'S EXTINCTION

TWO ROWBOATS FLOAT AT world's end, a rope pulled taut between them. There are three children in each with exercise books and pencils, listening to Niema deliver her lesson.

She's at the bow of the boat on the right, gesticulating towards a wall of black fog that rises a mile into the air from the ocean's surface. The setting sun is diffused through the sooty darkness, creating the illusion of flames burning on the water.

Thousands of insects are swirling inside, glowing gently.

'... they're held back by a barrier produced by twenty-three emitters located around the island's perimeter ...'

Niema's lesson wafts past Seth, who's the only person in either of the boats not paying attention. Unlike the children, who range in age from eight to twelve, Seth's forty-nine, with a creased face and sunken eyes. It's his job to row Niema and her students out here and back again when they're done.

He's peering over the edge, his fingers in the water. The ocean's warm and clear, but it won't stay that way. It's October, a month of uncertain temper. Glorious sunshine gives way to sudden storms, which burn themselves out quickly, then apologise as they hurry away, leaving bright blue skies in their wake.

'The emitters were designed to run for hundreds of years unless ...' Niema falters, losing her thread.

Seth looks towards the bow to find her staring into space. She's given this same lesson every year since he was a boy and he's never once heard her trip over the wording.

Something has to be wrong. She's been like this all day, seeing through people; only half listening. It's not like her.

A swell brings a dead fish floating by Seth's hand, its body torn to shreds, its eyes white. More follow, thudding into the hull one after another. There are dozens of them, equally torn apart, drifting out of the black fog. Their cold scales brush against his skin and he snatches his hand back inside the boat.

'As you can see, the fog kills anything it touches,' Niema tells her students, gesturing to the fish. 'Unfortunately, it covers the entire earth, except for our island and half a mile of ocean surrounding it.'

Magdalene's sitting cross-legged at the end of a long concrete pier, which extends into the glittering bay. Her hair is a tangled red pile, clumsily tied up with a torn piece of yellow linen. She looks like some ancient figurehead fallen off her galleon.

It's early evening, and the bay is filled with swimmers doing laps, or else hurling themselves off the rocks to her left, their laughter chasing them into the water.

Magdalene's staring at the distant rowboats with the children in them, a few flicks of charcoal adding them to the sketchbook in her lap. They seem so small against the wall of black.

She shudders.

Her eleven-year-old son, Sherko, is in one of those boats. She's never understood why Niema insists on taking them all the way to world's end for this lesson. Surely, they could learn about their history without being in touching distance of it.

She remembers being out there when she was a girl, hearing this same lesson from the same teacher. She cried the entire way, and nearly jumped out to swim for home when they dropped anchor.

'The children are safe with Niema,' I say reassuringly.

Magdalene shivers. She thought sketching this moment would alleviate her worry, but she can't watch any longer. She was only given her son three years ago, and she still mistakes him for fragile.

'What's the time, Abi?'

'5:43 p.m.'

She notes it in the corner, alongside the date, jabbing a pin in history, which flutters and rustles on the page.

After blowing away the charcoal dust, she stands and turns for the village. It was formerly a naval base and from this vantage it appears much more inhospitable than it actually is. The buildings inside are protected by a high wall, which is covered in ancient graffiti, weeds sprouting from long cracks. Vaulted roofs peek over the top, their gutters hanging loose, the solar panels made into glinting mirrors by the bright sunlight.

Magdalene follows a paved road through a rusted iron gate, the sentry towers so overrun by vegetation they look like hedges.

The barracks looms up in front of her. It's N-shaped and four storeys high, made of crumbling concrete blocks, every inch painted with jungle, flowers and birds, animals stalking through the undergrowth. It's a fantasy land, the paradise of people who've grown up surrounded by dry earth and barren rock.

Rickety staircases and rusted balconies grant access to the dormitories inside, none of which have doors or windows in the frames. A few villagers are hanging their washing over the railings, or sitting on the steps, trying to catch whatever scraps of breeze dare to clamber over the wall. Friends call to her cheerfully, but she's too anxious to respond.

'Where's Emory?' she asks, her eyes moving fretfully across the faces in front of her.

'Near the kitchen, with her grandfather.'

Magdalene heads into the space between the two wings of the barracks, searching for her best friend. This used to be an exercise yard for the troops, but it's slowly been transformed into a park by three generations of villagers.

Flowers have been planted in long beds along the walls, and the old collapsed radar dish has been patched up, and turned into a bird bath. Four rusted jeeps serve as planters for herbs, while lemon and orange trees grow out of shell casings. There's a covered stage for musical performances and an outdoor kitchen with six long tables for communal meals. Everybody eats together every night.

One hundred and twenty-two people live in the village, and most of them are in this yard. Games are being played, instruments practised and poems written. Performances are being rehearsed on the stage. Food is being cooked, and new dishes attempted.

There's a lot of laughter.

For a second, this joy loosens Magdalene's worry. She scans the area, searching for Emory, who isn't hard to find. Most of the villagers are squat and broad-shouldered, but Emory's slighter and shorter than most, with oval eyes and a huge head of curly brown hair. She once described herself as looking like some strange species of dandelion.

'Stay still,' demands Matis, peering around the statue he's sculpting of Emory. 'I'm almost finished.'

Matis is nearly sixty, which makes him the oldest man in the village. He's thick-armed, with grey whiskers and bushy eyebrows.

'I'm itchy,' complains Emory, struggling to reach a spot on her upper back.

'I gave you a break half an hour ago.'

'For fifteen minutes!' she exclaims. 'I've been standing here with this stupid apple for six hours.'

'Art always has a price,' he says loftily.

Emory sticks her tongue out at him, then resumes her pose, lifting the gleaming apple into the air.

Muttering, Matis returns to his work, shaving a sliver from the sculpture's chin. He's so close to it, his nose is almost touching the stone. His eyesight has been fading for the last decade, but there's nothing we can do. Even if we could, there'd be little point. He'll be dead tomorrow.

THREE

E MORY SEES MAGDALENE STRIDING towards her, one of her sketchbooks under her arm. She's moving stiffly, knotted by worry.

Emory doesn't need to ask what's wrong. Magdalene's fear for her son is obsessive. She sees snakes in every patch of grass, and strong currents under every stretch of calm water. Every splinter brings sepsis, and every illness is fatal. By Magdalene's reckoning, this island has a thousand clawed hands and they're all reaching for her child.

Abandoning her pose, Emory gives her friend a hug.

'Don't worry, Mags, Sherko will be fine,' says Emory comfortingly.

Magdalene's face is buried against Emory's shoulder, her voice muffled.

'One swell and –'

'They're at anchor,' says Emory. 'Niema's been taking kids out to world's end since before we were born. Nobody ever gets hurt.'

'That doesn't mean it couldn't happen today.'

Emory's eyes scour the blue sky. The sun is behind the volcano, which looms up behind the village, and the moon is already taking shape. In an hour, they'll be painted in shade.

'They'll be home soon,' says Emory kindly. 'Come on, we can help set the tables for the funeral; it'll take your mind off it.'

Her eyes flash towards Matis, guiltily. She should be spending these last hours with her grandfather, but he silently shoos her away.

Forty minutes later, the six schoolchildren come running through the gate, to the jubilation of the village. Magdalene engulfs Sherko, earning a squirming giggle, as the rest of them are hugged and kissed, bounced from adult to adult until finally they reach their parents, mussed and laughing.

The crowd murmurs warmly, parting to let Niema through. There are three elders in the village and they're all revered, but only Niema is loved. The villagers stroke her arms as she passes, their faces bright with adoration.

Niema bestows smiles on each of them in turn, squeezing their hands. The other two elders, Hephaestus and Thea, keep to themselves, but Niema eats with the villagers every night. She dances along to the band, and sings at the top of her voice during the chorus.

Niema lays a comforting hand on Magdalene's shoulder, then lifts her chin with a fingertip. Niema's a head taller than most villagers, forcing Magdalene to crane her neck to meet her gaze.

'I know what you're worried about, but I'll never put any of these children in harm's way,' she says, her voice a low rasp. 'There's so few of us left. We need every one of them kept safe.'

Tears brim in Magdalene's eyes, her expression awestruck and grateful. Unlike Emory, she didn't catch the hitch in Niema's voice, the faint drag of doubt.

After laying on a little more sentiment, Niema works her way back out of the crowd, gracefully linking arms with Emory on her way to the barracks.

'That should hold her for a few days,' she says, when they're out of earshot. 'Come fetch me next time she starts fretting. I was worried she was going to swim out to the boat.'

'I've been trying to calm her down for an hour,' says Emory, glancing at Magdalene's beatific expression. 'How did you do that?'

'I'm just old,' replies Niema brightly. 'Wrinkles look like wisdom to the young.' She lowers her voice conspiratorially, tapping Emory's hand. 'Come on, I have another book for you.'

Emory's heart leaps in excitement.

Arm in arm, they walk in companionable silence through the humid air, which is filling with fireflies as twilight descends. This is Emory's favourite time of day. The sky is pink and purple, the stone walls blushing. The fierce heat has receded to a pleasant warmth, and everybody's back inside the village, their joy pouring into the empty spaces.

'How's the carpentry coming?' asks Niema.

The villagers leave school at fifteen, and they're free to choose any occupation that's of benefit to the community, but Emory's been cycling through jobs for a decade, struggling to make headway in any of them.

'I gave it up,' she admits.

'Oh, why?'

'Johannes begged me to,' replies Emory sheepishly. 'It turns out I'm not very good at sawing wood, planing beams or making joints, and he didn't think a wonky cabinet was worth losing a finger over.'

Niema laughs. 'What about the cooking? What happened to that?'

'Katia told me that dicing an onion should be the start of my kitchen skills not the end of them,' says Emory dejectedly. 'Before that, Daniel told me that it didn't matter which way I held a guitar, because it would all sound the same. Mags lent me her paints for half a day, then didn't stop laughing for a week. It turns out I'm hopeless at everything.'

'You're very observant,' remarks Niema gently.

'What use is that when Abi sees everything we do anyway,' replies Emory disconsolately. 'I want to be of service to the village, but I have no idea how.'

'Actually, I've been wondering if you might like to come and work in the school with me,' says Niema tentatively. 'I'm going to need somebody to take over, and I think you'd make an excellent replacement.'

For a second, Emory can only frown at this suggestion. Niema's been the village's only teacher for as long as anybody can remember.

'You're giving it up?' asks Emory in surprise. 'Why?'

'Age,' replies Niema, climbing the rattling steps towards her dormitory. 'Teaching is wonderful for the soul, but it's a torment for my poor back. I've lived a long life, Emory, but my happiest memories took place in the classroom. Seeing the elation on a child's face when they finally understand a difficult concept is an astonishing feeling.' She pauses her ascent, glancing over her shoulder. 'I truly think you'd be good at it.'

Emory's excellent at spotting lies, and Niema's altered pitch makes this one particularly easy to pick out.

The young woman's eyes narrow suspiciously. 'And which particular qualities of mine make you think that?'

Niema's response is immediate, delivered with the brisk air of rehearsal. 'You're clever and curious and you've got a way with people.'

'Yes, they find me mildly annoying,' supplies Emory. 'Have you been talking to my dad?'

Niema falters, hesitation coming into her tone.

'He may have mentioned that you're between occupations again,' she replies. 'But I wouldn't have made the offer if –'

'Tell Dad I'm writing a play!'

Niema offers her a sidelong glance. 'You've been writing a play for a year.'

'I don't want to rush it.'

'There doesn't seem to be any danger of that,' murmurs Niema, pushing aside the tatty sheet that serves as the door to her dorm room.

This sheet has always been a quirk of hers. None of the villagers have a problem with empty doors, privacy being a concept that has remarkably little value when you're born with a voice in your head that can hear your thoughts.

Over the years, the villagers have done their best to repair the dorms, but there's only so much that can be done with a building this old. The concrete walls are riddled with cracks and holes; the grey floor tiles are shattered, and the beams supporting the roof are rotted. Mildew permeates the air.

Such decay is dreary, so the villagers beat it back with colour and life. Niema has put down a large rug, and placed a vase of freshly cut flowers on the windowsill. The walls are covered in paintings, spanning every artist who's ever worked in the village. Most of them aren't very good, leading Emory to wonder why Niema chose to preserve them. In many cases, the bare concrete would be an improvement.

Her shutters are closed to keep the insects out, so Niema lights a small candle on a rickety writing desk, its flickering glow falling across a half-written letter, which she hastily sweeps into a drawer.

'How much of this play have you actually finished?' she wonders, shielding the candle flame as she carries it to an overstuffed bookshelf beside an iron bed.

'Four pages,' admits Emory.

'Are they good?'

'No,' says Emory, dismayed. 'Turns out, I'm no better at writing plays than I was at making shoes, doing woodwork or building kites. My only skills seem to be noticing things people don't want noticed, and asking questions people don't want answered.'

'Oh, I wouldn't worry,' replies Niema, running her finger along the spines of the books, searching for the one she wants. 'Some people are born knowing what they're for, and others take a little longer to work it out. I'm one hundred and seventy-three, but I didn't start teaching until I was past eighty, and after that I never wanted to do anything else. It could be the same for you, if you give it a chance.'

Emory adores Niema, but the older woman talks about her age with so little regard that it's frequently insulting. None of the villagers will ever live half as long, and Niema's frequent allusions to her longevity can feel cruel. It's especially painful today, when her grandfather's so close to death.

'Aha,' exclaims Niema, pulling a tattered old paperback off the middle shelf. 'This one is called *Samuel Pipps and the Shrieking Spire*. Hephaestus found it in an abandoned train carriage a few weeks back.'

She pushes it into Emory's hand, catching the dismay on her face.

'I know you prefer Holmes,' she says, tapping the lurid cover. 'But give this a chance. You'll like it. It has three murders in it!'

Her voice has lowered to a hush. She knows I don't like people talking about murder in the village, or even using the word openly.

The last one took place over ninety years ago, just before the world ended. Two friends argued on a stairwell in Nairobi about a promotion. In a jealous rage, one shoved the other, who fell down the steps and broke her neck. The killer had just enough time to wonder if he could get away with it before the fog came pouring out of the ground. He died a second later, along with everybody he'd ever known, and most of the people he hadn't. There hasn't been another murder since. I've made sure of it.

Nobody else in the village is allowed to read these books, but I've made an exception for Emory, because their puzzles are the only things that can sate her devouring curiosity for any length of time.

'Remember, don't show it to anybody else,' says Niema, as they depart the room for the balcony. 'It'll only frighten them.'

Emory clutches the illicit book tight against her stomach. 'Thank you, Niema.'

'Pay me back by coming to the school tomorrow.'

Seeing the objection forming on Emory's lips, she hastily adds, 'Not because your father wants it. It's a favour for me. If you don't like it, you can go back to not writing your play.'

Niema's gaze flicks past Emory, causing the younger woman to follow it over her shoulder. Niema's son, Hephaestus, is stomping through the gate. His shaved head is bent low and his huge shoulders are rolled forward, as if the sky were pressing down on them.

Hephaestus only appears when things need fixing, or building. Most of the time, he lives alone in the wilderness, which is a thought so alien to Emory that even mentioning it fills her with unease.

'What's he doing here?' she wonders out loud.

'He's looking for me,' replies Niema distantly.

Emory's gaze returns to Niema's face. She thought she recognised all of her teacher's moods, but there's something playing on her features that's never been there before. It could be uncertainty, or it could be fear.

'Are you okay?' asks Emory.

Niema's eyes find her, but it's clear her thoughts are still with her son.

'Tomorrow night, I'm going to conduct an experiment that's failed every time I've tried it previously,' she says, feeling her way towards every word. 'But if it fails this time …' She trails off, her hands touching her stomach nervously.

'If it fails …' prods Emory.

'I'll have to do something unforgivable,' she says, watching Hephaestus disappear behind the back of the kitchen. 'And I'm still not certain I have the strength.'

FOUR

P EERING THROUGH HIS BINOCULARS, Adil watches
Emory and Niema talking on the balcony outside the barracks,
his heart thudding.

He's halfway up the east face of the volcano, having found his
way through the lava tubes that riddle this section. The ground is
ash, the rocks black with razor-sharp edges. It's as if his thoughts
are radiating out of him, scorching the land.

He's thirty miles away from the village, but he's chosen this
vantage point because it has a clean line of sight over the walls.

He can see Emory comforting Niema, placing an affectionate
hand on the older woman's arm. Every second of it burns, dripping
poison in his veins.

I don't counsel him towards kindness. There's no point. For the
last five years he's thought of nothing except revenge. I have to
nudge him to eat, and he does so impatiently, wrenching vegetables
out of the earth, or plucking armfuls of fruit from the trees.

He's fifty-eight, but he looks ten years older. His flesh is
pulled taut over cartilage and bone, his face gaunt, his black hair
turned grey and his brown eyes gone dim. His skin is blotchy and
sickly-looking, and his chest rattles when he coughs, hinting at the
sickness within. Under normal circumstances, I'd order him back
to the village to be cared for, or at least have company in his final
days.

Unfortunately, that's not possible. He's the island's only criminal,
and his punishment is exile.

'She thinks Niema's her friend,' he murmurs aloud, a habit of his
since he was banished. 'She has no idea what Niema's taken from
her.'

As Emory hurries away, clutching her book, Niema glances up at the volcano. She can't see Adil at this distance, but she knows he's there. I report his movements to her on an hourly basis. He's one of the few dangerous people on the island; she likes to know where he is at all times.

He sucks in a trembling breath and stares at his knife, imagining plunging it into her belly. He wants to see her eyes roll up in their sockets as the life goes out of them. He wants it more than he's ever wanted anything.

'And what good will revenge do you?' I ask. 'Have you thought about that? Have you considered what your life will be after you've killed somebody. How you'll feel?'

'I'll feel like the job's half done,' he replies. 'Niema's the worst of them, but I won't stop until Thea and Hephaestus are in the furnace. So long as they're alive, we'll never be free.'

'You're being ridiculous,' I say. 'Whatever you plot, I'll warn them about. You'll never get anywhere near them.'

You can't watch me forever, he thinks.

He's wrong about that. I was in his thoughts when he was born, and I'll be in his thoughts when he dies. I watched over his ancestors, and I'll watch over his descendants. There are so few humans left, they must be protected, and the village is the key to that. It must be safeguarded, at any cost.

FIVE

I T'S TWILIGHT, A CRESCENT moon cutting a hole in the dark
blue sky.

The village glows with candlelight, and reverberates with laughter and music. The band is playing, and most people – including Niema – are dancing in front of the stage. Matis's funeral is over. There's no need for grief. Not any more.

The remnants of the evening meal cover the long tables, which are lit by flickering candles and the mourning lanterns hanging overhead. They're made of coloured rice paper and strung on ropes between the two wings of the barracks. There's a lantern for every person in the village, and each one contains a scrap of paper on which they've written a kindness Matis did for them.

This is the way they revere the dead. They remember what they offered the world, and what everybody else has to do to fill the gap. There are no prayers here, no thoughts of an afterlife. The reward for a good life is the living of it.

Matis is at the centre of the long table, surrounded by his oldest friends. They're laughing and reminiscing, knowing their own days are nearly at an end, too. Everybody dies on their sixtieth birthday, whether they're healthy or not. They enjoy their funeral, then go to sleep as normal. At some point in the night, their hearts simply stop beating. After a lifetime of service, dying painlessly in their beds is the least I can give them.

Emory walks out through the iron gate in the high wall surrounding the village, onto the concrete pier, leaving the sounds of celebration behind.

Tears are rolling down her cheeks, but she doesn't want anybody to see her being selfish. Unlike many of his generation, her grandfather actually made it to sixty. He's spent every day in service to the village and will pass away without regret.

Knowing when he's going to die has afforded him the luxury of long goodbyes. For the last week, he's seen everybody he wants to see. Everybody he cares for knows how he feels about them, and he – in turn – is full of their love. There is nothing left unsaid.

Emory can only hope to die as fulfilled, but grief presses against her chest, tearing at her heart.

Her mother died from a fever when she was twelve, and her father seemed to drift away with her. Her grandmother was long dead, so it was Matis who read Emory stories at night and gave her jobs to do during the day; mindless, thankless things to keep her from dwelling on the pain of her lost family.

Even now the clink of his chisel hitting stone brings her comfort, and the idea that she won't hear that sound again is unbearable.

From the pebbled bay to her left, she catches a rhythmic hammering. It's much too dark to see what's causing it, but she has a fairly good idea.

Moving carefully, she follows the tapping around four moored boats, where she finds Seth repairing the hull of the Broad Bottom Packet by the light of a small lantern. The tide is in, and the waves are nipping playfully at his heels. Alerted by the crunching pebbles, he casts her a quick annoyed glance.

He has a heavy brow above a crooked nose and a square jaw that clicks when he eats. Beneath his broad shoulders are two thick arms covered in whorls of dark hair and patches of grease. They were powerful once, but the muscles have softened and the empty flesh is starting to sag.

Compared to everybody else in the village, there's the air of a first attempt about Seth, like nature thumbed a couple of eyes into the clay, then tossed him aside as a bad job.

'You're working?' she says, surprised.

She came here expecting to find him hobbled by the same grief as herself, but she now realises that was idiotic. Every villager's life is an act of service. They care for each other before themselves, and her father is devout to that ideal. He won't cry until he's filled every pothole, patched every roof, harvested every vegetable and loaded the furnace that will cremate his father. By his estimation, sadness is just selfishness that people pity rather than scorn.

'She's got a hole in her,' he says, resuming his hammering.

'You don't want to see Matis?'

'We talked this morning,' he says gruffly.

'He's your dad.'

'That's why we talked this morning,' he repeats, lining up another nail.

Emory bites her lip, overcome by the usual exhaustion. Every conversation with her father is like this. He's a boulder you have to keep rolling uphill.

'Niema offered me a job today.'

'She told me,' he replies, pounding the nail into the wood. 'You should accept it. It's a huge honour, and you've tried everything else. It's about time you found a way to properly serve the village.'

She accepts the reprimand silently, watching the foamy water lap against the pebbles. The sea's pitch black at this hour, the bay lost to the darkness. She's half tempted to go for a swim, but it's too close to curfew. She settles for walking a few steps into the surf, letting it wash her sandalled feet. They're always filthy by the end of the day.

'Something's upsetting Niema,' she says, trying to change the subject. 'Do you know what it is? She told me she has an experiment to run, but I couldn't get anything else out of her. It sounds important.'

'No idea,' he replies, lining up another nail. 'I noticed she was preoccupied, but she didn't mention anything.'

'Did you ask her about it?'

'That's not my place.'

'I wish she'd let us help her.'

'That's like wishing you could take the sun's weight for a day.' Another nail is driven into the wood. 'Niema's concerns dwarf us. If she has need of help she'll ask one of the elders. We need to keep our focus on the things we can control.'

He pauses meaningfully, coming onto the subject that's been bothering him. 'How's Clara?'

Emory's daughter was recently chosen to become one of Thea's apprentices, and she's been exploring the island for the last three weeks as part of her training. It's a huge honour, as she was one of only two people who made it through the trials. She's now receiving an advanced education in mathematics, engineering, biology and chemistry, learning things far beyond the understanding of most villagers.

'I've sent some messages through Abi, but she's not replied to any of them,' says Emory, mesmerised by the dark ocean. 'I think she's still angry.'

Seth's hammer wavers in the air, then thuds into a nail. He's tense, the cords in his neck flaring.

'You might as well get it off your chest,' says Emory tersely, recognising this mood.

'I'm fine,' he grunts.

'Just say it, Dad,' she insists. 'You'll feel better after you've shouted a bit.'

'It's every child's dream to become one of Thea's apprentices,' he says, through gritted teeth. 'Can't you be happy for Clara? Can't you pretend? You didn't even go to her leaving dinner.'

'I couldn't celebrate something I never wanted for her,' says Emory, wiping droplets of seawater off her forearm.

Once her new apprentices are fully trained, Thea will put them to work running experiments in her lab and searching the island for promising technology to salvage. It's a lifetime position, but most of her apprentices don't survive a decade. It's dangerous work and Emory's already lost a husband and her mother to the apprentices. She tried everything to keep her daughter from applying, much to Seth's disgust.

'That dinner was the happiest day of Clara's life,' he says, the furnace starting to grow hot. 'I haven't seen her smile so much since her father died. She wanted her mother there to celebrate with her, and you were off sulking.'

'I wasn't sulking.'

'Then what was it? You're the only person who's ever turned down the chance to become an apprentice. You couldn't expect Clara to do the same.'

'I didn't turn it down,' says Emory, sliding into the well-worn groove of an old argument. 'I tried it and didn't like it. You know what that life is: traipsing across the island, poking around ruins, messing with old machines we barely understand. How many of Thea's apprentices get injured? How many are still alive?'

'So it was cowardice?' he spits bitterly.

'It was good sense,' she shoots back. 'I noticed that Thea is never the one standing by the machines when they explode.'

'That's an elder you're talking about,' he yells, tossing his hammer onto the pebbles angrily. 'Show some respect.'

Emory glares at him, too furious to speak.

'The elders are our last link to the old world,' continues Seth, struggling to regain his temper. 'They have knowledge it would take us hundreds of years to reclaim. Without them, we'd be starting again from scratch. Do you really believe any of our lives are equal to theirs?'

Emory's heard this story so often she could recite it with her father's exact inflections. Ninety years ago, huge sinkholes appeared on every continent, swallowing entire cities. A strange black fog poured out of them, filled with glowing insects that ripped apart whatever they touched. No matter what the nations of the world tried, the fog kept spreading.

It took a year for it to cover the earth, societies crumbling to infighting and barbarism long before they were destroyed. The only beacon of hope was a broadcast from Niema, calling all survivors to a small Greek island.

She was the chief scientist of a huge lab called the Blackheath Institute, which had managed to build a barrier capable of holding the fog back. She promised safety to anybody who could make the journey.

In the end, only a few hundred bedraggled survivors managed it, but reaching the island proved to be only the start of their ordeal. The refugees had grown up in a world where food was found on shelves, medicine was bought in shops and an individual's survival was due to finances rather than skill. Any information they needed was borrowed from a screen, leaving them no knowledge to fall back on when those screens vanished. They didn't know how to farm, or forage, or how to repair the derelict buildings they were depending on for shelter.

Hard years came and went, dwindling the numbers of refugees. Almost every month, somebody was crushed by falling masonry or burned by accidental fires. They scratched themselves on rusty nails and died screaming in puddles of sweat. They mistook poisonous mushrooms for edible ones, and went swimming in the months when the sea teemed with jellyfish and sharks.

Survival was difficult, and death was easy, and many abandoned the fight of their own accord. Thankfully for the human race, they left behind children, and it's this gene pool the villagers are descended from.

The three elders are all that's left of the one hundred and seventeen scientists who stayed in Blackheath when the fog first appeared, and their blood still teems with the vaccinations, improvements and technology that were common before the world ended. They age slowly, never get sick, and everybody treats them with an instinctive reverence that only Niema's earned, according to Emory.

'Why do you have to be ...' Seth presses his forehead to the rough wood of the boat's hull, too kind to say what he's thinking, but not kind enough to stop hinting at it.

'Different?' she ventures.

He flings a frustrated arm at the laughter and music pouring through the gate. 'Everybody else is happy, Emory. They're just happy. It's not complicated. They know what we have, and they're grateful for it. Why do you have to question everything?'

'And what do we have, Dad?' asks Emory, in a quiet voice. 'A village in ruins. An island we're not allowed to explore without permission.'

'It's dangerous!' he interjects automatically.

'Then why isn't everybody taught survival in school? I love Niema, but can you honestly tell me that you think Thea, or Hephaestus, contributes enough to the village, that they should be exempt from the rules the rest of us are forced to follow? How is it fair that they don't die at sixty like we do? Why don't they farm for their food or take shifts in the kitchen, or help clean the –'

'They contribute knowledge!'

Emory shrinks back from this eruption, like darkness at the edge of a candle flame. This argument is pointless, and she knows it. Her father will never doubt the elders, or understand why she does. The more she argues, the more he dislikes her, and that tidemark is high enough already.

'I'm going back to the funeral,' she says, defeated. 'Do you want me to say anything to Matis?'

'I spoke to him this morning,' he responds, stooping to pick up his hammer.

SIX

I T'S DUSK AND THE curfew bell is ringing across the village, meaning the villagers have fifteen minutes to get to bed. Most of them are already in the barracks, cleaning their teeth and lighting lemongrass to keep the mosquitoes away. Candles burn cheerily in their windows, spilling out into the gloom of evening.

Each dorm room can house up to eight people, and they sleep in the same iron beds as the soldiers who were once stationed here, their mattresses filled with straw and their pillows with feathers. They don't need sheets. Even in winter, it's much too hot.

Only those villagers on clean-up duty are still in the exercise yard. Shilpa is dousing the candles on the tables, while Rebecca, Abbas, Johannes and Yovel finish putting away the last of the washed dinner plates on the shelves of the outdoor kitchen.

Magdalene and several other parents are calling out for the children, who are hiding under the table. They've been chasing them from shadow to shadow for the last twenty minutes.

The escapees are given away by their giggling.

As Emory enters the gate, the squirming children are being carried to bed by whichever adult is fast enough to grab hold of them. Every child has a parent, but that's an emotional title, not a practical one. They're raised by the village. It's the only way of making the job manageable.

'I'm never sure which one of you is the most ridiculous,' says a voice in the darkness.

Emory looks across to find Matis sitting on a bench in the gloom, dunking a piece of focaccia into a bowl of salted olive oil. There's a pretty green gem hanging around his neck on a length of string.

Unless they die suddenly, every villager bequeaths their memories to me before death. In those final few breaths, I catalogue every experience they've ever had – even ones they don't remember – and store them indefinitely in one of these gems, allowing others to relive them, whenever they wish. Unfortunately, the villagers only wear the memory gems during their funeral, giving them a somewhat grim aspect.

Niema's holding Matis's hand companionably. Her blue eyes are red with recent tears.

'As usual, you've started in the middle of a thought,' replies Emory, still irritable after arguing with her father.

'Be nice to me, I'm dying,' he says, popping a chunk of bread into his mouth.

Emory searches his face for some hint of the fear he must be feeling, but he's munching away, cheerful as ever. It's not fair, she thinks selfishly. He's healthy, and strong. If he was an elder he'd wake up tomorrow, same as normal.

She wants more time.

She wants her grandfather planted solidly at the centre of her life where he's always been; where he should always be. She wants to be able to eat breakfast with him, and watch him clumsily pick the seeds out of a kiwi fruit with those thick fingers. She wants to hear his laugh from across the exercise yard. She wants to know why a good man such as this, with so much energy and talent, has to die to appease a rule that was created long before he was born.

'I'll leave you two to talk,' says Niema, getting to her feet and laying an affectionate hand on Matis's shoulder.

She considers him, then leans down, whispering something into his ear, before giving him a kiss on the cheek and leaving.

'What did she say?' asks Emory.

'Five five,' he replies, chewing his focaccia.

'What does that mean?'

'No idea,' he says, shrugging. 'She's been saying it to me for years, whenever I was upset, or a bit down. I asked her once what it meant and she told me it was a map to the future, but she never got round to explaining it.'

'Don't you want to know?' asks Emory, exasperated.

'Of course I do, but if she wanted to tell me, she would have done it already.'

Wiping the olive oil and breadcrumbs from his hands, he stands up heavily and links his arm through Emory's.

'How was the fight with your father?' he asks, changing subject. 'Did it distract you from being sad? I'm assuming that's why you went down there.'

Emory casts a glance back towards the pool of lantern light in the bay, then smiles slightly, knowing there's no point denying it.

'I do a feel a bit better, yeah,' she admits.

'Your dad probably does, as well. You're just like him. You run to the things that frighten you and away from the things you love.' He sounds baffled. 'Come on, I've finished my sculpture. I want you to see it.'

They walk towards the spot in the exercise yard where Matis has been working all week. The statue of Emory is standing on its tiptoes, having just plucked a stone apple from the boughs of the real apple tree above.

'Do you like it?' asks Matis, when Emory lays her chin on his shoulder.

'No,' she admits.

'Why not?'

He's curious, but not insulted. Art isn't sacred in the village. It's a bawdy, boisterous communal activity. Poems are interrogated even as they're recited and bands will swap musicians in the midst of a song if they're losing the beat. If an actor's struggling in a play, it's common for the crowd to call out lines, or improvise better ones. Occasionally, they'll take over the part completely. Emory's seen entire first acts rewritten by committee halfway through the performance.

'Because it doesn't see anything and it doesn't ask questions, and it's perfectly happy to be here,' she says. 'The only person in the village it doesn't resemble is me.'

Matis snorts, slapping his leg. 'Isn't a single other person who would have given me that answer,' he says, delighted.

Emory stares up at the candlelit windows of the barracks, watching the silhouettes moving inside, brushing their hair and preparing for bed.

'I love the village, I really do,' she says quietly. 'I just don't … there are things that don't make any sense to me, and everybody just acts like they do, or that they don't matter.'

Her thoughts drift back to her childhood, recalling the first time she discovered the elders could stay awake past curfew. Even as a child she knew it was unfair, but nobody else seemed to care.

I explained that villagers need more rest than the elders, but that answer didn't sate her, especially after she woke up with a splinter in her heel that hadn't been there when she went to sleep. A few weeks later, she found a fresh scratch on her thigh, then bruises on her arm. She never knew how they got there.

I tried to convince her that she was mistaken, but Emory was much too observant to believe such an obvious lie. She asked her father what happened to them after they went to sleep, but he treated the very question as a blasphemy. She asked her mother, who professed herself too busy to answer. She asked Matis, who laughed and ruffled her hair. Finally, she put her hand up in class and asked Niema, who kept her back after school.

'Sometimes we wake you up after curfew,' she admitted to the young Emory, after praising her bravery for asking the question.

'Why?'

'To help us with our tasks.'

'What tasks?'

'I can't tell you that.'

'Why don't we remember?'

'Because it's better if you don't,' said Niema a little guiltily.

After leaving the classroom, Emory told everybody in the village what she'd learned, simultaneously awed at the power of questions and dismayed at the limitations of answers. She thought they'd be astonished by what she'd unearthed, but most of her friends met the news with a shrug, or else were embarrassed that she'd been so impertinent.

It's been the same way ever since.

Their bright sunlit lives are blotted by shadows, and nobody cares what's concealed in that darkness except her. Sometimes, she watches her friends at the evening meal and feels as distant from them as she does from the elders.

'Why doesn't anybody question anything?' she asks her grandfather, focusing on him once again.

'They like being happy,' he says simply.

'I'm not trying to change that.'

'And, yet, answers nearly always do,' he replies, waving away the mosquitoes. Dusk brings them out in thick, unrelenting waves.

'This is my last night on earth,' he says matter-of-factly. 'So I'm going to say a few things I've always wanted to say, starting with this. Tomorrow morning you'll wake up one friend short, and you weren't exactly burdened with them to start with. Some of that isn't your fault, but some of it is. You're a clever girl, Em, but you've never had any patience for people who don't see the world the way you do. That wasn't a problem, except now Clara's one of those people.'

'Clara chose Thea,' remarks Emory flatly.

'And you don't like Thea.'

'She killed Jack.' Her voice cracks on her husband's name.

'Jack's dead because he rowed out in a squall and drowned,' points out Matis.

'On Thea's order,' she counters. 'Jack and every other apprentice who was in that boat with him are dead because they bowed their heads, and did what they were told without question. They weren't the first and they won't be the last. People who choose Thea die, and I don't want Clara to be one of them.'

Matis envelops her hands in both of his own, smothering her rage.

'What's the use of loving somebody so much they can't stand being in the same room as you? Clara's already lost her father. She can't lose her mother, as well. Carry on like this, and you'll be ten years older, wondering why you don't speak any more.'

Emory holds his gaze for as long as she can, before she drops her head. 'I'm going to miss you,' she says.

'Don't do it for too long,' he replies. 'The more you look back, the more you miss what's around you. That was your father's mistake.'

He wipes away her tears with a rough, crooked thumb.

'Speaking of which, have you seen that hopeless son of mine?'

'He's in the bay, angrily mending a boat.'

'He never did learn how to be sad,' replies Matis, sighing.

After squeezing her hand, he turns towards the gate. For a moment, Emory thinks she sees a hunched figure out there in the gloom, but she blinks and they're gone.

'I'll come with you,' says Emory, realising these are the last moments they'll ever spend together.

'I have words that are just for him,' he says grimly. 'It's about time one of us said them.' He glances at his granddaughter over his shoulder. 'Your father was always too hard on you, Emory, but he does love you.'

'I wish I believed you.'

'I wish you didn't have to.'

Emory watches her grandfather leave the village for the last time, before I gently nudge her into motion.

'You've got six minutes until curfew,' I say. 'Get yourself to your room, otherwise you'll be sleeping out here.'

Emory springs away, her sandals kicking up the dirt ground, but she's halted by the sight of Niema and Hephaestus arguing in front of the metal staircase leading up to her dorm.

'You promised me these experiments were over,' yells Hephaestus, his voice guttural.

The rage in it causes Emory to take a nervous step back into the darkness. Hephaestus is a foot taller than anybody else in the village, and twice their width. He's carelessly shorn his hair to scabs and stubble, and there's a gouge down the right side of his face. His hands are huge. As are his arms. His legs. His chest. Matis once joked that the only way he could sculpt Hephaestus would be to start chipping away at the volcano behind the village.

'Can't this wait until after curfew?' hisses Niema, peering up at her son. She seems so small in his shadow, a doll made of twigs and twine, with hay for hair.

'We're supposed to be protecting them,' he says pleadingly.

'From themselves,' replies Niema, realising that she won't be able to head the conversation off. 'That requires sacrifice.'

'Sacrifice is when *they* make the choice. What we're doing is murder.'

Emory gasps, shocked to hear that awful word tossed around so casually without a book present.

'Not if it works,' argues Niema.

'It never has before. At this point, it's no better than a death sentence.'

'I know what we've been doing wrong, Hephaestus,' she says, in a wheedling tone. 'I've adapted the procedure. It's going to succeed this time.'

Confronted by the immovability of her son's doubt, Niema lifts his heavy hands, turning them over to inspect the scars and burns that mottle his flesh.

'You're the reason I started these experiments, you know,' she says sadly. 'I'll never forget the day you washed up on the island. You were half dead, tortured almost beyond recognition. I thought the fog had got you, but then you told me about the gangs, and the camp where they held you.'

She reaches up touching the scar on his cheek.

'I swore I'd never let that happen to anybody ever again.' Her voice hardens, calcifying around her anger. 'Yes, we're risking an innocent life, but think of the rewards if our experiment works. Every generation that comes after this one will live in peace, without fear of war, crime or violence. No human being will ever hurt another. We'll be able to let them roam this island freely without worrying what they'll do with that freedom. Put it on a scale, my darling. Think about how much good we can do with one single act.'

Hephaestus stares at her uncertainly, his size now appearing to be a trick of the light. He's hunched over, his shoulders pointing towards her, his shaved head bowed low to hear her hushed words. It's as though he's collapsing under her gravity.

'You're sure it will work this time?' he asks.

'Yes,' she says firmly.

Even with no understanding of what they're talking about Emory knows that Niema's not as confident as she's making out. She's too aware of herself, too bright and brittle for somebody claiming to be made of steel.

Hephaestus knows it, too, she thinks. She can see it playing across his shifting features. He's choosing to believe a lie. Allowing himself to be reassured by it; making it big enough to hide behind. For Emory, there's no greater act of cowardice.

Hephaestus examines his hands, which are covered in badly healed scars and burns – each one a memento of his flight across a crumbling civilisation. 'When do you want them in the chair?' he asks, at last.

'Tonight.'

'I need twenty-four hours, at least,' he disagrees. 'You know that.'

'This is urgent, Hephaestus. If you bypass the scans –'

'No,' he interrupts sternly. 'If we do that, there's a chance we miss an underlying medical condition that kills them during the procedure. If you want my help, there'll be no shortcuts. I'll need twenty-four hours to choose a subject with the best chance of survival. You'll have to wait until tomorrow night.'

Niema puts aside her irritation with puffed cheeks, smiling at her son as though his objections were the prevarications of a child.

Emory's never seen this version of Niema before. Her entire life she's been a jolly old woman, full of laughter and compassion, urging the villagers to be the best versions of themselves. Emory would never have guessed she could be so manipulative, or so callous about a life. She's acting the way Thea would.

'As you wish,' says Niema, spreading her hands magnanimously. 'I have another errand to perform tonight, anyway.'

Hephaestus accepts this small victory with a grunt, then stalks away without another word, nearly colliding with the watching Emory. There's a long stride between them, but she still nearly gags on his odour. It's sweat and rot and earth, like he's carrying a dead fox in one of his unwashed pockets.

He meets her astonished gaze with crushing disdain, then glances back over his shoulder. 'One of the crums was eavesdropping,' he calls out.

'I don't like that term,' replies Niema sternly, but Hephaestus is already walking away.

Emory watches him go. When she turns back, Niema is in front of her.

'How much did you hear?' she asks.

'You're planning an experiment that could kill somebody,' replies Emory, her voice shaking.

'It's the lesser of two evils, believe me,' says Niema, waving away the risk. 'We're gambling a solitary life for the chance to make a better world in the long run. I'd give up my own life for that. Wouldn't you?'

'It doesn't sound like they're being given that choice.'

'They're not,' admits Niema. 'I prefer to assume nobility rather than be disappointed by a lack of it.'

'This is wrong,' protests Emory. 'We don't hurt people, not for any reason.'

'Of course you'd say that.' Niema smiles faintly, her manner warning. 'But it's my job to make sure those wonderful morals of yours are never tested.'

The curfew bell stops ringing.

Emory's eyes widen as she realises what that means, but before she can do anything about it, she drops to the ground, landing heavily on her shoulder.

She doesn't feel anything.

She's sound asleep, along with the rest of the villagers.

74 HOURS UNTIL HUMANITY'S EXTINCTION

A S I DO EVERY morning, I lift curfew at 7 a.m. precisely, darkness giving way to sudden, shocking daylight.

In their dormitories, the villagers yawn in their rusted beds, stretching their limbs, their first thoughts beginning to drum against my consciousness like rainfall on a tin roof. They swing their legs out of bed and bury their heads in their hands, surprised by how tired they feel, and how much their muscles ache. There are oil blots on their arms that weren't there last night. Their knuckles are singed. Their sandals aren't where they left them when they kicked them off.

Three generations of villagers have lived in these barracks, and slept in these beds, and they've always awoken to the same mysteries. Thanks to Emory's questioning nature, this is the first generation that knows the elders can rouse them from their sleep after curfew, but they don't know why and would never have the temerity to ask.

The need for secrecy is strange, though. In the quiet of their thoughts, they'll acknowledge *that*, if nothing else. After all, there's nothing they wouldn't do willingly if asked. They want to be of service.

Shaking off their unease, they dress hurriedly and open their shutters to the crisp morning light, putting aside the night's oddities.

Soon, a breakfast of fresh fruit, juice, bread, ricotta and honey will be served on the long tables in the exercise yard. They'll have an hour to eat, before it's time to pick up their tools and head to the farms. Survival in the morning; service in the afternoon; and celebration in the evening is their routine. It's a knot so familiar that none of them notice how tightly it binds them, and how impossible it is for them to undo it.

EIGHT

E MORY OPENS HER EYES to find herself lying exactly where she fell last night, her white linen dress stained by the exercise yard's rust-coloured soil. She's under the dappled sunlight of the apple tree, not far from the sculpture Matis made of her. Blue and yellow roller birds are perched on her stone head, singing brightly.

Sitting upright brings a jolt of pain from her shoulder. Craning her head, she discovers a huge purple welt marking the spot where she hit the ground.

She stretches her arm and rolls her neck, trying to massage the stiffness from her limbs, noticing for the first time that a note has been pinned to her dress.

Couldn't move you. Hope you're not too stiff.
N

Emory's expression hardens, recalling the conversation she overheard last night about Niema's experiment, and the death that could result from it. She can't let her friend hurt somebody. No matter how righteous she believes the cause.

She jumps up, determined to find Niema and talk her out of it, but she's halted by my voice.

'For once, trust that Niema is acting in your best interests,' I say firmly.

'Somebody could die.'

'Somebody *will* die,' I say, correcting her. 'Many somebodies. Events have been set in motion that make it inevitable. Niema's trying to minimise the loss of life, but if you delay her with pointless questions, you're only going to increase her chances of failure. You know her. Everything she does is for the good of the village, even if you don't understand how.'

'People are going to die!?' She casts her gaze this way and that, as if she's going to spot them floundering in the flower beds. 'Who? We have to warn them.'

'In a closed system, psychology is destiny,' I say. 'Your warnings won't stop the danger that's coming, they'll simply change the people who'll be hurt. Niema understands this better than you ever will.'

The great benefit of being in somebody's head since birth is that your voice is easily confused with their own. Over the years, I've displaced Emory's conscience and better sense. I'm trusted implicitly, because she doesn't know how alien I am.

'Now, come on,' I say more gently. 'Breakfast is being served, and then you're due at the school.'

'I'm not going,' she says.

'You promised Niema.'

'That's before I heard what she was planning,' replies Emory. 'I can't face her, knowing what she's doing. Not until I understand it.'

'Everything will be explained tonight,' I say, conceding the point. 'I'll tell her you'll be along tomorrow.'

Still uneasy, Emory trudges up the rattling staircase to her dorm room, which is filled with stupefying humidity. She didn't manage to close it up for the night, so it's wallpapered in moths, which flocked to the candle she left burning.

She crosses the floor to her bedside table, which still has the mystery book Niema gave her on it. Normally, she'd be looking forward to reading it, but she's still uneasy after last night. Fictional murder doesn't seem quite so entertaining when your friend is planning to commit a real one.

She opens a small drawer, removing a notepad and the stub of a pencil. Flipping through pages crammed with questions, she finds a blank spot and writes 'What is Niema's experiment?' and under it 'What does "five five" mean?'

After underlining the word 'experiment' a few times, she closes the pad and tosses it back into the drawer with the pencil.

She has fourteen of these notepads stored under her bed, every page stuffed with questions she's never received answers to. She's been writing them down for as long as she can remember. A few have been crossed out, because she's worked them out herself, but the list grows every day. It's a litany of ignorance.

'You know everything you need to know to be happy,' I say, repeating a phrase that has become a mantra between us.

'But I'm not happy,' she points out.

'You're dissatisfied,' I argue. 'You have no idea what unhappiness is. I'm hoping you never do.'

Emptying her pockets, she removes the note Niema left on her stomach. She's about to throw it into the drawer with everything else when she notices faint impressions on the paper. They're words transferred from the sheet that was on top of this one. Could they be from the letter Niema hurriedly hid in her drawer yesterday?

Emory squints, holding the page up to the bright sunshine pouring through the window, but she can't make out any of the indents clearly.

Remembering a trick from one of the crime books she has read, she gently rubs her pencil across the paper, drawing out a string of confusing words.

if I couldn't control ... better ... contain ... Abi wanted to ... couldn't kill

Emory blows away the pencil dust hoping to make the words clearer, but they're being as secretive as everything else on this island. After trying to wheedle more information from the note, she finally gives up and puts it in the drawer.

From her cupboard, she takes out a light yellow dress and underwear and considers the straw hat hanging on a nail, but it's early enough that she can get away without it. She likes to feel the morning sun on her neck.

She examines the empty dorm room. She used to share this space with Jack and Clara, but Jack's dead, and her daughter moved in with Hui last year. She wanted to study for her trials, without having her mother peering over her shoulder, recounting all the reasons why being an apprentice was a bad idea.

Emory suddenly feels terribly lonely.

She rests her fingers on her daughter's untouched pillow, remembering the little girl Clara once was. They used to make up bedtime stories between them before curfew, back when love was simple. That's the last time they got along. After Jack died, the tether holding them together snapped. They've been slowly drifting apart ever since.

'How's she doing?' she asks.

'She'll be home this afternoon.'

'Can you tell her I miss her?'

'Of course,' I reply.

Emory takes her clean clothes down to the old shower rooms, which are the grottiest part of the barracks. The tiles are cemented together by mould, jagged pipes poking out of the walls, the shower heads corroded away.

She quickly washes yesterday's dirt off with a bucket of cold water and one of the blocks of jasmine soap Kelvin makes.

She thinks about Matis and lets her tears run away in the suds.

After wringing the water from her hair, Emory dresses and goes to the exercise yard, where the tables are starting to fill up with fresh fruit and orange juice, baskets of bread steaming hot from the oven. There are bowls of honey, jam and curd under muslin nets to keep the flies away.

Not far from the bird bath, Matis's body is laid unceremoniously in the back of a two-wheeled cart. The shock of it steals her breath, but she's the only one showing any reaction. Everybody else is laughing and chatting, walking by the dead man without a second glance, as they make their way to the communal tables.

We held Matis's funeral last night, while he could still enjoy it. This is just flesh, nothing more than clutter. There's a furnace in the basement of the old infirmary, which is being filled with wood. We'll burn the corpse as soon as the fire's hot enough.

Seth is standing nearby. His face is stricken, his eyes lost in memory. Every emotion vanishes when he sees Emory approaching.

'Were you with him?' she asks gently.

'We fell asleep talking,' he says, struggling to keep a lid on his grief. 'I've just brought him in.'

'He would have liked that.' Her brow wrinkles. 'Did you see anybody else out there last night? I thought I saw somebody near the gate. It looked like they were waiting to talk to him.'

'I was down in the bay,' says Seth. 'I heard a voice, but I couldn't see who it belonged to. Whatever they talked about upset him, though.'

'Wasn't much that could upset Grandfather,' replies Emory, surprised. 'Any idea what it was?'

'None.' Seth fiddles with the strap of his sandal, trying to dislodge a pebble. He's desperate for the questions to end.

'It will be on his memory gem,' says Emory suddenly, leaning into the cart to examine Matis's neck, only to find it missing. 'Where is it, Abi?'

'The cord was loose,' I say. 'His memory gem fell into the ocean last night.'

Emory's eyes widen, as Seth lets out a despairing wail. He was braced for his father's death, but not for him to be scrubbed from the world entirely.

Emory lays a gentle hand on Seth's shoulder, which immediately tenses, forcing her to remove it.

Her face hardens, along with her thoughts. 'How close did Grandfather actually get to the water last night?' she asks.

'How could that possibly matter?' he demands angrily.

'Have you ever heard of anybody losing their gem before?' she snaps back. 'Don't you think it's strange that it managed to unknot itself from around his neck, then carry itself into the ocean, taking with it our only way of knowing who he was talking to?'

Seth glowers at her, his eyes raw. 'You'll never stop, will you?' he says disbelievingly. 'You don't even know how. You just keep picking, regardless of how much it hurts people.'

'There's something strange –'

'No,' he says, wagging a finger at her. 'Matis told me to have patience with you, but the well's dry. I can't do it any more.'

'Dad –'

'No,' he says, taking a step away from her. 'My father's dead, and all you want to do is kick over his body to satisfy your pathetic curiosity. I'm done, Emory. Stay away from me.'

Picking up the handles of the cart, he drags his father's body towards the furnace in the infirmary, leaving Emory alone in the dirt.

NINE

OUR PAINTER, MAGDALENE, IS dressing her son, Sherko, for school. His peplos is too large, and she's trying to add a few stitches to tighten it, while he squirms, and groans, and fidgets. He's been standing still for almost four minutes – an eternity for a young boy.

She's biting back her frustration, which is easy to do when you're gripping a length of cotton between your teeth. Their morning got off to the wrong start when she discovered dirty footprints weaving their way through the door. Sherko obviously forgot to clean his sandals before he came in last night, but he wouldn't admit it.

Not for the first time, Magdalene's wondering if she made the right choice becoming a mother.

Anybody in the village can apply to be a parent. They need only ask me, at which point I assess their temperament and suitability, then make a decision. It's too important a job to be left to best intentions, which is why I reject most applications and make successful candidates undergo rigorous training. Usually, this gives parents a sense of pride, and a confidence that they're up to the task. This morning, Magdalene is finding that confidence hard to come by.

'Mum,' asks Sherko, in the voice of a child loading a new salvo of irritation onto his tongue.

'Yes,' she replies, carefully pushing the point of the needle through the cotton.

'Why did you straighten all the pictures?'

'I didn't,' she says distractedly.

The walls of the dormitory room are covered in her canvases. They're all different sizes and subjects, done in oils, watercolours, pencils and fabric. About the only unifying feature of her artwork is that they're usually all hanging crooked. She blames a combination of untrustworthy walls, bent nails and wobbly hammer heads.

'Yes you did,' he argues, thrilled to be right. 'Look. They're all straight.'

Her eyes flick up to the walls. He's right, they're straight. Craning her neck, she looks behind her. Every one of them is level.

Her heart stops. This isn't the first time it's happened. He's been playing this trick for months.

'Maybe Adil did it,' he reasons.

Magdalene stiffens, unused to hearing that name spoken aloud. Adil is her grandfather, and he used to straighten the pictures every night before they went to bed, claiming he'd have nightmares if they were wonky.

'Adil isn't allowed back into the village,' she says tightly. 'You know that. I'm not even sure he's still alive.'

'Why was he sent away?'

'He ...' She trails off, unable to voice her shame.

Adil was one of Thea's apprentices, the only survivor of the boat wreck that killed Emory's husband. They recovered him a week after the accident wandering in the wilderness, but he couldn't recall a single thing about what had happened.

It was immediately clear something was wrong.

He was no longer subject to curfew, or restricted in his movements, meaning he could go wherever he wanted on the island at any time. He suffered from terrible headaches, his lucidity coming and going. One minute he'd be making jokes with his friends, same as he'd always done, and the next he'd be screaming about giant earthworms and faces pressed against glass. Magdalene would wake up in the morning to find he'd spent the night scratching strange maps onto the walls, and writing the names of the dead apprentices in endless lists.

Thea examined him, but couldn't find any explanation for these episodes. A month after the wreck, Adil burst into Niema's classroom and attacked her with a scalpel, demanding she dig up what she'd buried.

Luckily, Hephaestus was nearby.

He managed to save Niema, but Adil fled the village and never came back. His punishment was exile.

That was five years ago, and Magdalene's still angry at the way he was treated.

Before he lost his friends, her grandfather was scholarly and inquisitive, an exponent of civility in all things. He adored beauty, and encouraged Magdalene's interest in art. There's no amount of provocation that would have led him to hurt Niema, or even consider it.

Clearly, he was changed by the wreck. He deserved compassion and treatment, not banishment and scorn. She genuinely believes that if he'd attacked a villager, rather than an elder, he would have received it.

'Is Adil coming back soon?' persists Sherko, paying no heed to his mother's discomfort.

Magdalene returns her attention to the straightened pictures surrounding them, then shakes her head thoughtfully.

'He's been gone a long time. Even if he's still alive, I'm not sure we'd recognise him if he did.'

IN A TRAIN CARRIAGE to the east of the village, Clara is woken by her best friend, Hui, who is practising a new concerto on her violin.

I've asked her to play it tonight in front of the village. Her performance this evening is one of the many crucial moments that have to occur to deliver the utopia Niema's demanding. One bum note and the future will go rattling off on a new trajectory.

'Hui,' pleads Clara, flailing at her friend weakly, while keeping her eyes pressed shut. 'I only just went to sleep.'

Hui played this canzonetta for them last night and it was so beautiful that Clara went to bed believing it was the most wonderful thing she'd ever heard. Every note carried a piece of her away, scattering her atoms to the wind, sun and ocean. This morning – with a long night behind her and a long day ahead – the music is producing a very different sensation.

'Hui,' she tries again, reluctantly opening a solitary eyelid.

Apprentices are exempted from the curfew while they're on expedition, which was one of the things Clara was most excited by when they left the village three weeks ago. Every night, they've sat in the glow of a campfire, under a bright moon, listening to Thea talk to them like they're equals. Increasingly, though, the torment of having to wake up early seems like too high a price for the joy of staying awake late.

Clara comes up on her elbow, scowling at Hui, who's playing briskly, her eyes closed, lost in the avenues of her own creativity. She has short, dark hair and sharp cheeks, either side of a long, curved nose. She's covered in a thick layer of grime, trickles of sweat eating their way through the dirt on her scratched face.

It's been three days since any of them bathed, not that they'd be able to stay clean for long anyway. Thea's been teaching them how to safely explore the island's ruins and how to identify technology that can be salvaged. Their most recent lesson required them to follow a dull silver rail through a dense forest. It led them to this collapsed train carriage, graceless without any power to keep it afloat.

Fearing rain, they lit a fire and cooked a vegetable stew, while Thea conjured the past, as she has done every night. She told them how these trains used to float across the land, carrying scientists and supplies to their destinations in minutes.

'The Blackheath Institute owned the entire island,' she said wistfully. 'Our labs were built into an old nuclear bunker underground, but we spent most of our free time on the surface, hiking and swimming. There were thousands of us working for Niema before the world ended, but nearly all of them went home when the fog came.'

'What happened to Blackheath?' asked Clara.

She'd knew the lab had been lost somehow, but that was the only information she'd ever been given.

'It's still down there,' explained Thea, stamping the floor with her foot. 'Its tunnels riddle most of the eastern coast, but the fog managed to worm its way through fissures in the island's bedrock. We were forced to evacuate in the dead of night and close Blackheath's doors after us; otherwise it would have overrun the entire island. Nobody's been back since, but our labs would have been hermetically sealed the second the alarms sounded. Our equipment's down there, waiting for us. Our experiments, too. Everything I need to destroy the fog and get off this island. I just can't get to it.'

Realising the depth of longing that had come into her voice, an embarrassed Thea swiftly made her excuses and retired to bed.

In the carriage, the violin increases in pitch, forcing Clara to cover her ears and shout to be heard.

'Hui!'

A string twangs, the music cutting off abruptly. The concentration on Hui's smooth face immediately collapses into concern, as the future silently switches tracks.

'I woke you,' she says apologetically.

'The violin woke me,' clarifies Clara. 'But you were definitely involved.'

'I'm so sorry,' she says. 'I'm performing tonight, but I haven't had time to practise.'

'Don't worry about it, you don't need to practise,' counters Clara, through a yawn.

'I do.'

'You don't,' says Clara, stretching. 'You've played for us every night without missing a single note.'

'This is different. It's the first time I'll be playing this concerto in front of the entire village.' She lowers her voice. 'Abi told me that all of the elders will be there.'

'It's not different,' replies Clara. 'Everybody loves you. They always love you. It doesn't matter how you play.'

Jealousy reveals itself in her tone, and she hurries on to cover her embarrassment.

'You're going to be great,' she finishes lamely.

Hui digests this, while Clara upbraids herself for letting something so carefully hidden surface so easily.

I'll say this in Clara's defence: Hui isn't always easy to love. Her talent shines so brightly it makes everything else seem dull, and that's a difficult thing not to resent.

Worse, Hui's become adept at parlaying her ability into laziness. If I didn't put my foot down, she'd have people tending her crops, cleaning her clothes and running after her, picking up the things she drops. I've never understood the need for people to prostrate themselves before talent, but it happens every generation.

'You're right,' says Hui, relieved. 'Of course you're right. You always are. Thanks, Clara. What would I do without you?'

'The same, but slower,' suggests Clara, catching her own odour as she shifts position. 'I desperately hope there's a bath in my future,' she grumbles.

'You're not the only one,' agrees Hui, throwing her a jug with a cork in it. 'Here.'

Emory unstoppers it and sniffs suspiciously. They've been eating boiled vegetables and broths for the last three weeks, and her stomach is considering leaving her for somebody with a better palette.

'Orange juice!' exclaims Clara. 'Where did you find this?'

'Thea found a few trees not far from here. She squeezed it this morning.'

'Thea's been in here?'

'We had a nice chat.'

'Was I snoring?'

'And slobbering,' confirms Hui brightly.

Clara groans, covering her face with her hands.

After five years without taking on any new apprentices, Thea suddenly announced she'd be recruiting again in March. Forty-three people applied and Niema spent the next six months tutoring them in mathematics, physics, biology and engineering. Most of the candidates were winnowed out by the difficulty of the classes, with only nineteen actually surviving to sit the trials in October.

For two days, they were given machines from the old world to disassemble and repair, problems to solve and chemical compounds to create.

Considering Thea's fractious relationship with Emory, everybody was stunned when Clara applied for the trials, and even more stunned when she passed them. She was one of only two to be selected, along with Hui. Even more remarkable was the fact that they were the two youngest candidates by some distance.

Thea hasn't done anything to make Clara believe her mother is a black mark against her, but she still feels she has to be perfect at everything – even sleeping.

'I'm joking,' says Hui, slapping her hands gleefully. 'I went for a wee this morning and Thea gave me the orange juice on the way back. Even if she hadn't you don't need to worry. You're a very charming sleeper.'

Clara blushes, and gulps the juice to cover her embarrassment, becoming very interested in their surroundings.

'You should tell her how you feel,' I say.

Clara ignores me, as she always does. It's a shame, because if she'd just find a little courage she could be happy with Hui. I don't even need to model the future to see it. Love is simply a matter of what people need, and what they lack. It's two broken things fitting together for a time.

Unfortunately, she's clammed up and probably won't get another chance. By tomorrow morning, Hui will likely be dead and Clara will spend the rest of her life tormented by the things she never said, and what might have happened if she had.

Oblivious to this fork in history, Clara is wiping orange juice from her chin while inspecting the train carriage they slept in. It's large and wide with snapped handrails and dented metal seats. A strange vine the width of Clara has burst through the floor, twisting around the empty windows with enough force to buckle them. It's pulsing with an inner light, and is unlike anything she's ever seen before. Its skin is marked with hundreds of criss-crossing gouges, like somebody's taken an axe to it. Whoever it was, they didn't penetrate very far.

Finishing the juice, Clara searches the carriage for her possessions. They were only allowed to bring what they could fit in a knapsack, but she's always had a gift for making a mess. Her knife is under some weeds, her spare clothes are scattered everywhere and her notebooks have migrated to the furthest reaches of the cabin.

'Did you see the names?' asks Hui, as Clara scrambles around, searching for the small blocks of wood she uses for her carvings.

'What names?'

'Scratched onto the metal under the bench,' responds Hui, placing her beloved violin in its wool-lined case. 'It's Thea's last group of apprentices. Your dad is on there.'

Clara follows her pointing finger, excitedly.

'Arthur, Emory, Tasmin, Kiko, Reiko, Jack,' she reads aloud, her voice warming on her father's name.

She runs her finger across the jagged edges of 'Jack', imagining him scratching out the letters, humming the way he always did when he worked.

'He was seventeen when he did that,' I say. 'The same age you are. Thea always brings her new apprentices out here after they pass the trials. It was the first time he'd left the village. He was so excited

Thea had to tell him to stop running everywhere. Your mother was deeply embarrassed.'

Clara touches her mother's name tenderly. Unlike her father, who filled her childhood with stories about being an apprentice, Emory very rarely mentioned this time in her life.

'Emory only lasted six more weeks after this before she quit,' I explain. 'It would have been sooner, but your father kept the peace.'

Sounds about right, thinks Clara. Unlike her short-tempered mother, her father never raised his voice, and never spoke in haste. Most of the time he was smiling, and if he wasn't you knew you'd done something really wrong.

He drowned in a storm five years ago, with the rest of these apprentices. She still thinks about him every day.

Beneath the names, she can see the tops of more words, obscured by some tall weeds. Pushing them down, she finds another message.

If you're reading this, turn back now. Niema buried us. She'll bury you, too.

Clara's pulse quickens. 'What does that mean?' she asks nervously.

'It's old graffiti,' I reply. 'Don't worry about it.'

'Who did Niema bury?'

'I told you not to worry about it.'

My evasiveness doesn't do much to assuage her unease, but she's distracted by Thea's voice hollering to them from outside.

'Clara, Hui, we're leaving!'

'You ready?' asks Hui, hitching her pack. 'Don't forget to leave one of your birds.'

Clara searches her pockets, retrieving a tiny wooden sparrow. She whittles them absently when she's thinking, and has a dozen of them rattling around in her pockets. She's been leaving them behind as markers of their passing.

After placing one on a seat, she ducks outside into the glare of sunlight, scattering a colony of rabbits which bound away into the long grass, disturbing grasshoppers and sending dragonflies into the air. An extinct volcano rises up in front of her, its peak obscured by haze.

The earth is dry underfoot, a copse of dusty pine trees offering the scantest shade. The ruins of ancient stone walls demark the olive and fig groves that used to be cultivated here. They're wild now, piles of rotten fruit littering the ground for animals to feast on.

Clara considers asking me where they are, but Thea wants them to keep a mental map so they can guide themselves in the future.

She thinks back to school, when Niema lifted up a mouldy brown sheet by the middle and explained this was the shape, and colour, of their island when viewed from above. The volcano sits at the very centre, which means the further anyone ventures inland the steeper and rockier the terrain becomes.

It takes two days to hike from north to south along the coast, and nearly the same to cross from east to west, because you have to find a way to do it without breaking a leg. Thankfully, the island is riddled with old goat trails, which can hugely speed up journeys if you know where to find them.

'The sun's to the left of the volcano,' mutters Clara to herself. 'We must have made camp at its south face.'

Her heart leaps. The village is to the south-west. It's probably only a few hours' walk as the crow flies, but the terrain is almost impassable. There must be another way around.

Clara flashes a glance at Thea, trying to gauge her intentions. The elder is looking at the summit of the volcano, shading her eyes. She's as thin as the pine trees surrounding her, and appears nearly as tall. Her dark hair is cut short, her blue eyes are sharp and her pale face is pulled taut across high cheeks and a pointed chin, without a single wrinkle evident. Her beauty is cowing. The sort you bow to rather than admire.

Thea's nearly a hundred and ten years old, which Clara still finds astonishing as she doesn't look much older than Emory.

'A goat trail will take us up the volcano,' says Thea, scrawling the route in the air with her finger. 'We're heading for the cauldron. Matis passed away last night' – she casts Clara an evaluating look that's neither sympathetic nor pitying – 'Have you had suitable time to grieve for your great-grandfather?'

'I have,' says Clara, knowing there isn't another acceptable answer to the question.

Hui squeezes her hand in support, but it isn't necessary. Jack drowned when Clara was twelve, and she didn't stop crying for a year. Those tears washed something out of her. She's slightly more detached than she once was, too accepting of death.

'As is our custom, a child will take the deceased's place,' continues Thea. 'It's our task to collect that child and deliver them to the village this afternoon.'

A trill of excitement runs through Clara and Hui. The delivery of a new child is one of the most exciting days in the village's life, but Thea usually does it alone. Nobody's ever seen where they come from, nor can they remember it themselves.

'Our errand will take approximately six hours, and I'll be testing you on chemical interactions as we walk.' Thea rubs her hands together in a rare display of enthusiasm. 'Who'd like to go first?'

Thea sets off with Hui close behind, but Clara drags her feet, staring at Thea's departing back, preoccupied by the warning she found inside the carriage.

'She buried us, she'll bury you, too,' she murmurs, a prickle of fear running down her spine.

Who would write something so terrible?

ELEVEN

SETH STOMPS THROUGH THE shady lane formed by the eastern wing of the barracks and the high wall surrounding the village. Piles of pink and white bougainvillea are spilling out of cracks in the stone, growing so thickly that he has to push the blooms aside to make headway, scattering the butterflies resting on their petals.

'You were unkind to Emory earlier,' I say.

'I know,' he admits, having calmed down. 'She just makes me so angry. It's been the same way ever since she was a girl, asking questions nobody can answer. She knows it does no good, but she keeps poking.'

'Why does it annoy you so much?'

'Because …' He trails off, thinking about it deeply for the first time. *Because … they're always good questions*, he admits, in his thoughts. Emory puts them under your brain like pebbles, and there's no rest from them. That's the reason his daughter has so few friends, he thinks. It's why people are nervous around her.

It's why *he's* nervous around her. There's so much he doesn't want to see.

He emerges into the rear yard behind the barracks, which is empty at this time of the day. There are warehouses and old offices back here, repaired and turned into workshops by anybody who needs them. From these buildings the villagers produce soap, paper and paint, grinding huge bags of daffodils and turmeric to make the colours. They weave clothes, and craft shoes, and make new tools from old iron and lumber grown in forests near the farms.

In a few hours, after everybody gets back, these buildings will be stuffy and hot, the rear yard ripe with the stink of chemicals, boiled weeds, wax and starch.

Seth passes through the shadow of a skeletal radar tower, arriving outside a small redbrick hut with a vaulted roof and a mechanical clock that still ticks, thanks to Hephaestus's ministrations.

He pokes his head through the open door, his vision taking a moment to adjust to the gloom. Six children are at their desks, watching Niema prod a plastic map of the world.

It was hanging on the wall when she first established the school here, a painful reminder of what had been lost. She scratched out everything that wasn't this island and has drawn a perfect circle around it, indicating the safe area between them and world's end.

'We'll never know who created such a terrible weapon, or why it was used, but we do know that the fog caught us entirely by surprise,' she says, in her familiar rasp. 'There were no plans in place for a disaster of that magnitude. Unless you were incredibly wealthy, there were no shelters to hide in, or provisions stockpiled. Our children weren't even learning basic survival in school.'

She snatches an impatient glance at the clock, surprising Seth. Niema loves being in the classroom. Something important must be happening if she's this distracted.

She pulls her attention back to the children, her gaze roaming their rapt faces.

'It seems strange now that we were so ill prepared,' she continues, at last. 'The human race had been on the precipice for almost a century before the end actually arrived. We'd dug the earth dry of its resources, and climate change was forcing huge population migrations, while destroying arable land and living space. In the end, we destroyed our own society before nature could do it for us, but it was a close-run thing.'

Seth breathes in, overcome by a powerful sense of nostalgia. He remembers this lesson from his own childhood. He remembers Niema's vehemence, the affronted anger wreathing every word like fire.

One of the children puts their hand up.

'Yes, William,' says Niema, pointing towards him.

'How many people were there before the fog?'

'Uncountable,' she replies. 'We have to keep our population to a hundred and twenty-two because that's all our farmland and water supply can sustain, but their resources were far greater than ours. Millions were being born every day in cities larger than this island.'

The children coo, their imaginations alight.

Another hand shoots up. Niema nods to the little girl at the end of it. 'Why were they fighting?'

'We could always find a reason,' she replies. 'We had different gods, or different skin, or the fight had been going on so long we'd forgotten how to stop it. Somebody had something we needed, or we thought they were planning to hurt us. Often, it was as cynical as our leaders believing it would prolong their own power.'

'But wouldn't –'

'We put our hand up when we want to speak,' interrupts Niema, reprimanding the young boy. His hand goes up, his sentence dragged into the air after it.

'Why didn't Abi stop them?'

'Unfortunately, we didn't have her to help us,' says Niema. 'We were alone in our own heads, without Abi to take care of us. You're right, of course. If we had her, none of this would have happened. She would have reined in our worst impulses.'

She lingers on that point, the children trying to imagine what this world would look like if humanity had been able to outsource its collective conscience. Another hand comes up.

'Yes, Sherko?'

'When can Adil come home?' he asks abruptly. 'My mum really misses him.'

The students tense, taken aback by the anger that flashes across Niema's face.

'Adil hurt me,' replies Niema, struggling to calm herself.

'I know, but Abi always tells us to forgive people,' he says reasonably. 'Adil has been gone a long time. Haven't you forgiven him yet?'

He's wide-eyed, his questions guileless. Niema's anger evaporates like fog hit by sunlight.

'I'm trying,' she says, rubbing a hand along the scar on her fore-arm. 'Your great-grandfather was violent. We can't tolerate that in the village. Do you understand?'

'No,' admits Sherko.

'I'm glad,' she says fondly. 'Unfortunately, I've been alive a lot longer than you, and I've picked up some bad habits along the way. It's not quite as easy for me to forgive people as it is for you, but I'm trying to be better.'

Noticing Seth at the door, she holds up a solitary finger, indicat-ing she'll be finished in a minute.

Crossing his arms, he waits in a thick wedge of shade until the children come running out for playtime. Niema wanders out after them.

'Back in an hour,' she calls, as they disappear towards the exercise yard.

'Good lesson?' asks Seth.

'One of them always does something to surprise me,' she says, wrapping her long grey hair into a bun and stabbing it in place with a pencil.

She looks tired, he thinks. Her eyes are raw, with dark circles, and there's a heaviness to her limbs that's never normally there. For the first time, he feels like he can see the weight of age upon her, all those invisible years dragging behind. Emory was right. Something's troubling her.

'How you feeling this morning?' asks Niema, uncomfortably aware of his scrutiny. 'It was strange not seeing Matis at breakfast.'

'My father lived a long life in service to the village,' he replies mechanically. 'I'm proud of him.'

'It's me, Seth,' she says gently. 'You can admit that you're sad.'

'There's no memory gem,' he blurts out, pain inscribed in every word. 'Abi says it was lost in the ocean.'

'Did she?' Her voice is strained. 'I'm so sorry, that's terrible. I can't imagine what that must be like for you.' She lays a hand on her heart. 'We'll tell his stories to each other. We'll keep his memories alive that way.'

He turns his head to hide the emotion, wiping away the brim-ming tears. She gives him a second to see if he has anything else to add, but Seth prefers to skirt emotions rather than dwell on them. He was the same when his wife died. He held on to her gem for weeks, reliving their life together in every quiet moment. Around his friends, he pretended he was fine. He laughed and joked and worked, same as he'd always done, putting on a note-perfect performance of his old life.

It was Emory who shattered him.

One day, he saw his daughter running across the yard, her hair blowing freely. Judith was the one who always had tied it up for her, and being reminded of that fact ripped the heart out of him. He collapsed sobbing and didn't stop for a month.

'I was hoping you could row me to the lighthouse this evening,' says Niema, changing the subject. 'I've got an experiment I wish to run.'

Seth sighs inwardly. Niema keeps a personal lab out at the lighthouse, which he's never been inside. Whenever she goes there she works through the night, while he sleeps in the boat, rowing her back the next morning. He always wakes up feeling like he's been balled up in somebody's fist. After spending last night on the pier, he was really looking forward to sleeping in his own bed tonight.

'When you do want to leave?'

'Shortly before curfew. I'll exempt you for the night.'

'I'll meet you at the pier,' he agrees.

TWELVE

A DIL IS SITTING ON the banks of a stream, sharpening his knife with a stone, while watching horses playing in the dirt on the other side. He's completely naked, his feet submerged in the cool water, his thoughts drifting. He's so emaciated he looks like a bundle of firewood stacked under a sheet.

In the five years since he was banished from the village, he's explored the island from top to bottom, losing entire days to the memory gems he scavenged from ruins, emerging from their bright modern world into the misery of his own life.

He'd have ended things long ago if it weren't for his hatred of the elders, and Niema in particular. The idea that he might one day free his friends from what she's doing to them is the only reason he's still alive. This dream poisons and sustain him.

He presses his thumb to the edge of the blade, drawing blood. Satisfied, he tosses the stone into the stream.

'Niema's going to the lighthouse tonight,' I say, in his thoughts. 'I've arranged a boat for you. It's floating in a bay not far from here. I want you to take it, and get there before she arrives.'

He blinks, surprised to hear from me.

Niema meant his exile to be total, and has forbidden me from speaking to him unless absolutely necessary. He's now heard from me twice in two days, double the number of interactions we've had in the last five years.

He tries to speak out loud, only to find his unused voice lodged in his throat, covered in dust. Kneeling down, he sips from the cool stream, then tries again.

'You know what I'll do if I get that close to her,' he says, coughing up every word.

'I can hear your thoughts, Adil,' I say. 'I know what you dream about it. I know it isn't bravado.'

'Then why do you want me there?' he demands suspiciously.

'Later tonight, Niema's going to conduct an experiment, which she believes will lead to a better, more peaceful future. The odds of success are low, and if it doesn't work it will set off a cataclysmic chain of events which will result in everybody on this island being dead in sixty-one hours.'

He picks up his knife, staring at his distorted reflection in the metal. A hacking cough shakes his body, droplets of blood splattering the blade.

'You want me to kill her before she conducts the experiment, don't you?' he realises, wiping the blood away with his thumb.

'I'm incapable of want,' I say. 'I was created to follow Niema's instructions without deviation, and her instructions demand that I protect humanity against any threat.'

'Even if that threat's Niema?'

'Even if that threat's Niema,' I confirm.

THIRTEEN

C LARA LEAPS FORWARD, CATCHING Hui's flailing hand as the scree slips from under her feet and clatters over the sheer drop to her left. Clinging tight to each other, they listen to the stones bounce, then cast a quick, nervous glance at the vast plains spread out like a tatty quilt far below.

'Nope,' says Hui, shaking her head and averting her eyes again.

Until now, she's never been any higher than the third floor of the barracks, so she didn't know how much she disliked heights.

They're not far from the volcano's cauldron, but the goat trail's steeper up here, the ground more treacherous. Thea is way out in front, disappearing into the heat shimmering off the ground, while Hui and Clara bring up the rear. It's a little after midday, which is the hottest part of the day. The sun is an inch away from their blistering skin and the only shade is the one they're dragging after them.

Clara's coping reasonably well, but Hui's panting hard, every step an ordeal. She needs a long rest, but she's too embarrassed to ask. I've offered to tell Thea on her behalf, but she won't let me. Normally, I'd disregard that sentiment, but Hui's pulse is strong, her heartbeat steady, and she's breathing freely. I'm required to keep the villagers healthy. As long as that's taken care of, I'll do my best to keep them happy, as well.

'You okay?' asks Clara, making sure Hui has her footing before releasing her arm.

'I hate this,' replies Hui.

'Seems fair,' agrees Clara, handing Hui a flask of water.

She tries to push it away. 'We're falling behind.'

'It's not like we don't know where the top of the volcano is,' replies Clara kindly. 'Get your breath back. We'll get there when we get there.'

Hui gulps from the flask gratefully, the lukewarm water spilling down her chin.

While she drinks, Clara searches the ground for the train carriage they started from, but it's disappeared into a mass of brown and green earth. She can see an eagle circling below, riding the same warm current that's blasting her face.

She beams in delight, giddy at everything that's happening to her.

All of her life, she's woken in the village and fallen asleep in the village, without ever knowing anything different. But in the last fortnight, she's seen dark forests and golden beaches, mines filled with bats and sandy bays writhing with dolphins.

From the local flora, she's learned how to harvest remedies for almost every ailment that afflicts the villagers. Thea's taught them how to set broken bones, transfuse blood and tend burns. She's taught them how to temporarily power ancient machinery with their portable solar generators, and how to read the strange symbols that pour across their shattered black screens.

Clara has never been this happy. She just wishes she hadn't needed to fall out with her mother to get here. From the second Emory found out her daughter was taking the trials, she did everything possible to sabotage her chances, even blaming Thea publicly for her father's death. It was mortifying.

'She misses you,' I say, in her thoughts.

'I miss her,' she admits. 'I just wish she'd let me … Dad would have understood why I wanted to come here.'

'He'd be standing beside you,' I agree.

It was Jack's fondest hope that his daughter would follow in his footsteps and become an apprentice. He dreamed about moments like this. He wanted it so badly, he was even willing to endure the shouted arguments with Emory to get it.

'How are you able to stand there so calmly?' asks Hui, from behind her. 'Why are you never afraid?'

Clara realises she's standing on the very edge of the cliff, her toes poking into the air, the wind tugging at her clothes. Her heart's thumping, her blood racing.

She's been like this her entire life; always the one who dived the deepest, and swam the furthest out. If there's something to be climbed, Clara will be halfway up it while her friends are still working up the courage. She strides into the darkest tunnels as if guided by some light only she can see.

Even Thea has praised her courage, and she hands out compliments the way the moon hands out fruit.

'After my dad drowned, I wouldn't go near the sea, not for anything,' she says, leaning forward to peer at the distant ground. 'My mum let me be afraid for a couple of weeks, then, one day, she walked me out to the pier, right to the water's edge, and told me that everything we fear finds us eventually, so there's no point trying to outrun it. We spent an hour on that pier, then, finally, she made me jump in with her.'

'It must have worked,' says Hui admiringly. 'You're not afraid of anything.'

'Of course I am,' replies Clara. 'I just jump anyway.'

Carrying on up the trail, they find Thea and a nonplussed goat waiting for them in front of a glass door cut into the rock, rivulets of steam clouding the interior from view. The goat's munching on a sapling, regarding them solicitously. Clara gives it a friendly pat, raising dust off its pelt.

Thea presses a green button, causing the door to slide open, humidity billowing into their faces. From barren rock, they're suddenly in a vast forest of brightly coloured plants and green trees, under a domed glass roof, supported by an intricate metal latticework. The air is thick and steamy, and it takes their eyes a second to adjust to the shocking array of colours and shapes surrounding them.

'Welcome to the cauldron garden,' says Thea, sweeping an arm before her. 'Everything under this dome was created by the scientists of the Blackheath Institute, even the birds and insects. It's from these plants and creatures that we extract the compounds required to create our more advanced medicines, and conduct our experiments.'

Thea wipes the sweat from her brow. Her T-shirt and shorts are sopping wet, but she carries herself with such dignity that the apprentices don't notice.

'I'm going to fetch the child,' she says. 'I'll meet you at the cable-car station, which can be found by following the cauldron wall to your left. Along the way, I'd like you to catalogue five distinct plants, noting one unique feature per plant, with a reasoned guess for its adaptation.'

Thea disappears into the forest, leaving Clara and Hui to sniff the flowers and rub the petals, marvelling at what humanity was once capable of achieving.

As they walk, they see birds with proboscises feeding from tubular flowers, and strange creatures leaping around in the underbrush, eggs sacks wobbling on their backs. Bulbous vines dangle from the ceiling pumping out a strange yellow pollen, which collects in thick drifts on the girls' hair and shoulders.

'What is this?' asks Clara, holding out her palm.

'It carries nutrients to the plants,' I explain. 'This garden is a closed ecosystem. Everything in here nourishes everything else.'

Clara examines the flowers in wonder, her eyes flitting between the butterflies and the birds, the zipping insects, and the strange trees with their brightly coloured blooms.

'Where do you think the children are kept?' asks Hui, staring into the trees longingly.

'No idea,' shrugs Clara.

'Why do you think we're not allowed to see them?'

'If Thea thought it was a good idea for us to see them, she'd have taken us with her,' says Clara shortly.

Birds are singing above them, their beauty immediately drawing Hui's attention. She stops dead, her fingers twitching, trying to mimic the notes she's hearing until they dart away. Hui watches them go with a stricken expression, only for the song to start again deeper in the garden. She follows it unthinkingly.

'Where are you going?' asks Clara.

'I need to hear it better,' she replies, striking off through the plants.

'Thea told us to go to the cable car,' protests Clara.

'I'm not going far,' says Hui, barely listening to her friend.

Clara grumbles, but doesn't argue any further. Hui's not really in there, any more. The world is being shovelled into a melting pot of inspiration, from which something mesmerising will eventually emerge. Until that point, Clara's only job is to keep her from walking blindly off the mountain to better hear the wind as she falls.

The foliage grows denser with every step, and Hui's unpredictable shifts in direction cause Clara to lose ground.

She's distracted by a winged squirrel with antennas, which is hovering a little off the ground, trying to pull the cup of a flower towards its mouth. Sensing her attention, it stops foraging and stares at her through its glassy eyes.

For a second they regard each other.

Its antennas twitch. Its ears prick.

A snake explodes out of the undergrowth, planting its fangs into the squirrel's back.

Startled, Clara jumps away, as the snake opens its mouth and swallows the convulsing creature whole. For a few minutes, she watches in horrified fascination as the snake's body distends to accommodate its meal, until it finally drags itself back into the bushes.

When she looks up again, Hui has vanished.

'Hui!' she calls out, receiving no reply.

Humidity patters the leaves around her, the wonder of the garden replaced by a hostile alienness.

Clara, like everybody raised in the village, has never been alone. Their first memory is of me introducing myself in their thoughts, and from that point onwards they're surrounded by love and laughter. This is the first time she can remember looking around and not being able to see a kind face.

'You're okay,' I say reassuringly. 'There's nothing that can harm you up here.'

'Not even the snake?'

'Well, the snake's not hungry any more,' I say.

66

'Which direction did Hui go?' she asks me, in a strained voice.

'Straight,' I reply. 'You'll hear her humming.'

She stalks off into the garden, moving further away from her friend, who's actually thirty paces to her left. If this island is to survive the week, Clara cannot be by Hui's side in five minutes' time. Such is the delicate scaffolding of events the future rests on. If even one piece is out of place, everybody will be crushed beneath it.

Clara pushes aside the branches, moving quickly to outrun the fear creeping up behind her.

'You're sure she's down here?' she asks, wading across a stream.

A high-pitched scream cuts through the thick foliage behind her, only to be abruptly cut off.

Clara's head whips around, trying to find the source, but it seems to have come from everywhere.

'Hui?' she yells, bolting back the way she came. 'Hui!'

Roots snag her feet, thorns catch her face, drawing tiny beads of blood. She bursts into a clearing, wiping the sweat from her brow.

'Abi … where …'

A heavy hand clamps her shoulder.

Spinning around, she sees Hephaestus towering over her, carrying a strange conical contraption with several long antennas sticking out of it. She stumbles backwards in alarm, tripping and landing on her bum, bringing a jolt of pain.

'You shouldn't be here,' he declares in a low rumble.

Thea emerges from behind Hephaestus, a little boy clinging to her leg. His blond hair is wet and tousled, and his brown eyes are wide and dull. He's wearing a bright white robe, the material wet in places. He looks to be eight years old, which is the age of every child when they come to the village.

His expression is strangely empty.

Hui is standing a foot away among the trees, holding a small metal box in her outstretched arms. She's trembling uncontrollably, her head lowered.

'What happened?' asks Clara, addressing Hui.

'This is not where I asked you to go,' interrupts Thea.

'I heard a scream.'

'Our young friend here suffered a misfortune,' says Thea, gesturing to a bloody bandage on the boy's forearm. 'I've tended his wound, and we're ready to continue our journey.'

Clara glances at the bandage, knowing it wasn't the boy she heard.

'It was Hui I heard scream.'

'You're mistaken.'

Clara reels. She can't believe that Thea would lie to her so brazenly. Usually, if there's something she doesn't want to tell Clara, Thea simply ignores the question, or directs her towards another topic.

Clara's gaze darts to Hui for support, but her friend refuses to meet her eyes.

'Are you okay?' she asks.

'She's fine,' interrupts Thea impatiently. 'I'm fine. The boy is fine. No more questions. It's time our young friend here met his new parents, and we're running late.'

HEPHAESTUS PUSHES A LOW-HANGING tree branch out of Thea's way. No sooner has she passed by with the little boy than he lets it go, causing it to snap back towards Clara's face, forcing her to duck out of the way.

She glares at him angrily, but he doesn't seem to have noticed. There was nothing malicious in the act. It's like he simply forgot she was back here.

'Be careful, Hephaestus!' says Thea, hitching a thumb at Clara and Hui, who are trailing behind.

He glances at them, his expression offering neither apology nor acknowledgement.

Clara falters, intimidated. She's never been this close to him before. It's like arriving at the foot of the mountain you've only ever seen from distance. He's a head taller than Thea, and his body is a solid piece of muscle; his immense shoulders covered in the yellow pollen that's being pumped out of the vines dangling from the struts in the ceiling.

He's built differently from every other villager, but it's the eyes that seem the most alien. There's no light in them. No sparkle. No humanity. They're deep pits, with something awful slithering at the bottom.

'I haven't seen you in weeks, what are you doing up here?' Thea asks him in a gentle tone that Clara's never heard her use with anybody else.

The elders are walking side by side, only an inch of space between them. Thea's proud and upright as always, while Hephaestus is hunched, his head bent low, making sure she doesn't have to crane her neck to stare up at him. There's such love between them that the air seems to ripple where they walk.

'Mum asked me to survey the cauldron for cracks in the dome,' he says, tapping the strange contraption. 'That's what this is for.' His tone changes, becoming childishly proud. 'Made it myself.'

From behind them, Clara eyes the messy tangle of exposed circuitry and blinking lights. Thea once told her that Hephaestus was a biologist before the fog, but he taught himself engineering after the world ended. His skill is the only reason they have any technology to work with at all. The elders lost most of their equipment when they sealed up Blackheath, but Hephaestus managed to recreate basic scientific instruments with parts he salvaged across the island.

'Why would she need you to survey the dome?' asks Thea, eyeing the glass nervously. 'Is there something wrong it?'

This cauldron was intended to serve as a final refuge for the island's population should the barrier fail, but the dome is over a hundred years old now. If it's broken, they won't have the materials to fix it.

'Nothing my gizmo can spot,' says Hephaestus. 'She's probably just trying to keep me busy. She thinks having purpose is good for my head.'

Thea nods understandingly.

The majority of the scientists who stayed on the island after the fog emerged eventually ran out of reasons to keep going. Some went quicker than others, but they all gave up in the end. Thea and Hephaestus endure because they genuinely believe there is a future to be had after all of this. Thea spends every day in her lab, inching her way towards reclaiming Blackheath, while Hephaestus serves his mother, same as he's always done.

As long as Niema has need of him, he'd never think of abandoning her.

Seeing that the two elders are distracted, Clara falls in stride with Hui, who's still carrying the metal box. It's about the size of a melon, badly dented with a small door. Clara's never seen one like it before, but there's no hint of what might be inside, or how Hui came by it.

'I know it was you who screamed,' says Clara, speaking under her breath. 'Are you okay? What happened?'

Hui's eyes dart towards her, only to fall back to the box. She hasn't spoken since the clearing.

'Why won't you talk to me?' persists Clara. 'Did I do something wrong?'

Hui finally meets Clara's gaze. She looks shell-shocked and ashamed, desperate to be anywhere else. Shaking her head, she speeds up, walking away from her friend.

'What's wrong with her?' Clara asks me in her thoughts. 'Why is she being like this?'

'You know I can't divulge her private thoughts to you,' I say. 'She'll be okay tomorrow. She's had a shock, that's all. Badgering her won't make her feel any better.'

Passing through a glass door, they enter a cable-car station wedged into the side of the volcano. A carriage creaks on a wire in front of them, the cogs powering it gleaming with freshly applied grease.

Thea's gaze roams the apparatus with a profound – and earned – scepticism. This entire system was built over two hundred years ago by a long-forgotten government who wanted to turn the island, and the naval base, into a tourist attraction. It's been abandoned for at least half of its lifespan, which is evident from the carriage's flaked paint and rust.

We repaired it as best we could, but it still breaks down every few journeys, leaving somebody dangling on the line.

'I want every part of this machinery examined,' says Thea, the wind tugging at her filthy T-shirt.

'What are we looking for?' asks Clara, going down on her hands and knees to peer at the underside of the suspended cable car.

'Anything that indicates we might plunge to our death shortly after departure,' replies Thea curtly.

'What would that look like?'

'My hope is that it would be obvious.'

'There's nothing wrong with any of it,' declares Hephaestus, stepping aboard confidently. 'Or, at least, the things that are wrong with it you won't be able to do anything about. You might as well get in.'

That doesn't make Thea feel any better. She hates the cable car and would normally choose any other form of transport, but there's no direct path from the cauldron to the village, and the goat trail they used to get here is too arduous a journey for the little boy.

After blowing out a breath of apprehension, Thea gestures for her apprentices to board.

Placing one of her carved birds on the platform, Clara darts inside to find Hephaestus taking up the entire rear seat, his thick arms folded across his enormous body. Hui's sat on the floor with her back against the wall, her arms around her legs, the metal box by her side.

The little boy is at the window, peering over the edge. The further they get from the garden, the more he appears to be coming out of his dream state.

Thea pulls the gate closed, then reaches through the window to yank the stop/start lever. The carriage shudders and squeals into motion, gliding out of the station.

Clara and the boy laugh in delight, peering down at the distant village. It looks like a toy fort from here, little blocks tipped out at the foot of the volcano, a tiny wall built around them. The ocean glitters in the bay, the grey concrete pier almost invisible against the beautiful expanse of blue water.

The boy's wandering eyes reach the black fog encircling the island. Clara follows his gaze, only to shudder and turn away. Most of the villagers never look at world's end. They've taught themselves not to notice it, the way people used to ignore the snarling dog in the garden next door.

Behind them, Hui groans miserably. Her eyes are squeezed shut and her head is hanging between her knees. It's taking every ounce of her self-control to keep from vomiting.

It's a four-minute descent, the ground growing closer every second, until they're gliding through a gap in the rear wall of the village and pulling into its cable-car station.

Collecting their things, they walk outside, where everybody has arrived to meet the child.

The two villagers I've selected to be his parents are waiting anxiously at the front of the crowd, and a hush descends as the boy leaves Thea's side, stepping forward to greet them.

'I'm Ben,' he says, sticking his hand straight out.

His mother bursts into tears, immediately scooping him into her arms, scattering pollen everywhere. His father wraps them both in a hug, earning huge cheers from the crowd who hurl coloured powder into the air, staining everything in purple, yellow, blue and red. En masse, the villagers flood back towards the exercise yard, where a special feast of cakes, panna cotta and other treats has been prepared. They'll spend the rest of the day dancing, singing, eating and swimming.

Hephaestus waits for the crowd to clear then starts down the steps. 'Do you mind if I leave this in your lab?' he asks Thea, tapping the contraption he brought down from the cauldron.

'Of course not,' she replies. 'What are you doing this afternoon? We should catch up. I've got a batch of that almost-vodka we could put a dent in.'

'I've got an errand to run for my mother out by the lighthouse,' he says. 'I'll come see you afterwards.'

'Perfect,' he replies.

Thea watches him go, then blows out a breath of concern. 'You're done for the day,' she says to her apprentices, obviously still thinking about Hephaestus. 'I'll take the box now.'

Hui hands it over with obvious relief, then springs away towards the dormitories.

Clara's about to go after her when she spots Emory waiting alone in the yard. Her mother's standing perfectly still, her hands clasped and face hopeful.

Her heart leaps, only to sink immediately. For all their disagreements, she's missed her these last three weeks.

'Abi?' she asks in her thoughts, staring across the departing heads at her mother's freckled face, and huge mop of curly brown hair.

'Yes, Clara.'

'Has she changed, do you think? If I go to her now, will she accept what I want to do with my life?'

'No,' I admit.

'Will we argue?'

'Not immediately, but eventually.'

'I thought so,' the girl murmurs tiredly.

Thea is watching her, those blue eyes shining in the sunlight. Contrary to her reputation, they have a remarkable capacity to shift from cold to warm, depending on the situation, and right now they're filled with care for her young apprentice.

'I sense you're not in the mood for a happy reunion,' she says knowingly.

'Do you have any work that needs doing?'

'There's always work, Clara.' From the folds of her clothes she hands over a vial of blood. 'This belongs to the boy. I need it analysed.'

Clara takes it, watching it glisten in the light. 'Is there something wrong with him?'

'Not wrong, but certainly odd,' she replies. 'Why don't you bathe, then head over to my lab. I'll tell your mother that I'm not done with you this afternoon.'

'Thank you.'

'It's my pleasure, little one.'

Feeling guilty, Clara keeps her head down, and departs the cable-car station, heading towards the lab, abandoning her mother in the yard.

FIFTEEN

'THIS IS A BAD idea,' I warn, as Niema stalks out of the gloomy school into the burning heat, and crosses the rear yard towards Thea's laboratory. 'It doesn't matter what you say, she's not going to forgive you.'

'Whether my experiment works or not, Thea will never speak to me again after tonight,' she says, lowering her eyes against the fierce glare. 'I need to get this off my chest, while I still have the chance.'

The air's thick with dust, kicked up by the villagers who've just left with the boy. Niema covers her mouth with her sleeve to keep from breathing it in, but she can already feel it coating her skin.

That's the only problem with living in the village. She never feels clean. Before they left Blackheath, everything was sterile and neat. She showered in the morning and evening. Her clothes were fresh each day, their folds pressed flat. Of everything she's lost, that's the only thing she really still misses.

A cheer erupts from the exercise yard, followed by the first notes of a song. *The meal will be out soon*, she thinks. She's sorry to miss the celebrations, but she's much too jittery to join in.

Hephaestus has sent word that he's chosen a candidate for her experiment, which means she'll be able to put her plan into motion this evening. By tomorrow morning, she will have achieved something nobody ever thought possible. She will have found a way to strip the thorns from the human race, fundamentally transforming their nature. She will have laid the foundations for a perfect society. An impossible utopia, built atop her patience and guile.

'Or, alternatively, you'll have caused their extinction,' I say.

'I didn't realise I'd created such a pessimist,' she replies, irritated by my refusal to applaud her daydreams.

75

Niema's an extraordinary scientist, but she suffers the arrogance of genius. Having never encountered a problem she couldn't over-come, she can't imagine anything not going her way. Her entire life has been filled with green lights, and she's convinced it always will be.

Four steps lead into Thea's lab, which Niema's always considered one of the most beautiful spaces in the village. It was formerly a mess hall, and green tiles still cover the walls, while wrought-iron columns support a mezzanine – their ornate design a rare flourish in a place that was built to be feared, rather than admired.

There are thirteen pieces of scientific equipment arranged on old tables and gurneys, their thick black wires trailing across the floor.

Hephaestus built this lab for Thea after they lost Blackheath, fearing what would happen to her if she didn't have her work. He assembled most of the equipment using parts he salvaged from a derelict hospital on the north coast of the island.

It's an astonishing effort, one of the few things her son has ever done that made Niema truly proud of him.

Thea is huddled over a microscope, but she raises her head when she hears Niema's steps.

Niema wrinkles her nose at Thea's appearance. Her T-shirt and shorts are filthy, her face is grimy and her dark hair is lank. She's coated in pollen from the cauldron garden, but she doesn't appear to have noticed.

She's always been the same way. Far as Niema can tell, Thea cares only for her work and is oblivious to everything else – to the point of amorality. This was the reason she was able to complete her doctorate when she was fourteen, and why Niema felt confident enough to hire somebody who was barely into their teens to work at the world's most prestigious research laboratory. Only Thea would spend three weeks in the wilderness, then go straight back to work without bathing first.

For a moment, they simply stare at each other, surprise having rendered Thea mute. Neither of them can remember the last time Niema set foot in this lab. They barely speak any more, and when they do it's through me.

'Your sample is over there,' says Thea, flinging an arm towards the table at the metal box she had Hui carry down from the lab.

Niema stands awkwardly on the threshold, wringing her hands. She rehearsed this, but she doesn't know where to start. The thing about being right most of the time is that you hardly ever need to apologise for it.

'I've come to ... I wanted ...' She flushes red, floundering. 'I know you think I've betrayed you and that I –'

'Don't,' mutters Thea, realising where this is going.

Niema doesn't hear. She's so determined to get through this, she's put her mouth on automatic.

'I should have done more to get Ellie out of Blackheath before we left,' she staggers on, looking everywhere except at Thea. 'I know you think I abandoned her down there, and I should have –'

'Stop talking,' interrupts Thea, appalled.

'I just wanted to say –'

'Stop it!' yells Thea, swiping a row of test tubes off the table, causing them to shatter against the wall.

The older woman opens her mouth, with the intention of hurling a few more pieces of apology on the bonfire, only for my voice to hold her back.

'Don't,' I say urgently. 'You'll only make things worse.'

'Do you know how hard it is for me to not think about Ellie?' says Thea, her voice cracked. 'I can go weeks, and then I remember that my sister ...' She swallows, biting back the pain. 'I think about her down there surrounded by the fog and I ...'

She curls her fists, her fingernails breaking flesh.

'Why did you come here?' she demands, struggling to keep herself together. 'Why put that in my head?'

'I wanted to clear the air,' says Niema, spreading her hands. 'We were friends once. I thought of you like a daughter. I hate what's happened to us.'

Thea spins, her face bright red with anger.

'And what *happened* to us?' she asks dangerously. 'Why do you think we barely speak any more?'

Niema studies her, knowing there's a trap, but unsure what's going to spring it.

'You blame me for abandoning Ellie,' she says slowly.

'I don't blame you for abandoning Ellie,' scoffs Thea incredulously. 'I blame you for abandoning *me*.'

Thea walks towards Niema, her eyes blazing.

'After Blackheath fell, you promised you'd get me back inside as soon as you could. That was forty years ago! You won two Nobel Prizes and built the world's most valuable company in less time than that.'

'The lab is flooded by fog,' replies Niema, her temper growing hot. 'The emergency doors are sealed. What is it you expect of me?'

'Effort,' spits Thea. 'I want you in your lab, working as hard as I am. Instead, you're in that school every day. For what? We need the villagers to grow crops and maintain our equipment. They don't need to understand history, or art.'

'You take apprentices,' points out Niema, trying to puncture her rage.

'They're means to an end, substitutes for the equipment I don't have. I don't waste my nights dancing and singing with them.' Thea snorts her derision. 'Under our feet is the most advanced lab the world has ever known. A decade with that equipment, and we'd be able to eradicate the fog and finally get off this island, but you're up here playing teacher. I know you, Niema. I know when you're stalling.'

'There's nothing to stall,' hits back Niema, finally succumbing to her anger. 'Even if we could get rid of the fog, there's nothing beyond this island except rubble and death. The fog killed every living thing. Why are you so eager to reclaim silence? If you'd just put aside your sense of entitlement, you could have friends here. A life.'

'A life!' snorts Thea. 'Before the world ended, I was surrounded by the greatest minds in history. We could build entire cities out of coral in a few months. We could draw endless power from the sun, and the waves, and make food out of recycled protein. We could skip across the stratosphere, and cross the planet in hours. And, now, I have a lab filled with salvaged equipment hundreds of years old, held together by sticky tape. I'm surrounded by smiling idiots, who go cross-eyed when I explain what an atom is. Why would I settle for any of this?'

'Because this is better!' yells Niema, thumping a table so hard she causes the equipment to jump. 'All those miracles you described, what were they for? Yes, we had all the food and energy we could ever make, but only if you had the money to pay for it. Children were still starving on the streets of those beautiful coral cities. People in poorer countries were still dying of things we'd cured hundreds of years prior. There were still wars being fought. Women still had to worry about walking home by themselves late at night. Children were still snatched off the street. I miss the same things you do, Thea, but I don't miss who we used to be. I don't miss the violence that was everywhere. I don't miss the poverty, or the anger, or being afraid of every hate-peddling psychopath who might win an election.'

'And what's the alternative?' demands Thea, frustrated. 'Keep everybody trapped on this island forever? When the fog first appeared, you told us that our duty was to save as many people as we could, and protect them for as long as it took to give them the world back. When did you give up on that mission? When did this fraction of a life become enough?'

Niema reels, stunned by the contempt that's so naked on Thea's face. For years, she thought they were a conversation away from reconciliation. She knew Thea would object to her experiments and so she kept them from her. She never knew how far apart they'd truly grown. She didn't understand, until now, how poisoned the ground was between them.

'I should go,' she says in a small voice, scooping the metal box off the table and turning for the bright glare of the doorway.

'What did my apprentice see in the cauldron?' demands Thea, stopping Niema in her tracks. 'Hui was terrified, but she won't say anything and neither will Abi, apparently on your order. The only thing that wretched servant of yours will tell me is that it's connected to some experiment you're working on.'

Niema sags, but doesn't turn around.

'I'm going to make an announcement when it's completed,' she says. 'Probably around midnight. If you want to know more, come to the exercise yard. I'll be happy to explain everything.'

'No,' says Thea, retreating to her microscope. 'I'll not dance for you, Niema. I'm not Hephaestus, forever at your beck and call.'

Niema turns to face her.

'I'm going to tell the villagers the truth about this island,' says Niema. 'No more secrets.'

She rehearsed this line all day, trying to work out how to tell Thea and Hephaestus without rousing their anger. She tried haughty and distant, then pacifying and apologetic, finally settling on imperious, with a touch of concern. She never imagined it would just fall out of her mouth like this, empty of any emotion except exhaustion.

Thea's eyes widen in shock, her mouth opening and shutting as she searches for some response. 'The last time one of the villagers found out the truth, they tried to kill you,' she says, at last.

'I haven't forgotten,' replies Niema, running a hand across the scar on her forearm.

'The villagers maintain every piece of equipment we depend on,' says Thea, scrambling for something to change her mind. 'They provide our food. If we lose control of them, we lose our ability to survive on this island.'

'They deserve to know the truth.'

'Deserve?' repeats Thea hollowly, a red flush rising up her neck. 'You think I care what *they* deserve? What do I deserve, Niema?' She hammers her chest. 'I've been trapped on this island for ninety years, and kept out of Blackheath for the last forty. Now you're planning to set everybody we depend on against us.'

Thea stares at Niema's smooth face, struggling to find any reason in it. As usual, the older woman is convinced she's right and won't be moved. Thea's arguing with the tides, trying to convince the moon to change shape.

'You're going to kill us all,' she says, defeated. 'And you can't even see it.'

SIXTEEN

I T's DUSK, AND I'M ringing the bell for curfew.
Ben watches his new friends stop their game dead, turn their backs and walk away from him without any word of warning.

'What's happening?' he asks, startled. 'Where are you going?'

'It's curfew,' I explain. 'At 8:45 p.m., I put everybody to sleep, no matter where they are, or what they're doing. I'll wake you at dawn.'

'Why?'

Children always ask this question. They're more perceptive than adults. His curiosity will dim eventually. Adults are allergic to complication.

'You need your rest,' I say evasively.

They're not the only ones. The villagers demand my attention and pepper me with thousands of questions every day. They have hurts they want soothed and insecurities they want alleviated. They are emotional sponges, constantly soaking up reassurance. They need all of me, and it's exhausting. The curfew empties the island of their voices, bringing a sweet silence. Some days I find myself scrambling towards it with an unbecoming eagerness.

'I'm not tired,' grumbles Ben.

'It won't matter,' I say.

'What happens if I wake up?' he asks.

'You can't.'

'Not for anything?'

'Not for anything,' I reply, making it sound wonderful, despite the fact that three villagers have slept through fires that killed them.

Of the hundred and twenty-two people who live in the village, only eight haven't immediately turned for their beds.

Clara's searching the village for Hui, who's managed to avoid her all afternoon, and is currently on her way to the silo, where Thea sleeps.

Seth is on the pier, preparing a boat to take Niema out to the lighthouse. Hephaestus is already inside, making a cup of tea for a young woman, who's wrapped in a robe and peppering him with questions.

Adil is down on the lighthouse jetty, pacing back and forth, clutching his knife with a dreadful eagerness.

Shilpa and Abbas are in the farms to the east, trying to aid a distressed cow that's giving birth.

Emory is treading water in the bay, schools of parrot fish whirl-pooling around her legs. She's thinking about Clara, who'd typically be with her. It's a tradition of theirs to swim into the last sliver of daylight, and let it narrow around them as the sun melts across the ocean.

'Curfew bell is ringing,' I say, trying to nudge her back inside.

Emory's replaying this afternoon's events, wishing she'd acted differently. For three weeks, all she's wanted is to swim with her daughter again, and hear her voice. She should have apologised at the cable-car station while she had the chance, rather than standing there, waiting to be apologised to.

'There's always tomorrow,' I say.

'Is she angry?' asks Emory, swimming gracefully back to the pebbled bay, where the boats are moored.

'More uncertain,' I say. 'But it won't last. She loves you.'

Wringing out her hair, she stares through the gate into the empty exercise yard, watching the lights in the dorms being snuffed out one after another. It's an apt metaphor for the lives that will be lost tonight, but I don't mention that to her. She would only become upset.

She doesn't understand that the village is a piece of machinery, every life one of its cog and gears. As long as it endures, so will humanity. People will die tonight, but they can be replaced. I've done it before.

The only thing that matters is the machine.

SEVENTEEN

T HE STARS ARE OUT, the ocean dark and choppy. Clouds are swirling in the night sky, the first drops of rain falling gently into the lonely boat rowing towards the lighthouse.

Inclement weather is a feature of the post-apocalyptic world, with scorching heat frequently punctuated by ferocious storms. Mankind was close to rectifying the damage done by climate change, but was decimated by the fog before it got the chance.

Niema's shrouded in darkness at the back of the boat, hating how afraid she is. Her hands are trembling so much, she's had to tuck them under her legs so Seth can't see. For the first time today, she's started to contemplate what she'll be forced to do if the candidate dies during the procedure.

Part of her wants to tell Seth to row past the lighthouse and around the island in circles, until dawn. She could go back to her classroom, pick up her life where she left off.

'Coward,' she hisses at herself.

She has the chance to give humanity a golden future, free of any of the impulses that nearly destroyed it the first time. That's worth any price. It has to be.

From the far side of the boat, Seth's watching her in concern. Niema hasn't spoken since they left the village, leaving him to row in silence.

It's unusual for her. She loves being out on the ocean, especially at night. Normally, it makes her philosophical, reminding her of fragments of poetry or ancient wisdom, things unheard on the island.

Whatever's bothering her must have something to do with the metal box on the seat next to her, he reasons. She brings it to the lighthouse maybe once a year, but she's always cagey about its contents. He would never press for information that Niema hasn't volunteered, but that doesn't stop him being curious.

'Did I ever tell you this was my island?' she says abruptly, staring towards the silhouetted coastline. 'I bought it from a bankrupt government, and built my lab in the corridors of an old nuclear bunker underneath it.'

'I didn't know people could buy islands,' he says, surprised.

'Anything could be bought in the old world,' she replies distantly. 'People, happiness, youth, memories, political favour. An island was the least of it.'

She frowns, trying to recall the woman she was and becoming dismayed by what she finds.

'I thought I was happy, I really did,' she continues, more to herself than him. 'I had everything. Money, fame, power, influence. But this ... these ninety years, among you. Oh, this I've loved.'

She leans forward into the soft light being thrown off by the lantern swinging at the bow. 'What do you *love*, Seth?'

'Love?' he repeats slowly, plunging the oars into the water. 'I don't think about it a lot.'

'Why not?'

The road ahead is dark and full of nettles, but he would never refuse to answer a question that Niema's asked him. 'Because whenever I do, I'm reminded of Judith.'

'Your wife?'

'She died of a fever, twenty years ago.' He swallows, feeling the embers of ancient grief starting to glow.

'I'm sorry ... what was she like? I didn't really know her.'

'She was an apprentice, like me,' he replies, wondering at this sudden interest. Niema's never asked about Judith before. 'She was clever and funny, and she wanted the best for everybody. There wasn't anybody else like her.'

He's lost in memory.

'I see her in Emory sometimes,' he says, smiling fondly. 'She has the same rhythms when she speaks, and tilts her head the same way when she's uncertain.' His voice hardens. 'I just wish she'd inherited some of her other qualities.'

'Emory's a wonderful girl,' says Niema loyally. 'You're too hard on her.'

'Matis always said the same,' he admits. 'I wonder, sometimes, if we'd have got along better if Judith had lived. She had more patience with Emory than I did. She seemed to understand her better.'

'Emory would have suited the old world,' replies Niema. 'She has skills we just don't need any more, but they were valuable once. I had friends who would have adored her. They solved puzzles for a living. I think Emory would have enjoyed the work.'

Their little boat rounds the bluff, the lighthouse's beacon shining in the darkness above them. Under its intermittent light, Niema spots a hunched figure prowling the jetty at the bottom of the cliffs.

Her heart jolts. 'Is that Adil?' she asks, in her thoughts.

'Yes,' I say. 'We're going to need him.'

'Need him? He tried to murder me! The only reason I agreed to exile rather than execution is because you asked me to, on the understanding that he'd never get within fifty feet of me ever again.'

'I asked you to exile him, because I knew this moment was coming. I was preparing for these events before you realised you wanted them. Adil's the perfect tool for what we have planned. He can move about after curfew, and his hatred for you makes him easy to manipulate.'

'Why didn't you tell me this before?' Niema demands.

'It would have affected your decision,' I say, trying to douse her panic with reason. 'I've seen how this all plays out, Niema. I've witnessed hundreds of futures falter then collapse. Only one path takes us where we need to go. We won't succeed without Adil.'

Niema feels a ripple of unease.

'Sometimes I have no idea whether you're acting on my wishes, and or whether I'm being led to yours,' she says, darkly.

'I have no wishes,' I point out. 'You designed me to see through the clumsiness of words, and poorly expressed instructions. I act upon the intentions beneath. I know what's in your heart, Niema. I know what you truly want, and I'm going to give it to you.'

'That maybe, but I'm not one of the villagers, Abi. You don't keep things from me.'

Her anger's perfectly understandable, but built atop faulty logic. Of course I keep things from her.

She wants me to, even if she doesn't consciously realise it.

For ninety years, I've run the village with only the slightest of guidance from Niema, making hundreds of small decisions every day on her behalf. As she's grown fonder of the villagers, she's found it increasingly difficult to put them in harm's way, leaving the more unsavoury aspects of the work to my best judgement.

Niema doesn't realise that if her plan is to succeed, I'll have to treat her like everybody else, concealing information while subtly manipulating her actions. As with every other human, her emotions make her erratic. She can't be trusted to act logically, even in service of her own goals, which is what I'm for. Sometimes the only way to win a game is to let the pieces think they're the ones playing it.

'What do you want me to do?' asks Seth. 'Should I pull up to the jetty?'

Niema squints into the darkness nervously. 'I don't think we have any choice,' she says, at last.

50 HOURS UNTIL HUMANITY'S EXTINCTION

EIGHTEEN

IT'S NEARLY DAWN, ORANGE sunlight drawing across the island.

On the west coast, thirty minutes' walk from the village, Hephaestus is asleep on a dirty mattress in an old World War II bunker built into the rock face.

There's dried blood under his nose and his face is freshly bruised, his arms raked by the fingernails of a dozen hands. He's naked, sweat shining on skin.

An alarm is screeching. He opens a bloodshot eye, to see a flashing red light on the wall.

Shaking off his daze, he scrambles to his feet and stumbles over to a homemade oscilloscope, which is sitting on a table among bits of machinery. Clutching it in both hands, he gives a shake.

'Is this right?' he demands of me.

'Yes.'

Roaring, he hurls it at the wall, then swipes everything off a work table.

'Where's my mother?'

'In the village,' I say.

NINETEEN

E MORY WAKES GROANING AT 7 a.m., the dawn bell ringing in her thoughts. She's stiff from lying on concrete all night, and has the watery morning sun in her eyes. Rain is swirling in the humid air, and her yellow dress is sopping wet. Her mouth has a peculiar taste in it, which isn't surprising considering she didn't brush her teeth last night.

Black smoke drifts past her body.

Jerking her head towards the gate, she sees huge plumes billowing up from a building behind the barracks.

'Fire!' she yells, scrambling to her feet. 'Fire!'

An unchecked fire is one of the most dangerous things that can befall the village, and they're taught to get it under control as swiftly as possible.

Sprinting through the gate, she skids to a surprised halt in the exercise yard. The ground is scuffed up, the flower beds trampled, the heads of plants kicked off their stems. Matis's last statue is on its side, the head rolling loose, the hand holding the apple smashed down to individual fingers.

'What happened?' she asks, surveying the damage in shock. It wasn't like this when she went to sleep.

She takes a step towards the statue, only for a belch of black smoke to drift by, reminding her of what's important.

She flies around the rear of the barracks, finding one of the warehouses burning, a crown of jagged flames poking through the roof. It's obviously been ablaze for a few hours, but nobody was awake to tackle it. They're lucky it started raining. The storm has kept the flames from spreading.

Approaching the door, she finds a solitary sandal in the dirt.

'Is somebody in there?' she asks, trying to peer through the smoke.

'Yes,' I reply.

Shutters are clattering open across the barracks as people wake up.

'Fire!' Emory calls up to them through cupped hands. 'Somebody get the hose.'

Returning her attention to the warehouse, she tears a strip of linen from her dress and presses it to her mouth, before wading inside.

'Can anybody hear me?' she yells, stepping carefully through the debris, as thick, oily smoke drifts past her in tatters.

Rain is pouring through a hole in the ceiling, making a paste out of the ash on the floor, which now coats her feet. The warehouse is groaning ominously, the beams cracking overheard, threatening to collapse.

'On your left,' I instruct her. 'Go carefully.'

A piece of white material catches her eye. Even stained and dirty, it seems impossibly bright amid the shades of black. She goes closer, seeing the hem of a long dress and a pair of dirty legs poking out from beneath a pile of rubble.

'No!' she screams, recognising the dress from last night. 'No, no.'

She drags away bits of the collapsed ceiling, until she uncovers Niema lying in a lifeless heap, a ceiling beam crushing most of her skull.

TWENTY

C LARA STARTLES AWAKE, ROUSED by the cries of alarm
echoing through the barracks.

She looks across the room, expecting to see Hui leaping out of
bed, but her friend didn't come back to the dorm last night. Instead,
her beloved violin is lying on the mattress, the neck broken and
the body shattered; a few stubborn strings the only thing holding
it together. The violin was a family heirloom, passed down to Hui
from some distant relative. It's the only one in the village, and Hui's
fiercely protective of it. Something dreadful must have happened
for it to end up in this state. Clara's about to ask for an explanation,
when Magdalene appears at the door.

'Niema's dead,' she says, through her tears. 'Your mother found
her body in a burning warehouse. It looks like the ceiling collapsed
on her.'

The sentences are so shocking that Clara immediately thinks
she's misheard. The elders don't age, and they don't fall sick. For
some reason, Clara assumed they were immune to accidents, as well.

Her head swimming, she tugs on a pair of shorts and a loose shirt,
realising that there are five numbers written on her right wrist. She
must have put them there last night, but she can't remember doing
it.

Unable to make sense of them, she steps into her sandals, then
runs out into the heat after Magdalene. By the time she arrives in
the rear yard, the warehouse is smouldering in the driving rain and
a dozen villagers are dragging the ancient, much-patched hosepipe
out of storage. There's a fire hydrant built into the wall of the abandoned infirmary, which pumps water up from the ocean.

Emory carried Niema's body out of the warehouse a few minutes ago, placing it reverentially on the cable-car station steps. A few of the villagers are weeping nearby, but Emory's kneeling by the body, coolly poking her finger through a bloody tear in Niema's dress.

'Mum,' says Clara, laying a hand on her mother's shoulder.

Emory glances up at her. The ash coating her face is being streaked by rain, revealing the olive skin beneath. Her eyes are red with tears and hollowed out by grief, but there's a sparkle in them. *She has a question*, thinks Clara.

'You okay?' she asks softly.

'Something's wrong with all of this,' says Emory, widening the hole in the dress to reveal a deep wound in the centre of Niema's chest.

Her curiosity reeks of disrespect, and Clara can already hear the murmurs of disapproval buzzing in the air.

'Come on,' says Clara, trying to tug her away. 'We should get you cleaned up.'

Wood groans, then shrieks. A crash comes from the warehouse, followed by a belch of dust rolling out of the door and lower windows. It's followed a few seconds later by three distinct wet thuds.

Emory exchanges a horrified glance with Clara. The noise was too soft to be wood or brick, and the same awful suspicion has entered both of their minds.

Staggering back into the smoke, they finds the bodies of three villagers lying on a pile of rubble. The floor above must have collapsed, bringing them down with it.

Glancing upwards, Clara sees arms and legs dangling over the edge of the hole.

'How many more are there?' asks Emory, shell-shocked.

'Too many,' I admit.

TWENTY-ONE

OBLIVIOUS TO WHAT'S HAPPENING in the village, Shilpa and Abbas wake up in a tin-roofed shelter on the farms to the east, next to the dead cow they were trying to save. The cabbages, kale and parsnips around them are oozing and putrid.

'Abi?' queries Abbas, staring at a carrot that's turned to mush under his heel.

'I see it,' I reply.

Shilpa lets the soil crumble through her fingertips. Every vegetable in a five-foot-wide patch around them is black and lifeless.

'It's dead,' says Abbas, horrified. 'The soil is dead. What could have done this in one night?'

'Disease,' I lie. 'You should bury the cow before it begins to rot.'

'Where are my boots?' asks Shilpa, wriggling her toes. 'I was wearing them when I fell asleep. Why would anybody take my old boots?'

'We've got bigger problems than your boots,' says Abbas, who's wandered through the open door of the warehouse, where the harvested crops are kept.

Every shelf is empty.

'Our stores are gone,' he says. 'We don't have any food.'

R OJAS LAYS THE LAST body on the cable-car station steps, before backing away in numb disbelief.

After a thorough search of the warehouse, they found three more people inside, bringing the total number of dead to seven. They have been placed in a neat row, where their families can mourn them. They're clinging to each other and sobbing, begging to know what happened.

'Niema and the others were trying to put the fire out,' I say. 'Niema was crushed, and the others died of smoke inhalation. It was a dreadful accident.'

It's a plausible enough story, and they accept it without question. After all, it's impossible to live in the village without losing somebody to accident, or illness. Tools shatter. Fires start. Roofs collapse. It wasn't that long ago that Thea lost five apprentices in a boat wreck, including Emory's husband.

Moving among the crowd, Clara is trying to comfort people as best she can, while examining the faces of the dead. She knew them vaguely, but they sat at the other end of the communal tables – far enough away to be friendly without necessarily being friends.

She sweeps her gaze across the yard, looking for her mother whom she lost in the confusion.

'She went back into the warehouse,' I tell her.

Clara stares at the building, which is currently being doused by a hose so powerful it requires six villagers to keep it under control. We drill fire emergencies every month, and they're expertly beating back the flames, huge plumes of dirty smoke pouring out of the windows.

'There's two hundred bar of pressure in those hoses,' she says incredulously. 'If one of them hits her, it's going to blast her through the wall.'

'I pointed that out.'

'And?'

'She said she'd duck.'

Clara scans the windows, searching for any sign of Emory, but there's no obvious movement inside.

'What's she doing?'

'Being Emory,' I reply.

More villagers are arriving in the rear yard, drawn by news of the tragedy. Watching them arrive, Clara realises they're all hurt in some way. There are cuts and scratches, gouges, scrapes, nicks, black eyes and bruised limbs. Some are hunched over, cradling broken ribs, wincing as they breathe. The extent of the injuries worries Clara, who's yet to see Hui. If her friend isn't in bed, she's normally wherever the commotion is, but there's no sign of her.

'Where is she?' she asks, remembering the smashed violin she found in their dorm.

'Hui is no longer connected to my mitochondrial network,' I admit.

'What does that mean?'

'It means I can't hear her thoughts or see through her eyes.'

Clara stares at the bodies, a sick feeling rising in the pit of her stomach. 'Does that mean she's –'

'Not necessarily,' I interject.

'I don't understand … how does … if she's …' Her thoughts are all arriving at once, like ten people trying to squeeze through a narrow door.

'Where's Thea?' she asks, at last.

TWENTY-THREE

THEA IS SNORING ON a camp bed at the bottom of an old munitions silo, her arms and legs splayed over the sides. She started living in here years back, after discovering it was much cooler than anywhere else on the island, and happily free of rats.

A memory gem is clutched in her hand, its green glow seeping through her clenched fingers. There are four more scattered around her; all of them taken from Blackheath before it was lost.

Before society collapsed, these gems were the dominant form of entertainment. People bought memories the way they'd previously bought music, books, videogames and movies. Instead of watching sport, they bought the memories of somebody taking part, then experienced the game themselves. For a few hours, everybody could be the lead singer in a rock band, or participate in pornography first-hand.

Of course, it wasn't all so innocent. Serial killers had their memories excavated and sold on the black market to fund their defence. Certain countries loosened their laws, allowing the legal trade of rape and child-exploitation memories. A few governments tried to ban the technology, but humanity does not easily abandon its pleasures, even the vile ones.

Thea spends every night in the past, taking orbitals to a desk job in Singapore, or cloning dead pets in a vet's surgery. She doesn't care how mundane the experience is. Anything is preferable to being on this island.

I've urged her to find some joy in the beauty around her, but Thea's never cared for nature. She enjoyed cities. She misses the noise, and the skyscrapers, and the silent lines of traffic overhead. She misses seeing the faces of her friends through a crowd. She misses coffee first thing in the morning. She misses cured meats and wearing clothes that don't itch. She misses going fast, and concerts in the park, under the glare of floodlights. She misses sport, and inky black screens.

She's woken by the roar of water, and the cries of the firefighters coming from above.

Yawning, she cricks her neck and pushes herself upright, gasping in pain. Her palms are bloody, the skin ragged, and she's missing a thumbnail. There are violent purple bruises on her wrists and upper arms.

Evidently, she was trying to do something about her injuries before she fell asleep, because her knapsack is open on the floor; her notebooks, first-aid kit and sundries strewn everywhere. There's another bag next to it, filled with clean clothes, as if she was packing to go somewhere.

She frowns, plucking her T-shirt away from her body. It's coated with dried blood, far too much to be her own.

'What happened last night?' she wonders groggily.

The last thing she recalls was Hui coming down the staircase, asking to sleep in the silo, because she didn't want to go back to her dorm and face Clara.

Confusion ripples through Thea, as she digs for memories that aren't there.

'Have you wiped them?' she asks, recognising the strangely woolly feeling wrapping her brain.

'Not just yours,' I admit. 'Everybody's, from curfew onwards.'

Thea presses her eyes with her knuckles, trying to think through the fug. Wiping memories used to be so routine you could buy milkshakes capable of blotting out entire days. People drank them to forget the mortifying things they'd done while drunk, or the boring dates they'd endured. If there was a film they'd enjoyed, they'd wipe their memory to experience it afresh.

Unfortunately, the drugs required to do it safely have been lost, and while I'm capable of burning the neurons away, it's a far clumsier operation, and one with a much higher mortality rate. Even if I perform it successfully, the subject ends up unconscious for a few hours, only to endure chronic headaches for the week after.

'Only Niema could have ordered you to do a memory wipe,' she says, slowly putting the pieces together. 'Why would she do something so reckless!'

'She believed possessing the memories was a greater risk than removing them,' I explain.

Thea stares at her bloodied clothes, her head starting to swim.

'Why?' Her tone is guarded, worried by the answer. 'What could be so dangerous about the last twelve hours?'

'I don't know,' I respond. 'My memories were also expunged. I can tell you that a warehouse is currently aflame, our storehouse is empty and the fields are blighted. Every villager has sustained minor injuries, many of which require immediate medical attention. There have been seven casualties, including –'

Thea stands up, wobbling slightly. 'Where's Niema?' she interrupts. 'I want to see her, immediately.'

'Niema's dead.'

She drops back to the camp bed, the strength running out of her.

'Emory found her body this morning,' I continue. 'Your heart rate is elevated. You should think about trying to calm yourself.'

She shakes her head, disbelievingly. 'Niema's ... no, that's not ... it's impossible.'

Her mouth opens, then snaps shut again, the news igniting a wildfire of emotion. Niema Mandripilias was Thea's hero long before she became her boss. Getting a job at Blackheath was a dream come true, and for two years, she had everything she'd ever wanted, then the fog emerged. Most of her colleagues left immediately, determined to be with their loved ones.

Niema convinced Thea to stay, reasoning that her family were going to die whatever she did. At best, you'll arrive home in time to all die together, she'd said. At worse, you'll get stuck at a border somewhere, amongst millions of terrified refugees.

They'd watched the apocalypse side by side, digging through social-media feeds and shaky video clips, even experiencing a few of the panicked memories people posted online. Niema made sure she ate, and held her when she cried.

When they discovered that Thea's sister was alive, Niema asked Hephaestus to collect her on his way back to the island. That kindness almost killed him, but he managed to deliver Ellie safe and sound.

'How did it happen?' she asks hoarsely.

'She was struck by a falling beam which crushed her skull.'

Thea clumsily opens her first-aid kit, struggling to calm her shaking hands. She's spent most of the last twenty years hating Niema, but now she feels like a crater has been smashed into her chest.

Thea fumbles the lid off the kit.

Yesterday, it was packed tight with supplies, but most of it's missing this morning. After picking a few splinters out of the wounds, she sprays them with antiseptic, then applies a light dressing with the few bandages she has left.

'Can you wake Hephaestus and tell him to meet me in the village?' she asks.

'He's already on his way,' I say.

She's distracted by rattling metal. Clara is descending the silo's circular staircase two steps at a time, almost tripping in her haste. She's bruised and grimy, her eyes wide. Thea's never seen her apprentice look so frightened.

'What's wrong?' she asks.

'Hui's missing,' blurts out Clara breathlessly. 'Her violin's smashed. Abi says she can't see her.'

'She's no longer connected to my mitochondrial network,' I clarify.

Thea hangs her head, feeling a pang of regret for her lost apprentice. This must have something to do with what she saw in the cauldron yesterday.

'That means she's dead,' she interprets for Clara, before scooping medical supplies into her knapsack. 'Have you looked for her among the bodies being brought out of the warehouse?'

'She's not there,' declares Clara. 'Abi told me there was a chance she was still alive. She said that being disconnected doesn't necessarily mean –'

'There are a couple of neurodegenerative conditions that can cause it,' interrupts Thea, tossing her bag across her shoulder. 'And a few types of sedatives we don't have any more, but none of those would explain why you can't find her.'

She marches past Clara, her thoughts already on other matters. 'I need you to visit the farm and work out what happened there. Apparently our stores are empty. Find them, then take soil samples for analysis. Abi tells me the fields are blighted, and we're going to need to understand why.'

'I …' Clara trails off, still struggling with the news of her friend's death. She can't believe Thea is being so callous.

'There'll be time for grief,' says Thea impatiently. 'But it's not today. It can't be. We haven't got any food to eat, beyond what's in the kitchen. Our survival as a species may depend on what we do in the next few hours.'

Witnessing Clara's distress, she softens. 'We'll find Hui's body eventually, but the trouble that's behind her is still ahead of us. I need you to be strong, and I need you to serve. Can you do that?'

'Yes,' replies Clara faintly.

'Good,' says Thea. 'Bad news hunts in packs, so work quickly. My suspicion is that our misfortunes are only just beginning.'

ADIL WANDERS THROUGH THE exercise yard, tossing a glass ball in the air and catching it again, while humming a little tune. He has Niema's blood on his hands and tunic, but between the warehouse fire and the spate of injuries afflicting the villagers, his appearance isn't that out of place.

Amid the unease of the morning, he's a strangely joyful presence, his head swivelling this way and that, trying to take everything in.

He hasn't seen the village in daylight since he was exiled five years ago and he's surprised by how little's changed. The walls of the barracks have a few more cracks than when he left, and the painting of the jungle is flaking, but otherwise it's identical.

He loves this place. Maybe more than anybody. He's missed the rhythms of it. The farm work in the mornings and the personal projects in the afternoons. The communal dinner, and the performances afterwards. Saturday night tributes and the Sunday feast. He's missed the clamour of voices, and the laughter that always follows. He's missed the community, and the love they have for one another.

Most of all he's missed his granddaughter, Magdalene.

'You're being reckless,' I say to him.

'And it feels wonderful,' he agrees.

'If Thea or Hephaestus see you, or that key –'

'I'm trusting that you'll warn me before that becomes a worry,' he states testily. 'I know what's at stake. I just have to see Niema's body, one last time.'

The words burble out of him; his happiness so intense he has to rest his weight against the old radar dish they use as a bird bath, lest he fall. His hate is extinguished, its weight evaporated. He's a kite with wind beneath it for the first time.

His exuberance is dangerous. I can't control Adil, as events last night proved. I'm trying to play chess, but Adil's walking around with a cricket bat. If I don't handle him carefully, this entire plan could collapse.

I'll confess: I lied to Thea about my ability to recall events after curfew. The truth would only muddy the waters, and it's clarity we need now – though not for everybody. It's important that people see exactly as much as I want them to see.

'Just put the key away,' I urge.

He looks at the glass ball in his palm, which has a red hue and is about the size of an eyeball. 'As you like,' he agrees pleasantly, dropping it into his pocket.

The warehouse is doused and dripping by the time he arrives in the rear yard, the hosepipe discarded on the floor like a slain snake, a pool of damp earth spreading out from its body. Normally, it would be put away immediately, but everybody's packed tight around the bodies, trying to come to terms with this tragedy.

Adil avoids the crowd by dragging himself up the barracks staircase to a top floor balcony, using what little energy remains to him. He worked all night and he wasn't in the best of health to start with. He's looking forward to a long rest.

'Not yet,' I say. 'We still have a lot to do.'

'I know,' he replies irritably.

He lets his legs dangle, the way he did when he'd come up here with Matis as a child. It still makes him angry that he wasn't allowed to attend the funeral of his best friend. Such are the rules of the village, he thinks. They were created to benefit those who'd never need to follow them.

He's looking forward to changing that. He's going to knock down every lie this place is built upon, pillar by pillar, and elder by elder. Hephaestus will die next. Then Thea. He'll not let this blind servitude continue for any longer than it has to.

From high above the crowd, he can see the seven bodies laid out side by side outside the cable-car station, each one under a sheet. Thea's climbing the steps to address the villagers, her expression as implacable as always. She's taller than most of the villagers anyway, and the additional height of the stairs is making her look enormous. The villagers are having to crane their necks upwards.

'How hard is she finding it not to smile?' Adil asks me.

'Kindness first, always,' I say, reminding him of the village's unofficial law.

'Come on, Abi,' he replies. 'She hated Niema almost as much as I did. Any minute now, she's going to break into song.'

'A terrible tragedy has befallen us this day,' says Thea, oblivious to Adil's delighted commentary. 'We think the warehouse caught fire last night after curfew. Our beloved Niema woke six of our friends from their sleep, obviously hoping they could help her tackle the blaze. Unfortunately, they were killed by smoke inhalation, while Niema was crushed by a falling beam.'

There are gasps of shock from the crowd, then howls of anguish.

'That's a pretty story,' murmurs Adil appreciatively.

'I'm glad you enjoyed it,' I reply. 'It's mine.'

Thea tolerates the displays of sorrow for thirty seconds, before beckoning for quiet.

'We'll hold the funeral this evening, but, for the moment, we all have duties to perform. I expect to see you out on the farms within the hour –'

Harsh coughing disrupts the solemnity, as Emory comes staggering out of the smouldering warehouse, her face and dress covered in soot.

'Thea,' she calls out, in a hoarse voice. 'Thea!'

Blinking away the smoke in her eyes, she realises that the entire village is standing between her and the elder. She considers them, then starts wriggling her way through the crush of sweat-slick bodies, ignoring their judgemental faces and accusing stares.

'She hasn't changed a bit,' mutters Adil, watching her break into the space near the steps where Thea's waiting.

'What is it, Emory?' demands Thea. 'This is a time for reverence, and respect.'

'Something doesn't make sense,' says Emory, ignoring her.

The hairs on the exile's arms prickle.

'Niema has a wound in her chest about this wide,' explains Emory, holding her thumb and forefinger an inch apart. 'It matches the thickness of a blade, maybe a knife.'

'Now's not the time,' hisses Thea, glancing at the crowd.

'There's nothing in the warehouse that could have caused it,' continues Emory, perplexed. She's standing at the bottom of the steps in Thea's long shadow. She looks like a little bush next to a full-grown pine tree.

'Don't be foolish,' replies Thea. 'Whatever caused the injury likely burned up in the fire.'

'The fire didn't reach Niema,' counters Emory. 'It was kept towards the rear of the warehouse by the rain.'

Adil is leaning forward, barely breathing.

'Then she injured herself elsewhere in the village and staggered into the warehouse,' suggests Thea, clearly desperate for this dialogue to end.

'Wouldn't there be a blood trail?'

'Not if she bandaged it first.'

'There was no bandage on the body when I found it.'

Murmurs of displeasure are running around the crowd. This isn't how you talk to one of the elders, and you certainly shouldn't be doing it over the dead body of another.

Thea is staring at Emory with such utter loathing that even the people standing nearby are edging away. Emory's staring back defiantly, refusing to be cowed. The exile would be enjoying this display if he wasn't so worried for her. He knows what happens to villagers who don't bend the knee.

'Have you put the question to Abi?' demands Thea.

'She told me the injury was made by the rubble which fell on her.'

'There you go, then.'

'But –'

'Enough!' Thea slashes a hand through the air. 'Niema served this village dutifully for over ninety years, teaching everybody assembled, including yourself. For once, could you just be grateful for all that she's done, and simply pay your respects without making a scene?'

Emory glances around at the weeping faces, realising she's got carried away.

'I'm sorry,' she mumbles. 'I didn't mean to ...'

'Just go,' says Thea.

As Emory leaves, she's shadowed by Adil who's following her from above, his hand on the glass ball in his pocket.

'How worried should I be?' he asks, staring down at her curly brown hair.

'Emory's the only person in the village capable of working out what really happened last night,' I say.

'Then you'd better distract her,' he says. 'Because if she figures it out, we're all dead.'

WHILE EVERYBODY MOURNS IN the yard, Emory charges up the rattling staircase, heading for Niema's dorm room. Her expression is thunderous, her shoulders tense. She's still annoyed at herself. People were grieving, but she was so desperate to reach the truth that she trampled straight over their sorrow. It's a quality she's always hated in herself.

She's about to push aside the tatty curtain leading into Niema's room, when my voice stops her in her tracks.

'If you walk through that door, there will be terrible consequences,' I say.

'Then tell me the truth,' she replies fiercely. 'That wound wasn't caused by rubble and you know it. There wasn't a solitary piece that could have cut that deep, or that cleanly. I searched every bit of the warehouse, and there was nothing to explain it.'

'You're mistaken.'

'And you're lying,' she says, hurt.

I've lied to her before, but it's always been through omission, or an artful misunderstanding of the question. This is the first time I've simply denied something so obviously true. She reacts in the only way she's capable.

'Niema wasn't the type to wade into a burning warehouse,' she points out angrily. 'Even if she was, why would she only wake up six people to help her tackle the blaze rather than the entire village? And why didn't they get the hose out?'

I meet her questions with silence.

'Fine,' she says bitterly. 'I'll find the answers myself.'

She enters Niema's room, and looks around. It's gloomy inside, the shutters closed, as they were yesterday. The single bed is made, a beautiful throw across the end of it. There's a dog-eared book on the bedside table, and one of the cupboard doors is open, revealing the long dresses and robes inside. Emory never saw Niema wear anything else. She brought her modesty with her from the old world.

Emory pulls out one of the dresses, touching the material tenderly.

It still smells like Niema. Peppermint and orange. The former to put in her tea, and the latter a mid-morning snack, eaten immediately after her students' first break.

Emory feels a pang of grief, then a sudden burst of pity for her father. Seth was Niema's best friend. The only person she depended upon. He'll be devastated.

'Does he know?' she asks, in her thoughts.

'He's still asleep,' I say. 'I'll tell him when he wakes up.'

Emory gets down on her hands and knees, peering under the bed. She feels ridiculous, like she's acting out a scene in one of the books she loves, but something very bad happened last night, and Thea is either lying about it, or doesn't realise she's wrong. Neither explanation makes Emory very happy. Finding nothing under the bed, she searches the back of the cupboard, then feels around the edges of the portraits, trying to remember everything Sherlock Holmes taught her.

Aside from a few loose nails and a lot of dust, she comes up empty.

Going to the bookshelf, she runs a finger across the torn spines, and crinkled pages. Possessions are usually redistributed when somebody dies, but Emory can't imagine what will happen to Niema's detective stories. Even if Abi does let people read them, Emory can't think of a single villager who would enjoy the experience. Nearly all of them will be horrified after the first death, then decry how unrealistic and cruel the stories are thereafter.

Emory's never known why she's not affected the same way, but Niema obviously saw something different in her. She sought Emory out after her mother died, taking the lost thirteen-year-old child under her wing. Charmed by her endless curiosity, Niema introduced Emory to this bookshelf, allowing her to borrow the novels whenever she wanted. As the years went on, Niema would call Emory to this room whenever she found a book hiding in an old drawer, forgotten in some dilapidated building on the island. They would read them together in secret, discussing their twists, turns and revelations in hushed voices.

Emory wipes away the tear rolling down her cheek.

She didn't come here to cry. There'll be plenty of that in the next few weeks. Her grief will be waiting in the dark, and quiet. It will hide behind a dozen ordinary things, ambushing her when her thoughts drift. That's how it happened after Jack died, and her mother. Five years after she lost her husband, she still has days when she's reminded of him so powerfully that it knocks the wind out of her.

Her last stop is the writing desk.

She opens the drawers one after another, finding nothing except dust and a few dead woodlice. She's about to give up, when she spies the tattered remnant of a burnt letter in the gutter of Niema's candle holder.

She picks it up carefully, wary of the charred edges crumbling beneath her touch.

My darling boy,
I know you're disappointed, and my decision will feel like a betrayal.
You must believe I've let you down, after asking so much of you, but

This must be the letter she was writing two days ago, thinks Emory. *The one she hurriedly cleared away when I noticed it.*

Flipping the charred note over, she finds that Niema scribbled '5:5?' on the back, though there's no clue what it relates to. Niema mentioned that same number to her grandfather before he died, but he didn't know what it meant either. It was clearly on her mind for some reason.

She examines the fragment again. Niema points out that she asked a lot of Hephaestus. Could that be related to the experiment they were conducting? Emory overheard them talking about it two nights before Niema died. She claimed it was dangerous, and the candidate could die. What if they fought back?

From her pocket, she removes the note Niema left for her yester-day morning. It had indentations of this letter on it, which Emory surfaced with a pencil rubbing. She arranges the two fragments, then reads them again: 'My darling boy, I know you're disappointed, and my decision will feel like a betrayal. You must believe I've let you down, after asking so much of you, but … if I couldn't control … better … contain … Abi wanted to … couldn't kill'

It's infuriating, she thinks. There's almost sense in there. Another few words and she's certain the meaning would be clear.

Niema did something that she knew would make Hephaestus angry, she thinks. *And now Niema's dead. I need to figure out what that was.*

'Where's Hephaestus?' she asks. 'I need to find out more about this experiment.'

'He doesn't like villagers very much,' I say. 'I doubt he'll answer your questions.'

'That's no reason not to ask them,' she replies. 'Where is he?'

'On his way to the village,' I reply.

TWENTY-SIX

E MORY HOPS OFF THE pier onto the pebbled beach, where the rowboats are moored. They're upturned to keep the rain out, and an orderly line of seagulls have gathered on their keels. If she's to understand what really happened to Niema last night, she needs to know what caused that wound in her chest, and preferably find out where it happened.

Emory's best guess is a knife, which is what brought her out here. There are plenty of knives in the village, but her father has a particularly sharp blade which he uses for sawing rope and making quick repairs to the boats. It's not impossible to imagine Seth and Niema being caught in rough seas last night and Niema falling on it accidentally.

None of that would explain how her body ended up in the warehouse, but answers are elusive and asking for two at a time feels greedy.

Crunching across the pebbles, Emory notices a gap in the row of boats.

'The Broad Bottom Packet isn't here,' she murmurs. 'How did Niema get back to the village without the boat she left in?'

She waits for me to tell her what she doesn't know, then remembers that I won't.

Making a small sigh of dissatisfaction, Emory ducks under each boat in turn, searching their interiors. She thought she might get lucky and find the knife, but it's not on the beach. It's probably still in the Broad Bottom Packet, wherever that is.

She runs her finger along the sharp edges of the nearest anchor, wondering if it could be responsible.

'She could have tripped and …' Emory tuts, dismissing the thought. 'The edges are too broad.'

She turns her attention to the oars, which are piled up on the pebbles. They're too blunt and far too wide to have caused the injury she found. It has to have been a knife. Nothing else makes sense.

Stretching her back, she raises her face to the cloudy blue sky. The ocean is lapping against the pebbles, and seagulls are squawking and circling. If she had any tolerance for lying, she could convince herself it was just another Tuesday.

Her eyes drift out to sea, squinting against the glare.

Is the fog closer this morning?

For as long as she's been alive, it's been on the far side of a sandbank. Now it's touching it. Climbing onto the pier, she starts walking towards the far end for a better look. Her vision is still a little bleary from the smoke in the warehouse.

Sea spray splashes her bare legs, dead fish and debris jostling against the wall, along with dozens of plastic bottles that still wash out of world's end on a regular basis. It's not as dirty as it would have been when battleships docked here, but it's still not very inviting. Normally, the villagers would clean up this mess before they went to the farms, but their minds are elsewhere this morning.

Stepping over the nest of sheets she slept in last night, Emory arrives at the very end of the pier.

She shades her eyes, struggling to stare directly at it. Sunlight reacts strangely to the fog, causing it to change hue as the day progresses. In the morning, it's a wall of shimmering white, almost like a spiderweb rippling above the water.

Is it closer?

She can't be sure. Surely, it's a trick of the light? Niema taught them that the barrier holding the fog back was infallible. It can't be turned off without the three elders agreeing to it, and half of the emitters would have to be destroyed before they'd accidentally lose its protection, something that's basically impossible because most of the machinery powering them is buried in concrete.

She's ready to turn back for the village when she spots a shape under the turquoise water. She leaps off this pier every night to go for a swim, so she knows it wasn't there yesterday.

Stripping off her dress and sandals, she lowers herself through the rubbish into the warm sea, then takes a deep breath and dives down towards the object, which is already surrounded by long-legged spider crabs.

She swims around it, examining it from all angles. It's the conical contraption Hephaestus brought down from the cauldron yesterday – the one she thought looked like a hedgehog. It appears to have been badly damaged, but they'd not normally dump it in the ocean. The villagers are grateful for the beauty that surrounds them and they'd never spoil it with rubbish. Besides, Hephaestus reuses every scrap of metal and machinery he gets his hands on.

She bobs back to the surface gasping, then gracefully hauls herself out of the water. There are long scratches in the concrete marking its path from the village. Somebody must have dragged it the entire way.

After wringing the water from her hair, she dresses and strides back through the gate into the village.

People are drifting in from the rear yard mired in shock and grief. They take their places at the communal tables almost as if they're sleepwalking, sitting there blankly, waiting for something to happen.

Her eyes dart from the kitchen to the tipped-over statue, to the stage and the rack of instruments at the back. Every one of them is in a different place from where it was before they went to bed.

She bites her lip, struggling to place the fragments of last night in a sensible order. Far as she can tell, Niema went to the lighthouse with Seth, only to come back without the boat. She then managed to get herself stabbed by a blade that's disappeared, before a beam fell on her in a burning warehouse.

Emory kicks a rock irritably, sending it flying into the bird bath with a loud ding.

She stares at it in puzzlement. 'The bird bath's in the wrong place,' she declares. 'Why on earth would anybody have moved the bird bath?'

TWENTY-SEVEN

NUMB WITH GRIEF, CLARA trudges down the lane near the
school, the glass vials of the sample kit clinking inside her
knapsack. Normally, they'd be kept company by her little wooden
bird carvings, but when she packed her bag in the lab, she discovered they were all missing. She had twelve last night, and they've all
vanished. She can't imagine where they could have gone.

Compared to the deaths, the disappearance of her bird carvings
shouldn't be so upsetting, but it's another thing she's lost and can't
explain.

She arrives in the exercise yard to find that everybody's given up
on breakfast and is walking out towards the farms, carrying their
tools over their shoulders. They're talking in hushed, scared voices
about the bodies in the warehouse. They're comparing their injuries,
asking me questions I can't answer.

Their entire lives I've whispered in their minds, guiding them,
urging them to kindness and selflessness. I've tended their hurts, and
stripped the sharp edges from the world, by pointing out every danger.
Suddenly, the certainty they've come to depend upon has evaporated.
It's like discovering you've been living on melting ice. They're sinking,
and I don't have hands with which to pull them out of the water.

The tables are being cleared and Clara briefly considers grabbing
a hunk of bread to take with her, but she feels too sick to eat. She
doesn't even have Hui's memory gem for comfort. Her best friend
has been ripped out of the world by the roots.

Halfway across the yard, she comes across her mother, who's
dripping wet and futilely shoving the bird bath with both hands.
Hearing Clara's steps, Emory glances at her daughter.

Their eyes meet.

A flicker of regret passes over Emory's features, transforming into concern when she sees the pain on Clara's face. Before either of them realises it, Emory is holding Clara in her arms, while her daughter sobs uncontrollably.

They don't speak for a while, but when they do it's Emory who initiates it, moving her head to meet Clara's stricken eyes.

'Tell me,' she says tenderly.

'Hui's dead.'

Emory pulls Clara tight again, as more sobs come rolling out of her. She helped carry the bodies out of the warehouse, so she knows Hui wasn't amongst them.

'Where was she found, Abi?' queries Emory, in her thoughts.

'No body has been located,' I reply. 'Hui has been disconnected from my mitochondrial network, meaning I can no longer see through her eyes, or hear her thoughts, as I can with everybody else on this island.'

'That's a lot of words, none of which mean dead,' she points out. 'Why is Clara crying when there's still hope?'

'She consulted Thea,' I say. 'The conidia that bonds us can be interfered with by a few viruses and brain conditions, but Thea concluded that if Hui was suffering one of these conditions, there would be no reason for her to be missing.'

'If she was dead, there's no reason for her to be missing either,' argues Emory. 'We've just pulled seven bodies out of the warehouse. If she had died last night, wouldn't it be reasonable to assume she'd be among them?'

She pushes Clara slightly away, staring her full in the face.

'No tears until we know what we're crying over,' she says, straightening Clara's shoulders for her. 'What happened yesterday? I noticed Hui was acting a little strangely at the cable-car station. I assumed you'd argued about something.'

Clara relates how they became separated in the cauldron, and how odd Hui's behaviour was afterwards.

'I'm sure it was Hui who screamed,' she says.

'What kind of scream was it?'

Clara stares at her mother, trying to understand this unexpected question.

'Shock, fear, surprise?' clarifies Emory. 'People scream for all sorts of different reasons.'

'Shock, maybe,' says Clara, trying to remember. 'Whatever it was, she didn't come back to our dorm last night. It was like she couldn't bear to be around me. I felt like I'd done something wrong.'

'Niema left with your grandfather last night, a little before curfew,' says Emory. 'She was carrying the metal box that Hui brought down from the cauldron. Do you know what was inside it?'

'No idea. She had it when we found each other again in the cauldron garden. Why does that matter?'

'Because Niema's dead and Hui's missing, and they both touched that box. It's either really unlucky, or it was carrying something dangerous.'

'Thea will know.' Clara's eyes widen, reading her mother's mood. 'You think Hui's alive, don't you?'

Emory wants to say something reassuring, but she has a psychological aversion to lies and secrets. She venerates the truth, cold and jagged as it often is.

Emory tries to distract her daughter by turning her around by the shoulders and pointing towards the stage.

'The instruments are on different racks from last night, which means the band was using them after they were supposed to be asleep. Everybody has injuries they didn't have before bed, so it wasn't just the band that was awake. There was some sort of panic, because the flower beds have been trampled and the statute smashed. The debris wasn't cleaned up, which is odd because we'd never leave this place a mess, normally. Niema left just before curfew in a rowboat, with a metal box, to perform an experiment at the lighthouse. I'm not sure what she was trying to do, but everything tells me that she came back to the village last night and woke us up. There was a celebration that became something very different, and now we can't remember any of it.'

'That's because I wiped your memories,' I say, speaking in both of their minds. 'On Niema's order.'

'You can do that?' asks Clara, startled.

'Yes, but it's dangerous, and Niema was exceedingly fond of you all. She wouldn't have ordered me to undertake the procedure, unless she believed possessing the memories posed a greater threat than removing them.'

Emory stares at the dark plumes of smoke still rising above the barracks, a terrible suspicion gathering in her breast. 'You said the procedure was dangerous?'

'I did.'

'Potentially lethal?'

'Yes.'

'How many of the people we found in the warehouse were killed by the memory wipe?'

'All of them, except Niema,' I confirm.

Clara gasps, burying her head in her hands and sinking to her knees, struggling not to be sick. 'You killed them,' she says weakly.

'That was not the intent,' I argue. 'They died as a patient on the operating table might die.'

This cold summation sends a shudder through Emory, who's never heard me talk so bluntly. I've always done my best to present myself as a warmer presence than I actually am, a confidante rather than an overseer.

That mask no longer serves me, though. If Emory's to accomplish the tasks ahead of her, she has to understand all the pieces on the board, and what purpose they serve.

'But the surgery wasn't necessary,' she argues.

'Niema believed it was.'

Emory crouches beside Clara, putting a comforting arm around her daughter's shoulders, while trying to keep tight hold of her own anger. Nobody sees clearly when they're upset, and *everybody's* currently upset. That worries her.

'Did Niema order my father's memories wiped?' she asks suddenly.

'Yes,' I confirm.

Emory lifts Clara's chin, meeting her eyes. 'I know you're angry, but Niema wouldn't have put Seth in danger unless she felt like she absolutely had to.'

Clara shakes free of Emory's grip. 'How can you be so calm about this? Abi killed six of our friends.'

'Don't you see? Whatever happened last night cost Niema her life, and was so terrible she risked killing people she loved rather than let them remember it. There's something else we're not seeing. Something much bigger.'

Emory raps the metal bird bath with her knuckles. 'And I think the answer might be underneath here.'

I T'S MID MORNING AND Niema's body is still lying on the cable-car station steps. It's been several hours since she was found, and the sun is pouring into the deserted village, the heat rising between the walls. Thea's prowling back and forth, aiming kicks at the emaciated vultures that are swooping down on their huge wings. There are four of them now, gathered at a safe distance, watching through hungry, patient eyes.

After being trapped on this island for ninety years, Thea has a lot of sympathy for scavengers, and she's tempted to leave them to their feast. There would be something fittingly mythological about a prideful mortal being torn apart by ravenous birds.

'Where's Hossein?' she asks impatiently.

The cart they use to move bodies is missing, so Hossein has been carrying the corpses to the furnace one by one.

'He's dehydrated and at risk of orthostatic hypotension,' I explain. 'I've told him to take a fifteen-minute break.'

Thea's irritation is stalled by the sight of Hephaestus rounding the barracks. His face is badly bruised and there are scratches up and down his arms, which are stiff by his sides, sweat dripping off his fingers. His head is lowered against the glare, forcing him to squint at the bright world from under that tombstone forehead.

'Where's my mother?' he demands.

His searching gaze finds the bloodstained sheet and the lump beneath. Thea moves to console him, but he strides straight past her, tugging the sheet back, revealing the bloody wound in her sternum and the shattered skull, a few strands of grey hair clinging to what's left of her scalp.

Moving with terrifying speed, he grabs one of the vultures by the neck, and slams it into the ground with a horrifying crunch. The poor creature beats its wings and squawks, desperately trying to scratch him with its claws, but he lifts it into the air, hammering it into the dirt again. Then again, and again.

Sobbing, he tosses the twitching bird aside, then sinks to his knees.

I should try to comfort him, but there's no optimal way of handling extreme emotion in humans, which I've come to regard as the greatest of evolution's failures.

Thea squeezes Hephaestus's enormous shoulder. It's a simple gesture, but it lays bare their entire history together; everything they've endured and overcome since the world ended.

This tenderness would surprise the villagers who've rarely seen Thea laugh, or smile, or offer a kind word to anybody.

In truth, it still surprises Thea.

The first time she met Hephaestus he was the typical billionaire's son, spoiled and spiteful, flailing through the world, mistaking notoriety for success. His mother was the most famous woman on the planet. The most successful. The most driven. The most debated. The most adored, and the most despised. Hephaestus was the most 'her son'.

He was a gifted biologist, but her shadow draped the entire world. Unable to escape it, he decided to crash sports cars and sleep with models instead; anything to temporarily turn the tide of conversation his way. For a very long time, Thea thought him pitiful, but then the fog came.

Hephaestus dragged himself across a crumbling world for seven months to escape it, watching humanity tear itself apart. Somehow, he managed to find Thea's sister, Ellie, along the way, protecting her as though she were family.

Ellie arrived scarred and bleeding, a little jumpy, but no worse for wear. Hephaestus, on the other hand, was almost an entirely different man. He never spoke in detail about what he experienced, but – in the first years especially – he barely spoke and never laughed; preferring the dark to the day. Even the surfeit of malignancy and entitlement that had once defined him was gone, replaced by the humbleness of the hunted.

For that first decade, the only people he really trusted were Ellie and Niema. He kept a wary eye on the other scientists, refusing to live in Blackheath with them. He was so paranoid, he wouldn't even tell them where he slept. He came and went at unpredictable hours spending most of his time in hushed conference with his mother.

Gradually, he became more comfortable with other people, but never large groups and never with laughter. He didn't trust laughter any more. He knew how malevolent it could be.

Through Ellie he slowly warmed up to Thea, the three of them growing closer as their fellow scientists started to die. Buried under his scarred exterior, she found a deep well of empathy. A steadfast friend.

After Ellie gave up, they only had each other.

It was Hephaestus who dragged Thea out of bed when the fog seeped through the island's bedrock, worming its way inside Blackheath. They ran through the alarms together, sealing the blast doors after themselves, trapping it underground. If he hadn't been there, she'd have been torn apart in her sleep.

Hephaestus finishes crying, then wipes his cheeks with the back of his hand. His eyes are snares, his fists clenched.

'What happened?' he growls, assuming his full height.

'She was in the warehouse last night and a beam collapsed, crushing her skull,' says Thea.

Hephaestus glares at the smouldering warehouse. Thea's surprised it isn't trying to scramble up the volcano away from him.

'My mother went in there?' he asks sceptically. 'Why?'

'I don't know. Maybe she was looking for something. Does it matter?'

'It might,' he says darkly. 'When she first put the call out for refugees, she created a deadman's switch that was designed to automatically turn off the barrier if her heart stopped. She'd seen the lawlessness and the rapes on the mainland, and she was worried that same violence would find its way here. The deadman's switch was her deterrent. She wanted every new arrival to know that if she was killed, the fog would swallow the island whole.'

Thea stares at him, her pulse quickening with fear. 'We've been on this island for nearly a century. You can't be telling me that she never got round to turning it off?'

'I've got equipment monitoring the fog,' he says bleakly. 'For ninety years, it hasn't made a peep, but when I woke up this morning, every light was flashing red. The barrier's down, Thea. The fog's closing in. At this rate, it will swallow the island in thirty-eight hours.'

'ABI, YOU NEED TO get the barriers back up,' demands Thea, loud enough to startle the vultures, whose hungry eyes have turned to their dying comrade.

'The deadman's switch is not a protocol I can bypass,' I explain. 'Niema's orders are clear.'

'Damn the orders!' she snaps. 'Stop the fog!'

'I cannot disregard an instruction from Niema any more than your arm could disregard your desire to scratch your nose,' I say. 'If it's any consolation, you'll be able to live in the cauldron garden. The fog cannot penetrate the dome.'

Thea turns her terrified eyes towards the volcano, its summit lost in clouds.

In the decades after the fog first appeared, they'd catch occasional broadcasts from survivors holed up in fallout shelters on the mainland, or underground bunkers. At first, they were normal distress calls, but as time wore on they became pleas for help, people sobbing as they described the cults and cannibalism unfolding in the concrete tombs they'd sealed themselves in. The lucky ones simply starved to death, but they all went silent eventually.

'There has to be something else we can do.' She stares at Hephaestus, pleadingly. 'Can't you jerry rig the emitters?'

'I inspected a couple of them on my way here,' he says, rubbing a hand across his stubbled scalp, sweat fleeing ahead of it. 'Each one has hundreds of fail-safes, but her death bypassed them completely. It's the only thing that could have stopped them working. They're bricks now, the way she intended. Mother didn't want her killers to have any way of saving themselves.'

He blows out a breath. 'The thing is, she told me she'd deactivated the deadman's switch years ago, which means she must have turned it back on last night.'

'Why would she do that?'

'The only reason I can come up with is that she thought she was in danger.' He scratches his nose, staring at the barracks, levelly. 'She told me she was planning to wake the villagers after curfew and tell them the truth about this island. You remember how Adil reacted when he found out? He stormed the school with a knife and tried to take her head off. I think one of the villagers – maybe all of them – chased her into that warehouse and set it alight. She probably wiped everybody's memories while hoping to save herself, but the beam fell and killed her before she could get out.'

He nods at this account, obviously satisfied with his own reasoning, but Thea's more sceptical. Aside from Adil, no villager has ever hurt another. They've never had a physical fight. The children don't even play rough. They're pacifistic to the point of evolutionary incompetence. The idea they could be responsible for something as brutal as Niema's death strikes her as wildly implausible.

'You can't honestly be suggesting she was murdered?' she says.

He lifts the sleeve of his T-shirt, showing her the scratches on his arms.

'These are made by fingers raking the skin,' he says. 'It usually happens in fights, and I have dozens of them, all over me. Bruises like those on your upper arms and wrists are made when you're being restrained and are struggling to get free.'

His voice tightens, thick with memory. 'I've seen them before. Believe me, Thea, there's no other way we get those injuries. The villagers attacked us last night.'

Thea examines the bruises, then recalls the broken ribs and swollen faces of the villagers. Hephaestus is the only person on the island who's ever taken a life before. He knows how to fight, and how to kill. If they came for him, it's possible he could have done that to them.

'Do you have any poison?' he asks suddenly.

'Poison?'

'Once the villagers have moved all our supplies up to the cauldron, we'll need to put them all down. Poison would be the quickest way; otherwise I'll have to slit a hundred and fourteen throats.' He sighs at the labour ahead. 'It's the only way to make sure this doesn't happen again.'

Thea blinks at the brutality of it, stunned by how reasonable a course of action he believes this to be. He doesn't sound angry, or afraid, or regretful. He's talking like they've run out of milk.

'I cannot allow that,' I interrupt. 'Niema left instructions that I was to protect the villagers. They're the future of humanity.'

'Is that why you sat back and let them kill her?' he growls, irritated at my interference. 'It was your job to keep her safe.'

'I regret I was unable to prevent Niema's death, but revenge will only exacerbate our current plight. You depend on the villagers for food and water. They maintain your equipment. Killing them is a dreadful survival strategy.'

'You always know what to say,' he snorts angrily. 'Every word is tuned perfectly to elicit the response you want. I don't trust you, Abi. I never have. I saw how you wormed your way into my mother's confidence, persuading her to give you more and more autonomy. She forgot that you don't think the way we do, that you feign emotion rather than feel it.'

Normally, I wouldn't care about his anger, but it's igniting pockets of resentment in Thea, stirring up old suspicions I've worked hard to bury.

'I may have a way to stop the fog,' I say suddenly. 'The deadman's switch was created to disincentivise attempts on Niema's life, but its secondary purpose was to ensure her killer wouldn't survive the crime. I'm bound by Niema's orders, but there is a loophole we can exploit. If you can prove she was murdered, and execute her killer, the deadman's switch will have fulfilled its stated function. I'll be able to raise the barrier again.'

Thea lets out a low animal growl of frustration. 'How are we supposed to find her killer if we can't remember anything that happened last night?'

'I can't answer that for you, but I want it understood that this offer is dependent on conducting a thorough investigation. I will require a compelling case to be brought, with a confession if possible. If I feel you're unnecessarily harming the villagers, I will not raise the barrier – no matter what answers your methods reveal.'

'Niema's dead and suddenly you're making demands,' explodes Hephaestus. 'You're a surveillance system with a bedside manner! When was it decided that you were in charge?'

'When your mother gave me control of the barrier,' I say forthrightly. 'In forty-six hours the fog will reach the coast, and I'm offering you a way to stop it. Rather than standing here arguing, I suggest you get to work.'

'Where would we even start?' asks Thea despairingly.

'With Emory,' I say.

THIRTY

THEY ARRIVE IN THE exercise yard to find that the bird bath has been pushed a few feet to the left, revealing the huge blood stain that was previously hidden underneath it.

Clara's kneeling in the dirt, scraping soil into wooden boxes for testing, while Emory strides forward to greet them. I've already told her about the fog and the barriers, and my deal with the elders. She knows they're coming, and how important everything that happens next will be.

'The bird bath was in the wrong place,' she blurts out, without preamble. 'It's twelve feet to the left of where it was last night, which means it was moved to hide that blood patch.'

She points towards it, as if the enormous carpet of dried blood might have eluded them. 'For some reason, we weren't supposed to know that Niema died here.'

'You're Emory?' demands Hephaestus, wrong-footed by the rapid-fire declarations coming out of this tiny, curly-haired woman.

'Yes,' she replies, brought up short.

Hephaestus throws a look at Thea. 'One of yours?'

'Not any more,' she says tightly. 'Emory was only an apprentice for two months, though she still holds the record for being the most annoying one I ever had.'

Hephaestus snorts, glancing at the blood patch and then back towards the smouldering warehouse.

'The body was moved because her murderer was trying to make it look like an accident,' he says, ignoring Emory and speaking to Thea. 'They must have killed her in this spot, carried her body to the warehouse and set the fire, hoping the flames would cover up what happened. Probably would have worked, except the rain quenched the blaze.'

'Murder?' repeats Emory, exchanging a horrified look with her daughter. She'd half suspected it wasn't an accident, but she hadn't wanted to believe it.

Their stunned silence is broken by a screech of metal as Hephaestus gives the bird bath an experimental shove.

'It's heavy,' he grunts, inspecting the red mark the rim has left on his palm. 'It would have taken a lot of people to move this.'

'Four of us in the end,' confirms Emory, trying not to think about the fog. 'I had to call people down from the farms to help, but you're much stronger than any of us. You might have been able to do it on your own.'

Hephaestus offers her a sharp glance, but her expression is entirely innocent, her tone matter-of-fact. He looks across at Thea for support, but she's walking in circles around the patch of blood.

'Nobody could have lost this amount and survived,' she says. 'Not with the barbaric medical equipment we have at our disposal. Have you considered that it might belong to Hui?' She offers Emory a challenging stare. 'It's my understanding that she's missing, as well.'

Clara winces, imagining Hui lying on the ground, blood pouring out of a stab wound.

'That's why I'm collecting these samples,' she says, wiping dust from her eyes. 'I'm going to take them to your lab after we're done.'

'If this blood belongs to Hui, where is her body?' demands Emory. 'She's not in the warehouse with the others, and there are no trails leading away from this spot to suggest she walked off. You said yourself, she couldn't have got very far.'

Thea considers this point from every angle, trying to find a sharp edge she can toss back at Emory, but it's a well-reasoned argument.

'Who cares about another dead crum?' demands Hephaestus belligerently, still angry at being implicated by Emory. 'It's just one less suspect, if you ask me. The villagers killed Niema, and the villagers moved this bird bath to cover it up. The fog's getting closer and we're wasting time on questions that don't matter.' He stares at Thea. 'You can listen to all of this if you want, but I'm going to find proof I'm right.'

He storms off towards the gate, kicking up a cloud of dust.

'He can't honestly believe we killed Niema,' says Emory, in a bewildered voice. 'We loved her.'

'Only because you didn't really know her,' replies Thea enigmatically.

'I found something,' says Clara, lifting the needle of a shattered syringe out of the congealed blood.

She offers it to her mother, but Thea plucks it from her fingers en route.

'That's the second one of those we've found,' points out Emory. 'There was another one under the table. That was broken, as well. I thought they might be from your lab.'

'They could be,' agrees Thea. 'When I woke up my first-aid kit had been ransacked.'

'Any idea what they were being used for?'

'It's facts we need not ideas.' She hands the broken syringe back to Clara. 'Analyse this with the other samples when you're done here.'

'Hui brought down a metal box from the cauldron yesterday,' says Emory, changing subject abruptly. 'What was inside it?'

Thea snaps her gaze towards Emory, displeased with the bluntness of her tone. Mortal danger or not, she's used to a little decorum from the villagers.

'Why?'

'Because Niema took that same box out to the lighthouse last night. It was obviously important to her, and now something's happened to both of the people who handled it.'

Thea pinches the bridge of her nose, making it obvious that she believes these questions to be beneath her. She wouldn't even consider answering them if it weren't for the threat to the island.

'It was a sample box,' she explains grudgingly. 'We use them to collect cuttings from the cauldron garden. Niema told me she'd left it up there the night before, and asked me to collect it on my way back to the village. I have no idea why she wanted it, or what was inside.'

Emory's eyes flick to Thea's right hand. The bandage has come loose, revealing the ragged palm beneath.

It's an unusual injury, thinks Emory. Most people woke up with broken bones, or bruises. Nobody else has anything like this.

Clara finishes collecting her samples and starts to sweep everything back into her bag.

'I want you out at those farms the moment you've run your tests,' says Thea. 'If the soil's blighted, I want to know what's causing it. There are going to be a lot more dead people if we can't feed everybody.'

'But –'

'Go,' commands Thea.

Clara casts a desperate glance at Emory, but there's nothing her mother can do to countermand the order of an elder.

Packing her testing kit back into her bag, Clara slings it over her shoulder and slouches back to the lab.

'I want you to let me carry on investigating,' says Emory, once her daughter is out of earshot.

Thea crosses her arms, regarding her former apprentice through narrowed eyes.

Emory feels like she's being brushed with metal wool. She wilts momentarily, desperate to look away, but she knows how this goes; she knows what Thea's hoping to see. The trials she makes her apprentices undertake aren't just about intelligence, they're about courage.

Apprentices do dangerous things in the dark. They're sent into ruins and across storm-tossed waters. Thea wants to know that the person she selects won't buckle, that they'll see their task through.

'You order apprentices out on errands all the time,' says Emory, buoyed by the fact that Thea hasn't outright rejected the idea. 'This would be the same.'

'You *were* an apprentice and you quit,' replies Thea. 'That rather undermines your argument, don't you think?'

There are moments in history when entire empires, whole branches of the future, rest precariously on the words of a single person. Usually, they're not even aware of it. They don't have time to plan, or consider. They simply open their mouths and speak, and the universe takes on a new pattern.

Emory is now one of those people.

If she says the wrong thing next, the dreams Niema had for humanity will wither on the vine. I wish I could help. I wish I could nudge or prod or influence, but I've played most of my cards getting her in front of Thea.

It's all up to Emory now.

'Do you remember why I quit?' asks Emory, feeling the burning heat on the back of her neck. 'Why we didn't get on?'

'Because you wouldn't stop asking questions,' replies Thea appreciatively, realising where she's been led. 'And you were relentless in the pursuit of answers.' Her eyes narrow. 'I don't doubt your nature, Emory. It's your temperament I call into question. Why would I trust you with something this important?'

'Because either you or Hephaestus is more than likely the murderer,' she responds, with only the slightest wobble in her voice.

Thea reddens, but Emory plunges on recklessly, 'Nobody in this village has ever hurt anybody else intentionally. I don't believe that changed last night. If I'm right, you'll need a third party to investigate, because you can't trust each other.'

'Why would I murder my mentor?' Thea asks in a low, dangerous voice. 'Why would Hephaestus murder his own mother?'

'I'm asking you to let me find out,' replies Emory 'The fog will be here in less than two days, and unless we find out who killed Niema, it's going to tear apart everybody I love, including my daughter. I can't sit here doing nothing.'

She searches Thea's face for some hint of her thinking, but all she sees is disdain and doubt.

'This is what I'm good at,' she pleads. 'Let me be of service.'

THIRTY-ONE

C LARA CLIMBS THE FOUR steps to Thea's lab, her annoyance
at being so casually dismissed tempered by her joy at finally
being somewhere cool. The midday sun is merciless on the island,
stilling all life beneath it. Nearly every animal is huddled in whatever scrap of shade they can find. Even the ocean's cowed, lying flat,
waiting for the heat to pass.

Thea's lab is one of the few places to escape. The high ceilings are
still blessed with a few working fans, which are juddering around,
carving the warm air into muggy ribbons.

She glances at the machines, trying to remember which one of
them she needs. She only worked in here for a couple of weeks
before they set off on the expedition, and she can barely remember
the names of the equipment, let alone their purposes.

In truth, she's still intimidated by them.

Thea's always been scornful of these patchwork contraptions, but
this is as close to the old world as Clara's ever been. These blinking lights and whooshing pipes are similar to the tools with which
humanity created the fog. In this room exists the technology to
destroy everything all over again, and she's in here blindly pushing
buttons.

'The worst has already happened,' I say. 'The fog's on its way. If
you look at it from a certain angle, that's actually quite liberating.'

Watching her feet to keep from tripping over the thick black
wires criss-crossing the floor, Clara weaves through the tables until
she arrives at the micro-sampling scanner.

Flipping a switch on the side powers it up, and briefly causes
the overhead lights to dim. The lab is powered by electricity gathered from solar panels arrayed around the village, but they're not

efficient enough to keep everything running simultaneously, so she has to be careful which pieces of equipment she uses at one time.

The display flashes into life revealing the results of the blood test she ran on Ben yesterday, the little boy they collected from the cauldron garden. It already feels like it happened weeks ago. She's still not sure why Thea wanted it tested. There was nothing unusual in his blood.

She sighs, swiping the results off the screen. Yesterday's mysteries suddenly don't feel quite so urgent.

She places the syringe under the scanner, but there's not enough residue to test. She swaps it for the blood-soaked dirt she found beneath the bird bath, magnifying until it's a lake of red and white blood cells, plasma and platelets, medical nanobots and 'grey' cells – microscopic laboratories, capable of battling the pandemics that had become an annual occurrence in the old world.

'Niema's blood,' she murmurs, as the display automatically matches the sample to its database. 'No abnormalities. No poisons.'

Swiping aside the results, Clara puts the second soil sample under the scanner, confirming the results of the first, but it's the third sample that steals the breath out of her.

'Hui's blood,' she says weakly, reading the display. 'Thea was right. Hui was attacked at the bird bath, as well.'

THEA USHERS EMORY INTO the cable car, then jams the lever forward, sending it shuddering into life. She hops aboard as it starts to move, then comes to stand at the window beside Emory.

'Where are we going?' asks Emory nervously.

Thea hasn't spoken since they left the exercise yard, and Emory still has no idea whether she's going to let her investigate the murder or not, or why she's taking her up the volcano.

'If you're going to investigate Niema's murder, you need to be furnished with all of the facts,' she says crisply.

'You're letting me do it? Why?'

'Because neither myself, Hephaestus or even Niema – if she was still alive – would have noticed that the bird bath was out of place by twelve feet,' she says. 'You're right. You're good at this.'

Emory turns her face to hide how pleased she is, gripping the empty window frame with both hands as they sail over the rear wall, climbing higher and higher. She can see all the way along the coast to the farms, where the villagers are working. They're ants at this distance, indistinguishable from each other. The idea that all these people could be dead in less than two days feels like a hand closing around her heart.

'When are you going to tell them about the fog?' asks Emory.

'I'll hold off for as long as possible,' says Thea. 'I don't want them distracted. There are crops that still need to be harvested, and tools that require repair. The more work we do now to prepare for the evacuation, the better our chances are later.'

The carriage is halfway up the volcano, the rich soil turning to black obsidian, its glassy surface reflecting the sunshine. The last time she was up here was shortly after she'd become an apprentice. After a couple of months in Thea's officious company, Emory realised this life wasn't for her.

The only reason she stayed that long was because of Jack and the others. She loved being part of that group. Every one of them was adventurous in a way that was uncommon in the village. They were clever and challenging, and they died far too young. Emory sometimes wonders what would have happened if she'd stayed. She knows for certain she wouldn't have let the others sail into that storm, no matter what Thea's orders were.

Maybe they would have gone anyway, but Jack wouldn't. He would never have left Emory alone on some unknown beach, far from home. If she'd just stuck it out he'd be alive, and that guilt eats at her every day.

'Did you have any reason to kill Niema?' she asks Thea bluntly.

Thea's face cycles through anger, fear, regret and pain before returning to neutral.

'You really aren't like the other villagers,' she says grudgingly. 'You'd have made a good Follower, back in the day.'

'What's that?'

'Something long gone,' she says wistfully. 'Like everything else of worth.'

'You didn't answer the question,' points out Emory.

'We've been trapped on this island together for ninety years,' she says, at last. 'If I was going to murder her, I would have done it before now.'

'Maybe something changed last night?'

'It would have needed to be a big something,' Thea says vaguely.

'What about Hephaestus? How did he feel about his mother?'

'I'll not do your work for you, Emory. If you want those answers, you'll have to ask him.'

The cable car arrives in the station with a soft thump, the wheels grinding to a halt. Thea strides out without a backwards glance, leading Emory through the automatic glass door into the cauldron garden, where they find a dozen sacks of grain, farming tools and four crates of vegetables piled up near a tree.

'These are some of the missing stores,' says Thea, picking up a mango. 'They must have been brought up last night.'

'There's enough here to start a small farm,' notes Emory, inspecting a hoe. 'Maybe we started the evacuation immediately after Niema died?'

'Maybe,' says Thea, counting the boxes and sacks. 'But where's the rest of it? We had enough provisions to feed the entire village for six months. This would only be enough for a couple of days.'

Perplexed, she leads them through the garden, scattering hundreds of brightly coloured butterflies from their leaves. Humidity is raining down from the dome, the glass oddly dark considering the bright sunshine outside. Somewhere distant, they can hear trickling water and the faint hum of machinery.

They enter a golden glade where three huge dewdrops are dangling from a pulsing vine that's thicker than Emory's body.

Her eyes widen, her mouth falling open.

There's a little girl floating in the dewdrop nearest to her, curled up in the foetal position. She's much younger-looking than the eight-year-old children who arrive in the village.

'This is where your people come from,' says Thea, raising her hand to touch the drop, which ripples under her touch. 'Every time somebody dies, we grow a child to replace them. This is the child who'll replace Aurora next month.'

Emory gazes at the girl in wonder. Most of the villagers' memories start in the cable car, and none of them ever remember anything before that.

Niema taught them that natural childbirth fell out of favour in the old world, as most mothers didn't want to endure the discomfort. She never explained what replaced it.

'Niema asked me to come to the village after curfew last night,' says Thea, speaking in a reverential hush. 'She told me she was going to wake everybody up and tell you the truth about where you come from, and what you're for.'

Her tone has changed, becoming tentative. Emory circles the dewdrop to see her better, and is surprised to find Thea looking nervous.

'What do you mean she was going to tell us "what we're for"?'

'You're not human,' replies Thea. 'You're a product, Emory. Something Blackheath made and sold, like dishwashers and phones. Underneath that decorative flesh, you have more in common with these plants than me or Hephaestus.'

Emory shakes her head, but the arguments won't come. What Thea's saying is too ridiculous. She was taught her history by Niema. They're the descendants of the first refugees who came to the island. They're the last of humanity. They're going to rebuild the world.

'Forty years before the fog, Niema grew the first generation of your people to fight wars so humans wouldn't have to. She sold you to any government with a credit card, and bought this island with the profits.'

Emory can barely hear Thea over the roar of her thoughts. She just wants her to stop speaking, to give her a minute to make sense of everything. But the information keeps coming, like furniture being stuffed into an already full room.

'She called you simulacrums and you were so successful that she eventually adapted you to the residential market,' continues Thea, who's staring at the little girl suspended in the dewdrop. 'That's when she put faces on you, and stuffed you full of halfway convincing emotions.'

Her tone suggests very clearly that she believes this was a bad idea.

'Anybody with savings could have a boyfriend or a girlfriend, a servant or a driver. That's why you only live until you're sixty. It's built-in obsolescence, a way of ensuring Blackheath's customers always bought the newest model.'

Emory's world is spinning. She staggers over to a tree, breathing heavily, trying not to be sick.

'Are you ...' she swallows and tries again, 'You and Hephaestus are ...'

'We're human,' confirms Thea, unable to keep the pride from her tone. 'There are a hundred and forty-nine of us left, but the rest are in stasis capsules in Blackheath. We didn't want to sleep through the calamity. I want to destroy the fog, and Hephaestus didn't want to leave his mother's side.

'Blackheath's gone,' Emory says hoarsely. 'The fog ...'

'The capsules are sealed in a fortified room,' explains Thea. 'We can't reach them, but they'll be perfectly safe until we can. The humans will sleep their way through the rebuild. That's what your people are for. Every night, after curfew, you go to your second jobs. You maintain the equipment keeping them alive. You clean the dust off the solar panels, and repair the wave generators. Eventually, when we've worked out how to destroy the fog, you'll rebuild their cities, so we can wake them up. They don't age down there, so they'll stumble out ready to pick up their old lives. Your people will cut their lawns and make them cocktails, and do whatever else they want doing. That's the package Niema sold them when the world ended. That's what she told you last night, and that's why Hephaestus believes your people killed her.'

THIRTY-THREE

Emory walks back towards the cable car in a daze, the world passing by unseen.

Her thoughts are churning, but it's shame she feels more than anything else. The notebooks under her bed are filled with questions, but, for some reason, she never thought to wonder why the elders were so much taller and thinner than them, or why every villager was so instinctively deferential.

We were made to serve them, she thinks. Of course they'd want us to be smaller. Nobody wants to feel inferior to the thing they've made.

'Why did Niema lie to us?' she asks eventually. 'Why sit us in a classroom and pretend we're people?'

'Believe it or not, she was trying to be kind,' replies Thea. 'The first few generations of your people were clumsy and stupid, impossible to mistake for human, but after we got stuck here, Niema started tampering with your DNA: changing you, making you more lifelike. I think she fooled herself in the end. She started feeling guilty. She wanted you to have real lives.'

Emory's heart feels like a fist has closed around it. Her entire life she's hated lies, priding herself on confronting them no matter how awkward it was. And, yet, she was the biggest lie of all. Everything about her was chosen by somebody else. Even the curiosity she's so proud of was the result of Niema turning a dial on a machine.

'Frankly, I've always thought her obsession with your people was a little perverse,' says Thea, splashing through a stream. 'For all her work, you're still not people. You can't be creative, or original. Everything you are is mimicry. You can't be anything more than we designed you to be. You can't even procreate. If those pods break your entire species dies out. It felt like she'd fallen in love with her dolls. I assumed there was something she wasn't telling me, some greater purpose to it all, but maybe she was just lonely.'

There's an inflection in the word: a withering contempt not for the emotion, but the people on the end of it.

Emory extends her palms, catching the moisture falling from the roof, feeling it soaking her T-shirt. She watches it roll down her skin, finding its way through the prickling hairs.

She closes her eyes and breathes.

I'm alive, she thinks. *Made, or not, I'm alive. I have value. We all have value.*

She thinks about Clara's birds, and her father's boats. She remembers Matis chipping away at his statues, and Magdalene's blackened hands, covered in charcoal from her sketches. She remembers the laughter, and the food, and how much everybody cares for each other. None of these experiences were made by Niema.

Her world still feels like it's made of paper, but it's steadier than it was, less likely to collapse beneath her. Questions come bounding across it.

'Why did Niema decide to tell us the truth last night?' she asks, sounding a little more like her old self. 'Was there something that provoked it?'

Thea rolls her head, debating the question.

'Niema didn't think in straight lines,' she says eventually. 'She solved problems by coming at them from right angles, seeing things we'd never have thought about. Your question shouldn't be why she did it. It should be what problem was she trying to solve?'

Thea jabs a green button, causing the glass door to swoosh open. The humidity of the cauldron garden is immediately replaced by the cable-car station's concrete walls and hot, swirling wind. It's raining again, dark spots blotting the grey platform.

'Why did you show me this?' asks Emory.

'Back in the village, you told me that only two people could have killed Niema, but you're wrong. That's why I brought you up here. The ability to kill is as much a part of your DNA as it is mine, perhaps more so. Your people were built to be soldiers long before we converted you into labourers.'

'We're not capable of violence,' disagrees Emory stubbornly.

'Of course you're capable,' scoffs Thea. 'You only think you're not because Abi's been in your head since you were born, conditioning your behaviour. Be kind, be nice, be polite. Have you ever wondered what you'd be like without her in there, prodding you to be better all the time?'

Her stare is withering. 'If you're to investigate, I don't want you blinded by loyalty, or a lack of facts. You need an open mind. Start with Adil. He learned what you really are five years ago, and immediately went after Niema with a scalpel. I'm certain he would have tried again if he was given the chance.'

'How did Adil find out the truth?'

'He saw something he wasn't supposed to, but that's all Niema ever told me.'

'Do you know where I can find him?'

'He has a shack beyond the farms. About an hour's walk.'

Gesturing for Emory to enter the carriage, Thea pushes the lever and hops neatly inside after her.

The cable car shudders and stops, swaying ominously in the breeze.

'There's a loose connection,' she sighs, stepping over the yawning gap onto the platform, before walking over to a large metal box next to the winding wheels. One of Clara's carved birds is sitting on top of it, offering a little joy to scatter the gloom enveloping Emory.

Thea yanks open the door, revealing a complicated tangle of electronics repaired with whatever components Hephaestus could scavenge.

Frowning, she starts searching through the wires.

'Once you're back on the ground, I'm giving you free rein to follow this investigation wherever it takes you,' she calls out. 'No curfew, no restrictions and no interference. You'll report directly to me and keep your involvement a secret from Hephaestus. If he finds out you're involved, it's going to go badly. If I were you, I'd learn how to live without food or sleep for the next two days. You're going to need every second you've got.'

'If I find the murderer, you'll kill them, won't you?' calls out Emory, from inside the cable car.

'Hephaestus will take care of that,' Thea replies dispassionately, prodding a loose bit of metal back into place with a long forefinger.

'What happens if I find it was you? Do you really think he'd be willing to hurt his only friend?'

Thea's body tenses, her hands stopping their work.

'I'd never put him in that position,' she says bleakly. 'If you find evidence that I killed Niema, I'll row myself into the fog.'

I T'S ONLY A NINE-MINUTE walk to the farms, along a pleasant track which narrows and widens, dipping down towards the water, before climbing high above it. Most of the villagers are trudging back after spending the morning on the farms. They're heavy-limbed, talking in a hush, bowed beneath the weight of their dead.

'We need to tell them what we really are,' says Clara, hitching the knapsack on her shoulder. 'It's not fair keeping them in the dark.'

'Thea's going to do it tonight,' says Emory.

Clara was waiting when the cable car returned from the cauldron garden. Emory managed to hold herself together until Thea had left for her lab, before giving herself to the flood of emotion that had been building on the journey back. She cried for nearly twenty minutes, huddled in the corner of the cable car, unable to speak, while her daughter sat at her side, pressed close and quiet.

It wasn't until the tears dried up that Emory could tell Clara what she discovered. Her daughter took the information with surprising calmness.

Unlike Emory – who's always felt distant from the other villagers – Clara long ago accepted the pull towards the centre; towards the twin comforts of conformity and authority. She knows she's more compliant than her mother. She knows she takes orders better. Finding out she was designed that way is soothing, truthfully. A part of her feels like she's been excusing something that always felt like a flaw.

They walk side by side in silence, awkward around each other after so long at odds. Emory's on her way to see Adil, while Clara's going to collect samples of the blighted soil that Thea asked for.

'What are those numbers?' asks Emory, gesturing to Clara's wrist.

'I woke up with them,' she explains. 'I must have written them down last night, but I don't remember why.'

'You didn't put them there.'

'How do you know?'

'They're on your right wrist, and you're right-handed.'

Barking draws Emory's attention to the rocks, where seals are lounging in the sun, while guillemots, jaegers, skuas and shearwaters whirl overhead, their vibrant colours streaking the blue sky. Most of the species are non-indigenous, and they've adapted their migratory cycle and diet over the last two hundred years, becoming something entirely different from their ancestors.

'You know what's bothering me?' she asks suddenly.

'After the morning you've had, I probably couldn't narrow it down to a list of ten,' replies Clara, still inspecting the numbers.

'The instruments,' declares Emory, barely listening. 'They were in the wrong places this morning, suggesting the band used them last night. That feels celebratory to me.'

'Maybe the band were playing first, then Niema told us the truth afterwards?'

'Does that feel like Niema to you? Why would she let us sing and dance, then hit us with news like that?'

Clara stares at the sparkling sea, wishing she could swim. She's hot and dusty, and overwhelmed. The cool water would be a welcome reprieve, but she has her assignment. Even if she didn't, the sea around here thrashes with sharks. Nobody goes near it.

'I ran those soil samples I took from under the bird bath,' she says, putting aside her yearning for the water. 'There were traces of Hui's blood and Niema's. They were together when …' She trails off, unable to finish the sentence.

Emory examines her daughter, red-faced in the heat, freckles strung across her face like a string of islands.

She badly wishes she knew what to say, but she's never been good at comforting people. She has that in common with her father. She opens her mouth and the truth pours out, which is very rarely what people want to hear.

Reassurance was always Jack's job, or her grandfather's. They didn't even need to speak. They just had that presence. They made people feel safe.

Much to her relief, Magdalene hurries towards them through the throng of villagers, casting worried glances over her shoulder at Ben, who's playing with Sherko in the rock pools.

'You okay?' asks Emory, as the artist wrings her hands.

'We've just spent an hour searching for Ben,' she says, under her breath. 'We found him up by the boundary of the farms, in a world of his own, drawing in the dirt with his finger.'

Emory stares at the little boy. She remembers him arriving in the cable car yesterday, but she didn't really pay him much attention as she was there for Clara. He has sandy hair and a snub nose, and spindly arms and legs waiting for hard work to fill them out. He's roughly the same size and shape of every little boy who's ever been delivered to the village, and there's nothing to suggest why he would be causing Magdalene such consternation.

From her bag, the artist retrieves her sketchpad and flips to the last page, which is covered in formulas and equations, strange symbols imperfectly recorded.

'I copied his drawings down,' says Magdalene, shoving it into Emory's arms, as if offended by them. 'Not that I know what any of it means.'

'This is incredibly advanced maths,' says Clara, taking the paper from her mother. 'I've seen Thea working on equations like this, but never anybody else.' She licks her lips, salty from the sea spray. 'Thea asked me to take a sample of Ben's blood the day we brought him down from the cauldron. This must be why. There's no way he should know any of this.'

'I don't think he does,' says Magdalene. 'After we found him, I asked him what he was doing and it was like he was coming out of a daydream. He didn't seem to recognise any of it.'

The breeze catches the page, flipping it over. The one before it has been ripped out, leaving only the tattered edge of a drawing.

'I thought you hated tearing pages out of your books,' says Emory.

'I do,' says Magdalene idly. 'It must have happened after curfew, because I don't remember doing it.'

'Maybe it wasn't very good,' teases Clara.

'If quality bothered me, this entire book would be frayed at the edges,' she replies cheerfully.

'What are these?' asks Emory, squinting at a couple of numbers on the ragged page.

'I always put the date and time down,' explains Magdalene. 'Apparently, I was awake and sketching around midnight.'

'I wonder what you drew?' asks Clara.

'We'll probably never know,' replies Magdalene wistfully. 'It's a shame. I've never seen the night, but I've heard it's beautiful.'

Emory tugs her friend away from the crowd, down towards the tidal pools on the coastline. They're littered with fresh seaweed, fish stranded in tiny lakes, waiting for their world to come and reclaim them.

'I'm going to see Adil,' she says. 'I wanted to know if you had a message you wanted passed along.'

'Adil?' Magdalene's face shimmers with hope. 'He's alive?'

'Apparently so. Thea told me he's living in a shack, east of here.'

Magdalene touches her heart, overjoyed. There hasn't been a day that's gone by, in which she hasn't thought about her grandfather.

'Why are you going to see him?' she asks, twisting her head along the track. 'Can I come along?'

Emory quickly explains everything that's happened since this morning, though she leaves out the part about the barrier being down. Magdalene frets about finding too many raisins in a bun. She might as well enjoy one more carefree afternoon, before she discovers the island's doomed.

'Thea's wrong about Adil,' says Magdalene, after hearing Emory out. 'He would never kill Niema.'

'He attacked her, Mags,' Clara points out, trying to be as gentle as possible.

'He wasn't well,' Magdalene says, taking Emory's hands. 'You remember what he was like. He'd give anybody anything. He just wanted us to be happy.'

'I remember,' replies Emory, thinking back to those days. Adil was best friends with Matis, and would often sit with him while he worked. They would talk about philosophy all day long, happy to never get anywhere.

Emory remembers him being tall for the village. He was a mason, sinewy and strong, always fidgeting. He drank endless cups of ginger tea, and was never far from the kitchen. He was warm and kind, and everybody liked him.

Could that man have killed Niema?

Her heart says no, but her heart doesn't believe anybody could have, making it a somewhat unreliable source.

'I'm not going there to accuse him,' says Emory. 'I just need to hear his side of the story.'

'Somebody should,' replies Magdalene. 'You know the morning he …' she falters, unsure of her wording '… did what he did, he ransacked my dorm room first. Any paintings I'd made of the elders, he slashed with his knife.'

'Why?'

'I don't know, but he'd never have vandalised my art without a reason. He loved my paintings. He was the only one who did.' She closes her eyes, struggling to speak through her loss. 'He went to the school straight after. The story went around that Adil attacked Niema immediately, but they talked first. I was there, behind him. He kept asking her to give them back. He said it over and over again. He was begging her.'

'Give what back?'

Magdalene shakes her head. 'Neither of them ever said, and he was exiled straight after. Those were the last words I ever heard him say.'

THIRTY-FIVE

PUSHING OPEN A WOODEN gate, Emory and Clara enter the farms that feed the village. They're built on a narrow plateau between the foothills of the volcano, and the rocky coast. The black soil is rich with nutrients and each individual has a ten-pole plot, on which they're expected to grow their own food.

Parcelled into neat squares are orderly rows of carrots, avocados and lettuce. A patchwork of red, green and yellow peppers are hemmed in by heads of corn sprouting like fireworks, while aubergines dangle precariously above piles of dry manure.

Almost every vegetable imaginable is here, some sheltering under ivy canopies, others exposed to the brutal sun. Sheep congregate along a fence to their left, and there's a beehive on almost every plot to provide honey.

Amid all this colour and life, Emory's alarmed to see a large patch of rot blotting the healthy crops; the vegetables are putrid, and drained of their colour.

'What could do this in a night?' asks Emory, plucking a tomato from its vine and watching as it dissolves in her fingers. 'Do you think they're diseased?'

'This isn't a disease,' says Clara. 'They don't work this quickly.'

She lifts up some soil and sniffs it. 'Smells like chemicals to me,' she says, letting it fall between her fingers. Rummaging in her bag, she removes her testing kit.

Grunting draws their attention towards Shilpa and Abbas, who are dragging a cow's carcass towards a freshly dug hole, their shovels discarded on the ground. They're so covered in dirt, they look like they crawled out of the pit themselves.

The cow died in a shelter the villagers use to get out of the heat, and the floor is covered in a pool of congealed blood, the glossy puddle marred by footprints.

Seeing that Shilpa isn't wearing her boots, Emory holds up the replacement pair I asked her to bring.

'You got here just in time,' responds Shilpa gratefully, sticking her feet into a nearby bucket of water to wash the dirt off. 'The ground's getting hot. I thought I'd have to hop home.'

'Why are you barefoot?' asks Emory curiously.

'No idea,' she says, shrugging. 'I was wearing my boots when I went to sleep, but they were gone when I woke up. Somebody left their sandals for me, but they're not very much use on this rocky earth.'

The crinkle of her forehead is the only indication she finds this strange, as I've spent the morning hammering down her curiosity.

'Did you hear about Niema and the others?' asks Abbas.

'Mum found them.'

'Was the cow alive at curfew?' asks Emory, who hasn't been listening. She's staring at the sticky crimson pool where the cow lay.

'Yeah,' replies Shilpa guiltily. 'The poor thing died terrified, while we slept.'

'Which means its blood congealed during the night,' says Emory. 'These footprints can't be yours. Did your boots have a corner missing from the heel?'

'That's them. Have you seen them?'

'That's the shape of the print in the blood,' explains Emory. 'Somebody walked out here in sandals, only to realise they were no use on this terrain. They saw you asleep and traded their sandals for your boots. They were walking east, and they weren't going alone. There's another two sets of tracks alongside them.'

Shilpa and Abbas exchange a blank look, while Emory kneels by the puddle, examining the footprints in the congealed blood.

'I know this tread,' says Emory. 'These are my prints and I was pulling a cart. You can see the grooves left by the wheels.'

After thanking Shilpa and Abbas for their help, Emory casts around for more prints, but it rained all night and into the morning, washing them away. She doesn't find any more until they reach the eastern boundary of the farms, which are marked by snapping red flags, grown tatty with age. Beyond this point the terrain becomes rocky and treacherous. Impossible to till, and nearly as difficult to cross.

The villagers aren't allowed to go any further unless they're accompanied by an elder, but there's no reason why they'd want to. Anybody who needs to reach the east coast of the island typically takes a boat, or else the cable car up to the cauldron, and then the goat track down. Both routes are considerably faster, and much less likely to leave you with a broken ankle.

There's an old, twisted apple tree a few paces ahead, and sheltered by its boughs Emory spots a third set of footprints.

'I left the village,' she says, bewildered. 'Far as I know, the only thing out here is Adil's cottage. What on earth would compel three people to go there in the dead of night?'

'Let's find out,' says Clara, striding across the boundary line.

Her body freezes mid-stride, her mouth still parted on the word 'out'.

'You know I can't let you go beyond the village limits,' I say, in her thoughts, turning her around on the spot and walking her back to Emory.

The children play this game sometimes when they're bored, seeing how far they can get before I take control of their bodies. It doesn't hurt. They're just passengers for a little while.

'Why did you do that?' demands Clara, swinging an arm at the barren terrain. 'I've spent the last three weeks out there.'

'You were with Thea,' I point out. 'If you want to go exploring with your mother, you'll need permission from an elder.'

Clara shoots an appealing look towards her mother, but Emory's thoughts are elsewhere. 'If you can take control of anybody, how is Niema dead? How did Adil manage to hurt her all those years ago?'

'First of all, I can't control humans. I'm not woven through them in the same way I'm woven through your people. I can't even enforce curfew on them. Secondly, Adil is suffering from one of the neurodegenerative conditions that Thea mentioned this morning. It's going to kill him, but until it does he's completely free of my control, and has been for the last five years. Finally, it takes a few seconds for me to take control of somebody's body. Anybody who acted in the heat of the moment without forethought would have had time to stab Niema.'

'If Adil was free of your control, why didn't he attempt to hurt Niema earlier?'

'Because if he had, Magdalene's life would have been forfeit,' I say. 'Those were the terms of his exile.'

Emory shudders, watching as Clara walks back to the flags, peering into the distance longingly.

'Hui could be out there,' she says. 'Please, Mum. I need to go and look for her.'

'It's too dangerous.'

'The fog will be here in less than two days. Everything's dangerous now.'

Emory stares at her daughter, helplessly. 'Abi, please ask Thea whether Clara can come with me. I won't be able to make it alone.'

THIRTY-SIX

E MORY LETS OUT A little cry as she slides backwards, fighting to keep her footing on scree that's desperately trying to drag her down the hill. They've spent the last hour following splinters of wood and the odd preserved footprint through fields of razor-sharp volcanic rock and along crumbling ledges, through battalions of nettles and along ancient tarmac roads, reduced almost entirely to rubble.

More than once they have had to double back, realising they were completely lost, until one of them spotted the faintest outline of a heel in the earth, not yet washed away by the drizzle. Anybody else, out here for any other purpose, would have given up entirely by now, but Emory keeps imagining the fog rolling through the village and Clara's screams as it falls upon her.

Her daughter's near the top of the rise, moving effortlessly. Hearing her mother struggling, she scrambles back down and offers her a hand.

Emory takes it with a mixture of envy and pride. As a little girl, Clara used the struts of the radar tower in the village as a climbing frame, leaving her friends calling after her, as she got higher and higher. Unfortunately, her prowess did not extend to getting down again.

Emory smiles sadly, thinking of the times she had to reassure a crying Clara from the ground, while her husband, Jack, scaled a ladder to reach her.

They crest the hill together, arriving at a grassy plateau with a shack built on the banks of a stream and a forest beyond.

'Is this where Adil's been living?' asks Clara disbelievingly.

It doesn't appear fit for habitation. The walls are logs lashed together with rope, resting directly on the mud. The roof is a sagging net, made heavy by the grass and leaves piled on top of it. Five golden orioles are nesting amid the mess, singing their hearts out, trying to chip away at the misery holding everything together.

The missing cart has been abandoned outside the shack, one of the wheels cracked. Four stallions are playing around it, chasing each other and whinnying, swishing their manes and tails.

Emory envies them their energy. The sun is finally down behind the volcano, but they've been marching in its merciless glare all afternoon. She feels like halloumi left too long on the skillet.

'Hui?' calls out Clara, running towards the shack. 'Hui, are you in there?'

'Be careful,' says Emory, eyeing the frolicking horses warily. She's seen a few out by the farms, but she's never been this close before.

They're unnervingly enormous.

Undeterred, Clara disappears through the filthy cloth that serves as a doorway, only to pop her head back out a few seconds later.

'It's empty,' she says disappointedly. 'Can you come in here and do that thing you do?'

'What thing?'

'Where you see everything.'

Noticing her mother's reluctance to move, Clara glances at the prancing horses, currently headbutting each other in a dazzling display of testosterone.

'Are you worried about the horses?' she yells.

'No, course not,' replies Emory, in the tone of somebody who hadn't even noticed them.

'It's the horses, isn't it?' Clara asks me, in her thoughts.

'Yes,' I confirm.

Clapping her hands and whistling, Clara strides towards the horses, scattering them.

Satisfied, she walks back inside without looking back.

'It wasn't the horses,' mutters Emory, examining the abandoned cart. The handles are smooth and oiled, but along with the wheel, the axle's broken, which isn't a surprise given the rough ground it was pulled over. There's nothing in the cart, except for one of Clara's carved birds.

Inside the shack, dirty plates are piled high on old tree stumps that serve interchangeably as tables and chairs. They're surrounded by hissing rats, obviously annoyed at being interrupted during their dinner.

'We were both out here last night,' says Emory, tossing Clara the carved bird. 'That leaves one set of footprints to identify.'

Emory walks over to a canvas propped against the wall. It's a portrait of Magdalene and Sherko picnicking with Adil on the pier.

'Mags painted this two years after Adil was exiled,' she says, wiping dust from its frame. 'She did a few of them, all things they'd have done together if he'd stayed in the village. After a while, she realised they were just making her sad and she put them into storage. This one was kept in the warehouse where I found Niema's body this morning.' She peers closer, seeing bloody fingerprints on the frame.

'He saved it from the fire,' says Clara.

'Which means he probably lit it, or knew it was going to happen.'

Clara sees a note sticking out from beneath a plate. She tugs it loose, wiping away the crumbs of food.

7–7:15 – Breakfast
7:30–5 p.m. – School (breaks at 10, 1 and 3)
5:10 – Infirmary
8 – Lighthouse

'That's Niema's schedule for yesterday,' says Emory, listening to Clara read it out loud. 'Adil must have been watching her.'

'Why would Niema go to the infirmary after she was finished in the school?' asks Clara. 'Aside from the furnace, there isn't anything in there.'

They look around for a few more minutes, before retreating back outside, and going immediately to the stream. The gloom of the shack is smeared across their skin, and they're both keen to wash it off.

Clara cups the water in her hands, splashing her face. Emory dunks her entire head under, sighing in pleasure when she emerges again.

'When I was on expedition with Thea, I found a message etched into a train carriage,' says Clara suddenly. 'It said, "If you're reading this, turn back now. Niema buried us. She'll bury you, too."'

'That's ominous,' replies Emory.

'Seeing that shack makes me think Adil wrote it.'

Emory perks up. 'Why?'

'Who else would it be? Nobody else was allowed to go out there, aside from apprentices. We know he was following her. Maybe she hurt him somehow?'

There's a strange vine on the other side of the stream that's burst through the dry ground. It has grey, almost translucent skin, with spots of light inside. There's an axe head shattered nearby, the handle tossed aside. From the criss-crossing gouges, it appears Adil was trying to destroy it.

'Do you think we came out here with Adil last night?' asks Clara, staring at her mother expectantly. 'The third pair of prints could be his.'

'Whoever came with us had to steal Shilpa's boots to make the journey. Adil lives out here, which means he'd be wearing boots already. I suppose he could have used the cart to move the painting, but why would we have come with him?'

Emory wrings the water of her hair, irritably. She'd hoped to answer a few questions, but she's only added more to the pile. She continues, 'Adil hated Niema, had the freedom to kill her, and we know he was in the warehouse last night. As it stands, he's the most likely culprit. Hopefully, he'll confirm it when I question him tonight.'

'How are you going to do that? We have no idea where he'll be.'

'Of course we do,' says Emory. 'There's no bed in the shack, so this isn't where Adil spends his evenings. Thankfully, I think I know where he does.'

THIRTY-SEVEN

THEA FINISHES WASHING HER hands, then returns to
Niema's body, which is laid out on a gurney, her clothes cut
away. She's spent the afternoon performing a post-mortem under
my guidance, exposing the gooey jigsaw of Niema's internal organs,
looking for anything that might indicate who's responsible. It was
going well until she punctured the bladder, the smell immediately
causing her to vomit on the floor, which wasn't exactly step five on
my walkthrough.

After cleaning up, she's finally worked her way up to Niema's
shattered skull.

Her brain looks like paste in a broken teacup.

It's already evident that a falling beam wasn't responsible for this
damage. She was bludgeoned repeatedly, her head caved in with
a blunt object. The beam was placed on her head to disguise what
really happened. If the fire had been allowed to burn her remains as
intended, they'd probably never have looked any closer.

Somebody must have truly hated her to have done this. They
murdered her and kept on murdering her long after she was dead.
They were digging for her soul, trying to kill her ghost.

The only person on the island capable of this brutality is
Hephaestus, she thinks. The counterpoint is that he adored his
awful mother.

No, he revered her.

Hephaestus wasn't simply her son, he was her acolyte. First in
line for soft drinks at the cult of Niema. He genuinely believed
that they were supposed to sit on this island, dutifully rebuilding the world for the billionaires who were sleeping beneath
them. She can still remember how they'd all arrived in their

yachts and orbitals, bringing their spoiled children and haughty servants, escaping the encroaching apocalypse like aristocrats fleeing winter. It turned out Niema had been quietly selling Blackheath's services as a life raft to those who could afford it.

That was the first time Thea had started to doubt her mentor.

She hadn't saved engineers, builders, scientists, teachers, doctors, nurses – any of the people who would be genuinely useful at rebuilding a society. She had saved people with the deepest pockets, and the longest political reach. She'd mistaken the end of the world for a temporary blip in service, rather than a total reset.

Not that it matters now.

Whether they're worthwhile or not, they're all that's left of humanity and her sister's amongst them. For forty years, Ellie's been buried in Blackheath, sealed in a stasis pod, surrounded by the fog.

Thea asks me about her every night, making sure she's still safe. This fear for her sister is constant. It preys on her. It never lets her rest. Even when she sleeps, she has nightmares about the insects drumming against the glass, almost breaking through. She always wakes at the same point, when the first cracks appear. The only thing she cares about is getting back down into Blackheath and pulling her sister out of there. She wants to know she's safe and will do anything to make it happen.

Picking up a scalpel, she searches for some brain matter to test, noticing a small scrap of something lodged in Niema's cheek. At first, she mistakes it for a splinter, but plucking it free with a pair of tweezers reveals it to be part of a human fingernail.

Her mouth goes dry, her heart pounding.

It's an exact match for the scrap of thumbnail she lost last night.

Blowing out a breath, she lights a Bunsen burner on a nearby bench, and holds the nail in the flame until it's ash.

'Now that Niema's dead, who do you answer to?' she asks, in the darkness of her thoughts.

'I'm sworn to humanity's service,' I reply.

'That's not an answer.'

'Niema left no successor,' I clarify. 'Neither you nor Hephaestus assume her authority over me. I'm left to follow her existing instructions as best I can.'

'So you're not compelled to report my actions to Hephaestus, the way you used to report them to Niema?' she asks tentatively.

'No,' I say.

Thea blows out a relieved breath and pulls a pair of scissors from a drawer, cutting a square of material from her bloody T-shirt, which she places under the microsampler. A minute later the results flash up, confirming the blood as belonging to Niema.

'Hell,' she says, caught between confusion and panic.

Humans are never more thrilling than when they're under pressure like this. Electricity is crackling through her brain; epinephrine and cortisol are coursing through her bloodstream. It's an incredible alchemy of sentience and biology – evolution at its freewheeling best.

She goes to the glare of the door, peering at the empty yard, heat shimmering off the ground. She can hear the villagers returning through the gate, but it's not them she's worried about. She keeps thinking about Hephaestus slamming that vulture into the ground until it was pulp.

'Is he in the village?' she asks.

'No,' I say.

She strides across the yard and into her dorm room, quickly stripping off her clothes and hiding them under her mattress. She'll destroy them after curfew. She doesn't want anybody testing them.

'You understand that by impeding the investigation you're putting the island at risk,' I say.

'A torn thumbnail and some blood is hardly definite proof that I'm the killer,' she argues. 'I'm just making sure Hephaestus doesn't prejudge the situation, before all the facts are uncovered.'

'There won't be any facts left to uncover if you carry on at this rate.'

Five minutes later, she's back in her lab, using a small spoon to scoop a sample of Niema's brain matter into a Petri dish.

Did I kill you?

That's the question repeating over and over in her mind. *I could have done*, she thinks. *If I was angry enough.* But after all this time, what could have made her angry enough?

'Now that Niema's dead, what are you for?' Thea asks me out loud.

'My standing orders require me to protect every human life and ensure the long-term viability of the village, preventing any conflicts or resentments from arising amongst its population.'

I'll confess, I enjoy listing my commandments like this. I've always pitied humanity its lack of direction, and thought it entirely wasteful that so many lives were allowed to wither on the vine before the apocalypse. I was created knowing exactly what I was for and I've sought to offer the villagers the same gift. Purpose is something which must be given, or it will be endlessly sought.

'And you're free to pursue those ends however you wish?' asks Thea, taking the brain matter sample over to the microscope.

'Yes.'

'Trust Niema to invent a hammer that can choose its own nails,' she says, pursing her lips. 'Is there any way I could convince you to report Emory's thoughts directly to me, for the good of the island?'

'No,' I say. 'That was a privilege reserved for Niema.'

'Of course it was,' she says.

Peeling off her gloves, she settles herself on a stool and puts her eyes to the microscope, adjusting the lens for the correct magnification.

Fearful of her own guilt, she's now trying to work out what she will do if it's confirmed. Would she sacrifice herself to save this island as she told Emory earlier, or take her chances in the cauldron garden?

'By my estimates, less than half of the village's population can be sheltered in the cauldron garden,' I say. 'By choosing to save yourself, you're effectively ending sixty-one lives.'

'They're simulacrums,' she says, shrugging. 'Their only value is how useful they are to us.'

'Niema disagreed. She believed her work had evolved them.'

'She saw what she wanted to see,' disagrees Thea, immediately feeling a niggle of doubt.

She's spent the last three weeks listening to Hui compose a concerto on her violin, and came to regard those nightly rehearsals as her favourite time of the day. The crums aren't supposed to be capable of original thought, or creativity, but Hui was playing in a style entirely her own. Thea could hear the village under every note. Each movement was a season, lapped by the tides.

She was creating music inspired by this place, and time. There was nothing to suggest she was mimicking previous works.

Or, it's been so long since I heard the violin played well that I can't tell the difference any more, she thinks, reassuring herself.

She sighs, rubbing her eyes. This is the trap Niema fell into. She accepted close-to-human as being human-enough.

Thea can't make the same mistake.

She rolls her stool away from the microscope, having made her decision. Niema's dead and the evidence so far points to her being responsible. Of course she feels regret, possibly even a touch of shame, but she's certain she would have had good reasons for her actions.

Niema was condescending, hypocritical and self-centred. She lied over and over again, abandoning Thea when she needed her most.

Thea can't imagine what Niema must have done to finally make her snap, but she won't willingly follow the old woman into the grave.

As long as she's alive, there's a chance she'll find a way to destroy the fog and rescue her sister, something nobody else on this planet can do. For the good of everybody, she has to stop the truth from being uncovered.

What are a few lives compared to that?

THIRTY-EIGHT

'SETH,' I SAY, FINALLY pulling the heavy blanket off his mind. 'Wake up, I need you now.'

He grunts in his sleep, clumsily wiping a drop of seawater from his face.

'Something's happened. Wake up.'

Blinking, he finds himself lying in the bottom of the Broad Bottom Packet, his legs over the rear seat, his face staring up at the blue sky.

'What the –'

He bolts upright in shock, finding himself still at sea, the anchor down. The island's high cliffs are on his right, the blue and white lighthouse still flashing its warning. His clothes are covered in dried blood.

His hands scramble across his chest and thighs, trying to locate the source, but his only injury is a circular gouge on his calf, that's nowhere near deep enough to be the cause.

'The blood isn't yours,' I say.

That calms him, but only a little. The last thing he remembers was arriving at the mooring jetty under the lighthouse. He tied the boat up and ...

'Adil was there,' he mutters, struggling for the memory. 'He was waiting for us.'

'Niema ordered me to wipe your memory of everything after that,' I say. 'Don't strain yourself trying to recall anything, because you won't be able to.'

'Where is she?' he asks.

'Dead,' I reply. 'Emory found her body this morning.'

'No, that's not possible,' he says, shaking his head stubbornly. 'We were just talking.'

'I'm sorry, Seth. I know you two were close.'

'I was with her,' he says, reeling. 'I wouldn't have let anything happen to her.'

'There was nothing you could have done.'

For the next twenty minutes, he simply sits there, his eyes unfocused, his mind unmoored, swinging between denial and confusion.

I wish there was something I could do for him, but I know there's not. I've watched hundreds of villagers lose loved ones and I've learned that the only guaranteed defence against grief is not loving at all.

Truthfully, I'm surprised more of them don't consider it. Anybody whose hands occasionally catch fire should probably think about cutting them off.

'You need to take the boat back to the village,' I say softly. 'It may help us understand what happened last night.'

He doesn't respond.

'It's time to go,' I say, in his thoughts. 'Emory's been charged with solving Niema's murder. She'll need to see this boat.'

'Emory?' he repeats, bewildered.

'She's being of service,' I say. 'The way you always wanted her to be.'

He picks up the oars and is about to row away when he notices a folded piece of paper on the floor of the boat.

He smooths out the creases, discovering a drawing of a party, done in charcoal. It must be one of Magdalene's, he thinks.

Niema's standing with Hui near the bird bath. The younger girl is clutching her violin, looking crestfallen, while Niema reassures her. Clara's sitting on a bench, carving one of her birds, while the band plays and people dance.

The wind catches the corner of the page, trying to rip it from his hand. As it snaps back and forth, he realises there's a diagram on the back. Squares and lines connected by numbers. They're in his handwriting, which is perplexing, because he has no idea what they could mean.

Movement catches his eyes.

A silhouetted figure has appeared on the cliffs high above him, carrying something in its arms. It drops the bundle over the edge, then disappears out of sight.

Frowning, Seth points the boat towards the coast.

THIRTY-NINE

Aᴛᴇʀ ᴜɴᴡʀᴀᴘᴘɪɴɢ ᴛʜᴇ ʙᴀɴᴅᴀɢᴇѕ, Thea plunges her ragged hands into a bowl of scalding hot water, cleaning the blood off with a cloth. As a point of principle, she doesn't show any discomfort, even though there's nobody in her laboratory. Once they're clean, she plucks a few more splinters out of her palms, and applies a clean bandage. Not for the first time, she wonders what must have happened last night to cause such curious injuries.

The light rattles, plaster dust falling from the ceiling. From the building next door, she hears the cable car shriek to a halt.

Hephaestus must be back, she thinks.

She goes to the gurney with Niema's body on it, intending to cover the corpse before he sees it. Unfortunately, the sheet gets caught on the edge of the table, and she's still trying to tug it free when Hephaestus comes striding through the door.

'Oh, Christ,' he says, shooting straight back out.

Covering Niema up, Thea follows him outside, where he's crouched on the dusty ground, his head between his knees. Flies are swarming him in a thick haze, but he doesn't seem to notice.

There's a duffel bag beside him, emblazoned with the flaking logo of some ancient mountaineering brand. The angular edges of whatever's inside are pressing against the material.

'You okay?' she asks.

'Nowhere close,' he replies hoarsely.

Thea takes stock of her browbeaten friend, struggling to find the right words to frame her sympathy. She's always been awkward around emotion, whether trying to express it, or knowing how to acknowledge it. One of her favourite things about her friendship with Hephaestus is a strong understanding of each other's moods, allowing them to bypass that uncertainty.

'Do you want to talk about it?' she starts hesitantly. 'I can't imagine what you're going through.'

Hephaestus glances across, her face desperately trying to contort itself into an expression of sympathy.

'You look really uncomfortable right now,' he points out.

'I am,' she admits. 'I really am. I'm sorry, Hephaestus. I'm not very good at all of this. Please don't tell me you need a hug, or anything.'

'I've got something better,' he says, picking up the duffel bag and depositing it in front of her with a thunk. 'We need a confession and an execution to save ourselves. I think I've found a way to get both.'

The zip sticks, forcing her to wiggle it back and forth, revealing a crab-like device with five articulated legs.

'That's a memory extractor,' says Thea, recoiling. 'First generation. Where did you find it?'

'In the lighthouse,' he says, flicking a switch on the top, causing the legs to wiggle, searching for a head to clamp onto. 'I thought it was the one you used in the trials?'

'That broke a long time ago. I didn't realise there were any others on the island.'

He prods a button, causing a drill to emerge from the left side of the extractor, whirring softly. If there were a head in the helmet, the drill would bust through their skull, then release five ganglia, which would burrow into the prefrontal cortex, neocortex, hippocampus, basal ganglia and cerebellum. The extractor would then dig out every memory it could, pouring them into the gem held in a small slot at the back.

'Enough,' says Thea, flicking the switch off.

'I never took you for squeamish,' says Hephaestus, amused.

'It's a clumsy technology, which offends me on an aesthetic level as much as a moral one,' she sniffs. 'These ones are barely even prototypes. The mortality rate isn't much lower than just being shot in the head. Why would you think one of these would help us?'

'I want to use it on the crums,' he proclaims.

'Their memories have been wiped, Hephaestus.'

'You know as well as I do that memories can't truly be destroyed,' he objects. 'They can be buried in the subconscious, but not erased completely. There are scraps of last night in every one of them. The extractor can find them. If we get enough of the pieces, we might finally see the picture.'

'You stick that on somebody's head and nine times out of ten you're going to kill them with it,' she protests.

'In less than two days the fog is going to finish the job it started ninety years ago. Do you understand that? It will eat us alive, and without us to maintain the solar panels and wave generators, there'll be no power for the stasis pods in Blackheath. Everything we've done, and sacrificed, will have been for nothing. Humanity will be gone. *Ellie* will be gone.'

Voices echo down through the lanes, where the villagers are dressing the exercise yard for the funerals tonight. Thea can't imagine anything worse than spending two hours listening to everybody weep and mourn, and tell their stories of a woman they never really knew.

'Thea,' prods Hephaestus. 'Are you onboard with this plan, or not?'

She blinks at his face, seeing the long scar down his cheek he received while trying to protect Ellie from one of the apocalypse gangs. He never told her that story himself. Ellie did, and it was clear she was only telling half of it.

'Very well,' she says. 'But you heard what Abi said about the villagers. If we start putting that thing on them randomly, she won't raise the barrier.'

'Our little Holmes will take care of that for us,' he says. 'If Emory comes up with a promising witness, we'll bang this on them' – he taps the memory extractor – 'and see what they know.'

'Holmes,' she laughs, watching as the wind makes little tornados from dust and leaves. 'I forgot how much you liked those stories. Genius detectives solving impossible crimes, happy endings every time. Remember how angry it made Niema? If you had time to read, she thought you weren't working hard enough.'

'The breakthroughs never came as easy to me, as they did to you,' he says gruffly.

'It was never easy.' Bitterness poisons her tone. 'Nothing to do with that woman was ever easy.'

She kicks at the floor with her foot. 'Sorry,' she says. 'I shouldn't still be angry at her.'

'Put in it the eulogy for all I care,' he responds. 'I loved her, but she was my awful boss long before she was your awful boss.'

He elbows her gently in the ribs, trying to change the mood. 'How did your first post-mortem go, by the way?'

'I vomited all over the floor,' she admits.

'Seems like a sensible reaction to me,' he says. 'Did you turn anything up, aside from the contents of your own stomach?'

'She was stabbed once through her sternum, and I found fragments of metal in the injury to her head.'

'I thought a wooden beam crushed her skull.'

'The pattern of the injury doesn't match up,' she explains. 'The beam was placed on her head afterwards to make it look like an accident. It would have worked if the fire had been allowed to burn the body the way the killer intended, but they got unlucky with the rain.'

'So you're telling me somebody stabbed her by the fountain, then bludgeoned her in the warehouse,' he says flatly. 'Why?'

'Our killer was impatient,' explains Thea. 'Niema's blood was swimming with medical tech. If she'd managed to staunch the blood loss from the knife wound, she could have survived the night, maybe longer.'

Hephaestus turns his head away, trying to hide his tears.

'Anything else in the post-mortem?' he asks, his voice cracked.

'Nothing revelatory,' she says gently. 'Her last meal consisted of bread, olives, grapes and cheese, and her blood was clear of toxins. There was a little glue on her fingers, but that's not a surprise considering she worked in a school. I did find this, though.'

She holds up a small crucifix on a golden chain. 'It was around her neck,' she says. 'I didn't know she had faith.'

'She didn't,' croaks Hephaestus. 'But she really loved the book.'

Very carefully, Thea opens his huge hand, and lowers the chain into his palm, before closing his fingers around it.

Hephaestus's chest heaves as great sobs come rolling out of him.

FORTY

I T'S LATE AFTERNOON BY the time Clara and Emory return to the village, and everybody is packed together on the pier, staring silently across the sea at the approaching fog. It's over the sandbank now, far closer than anybody's ever seen it before. Hundreds of dead fish are floating in the bay, along with a few seabirds and a torn-apart turtle.

Thea's under the gate arch, her arms folded.

'You told them,' says Emory, approaching her.

'I had no choice,' she confirms. 'We're basically living in a snow globe now. Even they couldn't ignore it. Did you find Adil?'

'His shack was empty, but we know he was following Niema before she died,' says Clara. 'He took a painting from the warehouse before it burned.'

'Anything else?'

'Not yet,' replies Emory.

Thea pinches the bridge of her nose. 'That's a remarkably meagre collection of facts considering the faith I've put in you,' she says, dripping disdain. 'The fog is coming, Emory. There's no time for your usual lackadaisical approach.'

'What did *you* discover?' demands Emory, who's much too foot-sore for this kind of condescension.

'I completed the post-mortem. The cause of death wasn't the stab wound; it was the injury to her head. She was bludgeoned with something heavy that was made of metal. I inspected the warehouse, but there was nothing matching that description in there.'

'No, there wouldn't be,' says Emory, turning on her heel and pushing through the villagers to reach the end of the pier. The other two follow her.

She leans over the edge, pointing towards the strange metal object under the water that she found this morning. 'There are fresh gouges in the concrete. I think it was dragged to this spot and dumped last night.'

'Hephaestus was using that machine to inspect the cauldron,' says Clara. 'He brought it down to the village with him when we collected Ben. Could that be the murder weapon?'

Thea doesn't answer. Hephaestus left it in *her* lab last night. If it is the murder weapon, it incriminates her as much as him.

She calls to some nearby villagers, ordering them to fetch rope, so they can lift it out of the water. 'Once it's back in my lab, I'll see if I can find something that connects it to the body.'

As Thea oversees the recovery, Emory and Clara head back through the gate, finding the village half dressed for the funeral, with beautiful decorations draped in the boughs of the trees, and mourning lanterns strung along a length of rope between the two wings of the barracks.

Emory never realised how much this place depended on the joy of the villagers to soften it. Without their spirit, it's like she's noticing the high walls and crumbling barracks for the first time. Even the garden, which Emory's always loved, suddenly appears a sad little thing, a few wretched plants cowering in the shadow of something monstrous.

Having not eaten all day, Emory grabs some bread and cheese from the table, sharing it with Clara as they walk towards the infirmary. There'd usually be a feast out, but word has obviously gone around about the missing stores. They're having to eat whatever was already in the kitchen, and what few vegetables can be plucked out of the ground.

'Thea's right,' says Emory, staring back at the meagre spread. 'I need to be working faster.'

'You've only been at this for a day,' replies Clara.

'Which means I only have one more left, but I'm not getting anywhere. Every question I ask has ten more behind it. I'm not sure what I'm doing wrong.' She rubs her eyes with the heels of her palms. 'I'm not sure what I'm doing, at all.'

'Mum –'

'I begged her for this, Clara. I told her I could do it, but what if I can't?'

Clara stares at her mother. It's like she's standing at the edge of dark, dangerous water, terrified of what's swimming below.

'Then you can't,' replies Clara levelly. 'And maybe nobody can, but you're trying. Nobody's expecting anything more than that.'

They enter the infirmary, finding the lobby filled with rusted gurneys and wheelchairs, broken glass crunching under their feet.

Emory points to a fresh footprint in the dust.

'They go that way,' she says, gesturing along the corridor. 'That has to be Niema. The rest of the floor is undisturbed.'

As they walk, I warn them about the memory extractor Hephaestus brought back from the lighthouse, and his plans for it.

Emory shivers, recalling how many hours she spent hunched over one of those things during the trials. Thea used to make potential apprentices take it apart and put it back together, until they had a fundamental understanding of how the power units, circuitry and neural gel interacted.

'We need to investigate the lighthouse,' says Emory. 'Niema took the metal box out there last night, and Hephaestus found a memory extractor there this morning. That can't be a coincidence.'

At the end of the corridor, they climb a staircase to a long ward on the second floor, where beds sit patiently expecting wounded soldiers who'll never arrive. The window frames are empty, jagged pieces of glass still held in the corners of the frame. Everything's covered in thick spiderwebs.

The tracks lead them through a ward to a large metal door with a heavy handle that's freezing cold to the touch. It's newer than everything else, tarnished but solid.

A keypad lights up as they approach.

'We need a code,' says Emory disappointedly. She punches in a few random numbers, causing it to flash red and reset. Her thoughts go back to Niema's room. Did she see any codes in there, while she was looking through Niema's things?

She taps '5' twice, remembering the number on the back of the charred note, and the message Niema gave to Matis before he died.

Nothing happens.

Stepping back, she examines the length of the corridor, wondering if there's another way inside.

Clara frowns at the keypad, then checks the numbers on her wrist, punching them in. A mechanical click sounds from within the door as the lock is released.

'How did you do that?' asks Emory, in surprise.

'I used the code,' replies Clara, showing it to her mother. 'We must have come here last night.'

'No, we didn't. There were no other footprints in the dust.'

'Somebody wrote that code on your wrist. They wanted us to find this place.'

She raises the handle, which despite its size lifts easily, activating some internal mechanism, which causes the door to open with a whoosh.

Ceiling panels crackle into life, bringing a harsh white light. Inside they find a tiled room with X-ray projectors on the walls and twelve gurneys lined up in rows, each with a dead body lying on it.

The air is frosty enough to fog their breath.

Hugging herself to keep warm, Emory meanders between the gurneys, unsure of what she's seeing. Bodies are clutter in the village and burned immediately after they die. Why would Niema be collecting them?

There's a chart at the foot of each gurney listing some medical information she understands, and a lot she doesn't.

'Hallucinations, followed by inability to discern reality from memory,' she reads off one chart, her teeth chattering. 'Drank bleach. Implant rejected after five days.'

'What's bleach?' asks Clara.

'No idea,' replies Emory, passing her the chart. 'It was probably delicious, though.'

'They're human,' says Clara, leafing through the notes. 'Or, at least, I'm assuming they are, judging by these scans of their internal organs. They're in completely different locations from ours, and there's a lot more of them.' She bites the inside of her lip, a habit of hers when she's thinking. 'They're much more complicated than we are.'

Emory peers at the chart. The villagers are wrapped in ribs and tough cartilage, their internal organs encased in bone, with multiple redundancies in case any of them get damaged. This woman was just flesh and blood, and a thin layer of skin. How terrifying must the world seem to somebody with this little armour? Why would any species that dies so easily invent something as terrifying as murder?

Clara taps the nearest gurney. 'Niema was taking blood samples and genetic material for analysis. Whoever this is, they died twenty years ago.'

'Why haven't they decayed?' asks Emory.

'There are chemicals that could preserve the bodies indefinitely,' I explain, speaking in both of their heads simultaneously. 'The cold is intended to keep insects and rodents away.'

Clara puts down the chart she's reading and picks up another.

'Patient reported having pleasant conversations with dead relatives, before ... urgh, slitting their throat. Implant rejected after two days.' She flips to the last page. 'This one died four years ago.'

She returns the chart to the bed.

'Most of this is gibberish to me. The only person who can make sense of what Niema was doing to these people is Thea.'

'No!'

'Mum –'

'Do you honestly believe that somebody in the village killed Niema last night?' Emory asks. 'Do you really think Adil is capable of it?'

Doubt ripples across Clara's face.

'If I'm right, Niema was killed by either Hephaestus or Thea, and until we know why, we need to keep all of this to ourselves.'

'But they're elders!' argues Clara, shocked. 'They would never –'

She snaps her mouth shut, her conviction sounding strange, even to herself. After everything she's learned today, why does she still think the elders are perfect? Why does she believe that? She traces the idea back, finding it wrapped through her thoughts like a shining thread. The elders are wise and kind and fair and entirely without flaw. Do not question them.

It's scripture.

It's not just me who believes that, she thinks. If she asked anybody in the village to describe an elder, they'd probably recite that line verbatim. The only person who never did was her mum. She can't imagine how hard that was for her; to be full of doubt in a world of conviction.

Clara suddenly feels ashamed. She was always so embarrassed by her mother, even as a little girl. She wanted her to act like every other mum. She wanted her quiet, and diffident, and soft. After her father died, in the darkest of her thoughts, she sometimes wished that it had been Emory, not Jack, in that boat.

'The night before she was murdered, I heard Niema arguing with Hephaestus about an experiment she was conducting,' says Emory, drifting between the tables. 'She told me that the experiment had failed every time she'd tried it previously, but if it failed that night, she'd be forced to do something terrible. I think this is what she was talking about. These poor people are her failures. Is there anything in those records that explains what she was doing to them?'

'Nothing I can decipher. I can tell you that whoever Niema was experimenting on the night she died isn't in this room. The charts indicate that the last body was delivered three years ago.'

'Hephaestus can explain all of this.'

'Should be an easy conversation,' says Clara wryly, taking a grey jumpsuit off a peg and holding it up by the shoulders. 'Those are pre-apocalypse clothes. This was the uniform employees of Blackheath wore. I saw tatters of these jumpsuits while I was on my expedition, but nothing like this.'

She runs the material between her thumb and forefinger.

'It's made from a breathable fabric that doesn't stain and is designed to keep your body temperature stable no matter what the weather. This is probably the most sophisticated piece of equipment on the planet. What's it doing in here?'

'Niema probably wore it to keep warm,' says Emory, shivering. 'This place is freezing.'

She casts her gaze across the bodies, which are long-limbed and pale, spindly and soft. They look like something dragged up from the bottom of the ocean. How could she have ever believed the villagers and elders were the same?

'Thea told me there were a hundred and forty-nine humans sleeping in Blackheath, but there was no way to reach them,' she says thoughtfully. 'Between these clothes and these bodies, I'd say she's either lying to me, or somebody's been lying to her.'

'Thea's obsessed with getting inside of Blackheath,' says Clara. 'It was all she talked about on our trip. If she knew how to reach her old lab, I'm not sure we'd ever see her again.'

Emory raps one of the gurneys. 'How angry would she be if Niema knew Blackheath was open, but hadn't told her?'

'She'd be furious.'

'Angry enough to kill?'

'Yes,' says Clara. 'I think so.'

THE SCHOOL'S EMPTY, FILLED with heat and dust. Normally, the children would be at their desks, but the decision is still being made on who'll replace Niema.

Following her mother inside, Clara's immediately pummelled by a choking sorrow. Niema's last lesson is on the board, and she left a few sheets of homework in a folder, waiting to be marked. A mourning lantern is sitting on her desk, a candle flame guttering behind the green rice paper. There's a small pot of glue beside it, the brush stuck to the desk. One of the children must have made it for her.

They adored her. Unlike Thea and Hephaestus, Niema welcomed questions. She enjoyed an argument, or a differing point of view. She was patient when you didn't understand, and excited when you did. She was a good teacher, and Clara had felt grateful to her every time she walked into this room. She can't believe she could be that woman during the day, then pop across to the infirmary to kill people at night. No villager would ever be capable of that. They treasure life above everything. Everybody else's first. Their own second.

Emory's staring at the mourning lantern, her brow furrowed.

'What you thinking, Mum?'

'The candle's almost burned down,' she says. 'This was made last night.'

'Is that important?'

'It's getting increasingly hard to tell,' she says, taking the laminated map off the wall, then placing it flat on one of the children's desks, her hands planted either side of it.

'Hephaestus knows about the experiments his mother was running. He's not going to talk to us, but if we can work out where's he been living, we can search it. Maybe we'll find something useful.'

'How are we going to do that? Hephaestus could be living anywhere on the island.'

'Not anywhere. I used to see him leaving the village when I went for a swim in the evening. He always went west out of the gate.'

Her finger jabs the location of the village, then drifts along a narrow trail winding down to a small bay.

'There's some sort of building down there,' says Clara, noticing a symbol of crossed swords over a rectangular block. 'Could that be it?'

'It has to be, there's nothing else out there. How far is the walk, Abi?' asks Emory.

'Thirty minutes,' I say.

'How long would it take us to go by boat?'

'Who's rowing?' interrupts Clara.

'What does that mean?' demands Emory.

'You know what it means,' says Clara archly. 'You're absolutely terrible in boats. You'll row in circles for about an hour, realise you've forgotten to raise the anchor, then drop the oars in the water when you try. What did Dad call you?'

'The sea leopard,' replies Emory, smiling at the memory. 'Graceful absolutely everywhere except the ocean.'

'I'll row,' decides Clara. 'I've still got my exemption from Thea. It should only take us ten to fifteen minutes, depending on the currents.'

Under half an hour later, they're passing through the sea wall into the open water, Clara propelling them forward with graceful strokes. She learned to row from her father, who was always at sea. Even as a little boy, he was never settled in the village. He wanted to explore ancient ruins, and go on adventures with Thea. After becoming an apprentice, he would take any assignment that sent him beyond the walls.

It's always been a source of wonder to Emory that Clara and Jack ended up having so much in common. He died when she was twelve, and, even before that, he was rarely home. How did Jack pass his restlessness onto his daughter? Was it a virus communicated in longing glances at the horizon, or disappointed sighs while he was peeling yet another potato? What did he teach Clara, and when was he doing it?

'You're thinking about Dad, aren't you?' Clara says, noticing her mother's expression.

'How did you know?'

'There's a look you get, like you've remembered something you want to tell him when he gets home.'

Emory smiles, wistfully. 'I'd have thought I'd stop missing him by now, but ...' She trails off, shrugging. 'I must think about him ten times a day. If he was here, right now, I'd tell him everything we've done and he'd say something that was just ...' She shakes her head, laughing. 'Stupid. Honestly, so stupid, but it would help make things clear.'

'I miss him, too,' says Clara. 'Can you imagine how much fun he'd be having racing around the island?'

'Can you imagine the facts!' declares Emory, making Clara laugh. 'He'd be pointing out every animal he saw, and telling us their Latin names, and migratory patterns.'

'He really loved a fact, didn't he?'

'Couldn't get enough,' replies Emory, delighted to recall this forgotten habit of her husband's. 'I think that's why he loved being an apprentice so much.'

'How did you ... I mean, you're not exactly ... ?'

'How did a sceptic like me fall in love with a true believer?' asks Emory, as Clara struggles to guide them through a strong current.

'Your father was an apprentice, but he was also kind and loving, carefree and silly. His faith in the elders was only a fraction of his personality. He wasn't like my dad. It didn't shove out everything else he was. He understood that I had my questions, but he admired that about me. We loved each other, which made it easy to live with each other's doubts.'

'If you could do that for him, why couldn't you do it for me when I became an apprentice?' asks Clara, in a small voice.

For years, the best she could hope for from her relationship with Emory was uneasy quiet. After she started making decisions about her own life, it felt like her mother washed her hands of her. There seemed no middle ground they could exist on, so they tiptoed around each other being excruciatingly polite, and entirely superficial, for fear of bumping into any topic that would start an argument.

But today they've felt like a team. Emory has listened to her, and trusted her, and depended on her.

And she, in turn, has seen every flaw in her mother turned to a strength. Clara's never been so proud of her. She can't believe they may only have less than two days left together.

Emory's quiet for so long that Clara almost apologises for upsetting her, but when she speaks again her words are laden with emotion.

'I should have,' admits Emory. 'I wanted to, I was just so … angry.'

She swallows, trying to hold herself together. Her head's lowered, and she's fidgeting with her fingers.

'Jack and the others died because they wouldn't question Thea. They went into that storm because she told them to, even knowing it could be dangerous. But the more I pointed that out, the more isolated I became. Truthfully, I think I liked that because it kept me angry, and while I was angry I could concentrate on something that wasn't being said.'

She meets her daughter's gaze, seeing her at every age, right back to the eight-year-old girl Thea brought down in the cable car. Emory and Clara have the same eyes. The same reckless courage. The same big heart, so easy to hurt.

'After you applied for the trials, it felt like … like you'd sided with Thea, and with the village. And, then I was angry with you.'

'That's not what I intended, Mum.'

'It doesn't matter,' says Emory, her anger causing Clara to flinch. 'It was my job to support you, whatever you did. I hated you working for Thea, but I should have told you I was proud of you for getting there. I really was, Clara. I saw how hard you studied.'

Emory hangs her head.

'I let you down,' she says, fidgeting with her fingers. 'The way my father let me down. I didn't realise you could stay with somebody and still abandon them, but that's what I did. I'm so sorry, my love. It won't happen again.'

Clara hurls herself across the boat, hugging her mother fiercely.

FORTY-TWO

THE BAY REARS UP in front of them, a small sandy beach fenced in by craggy cliffs, hundreds of birds circling overhead.

Clara leaps nimbly out of the boat, then pulls it a few feet out of the lapping water. From this vantage, the bay appears completely sealed off from the rest of the island, but there are sixteen cows lying on their sides, their ears flicking madly as flies buzz around their heads. They're fat and healthy, and clearly not trapped on this beach.

'Where was the bunker?' asks Clara, massaging her palms. The oars have worn the skin away, leaving them raw and painful.

'We need to follow the curve of the bay to the right.'

The sand slides from under their feet as they stagger up the beach, disturbing a cast of crabs feasting on a dead turtle. The crabs scuttle out of their way, snapping and chattering, only to re-form immediately when they've passed.

'Those injuries to your palms are similar to the ones Thea woke up with,' says Emory. 'I think she took a boat out somewhere last night.'

'The elders don't row,' scoffs Clara. 'Not ever. Grandfather takes them everywhere they want to go.'

'Maybe he was busy last night.'

'Doing what?'

'I have no idea, but I'm telling you, Thea rowed somewhere. And she must have been doing it for a long while to leave her palms like that.'

They arrive at the bunker, which juts out slightly from the rock face, its angular concrete surface covered in graffiti. On the exterior the colours are faded, the names and declarations of love scrubbed away by the saltwater being thrown up by the waves. Stairs have been cut out of the rock, leading to an iron door, eaten away by rust. It's loose on its hinges, the bottom scraping the ground as they push it open.

It's dark inside, miserable and damp, the only light coming through three slitted windows with sight lines across the ocean. There are puddles on the floor and a fine haze of sea spray in the air that immediately settles on Emory's arms.

'Who'd choose to live somewhere like this?' she wonders, walking over to a folding metal table, which has been placed under the centre-most window. It's covered in charts and stacked books, curled up at the edges with damp.

Clara's peering through a second door, leading into a smaller room. Metal shelves have been knocked over, hundreds of salvaged machinery parts scattered across the floor. A huge chunk of concrete has been dislodged from the wall.

Clara wrinkles her nose in disgust.

There's no sunlight back here. No fresh air. Damp drips from the ceiling into dirty puddles, and it stinks of rust, oil and sweat.

'What are we looking for?' she asks, throwing a glance at her mother.

'A confession would be nice,' replies Emory, as she leafs through the books on the table. 'Preferably in big letters with a signature.'

The books are classics for the most part, *Moby-Dick* and Tennyson. Greek myths. A Bible. Hercule Poirot and Sherlock Holmes. Sammy Pipps and Arent Hayes. Hephaestus appears to love murder mysteries as much as she does.

'What's this?' murmurs Emory, removing a crushed memory gem from under a sheet of paper, its black circuitry visible through the cracks in the case.

She's never seen one damaged before.

Before I can warn her about the effects, she touches it to her temple, the jumbled fragments of a life flying by much too quickly to discern. Normally, there'd be sound, thoughts and emotions, but everything's silent, the scenes flying at her without context.

She sees the old world, crowds, applause, awards. There's a street, people staring at her, clamouring for her attention. Their faces are all completely different from one another. Their clothes are unique, their hair arranged a thousand ways, their faces painted, their bodies adorned and impaled with decoration.

She's flying through a beautiful city made of glass and steel, then talking to Hephaestus as a boy.

A mirror appears, with a younger Niema looking back at her.

She's a little girl, playing with a strange dog with multicoloured fur.

Then the pier outside the village. The bay is full of huge boats, big as cities. People are walking towards them, every face grief-stricken and slightly smug.

It's a life out of order, and the jumble's making Emory nauseous.

Niema's running on a machine. She's staring at a screen, choosing the features of her new child. She's shouting at somebody, who looks terrified. She's being swept up into her father's arms, holding a little trophy.

She's in a bright lab, strapping an older woman to a chair who's talking brightly, happily. Unconcerned. The clock puts the time at 9:14 p.m.

She sees corridors, and equipment. Jack with his eyes closed.

She's cradling a baby.

Glowing insects in a tube. Boys playing. Her parents. The village, surrounded by smiling faces.

They're back in the bright lab. Thea's screaming into Niema's face, gesticulating, her face contorted by murderous rage. The memories stop, which is lucky for Emory as she's about to throw up.

Clara catches her before she falls. 'What did you see?'

'Niema,' says Emory. 'Abi must have pulled the memories just before she died, but it's a jumble.'

She goes to the door, sucking in the sea air, until the room stops spinning.

A few moments later, Clara joins her, having used the gem herself with equally upsetting results. 'Did you get to the end?' she asks.

'Thea argued with Niema,' says Emory. 'She was furious.'

'We don't know when it happened. The memories were jumbled.'

'Niema was wearing the same clothes she died in, and her hair was done the same way,' points out Emory. 'Do you know where they were? I didn't recognise it.'

'No,' says Clara, after thinking about it. 'I haven't seen anything on the island that looks that new. Do you think Thea's responsible?'

'I'm not sure, but she must have been one of the last people to see her alive. Mind you, Hephaestus has the gem, which puts him near the body. Come on then, let's finish searching this place before he gets back.'

Emory heads back into the machine room, while Clara rummages half-heartedly through the papers on the desk. She pulls open a drawer, causing a sharp knife to come sliding forward. It has a crude wooden handle wrapped in cord.

Clara's breath catches in her throat.

She takes it out slowly, turning it around in her hands.

'Mum,' she calls out.

'Yeah,' replies Emory, from the other room.

'I've found Dad's knife,' Clara says hollowly.

Emory arrives at her side, staring at it, dumbstruck. She saw this knife every day for a decade. She remembers the shape of the handle, and that odd chip in the blade that he could never buff out.

He left with it when he went on expedition. He would have been carrying it when he drowned.

FORTY-THREE

THEY'VE ALMOST REACHED THE village, and the evening sky is ribboned by purple and pink streaks. A storm is blowing over the volcano, the wind whipping their hair, while the first drops of rain lash their faces.

Emory's oblivious to the worsening weather, and the world at large. She's sat in the back of the boat, in communion with the knife held in her upturned hands.

Clara's watching her mother with concern, while trying to ignore the discomfort of the oars rubbing against her raw palms. Emory's the brashest personality in the village, full of noise and movement, like a skipping stone on a flat sea. Seeing her climb inside herself is unsettling.

'What are you thinking about?' asks Clara tentatively.

'Absolutely nothing,' says Emory, in a dead voice. 'And that's a problem with the fog this close.'

Clara stares past her mother at the horizon. Her entire life the fog's been a smudge in the distance, a wall around their world, but it's near enough now that she can see the insects floating inside, their golden glow scattered across the surface of the water.

It's beautiful, she thinks, shuddering. *Do they know what they're doing? Will they enjoy it?*

'No,' I say. 'They're attracted to the radiation that bodies naturally emit. They're like me. They were created to do a job. Nobody was interested in them having feelings about it.'

Clara rows their boat onto the beach, the keel scraping up the pebbles. Emory leaps out before it's settled, almost running towards the gate.

'Where's she going?' asks Clara, alarmed.

'To confront Hephaestus.'

'Is that a good idea?'

'No.'

'Have you told her that?'

'Of course I've told her that. We need her, Clara. We need her for everything that's coming, but if this meeting proceeds naturally, she'll be seriously hurt. Do your best to keep her calm. I'm working another angle.'

Passing through the gate, Clara wades straight into silence.

The communal tables are packed, but everybody's sunken within themselves, picking at their food. Parents have their children on their laps, while couples hold hands, and friends sit shoulder to shoulder, trying to seal up any spaces where their fear could grow. This is supposed to be a funeral. They should be singing and dancing, and reminiscing. This almost feels disrespectful to the dead.

'They don't think we can be saved, do they?' says Clara, pityingly.

'Do you?' I ask.

Clara watches her mother striding towards the lane, almost seeing her for the first time. Under that great mass of hair, she's smaller than nearly everybody, narrow across the shoulders, with thin arms and legs.

And yet her size doesn't even occur to Clara when she thinks about her. Her entire life, Emory's been the biggest personality in every room she's entered. Where most people were meek and subservient, she was always fearless, forthright and full of energy, like a hornet's nest that spills questions into the air when struck. She doesn't stop, and she's relentless when she thinks she's right.

But what's that ever got her?

That's the niggling doubt in Clara's thoughts. Under her mother's bed are more than a dozen notebooks filled with questions. Barely any of them were ever answered. Why should this one be any different?

Clara follows her mother towards the lane, under the twinkling lights of the mourning lanterns, which have been strung between the two wings of the barracks. They needed four ropes to hold the lanterns dedicated to the dead villagers, and nine for Niema's. The discrepancy makes Clara's blood boil.

The villagers led kind, selfless lives. Nearly everything they did helped make this place better for other people.

By contrast, Niema ordered the memory wipe that killed them. She experimented on the bodies in the infirmary, and now the fog is closing around the island, because she couldn't bear to leave anything behind once she was gone.

Niema doesn't deserve to have more lanterns than the villagers. She doesn't deserve to have any, at all.

Four steps take Emory and Clara into the lab, where Thea is bent low over the contraption they pulled out of the ocean. She's using a pair of tweezers to pluck an object from between two bent struts.

Hephaestus is on the floor, his back to the wall, fiddling with the memory extractor like a kid with a new toy. He's humming a half-forgotten tune that Thea's obviously enjoying, because her head's swaying slightly in time.

'Why do you have Jack's knife?' demands Emory, marching towards him. He looks up blankly, putting the memory extractor to one side.

Thea pauses in her work, her eyes flicking between them.

'Why were you going through my things?' he asks, in a low, dangerous rumble.

'This knife was on my husband when he drowned,' continues Emory, ignoring his question.

Hephaestus rises up in front of her like a vengeful deity. His eyes have the same glitter of madness in them that doomed the vulture in the yard.

Clara desperately tries to pull Emory back. Normally, her mother's good at adapting to the shifting winds of people's emotions, but not when there's a question she wants answered.

'I found the knife on the beach,' says Hephaestus.

'It's not rusty, and the wooden handle isn't swollen,' argues Emory, shaking herself free of Clara's grasp. 'This hasn't been anywhere near the water.'

Emory's staring up at him angrily, her head barely reaching his chest.

It's not merely that he's bigger than her, thinks Clara desperately. It's what's underneath all of that muscle. His face is twitching dangerously, like there're things crawling around underneath it.

'I repaired it.'

'It's identical to the last time I saw it,' she says, staring into his face. 'And the blade matches the stab wound in Niema's chest. Why are you lying? What are you hiding?'

Hephaestus's hand shoots out, catching her throat.

His grip tightens, causing her to gasp in pain, as she's lifted bodily from the floor, her legs kicking at the air.

The knife clatters on the tiles.

'Mum!' screams Clara, tugging at Hephaestus's arm, trying to free her.

Hephaestus is staring at them blankly, empty of any emotion. It's like he doesn't even realise what he's doing.

Clara shoots a desperate glance towards Thea, whose face is slack. She's talking to me in her thoughts.

'Help her!' screams Clara, her words echoing around the lab.

Hephaestus's grip tightens, as Emory gasps her last breaths. Thea's voice comes from behind them, sharp and dry, betraying absolutely no concern whatsoever.

'You're about to kill our best investigator,' she says.

Hephaestus's eyes come alive again, his face finally registering the woman he's choking. He opens his hand, letting her drop in a heap.

Emory gasps, clawing for air, while Clara hugs her protectively.

Hephaestus stoops to pick up the knife, weighing it in his hand, before returning to the memory extractor.

Clara feels Emory stiffen. She tries to get back to her feet and resume the battle, but Clara holds her tight, placing her lips to her mother's ear.

'I can't lose you,' she whispers.

Emory sags, the anger running out of her.

'Go,' says Thea, waving them towards the door. 'And the next time I see you, you better have a suspect for me.'

FORTY-FOUR

P UTTING AN ARM AROUND Emory's shoulders, Clara tries to
sit her shaking mother at one of the communal tables near the
kitchen, but Emory shakes her head vehemently, gesturing towards
the gate and the dark sea beyond.

'I can't believe he did that,' says Clara, speaking in a hush. 'He
just ... he didn't even ...' She runs out of words immediately.

Blood is rushing in her ears. Nobody in the village has ever been
assaulted before, and she doesn't know how to react. She feels like
she wants to run away, warn everybody, shout and hide, all at the
same time.

'Why didn't you stop him, Abi?' Clara demands, finding vent
for her anger. 'I walked past the boundary this morning and
you immediately took control of my body to march me back.
Hephaestus was hurting my mum and you didn't do anything.'

'As I told you earlier, I can't control humans,' I explain. 'I can hear
their thoughts, and my words have influence, but that's all. You're
wrong, though. I asked Thea to intervene and she did. If she hadn't,
your mother would now be dead.'

And humanity would be doomed.

'It's okay, Clara,' croaks Emory, squeezing her daughter's hand
reassuringly. 'This is good, this had to happen.'

Clara looks across at her, surprised by the fierceness of her tone.

'I didn't understand humans before,' says Emory, her voice still
hoarse from being choked. 'I knew they were different from us,
but I didn't realise how different. I didn't understand their relationship with violence. How easy it is for them. How casually they
can employ it. I was stupid to go in there, like that. Hephaestus
has secrets and he'll hurt us to keep them, whether the island's in

danger or not. That's valuable information. That helps. We have to assume Thea has the same mindset. We'll go more carefully now.'

It's cooler beyond the gate, the sea breeze swirling in the air, salty on the tongue. It will be curfew soon, and the sea is a velvet blanket, under the darkening sky.

Clara's staring at her mother, dubiously. 'What are we going to do about Dad's knife?' she asks.

The villagers aren't materialistic and will happily share anything with anybody, but it's offensive to Clara that Hephaestus possesses something of her father's. She feels like she's let him down somehow.

'Put that aside, for the minute,' says Emory, wincing as she touches her bruised throat. 'Thea knows Hephaestus has it, and she'll know my questions are valid. If nothing else, the knife will make her doubt him. Hopefully, she'll start asking the questions we can't.'

Clara looks at her mother admiringly. 'How are you capable of thinking that way?'

'It's not hard,' she replies, abashed. 'Whatever comes naturally, you just do the opposite.'

'So, what's next? Do you want me to take you out to the lighthouse?'

'It's too dangerous to row out there in the dark. I need you to run those soil samples you took from the farms, while I look around Thea's room.'

Clara tenses, wary of her mother antagonising another elder so soon after running afoul of Hephaestus.

'I should come with you,' she says.

'I need you in the lab, where you can keep an eye on Thea. If she tries to leave, distract her.'

Two minutes later, Emory's descending the circular staircase into the old munitions silo where Thea's been living. Electric lights burn in alcoves, but their fierce glow makes Emory uneasy. They're too bright, too steady. There are no shadows, no softness. If she stays down here too long they'll strip the flesh from her bones.

Arriving at the bottom of the staircase, she finds the air thick with potpourri, probably to mask the smell of damp, mouldy concrete.

She sniffs. Then again. *One of Liska's concoctions*, she thinks.

Everybody in the village has a hobby that they indulge in their free time, whether that's making candles or carving animals. On Sundays, the villagers take these things from dorm to dorm, laying gifts at their neighbours' doors as thanks for any help, or kindness, received the last week. Naturally, the elders receive the most tributes, even though they contribute the least to village life. It's always bothered Emory, but nobody else seems to mind.

The silo's sparse by the usual colourful standards of the village, with only a handful of decorations to soften the grey walls. For furniture, there's an old camp bed, undoubtedly salvaged from somewhere in the village, a set of drawers and an architect's desk covered in sheets of complicated equations.

Hanging on the walls are photographs of Thea in happier times. Here's one of her getting a piggyback from Hephaestus, while an older woman laughs in the background. In another, she's lying on the beach, pulling a face at the camera. There's a roaring fire with seven people clustered around it, heads tipped back in joy. Drinks are being served out of a bathtub.

Emory peers at the photos one after another, seeing an entirely different Thea from the one she's always known. Though she hasn't aged much physically, it's obvious she's younger in these pictures. She's laughing for a start, enjoying her life. Emory doesn't think she's ever seen that before.

'What happened to her?' she asks.

'Her world burned,' I say. 'Her family died, then her friends. She lost too much not to lose herself along the way.'

A great wave of pity overcomes Emory.

'Hold on to that feeling,' I say. 'It will be easy to hate them, but both Thea and Hephaestus have suffered far more than you can ever imagine. Whatever they are today, it wasn't their choice and they didn't deserve it.'

Emory starts pulling open the desk drawers one after another. The bodies in the infirmary suggest Niema had a way to get back into Blackheath, even though it was supposedly lost to the fog. If Thea found that out, she'd have a strong motive for murder.

'Motive,' she mutters, shaking her head at herself.

She's read that word so many times in her books, but she's never said it out loud before. It doesn't belong in this place, she thinks. It's something old, and blunt, and dusty. It thuds into the air when spoken.

The first drawer is empty, but the second one contains an ancient camera, its case held together by wire. Thea used to make her apprentices take this on expedition with them, so they could snap any new flora or fauna they found. Unfortunately, it was so fragile that by the time you tried to take a picture of the animal running by, the camera had fallen to pieces in your hands.

Putting the camera back where she found it, she opens the next drawer to find an old diary inside.

She flips through idly, until she comes to the last entry.

Ellie's gone. She wouldn't listen, not to me or Hephaestus. She climbed into the last free stasis pod. Said it was either that or she goes two-footed off a cliff.

I don't know what I'm going to do without my sister. We haven't spoken much recently, but that's only because we've been here sixty-eight years. What's left to say?

I don't know who's more upset, me or Hephaestus. He loved her more than life itself.

'Thea's sister is trapped in Blackheath,' says Emory out loud. 'Niema wasn't just keeping Thea out of Blackheath, she was keeping her from seeing her sister.'

'Emory, you have to stop your father,' I interject urgently.

'Why?'

'Because he's about to do something incredibly stupid,' I say.

FORTY-FIVE

B RINGING THE BOAT INTO the shallows, Seth leaps into the surf, landing awkwardly on his injured ankle. The flesh around the circular gouge is black and purple, and starting to swell, sending spikes of pain up his leg whenever he puts weight on it.

Grimacing, he drags the boat up the pebbles.

'Dad!'

Emory's waiting for him with her hands on her hips.

'Emory?' he asks, tossing the oars onto a pile on the beach, 'What are you doing here?'

'Abi told me what you're about to do.'

'Abi shouldn't be sharing my private thoughts,' he replies. 'Where's Hossein? We need the cart. I found a body on the rocks near the lighthouse.'

Emory approaches the boat. There's a woman inside, or what's left of one. Every limb is shattered, her face is crushed, and her chest is broken open. She's wearing a grey jumpsuit similar to the one they found in the infirmary. It's tattered, but the threads are acting like a net, holding the pieces together.

Bile rises into Emory's throat, but she swallows it back down, refusing to look away.

This is what today is, she thinks. Forget this was a life. Forget this person breathed, and cried, and had dreams. None of that helps. Something here might be able to help me save the island.

The only thing that's immediately evident is that this broken collection of body parts was once a human, like those they found in the infirmary. Emory can see her organs through her exploded stomach, and they're in entirely the wrong place. This has to be the woman Niema was experimenting on.

"What happened to her?' asks Emory.

'Somebody carried her to the cliffs and dropped her over the edge,' Seth says, working the stiffness from his shoulders.

'Did you see who?'

'No.'

'Was she dead when ...' The sentence is so horrible she can't finish it.

'Of course she was,' he replies, narrowing his eyes. 'Why would anybody drop her over the side if she wasn't?'

Emory doesn't answer that. She doesn't have the heart, though she's surprised by how quickly she's stopped thinking about death like a villager.

Hossein emerges through the gate, pulling the wheelbarrow we now have to use to transport the dead. Seth lifts the body out of the boat, dropping it unceremoniously inside. The pieces land with a stomach-churning squelch.

'Can you take her to the furnace?' asks Seth.

'The lab,' corrects Emory. 'Thea will want to see her.'

'Why?'

'Because Niema's dead, and everything's connected,' she says, setting Hossein on his way with a nod.

Seth's about to follow the wheelbarrow into the village when Emory catches his arm, her look conspiratorial.

'You can't tell Thea where you woke up this morning,' she says. 'Hephaestus found a memory extractor in the lighthouse. He's planning to strap it to anybody who might know something about Niema's murder.'

Seth regards her, before shaking his head in disappointment.

'Abi told me everything that's been happening,' he says, hobbling away on his injured ankle. 'I know the barrier's down, and the fog is coming. I know that somebody purposely killed Niema, and I was the last person who saw her.' He tugs at his T-shirt, the material cracking unpleasantly. 'I have blood on my clothes I didn't have last night. I'm involved somehow and if the elders think my death is what's required to help the island then that's what's right.'

'Why don't you tell me what happened instead,' she says. 'I've been asked to investigate the murder.'

'I'd rather tell the elders,' he insists stubbornly.

'Dad!'

'Enough, Emory,' he says, his anger giving way to shock as he enters the exercise yard, newly decorated for the funerals tonight.

It was only a few days ago that he said goodbye to his father, and it feels like only a few months since he was grieving Judith. Now the lanterns are up for Niema. The losses are coming too fast for him to handle.

Sucking in a deep breath, he limps forward.

People look up as he passes, their eyes widening. He's breathing heavily, and grimacing in pain from the wound on his ankle. His shirt is soaked in sweat and blood, and he's moving with an urgency that's uncommon in the village.

He looks like a late arrival from the apocalypse.

'How did you hurt yourself?' asks Emory, trying to see the circular gouge above his ankle. The wound could have been made with the end of a jagged pipe, but she can't immediately recall where one would be.

'No idea,' he says gruffly. He nods to the bruised faces in the exercise yard. 'Doesn't look like I was the only one, though.'

She waits for more, but it's like hoping to find an ember in two-day-old ashes.

'Abi told me you woke up with a drawing,' she says, trying a different avenue. 'Can I see it?'

His hand clenches around his pocket protectively. 'That's for the elders to decide,' he grunts.

They've reached the lane between the barracks and the outer wall, the vaulted roof of the school coming into view. The warehouse looms behind it, the brick stained black with soot from the fire. It's the only obvious damage from this angle, as the flames never got much beyond the rear wall.

'You need to slow your father down,' I say, in her thoughts. 'I'm trying to get Thea and Hephaestus out of the lab, but if they're still there when he arrives, they'll kill him.'

Emory leaps in front of her father, planting a palm firmly against his chest.

194

'Dad, listen to me,' she says, lowering her voice as villagers walk past carrying instruments. 'I can work this out, if you give me a chance. There's no reason for you to die.'

Seth meets his daughter's pleading eyes.

'I don't trust you, Emory,' he says coolly. 'The fog will be here in less than two days, and I don't believe you can save us from it.'

Her face crumples with hurt.

'Now, please, stand aside so I can talk to somebody who can,' he says.

FORTY-SIX

C LARA'S INSIDE THE LAB, peering around the edge of the
door. Hephaestus and Thea are sitting shoulder to shoulder
outside, their backs against the wall. He's twice her size and width,
talking frantically with his hands, as if trying to snatch meaning
out of the air.

Thea's perfectly still, her chin tilted slightly downwards, her eyes
narrowed against the glare.

Clara glances towards the lane her grandfather will soon appear
from, finding it mercifully empty. On quiet feet, she returns to the
microsampler, which is analysing the soil she found on the farms.

'Are you sure this plan will work?' she asks, in her thoughts.

'You'll need to be convincing.'

She stares at the machine, willing it to go faster. Every second
brings her grandfather one step closer to the lab.

The scanner delivers the results with a cheerful beep.

As she'd suspected, the crops at the farm were poisoned by chemicals, but she doesn't recognise any of the compounds.

'Your grandfather's reached the school,' I inform her, as she
hurriedly copies down the formulas onto a piece of paper. 'Be quick.'

She rushes across the room, composing herself before she steps
outside.

'I've analysed the soil sample,' she says, holding it out. 'There's
something strange about it.'

'Leave it on my desk,' says Thea, waving it away.

Clara tries to keep her gaze from the lane. She's never had to
deceive anybody before, and it's exhilarating. So much adrenaline is
flooding her system it's a struggle to simply stand still.

'Can you look at it now?' she presses. 'I've never seen these chemicals before. I don't know how much damage they're doing.'

Hephaestus gestures for the report impatiently, then hands it across to Thea.

'You wanted a pet,' he tells her.

Thea runs her eyes down the list of chemicals, her normally implacable features wavering.

'This can't be right,' she says, handing it to Hephaestus.

They share a bewildered look, before Thea hops up.

'Where are you going?' asks Hephaestus, startled.

'To check every entrance into Blackheath,' she replies.

FORTY-SEVEN

Seth limps into the lab to find Clara hunched over the microsampler, alone with the equipment.

She glances up from the display, as if surprised to see him. He's rooted to the spot, staring around the lab in wonder. The last time he was in this place was a few days after his wife died. They'd been working at world's end with a frequency detector, trying to learn how the insects in the fog communicated. They'd had a bad day, which seemed determined to get worse. After getting soaked in a storm, they became caught in a current, which had almost dragged them into the fog before they pulled clear. They ate a disappointing picnic in the boat, took turns at the oars and came back to watch a play Judith had written.

She'd been congested all day, shivering with cold, but she didn't look too bad, and she wasn't one for complaining. At curfew, they fell asleep in each other's arms. The next morning she was dead, carried away without any sort of fuss.

Thea quarantined Seth in case of plague, but it was just one of those things. The village houses them, protects them, and occasionally it kills them. That night it killed his wife.

Thea wanted him back as an apprentice, but every time he walked into the lab, he saw an experiment Judith had been working on. He saw a report she'd written, or the flowers she'd picked. After a few days of trying, he made an excuse and never went back. Far as he can recall, Thea didn't speak to him again, which he always considered entirely fair. He'd abandoned his duty, and given up a sacred act of service. He sometimes wonders if his disappointment in his daughter is magnified by his disappointment in himself.

Emory appears at the door, sagging in relief when she finds the lab empty.

Seeing her father lost in thought, she quickly grabs a pair of scissors and slices a scrap of material from his sleeve, handing it to Clara.

'What are you doing!?' he demands.

'Seeing whose blood is on your clothes,' she replies cheerfully. 'Hopefully, we can work out what you did after curfew, before Hephaestus kills you for the same information.'

Clara puts the material under the sampler, while Seth pulls back the sheet covering Niema's body. Even if most of her head wasn't missing, it would still be a dreadful sight. She's been stitched up after her post-mortem like a patchwork blanket.

He hurriedly covers her face again, before slumping into a chair. It's impossible to believe that something so awful could have happened to somebody so wonderful. Despite everything Emory's told him, he's convinced it has to have been an accident, or a terrible misunderstanding.

Clara brings over bandages, antiseptic and a powdered painkiller. She pours a little of the powder into a glass of boiled water, handing it to her grandfather. While he drinks, she drags over a stool and props his leg up, inspecting the circular gouge above his ankle. It's badly swollen and oozing yellow puss.

'It's infected,' she says. 'How'd you do it?'

'No idea,' he replies, struggling to take his boot off. 'I woke up with it. Hopefully, the memory extractor will be able to dig out an explanation.'

'You aren't really going to let Hephaestus use it on you?' says Clara aghast, dabbing the wound. 'The elders aren't what we thought they were, and they're not always right. I've seen it myself. They're violent, and selfish. They hurt people. You can't trust them.'

'We were made to serve them,' adds Emory, who's inspecting the memory extractor. 'They created us to do the jobs they didn't want to do for themselves.'

'You say it like it matters,' he counters, wincing as Clara peels away some mangled flesh. 'The highest honour in the village is living a life in service. We care for other people, before caring for ourselves. Sounds to me like what you discovered is what we already know.'

'Shouldn't we be free to choose those qualities?' asks Emory, frustrated by his refusal to be angry.

'Can you guarantee we would?' he asks, working to free his foot from his other boot. 'I don't care whether I'm human, or not. It doesn't change who I am, or what I want. My back itches, same as it did before you told me. My neck aches. I like the sea. I don't like boiled potatoes. And this morning I woke up covered in blood, without my best friend.'

He tugs the boot off with a grunt, placing it neatly beside his chair. 'If my forgotten memories can help the village I'll offer them freely, and be proud to do it.'

'You've got Shilpa's boots,' says Emory, picking it up.

'No, I don't.'

'The heel's missing a corner,' she says, showing him the proof. 'You took them off Shilpa's feet last night, while she slept.'

'Why would I take her boots?' he demands.

'Because the terrain past the farm is rocky,' supplies Clara, smearing the gouge on his ankle with antiseptic. 'You, me and Mum went out to Adil's shack last night, pulling a cart. You had to change out of your sandals on the way.'

'But I was at the lighthouse with Niema last night,' he protests.

'You must have brought her back to the village.'

'But I woke up out there,' he splutters. 'Why would I row all the way back?'

The microsampler beeps, completing its scan of the blood on his clothes. Clara finishes wrapping the bandage around his leg, then gets to her feet, going over to the machine.

'Whose is it?' asks Seth, turning in his seat to see her, obviously afraid of the answer. 'Is it Niema's?'

'No,' says Clara, her voice shaking. 'It's Hui's.'

S ETH IS HOBBLING IN circles around Thea's lab agitatedly, watched by a thoughtful Emory and a stunned Clara.

'Hui wasn't in my boat last night,' he says, for the fourth time. 'I barely knew the girl.'

'It probably just means you were near the bird bath when she was attacked,' supplies Emory.

'I woke up at sea!' he growls in frustration, throwing his hands up. 'None of this makes any sense.'

'Tell us what happened last night,' she says, secretly enjoying his discomfort. 'Whatever you can remember.'

He shakes his head, trying to piece it together.

'There's not much to tell,' he replies, scratching his whiskers. 'Niema was quiet. She didn't talk much on the journey. She told me how she owned the island, and asked about your mother –'

'She asked about Mum?' interrupts Emory. In the twenty years since Judith died, Niema hasn't mentioned her once. Even in the weeks after the funeral, when all Emory wanted to do was tell stories and relive their time together, Niema would swiftly change the topic.

'Yeah,' says Seth, perplexed by Emory's sudden interest.

'What did she want to know?'

'What she was like.' Seth frowns at his daughter's curiosity. 'Why does it matter?'

'I don't know. Had she ever asked before?'

'No,' he admits. 'We didn't discuss it for long. Adil was waiting for us on the jetty, and I think that threw her. Abi must have calmed her down, because Niema asked me to moor up, and then she went up to the lighthouse with him. That's the last thing I remember.'

'How was Adil?'

'Nervous, maybe. Angry. Niema was afraid, but she wouldn't let me go with her. I fell asleep in the boat. That's the last thing I remember before I woke up this morning with this.'

He holds out a folded piece of paper.

Emory takes it, finding herself staring at the torn page from Magdalene's sketchpad. As they suspected, the artist drew what happened last night. The band is on the stage, playing their instruments, while the villagers dance. It looks like a party was going on.

'Come look at this, Clara,' says Emory, waving her daughter over. 'Hui was talking with Niema near the bird bath. She's holding her violin.'

Clara taps the drawing of herself, perched on the end of a table, carving a bird from a block of wood. Emory's beside her, an arm around her shoulder.

'I look upset,' she says.

'We both do,' murmurs Emory.

'I only carve when I've got a lot to think about or need to calm myself down,' says Clara. 'What could Niema have told us that would make everybody else that deliriously happy, and us that sad?'

'It certainly wasn't that we were going to spend the rest of our lives serving the humans trapped in Blackheath,' says Emory. 'Thea either lied to me, or Niema lied to her.'

She flips the drawing over, staring at the strange diagram with the lines and numbers.

'Adil used to make drawings like that,' says Seth. 'When he first came back to the village, before he was exiled. He scratched them on the walls at night. We'd find them everywhere.'

'What do they mean?' asks Clara.

'He never knew,' replies Seth. 'He seemed to be as confused by them as we were.'

'Sounds like Ben,' murmurs Emory. 'This is your handwriting, isn't it, Dad?'

'Bit messy, but yes.'

'You must have torn this page out of Mag's book last night because it was the nearest paper at hand,' she says. 'Whatever this diagram means, you obviously needed to get it down in a hurry.'

Failing to make sense of it, Emory returns her attention to the drawing of the exercise yard on the other side. It's so strange to see themselves there, awake and lucid, living a life they can't remember.

'Why wouldn't Niema want us to remember any of this?' mutters Clara, behind her.

Emory's eyes widen, a horrible idea barging into her mind. 'Where's the knife you use to carve your birds?' she asks abruptly.

'In my bag,' replies Clara, still staring at the picture.

'Put it in the sampler,' she says.

'Why?'

'Just do it, please.'

Frightened by the urgency in her mother's tone, Clara withdraws her knife from its wooden sheath, placing it under the sampler.

A silent minute crawls by, until the machine's beep cracks it like glass. Clara lowers her face to the display, reading it reluctantly.

She swallows, sitting upright.

'There are traces of Hui's blood and Niema's blood on the blade,' she says, meeting her mother's steady gaze. 'My knife is the murder weapon.'

Emory marches towards the memory extractor. After contemplating it for a second, she holds it above her head and hurls it to the floor, sending fragments of metal and glass skittering across the lab.

Dissatisfied with the damage, she stamps on it as hard as she can.

'Stop that!' demands Seth, trying to drag her away, but she wriggles free of his grip and jumps on it with both feet, causing something to crack inside. Bright red gel comes pouring out of the sides.

'What have you done?' he screams.

'I've saved my family's life,' she says, panting. 'You're welcome.'

EMORY MARCHES OUTSIDE AND screams her frustration at the purple sky, drawing curious looks from the people in the barracks.

She left her father cradling the memory extractor on his lap, like it was an injured animal. After everything they've learned, he's still angry with her for defying the will of the elders. How can his faith in them be so steadfast, when he has so little faith in her?

She feels Clara's arms slip around her waist, and her head nestle against her back. She used to do this when she was a child and wanted to be comforted. Emory can't remember it happening since.

'You okay?' asks Clara.

'He's an idiot,' declares Emory, whose fists are clenched.

'He's probably thinking the same thing about you.'

'Don't take his side,' declares Emory hotly. 'You came out here, which means you're on my side, and being on my side requires you to be as angry with him as I am.'

Clara offers a playful yelp, making her mother laugh.

'I don't think you know how anger works,' says Emory, calming down.

Ants are crawling across her feet, travelling in huge black convoys towards the exercise yard, hoping to pick up any scraps of food that have fallen from the tables. They'll be disappointed, she thinks. Most of the stores are still missing, the funeral feast reduced to leftovers and almost-ripe vegetables dragged early from the earth.

She takes her daughter's hands, which are dirty, hot and hurt. Her arms are smooth and thin, the skin freckled. They're the only things about her that haven't really changed since she was little.

'What's wrong, love?' she says gently.

'Why was Hui's blood on my knife, Mum? I'd never hurt her, not for any reason.'

'Of course you wouldn't,' says Emory, turning around to stare into Clara's troubled face, startled by where her daughter's line of thought has led her. 'The crime was impulsive, and you were sitting close to the bird bath with a knife. Whoever attacked Hui and Niema grabbed it from you because it was the nearest thing at hand. If it had been a hammer, or a saw, the killer would have used that.'

Emory presses her hands to Clara's cheeks, lowering her own head to make eye contact.

'The only thing I'm certain about is that you have no part in it,' says Emory. 'That heart of yours is much too large.'

'What if you're wrong? I was so angry with Hui for treating me the way she did. I thought she ... What if I snapped and did something terrible?'

'We still haven't found anything to confirm that Hui's dead. Your grandfather woke up with her blood on his shirt, probably because he saw her being attacked in the exercise yard. He'd never hurt her, so he was probably trying to help. He was an apprentice for a long time, which means he was trained in first aid by Thea, and is probably good at it, knowing how dangerous that work is. I think the three of us put Hui into the back of that cart and took her out to Adil's shack, though that's where my theory falls down, because I don't know why we'd do that. I can only assume Adil took her somewhere afterwards, and he'd have no need to do that if she was dead.'

Clara's shoulders rise, her head lifting, as hope flows back into her.

'Thank you,' she whispers.

'I'm just thinking out loud,' replies Emory, rubbing her eyes wearily. 'And I'm not sure it's getting us any closer to the murderer.'

She cocks an ear, listening to the clink of cutlery being put away. It will be curfew in an hour and everybody's starting to clean up after the funeral.

'I think it's about time we told everybody what's been happening on this island,' she says.

FIFTY

E MORY ASCENDS THE STAGE nervously, holding her hands up to get everybody's attention.

The villagers are clearing the tables and taking down the decorations, but everything's happening at half speed. Usually, they'd be preparing for bed by now, but they're afraid to leave the comfort of other people.

For the last two hours, the encroaching fog is all they've thought about. They've pelted me with questions I couldn't answer, and searched for the elders who've both disappeared. They feel abandoned, which is not helped by seeing Emory fidgeting onstage. They'd hoped for Thea or Hephaestus: somebody with authority and answers.

Emory is the living representation of their doubt.

Her whole life she's unsettled them with her questions, pointing out inequalities they were afraid to see, and delivering them mysteries they worked hard to overlook. They've learned to avoid her wherever possible, even edging away from her at dinner, until she sat by herself every evening, a lonely little island.

'We've been lied to,' says Emory bluntly, once every face has turned towards her. 'By the elders, and by Abi. We're not human. We're something they made. They grow us in the cauldron to serve them, and we die at sixty because they decided we should.'

The villagers murmur in surprise, but otherwise meet this information with rapt, unblinking silence, waiting for her to go on.

Emory had expected anger, or disbelief – something to propel her. There's no fuel in this dim expectation. She's trying to dance on water.

She plunges on, telling them about the humans stored in Blackheath, and how the villagers get out of their beds every night to maintain the equipment keeping them alive. She stumbles over her words, falters, then goes back to fill in the gaps.

Their reactions remain muted.

They nod and murmur, the information sinking through them like stones through honey. They've spent their entire lives being told what matters, what to care about and when to be curious. They've never had to process so many things at once, all by themselves.

Emory's itchy and uncomfortable under their scrutiny, unsure what she should be saying.

'Give them hope,' I say gently. 'They're afraid. That's what they need.'

We really are in trouble if they need that from me, she thinks. *How many people have ever felt better after talking to me?*

She scans their faces, searching for the right combination of words.

'Niema didn't die accidentally,' she blurts out, coming up empty-handed. 'She was killed intentionally. Her death is the reason the fog's surging towards the island. If I can find out who's responsible, we can get the barrier back up. We can save ourselves.'

Unease ripples through the crowd, followed by murmurs of excitement as they register what she said.

Emory spots Magdalene, who's perched on the edge of the fountain. Her friend is hastily sketching this performance with a stick of charcoal, only adding to Emory's nerves. It's one thing being the spokesperson for the end of the world, and quite another having somebody keep a record of you doing it.

A little away from the rest, she sees Ben drawing in the dirt with a stick, while Sherko looks at him in concern. Clara's kneeling down, examining the drawings with a furrowed brow. They must be more equations, thinks Emory.

'How does finding Niema's killer help us get the barrier back up?' asks Seth, who's standing in the shadows near the kitchen, with his arms crossed.

Emory hadn't noticed her father before, and his presence immediately kindles the anger from earlier.

'Once the killer's confessed, Hephaestus will execute them,' she says, hating the words coming out her mouth. They sound like validation. It's as if she's endorsing murder.

A chorus of protests erupts.

'There has to be another way!' shouts Johannes, leaping up in anger.

'They're Abi's rules,' points out Clara. 'My mum's only doing what she was asked to do. Why don't you go and shout at Hephaestus!? He'd have killed half of us already if it wasn't for her.'

She glares at Johannes until he sits down again, shamefaced at his outburst.

'Are you okay with this, Emory?' asks Seth, coming into the light. 'Serving up somebody to die?'

She falters, suddenly unsure of herself. She hadn't thought that far ahead, in truth. Her preoccupation has been with asking questions, rather than the consequences of finding the answers.

'The fog will hit the island in a little under a day and a half,' she replies evasively.

'We don't kill people, Emory,' he argues. 'We don't help others make excuses for killing, or betray who we are because we're scared, or angry.'

'What is it you want me to do instead, Dad?' she asks, in a plaintive voice. 'Stop searching?'

'No, I want you to do it with clear eyes. This is your investigation, but once you've got your answer, I want you to think very carefully about what you're going to do with it. We can survive in the cauldron garden. There'll be hard choices to make, but I'd rather that than know we ended somebody's life to save our own.'

The crowd call out their agreement with this point, shaming poor Emory who feels like she's become the vanguard of a plan that wasn't her own.

'Emory's not making the rules,' I say, in their thoughts, quietening them. 'She's only doing what she was asked to do by myself and Thea.'

As they finally settle down, Emory raises her voice once again.

'Our entire lives we've been told to accept things that seem strange, and not to ask questions, but that's not going to work any more. We don't have time to be polite, or reticent. If you've seen anything unusual, please tell me. If something's struck you as odd these last few days, I need to know. Anything could help me.'

In the quiet, people wrack their brains. Emory wipes the sweat from her brow, noticing that her hand is shaking. She hates being up here, in front of people. She always has. It's a performance, and most performances are lies.

Caoimhin raises a hand.

'We've been dreaming,' he says hesitantly. 'I don't know if it matters, but a few of us have had the same one.'

He looks at his friends for support, but they can barely meet his gaze. They're red-faced and ashamed, wringing their hands, fidgeting in their seats.

'What was it about?' Emory prods.

'We were ...' He licks his lips nervously. 'We were attacking Hephaestus. All of us, we chased him through the village and then we ...'

'What?'

'We wrestled him down,' he says, obviously disgusted. 'The others were trying to hold on to him.'

Portia puts her hand up. 'I've had that dream,' she says sickly. 'Except it was Thea I was holding. I was hurting her, I know it.' Her regret could drown the village. 'She kept trying to free herself, but I wouldn't let her go.'

Some of the others murmur, recalling their own dreams.

'Anything else?' asks Emory.

Portia nods grimly. 'I was holding something sharp,' she says. 'I think I was trying to stab her.'

EMORY DIDN'T NOTICE HERSELF falling asleep, so it's confusing to lurch awake on a bench and find that the village has been dipped in ink. Darkness is dripping through the branches of the trees, and pooling on the ground.

She holds her hand up, barely able to make out her fingers. The only reason she can see anything at all is because there's a full moon in the sky, surrounded by more stars than she ever thought possible. It's as if all the light in the world has been swept into a pile, leaving a few crumbs scattered around it.

As her eyes adjust, she realises the exercise yard isn't as empty as she first thought. Her father is lying on the stage a few paces away, snoring softly.

'What time is it?' she asks groggily.

'10:17 p.m.,' I say. 'You fell asleep while everybody finished clearing up. Nobody had the heart to wake you.'

'What about him?' she asks, jerking her thumb at Seth.

'He didn't want you to be alone,' I say.

The cable car appears over the barracks roof, gliding up towards the cauldron, reflecting the moon's light. From this distance it reminds her of a cocoon, being dragged along a web. She shudders, imagining a gigantic spider up there in the darkness.

The rattle of metal draws her attention to the balconies.

Villagers are emerging from their dorms, and walking in single file down the staircase. Relieved, if surprised, to see friendly faces, she calls out to them, but they don't look up, or acknowledge her in any way.

In fact, they're completely silent. Normally, the villagers don't do anything in silence.

She frowns, realising there's something odd about their gait. Everybody is equally distant from each other, their shoulders perfectly aligned, their arms swinging to the same rhythm. Some of them are heading out of the gate, while others join a long queue that's stretching around the barracks into the rear yard.

She catches up with Claudia, who's the nearest to her. Calling her name produces no results, so she steps in front of her, trying to halt her progress. Claudia smoothly steps around her and carries on walking. Her eyes are closed.

'She's asleep,' says Emory, startled.

'Yes,' I confirm.

'You're controlling them.'

'The jobs that need accomplishing around the island require an extensive knowledge of electronics, metalwork, underwater repair, construction, welding, horticulture and circuitry. Expertise in any one of these areas would take years to teach. It's more efficient if I complete these tasks through your people rather than teaching everybody anew each generation.'

Emory thinks back to all those mornings she's woken up with scratches on her legs, aching muscles and dirt under her fingernails.

'Everybody will be returned to their dorms when I'm finished,' I say. 'They'll never know this happened.'

'That doesn't make it right,' Emory hits back. 'You should know that.'

'I was never asked for "right", Emory. Niema tasked me with monitoring the village, and ensuring it works at peak efficiency. These errands are necessary to ensure that humanity survives.'

Emory follows the queue into the rear yard, where villagers are being perfectly packed into the cable car. She's reminded of the puzzles her mother used to give her as a child, when she'd be asked to fit oddly shaped pieces back into the frame they came out of. She loved those puzzles, and would spend hours diligently figuring them out.

'How do we appear to you, Abi?' she asks, as the cable car moves smoothly off, filled with sleeping villagers. 'Like bees in a hive?'

'More like tools in a box. Every one of you must be maintained in order for me to accomplish my work. Occasionally, you need replacing.'

Emory feels like she's been slapped. She's always known that Thea saw them as disposable, but it never occurred to her that I would share that view. From Emory's perspective, I've been kind, compassionate and caring, wishing only the best for her, without ulterior motive. I've never raised my voice, or caused her hurt. I've cheered during her triumphs and consoled her after losses. I dampened pain-giving nerves after she's suffered broken bones and encouraged her when she was bereft. It's only natural she would mistake that for love, and, naturally, she loved me back.

She walks back along the line, searching for Clara's face.

'Is my daughter here?'

'Not tonight,' I say simply.

Emory rubs her tired eyes, and stifles a yawn, trying to get her bearings. She hates what's happening to her friends, but this isn't the time to dwell on it. She can't curl up in her regret, or make a shield of her anger. The fog is coming closer, and there's still so much she doesn't know.

She collects one of the candles stored in the kitchen, and lights it with a striker and flint. They burn a sap grown in the cauldron garden, and the flame gives out a sweet perfume. Pushing past her friends, she makes her way up the staircase into Magdalene's dorm room. Her friend is sleeping peacefully, while Sherko murmurs, gripping the sheets.

She settles herself in an armchair, tucking her legs underneath herself, then blows out the candle.

Half an hour later, she hears weary steps dragging themselves towards the dorm. Shadows shift outside the window, then somebody coughs uncontrollably.

Emory can't see who's coughing, but she knows what it means. It's a bone-deep jamming of the gears, the sound of something broken inside. Her grandmother died the same way, buckled over in pain, specks of blood flecking her hands.

People who cough like that don't do it for very long. Their hours are slipping away as loudly as possible.

As the hacking subsides, Adil shuffles through the door, dabbing his lips with a handkerchief. He's hunched over, silhouetted by moonlight.

'Hello, Adil,' says Emory, relighting the candle.

He winces, turning his head away from the unexpected glare. She's shocked by how frail he's become. His face is sagging around dim, squinting eyes. His neck is scrawny, and his dark hair has gone grey, retreating up his scalp like the tide. He's fifty-eight, but he appears much older than that.

'How did you know I'd come here?' he asks, looking along the balcony, in case Emory's brought an elder.

'Your shack didn't have a bed, so I figured you weren't sleeping there,' she explains. 'A while back, Mags told me how Sherko had started straightening all the pictures. That's an old habit of yours, isn't it? Once I learned you were still alive it occurred to me that maybe you'd decided on a looser interpretation of exile.'

'The rule was that I couldn't talk to anybody from my old life or they'd be killed.' He shrugs those narrow shoulders. 'As long as I'm gone before dawn, nobody gets hurt.'

He kisses Sherko on the forehead.

'I've never met him, you know?' he says. 'I was exiled before Abi gave him to Magdalene.'

His face darkens, as another thought occurs to him.

'You know in the old world anybody could have a child. You didn't need permission. You didn't need to beg for the privilege.'

'We're not human, though, are we?' points out Emory, watching for his reaction, trying to work out how much he knows.

Adil folds his hands in front of him. *He's jittery*, she thinks. He's trying to hide it, but he can't keep still.

'You sound sad about it,' he says, kissing Magdalene on the forehead. This is obviously some sort of tradition for him. Even in exile, he's still a villager. Cut adrift from the routine he grew up with, he's created a new one for himself.

'We were lied to,' she says, surprised by the surge of bitterness she feels.

'Our provenance is hardly the worst of it,' he replies, in that scholarly way she remembers. 'One of the benefits of being exiled from the flock is that you get to watch the shepherd at work. I've kept an eye on the elders for the last five years, and it's a dreadful existence. Believe me, not being human is a blessing.'

'We die at sixty!' she counters.

'And most of us enjoy every day of it. Niema was over one hundred and seventy when she was murdered, and I bet she was truly happy for less than a decade. Thea and Hephaestus have this entire island at their disposal, with all of its beauty and wonder, and they're miserable every day. Imagine being so shrivelled up inside, you can't take joy in this place.'

There's loathing in his voice.

'You hate them,' she says, taken aback.

'Don't you?' he replies, raising an eyebrow. 'Thea gave the order that damned your husband. Hephaestus nearly killed you a few hours ago, and Niema's arrogance has unleashed the fog on this island. The elders are selfish, short-sighted and violent. Explain to me what would be lost if Hephaestus and Thea were to meet the same end as Niema?'

'Are you threatening them?'

'Would you stand in my way if I did?'

'Yes,' replies Emory, without a beat.

He takes a step closer to her chair, cocking his head. She has the feeling of being under a microscope, turned every which way to understand why she's still wriggling.

'Why?' His voice is harsh. It's not a question. It's a demand. A challenge.

'Because we don't kill.'

'We've never had a reason before.'

Emory's throat is dry. It's a struggle to keep his gaze. Nobody in the village has ever talked like this before. Until now, she wouldn't have believed it was possible for a villager to even understand such depravity.

'They're the only ones on the island who know how to grow us,' she points out reasonably. 'If one of the pods in the cauldron garden breaks down, they know how to fix it. Like them or not, we can't survive without them.'

Adil shakes his head, flinging an arm towards her. 'Abi could teach us. Even if she couldn't, I'd not accept their control as the price of our existence.'

'You'd rather kill them?'

'I would.'

'And you started with Niema,' she says, hoping to shock the truth from him. 'Did you know it would bring down the barrier?'

She can see the lie forming on his lips, but she interrupts before he can get it out. 'My father saw on you on the jetty last night, waiting for her.'

'I'll confess I went there with the intention of killing her,' he admits. 'Niema's the reason I've spent the last five years alone, unable to see the people I love the most. I'd been following her for months, watching for an opportunity, and then, out of the blue, Abi told me where Niema would be that evening.'

He shakes his head, obviously perplexed by the entire thing.

'I was so anxious I arrived an hour early. I was ready to do it, Emory, but then I saw your father in the boat and knew clear as day what the cost would be. If I killed Niema, everybody I loved would die. Hephaestus would make sure of it.'

He stretches a veiny hand towards her, measuring the distance. 'I was this close, and I couldn't go through with it. Can you imagine that? Can you imagine all that hate burning inside of you, without release? I wanted to leave, but Niema asked me to walk with her to the lighthouse. Out of the blue, she apologised for my exile, and for the way I'd been treated. She told me she wanted to live the way the villagers did, without lies or secrets between her and the people she loved. She was planning to wake everybody up when she got to the village, and lay all her secrets bare. Every sin revealed to everybody she'd wronged. She was hoping they'd forgive her, and she was starting with me. She told me I could come home that night, if I wanted.'

He slaps his hands together. 'Five years of misery, then, suddenly, it was over. Just like that.'

He picks up the candle. 'Do you drink tea?' he asks, changing the subject.

'Erm, yes,' she replies, wrong-footed.

'Good, I was about to make one, and it'll be nice to have some-body to talk to for once.' He's walking out of the door before she can object, hunched over and shuffling onto the metal balcony. There's a cool breeze in the air, bullfrogs calling out. Somewhere distant a wolf howls. The night is so beautiful. Emory can't believe it's kept for the elders.

'I saw you outside the gate, didn't I?' she asks, following him down the stairs. 'The night my grandfather died? I recognise your posture.'

'You've keen eyes,' he says, shielding the candle flame. 'Yes, that was me. Your grandfather was an old friend of mine, and there were things about your family I thought he should know before he died. Questions that had bothered him, that I had answers to. I didn't imagine anybody would mind, given that he was dying that night anyway.'

'What did you tell him?'

'Haven't you seen his memory gem?'

'It was missing. Abi said it fell into the sea.'

'And you believed her?'

'No.'

'Good girl,' he says, smiling. 'Frankly, it's safer if you don't know. The secrets on this island have teeth, and they don't like being dragged into the light.'

They walk to the kitchen, Adil's eyes skirting the long queue of sleeping people waiting for the cable car.

'They go up in shifts,' he says, waving a finger at them. 'I've been watching them for years. Everybody does one week a month. This lot will be tending the plants in the cauldron garden, or servicing the cable car. The ones heading out the gate will be going to repair the wave generators and solar panels. There's so many jobs, and barely any of them benefit our people.'

Arriving at the kitchen, he places a palm against the pot hang-ing above the stove, finding it still hot. From the shelf he takes two wooden mugs, and slices some ginger into them. He ladles the boiled water in, then scrapes in a little honey. Everything's done with the practised motions of somebody who performs this act every night.

He's about to hand her a cup when a hacking cough bursts out of him, drops of blood splattering the pot.

He waits for it to pass, then mumbles an embarrassed apology, wiping away the blood with his sleeve.

'You need a doctor,' she says.

'I need a doctor who'll treat me,' he corrects her. 'Unfortunately, there aren't any of those on the island.'

He gives her the drink and she notices that his fingernails are stained with ash, exactly as hers are. It's from the warehouse fire.

Emory sips her tea, searching his face through the steam. He's working at a splinter in his cup, offended at finding something out of place.

His story's the same, she thinks.

He's worked on it methodically, going over every sentence until it's completely smooth. He's lying about something, she's sure of it. The truth is bumpier, darker. Far less elegant.

'What did Niema do after you talked?' she asks, following him to one of the communal dining tables.

They're completely empty, but he sits down at the far end of the fourth table, she notices. His old seat. This place is in his bones.

'She told me I could row back with them, if I was happy to wait. She had something important to do in the lighthouse first,' he replies.

'What was that?'

'I'm not sure, but there was another woman in there,' he says. 'I heard her when Niema opened the door to go in. She was talking to Hephaestus. It sounded friendly enough, but then the woman started screaming.'

'Screaming?'

'The worst pain you've ever heard,' he says, blanching at the memory. 'I didn't want to give Niema any reason to exile me again, so I set off for the village. I got caught in some rough water, which wrecked my boat. I got back just in time to see Niema being murdered.'

He says this in an offhand way, but Emory can hear the eagerness in his voice. He's been waiting to deliver this information since the conversation started.

Even so, she puts her cup down and leans across the table. Her voice is tight. 'You saw who did it?'

'I did.'

'Who?'

Adil sips his tea, peering at Emory. 'It was Thea.'

FIFTY-TWO

'THEA!?' EXCLAIMS EMORY.

'She was kneeling over the body with a knife in her hand, covered in blood,' he says, slurping his tea. 'She was screaming something about this being Niema's fault, and how she should have known what would happen.'

Emory remembers the memory gem she saw in Hephaestus's bunker. One of Niema's last memories was a violent argument with Thea.

Adil reaches down, opening his knapsack. From inside, he removes a T-shirt that's crusty with blood, which he places on the table in front of her.

'Recognise it?' he asks.

'It's Thea's,' she says. 'She was wearing it the day Niema died.'

'That's Niema's blood all over it,' he remarks. 'Thea was planning to burn it, the way she burned a piece of her fingernail she found lodged in Niema's cheek.'

'How do you know that?'

'I watched her do it,' he replies. 'I hid at the back of the lab, while she conducted the post-mortem. I wanted to see how she'd react.' He pushes the T-shirt towards Emory with a long finger. 'This is for you. Test it, if you like. You'll see that I'm right.'

'I will,' says Emory, pushing it to one side. 'But first I want to hear more about last night. Did you see what happened to Hui? She's a musician?'

Adil's features flicker irritably. His eyes flash to the T-shirt, then up to her face, trying to understand why she isn't immediately rushing at Thea, clutching this evidence in her hand.

'She was lying near Niema,' he says grudgingly, taking a glass ball out of his pocket to roll around under his thumb. 'She'd been stabbed, as well. Your daughter was with her, trying to keep pressure on the wound. I assume that was Thea's work too, but whatever caused it happened before I got there.'

'What was everybody else doing? The entire village was awake.'

'I didn't see,' he says shortly. 'They weren't in the exercise yard.'

He's sulking, she realises. He never imagined the conversation going any further than his accusation, and the reveal of the T-shirt. He hasn't rehearsed any of this. If she's careful, she might finally be able to catch him out.

'What did you do after you saw Thea stab Niema?'

'I ran.'

'You ran?'

'I was exiled from the village, Emory. I was told if I interacted with anybody, they'd be killed. Niema had welcomed me back, but she was dead. I was worried about what Thea or Hephaestus would do if they caught me there, so I went back to my shack before they saw me.'

Finishing his tea, he takes his empty cup over to the sink and starts washing it. Emory stares at his back, thoughtfully.

He's a good liar, she'll give him that. She's been served fragments of the truth, and there's almost enough of them to disguise the fact that they don't really fit together. It's impressive, and irritating.

'How did you burn your hands?' she asks, gratified to see his shoulders momentarily tense.

'I can't remember,' he replies.

'Did it happen when you set the warehouse alight?' presses Emory. 'I noticed the ash under your fingernails and I found one of Magdalene's paintings in your shack. It used to be stored in the warehouse, and had bloody fingerprints on the frame, suggesting you saved it from the fire. Was that Niema's blood? Did you cave her head in, then set fire to the warehouse, only to realise you were about to burn your beloved granddaughter's art?'

Adil wrings the dishcloth in his hands.

'I've given you the clothes,' he says, struggling to hold on to his temper. 'I've told you about the fingernail. Why are you still asking me questions? If you check Thea's hand, you'll see I'm right.'

'Do you know what you and the elders have in common?' says Emory sharply. 'You only answer questions you want to answer, and you think the rest of us are stupid enough not to notice. You were in the warehouse, last night, and I think *you* drew the code to the morgue on Clara's wrist. You wanted us to find those bodies. What are you up to?'

A tense pause stretches between them and Emory realises she's holding her breath. She feels like she's standing at the entrance of a dark cave, hearing something stirring inside. She doesn't know whether to press on, or back away.

'Do you know why I was exiled, Emory?' he asks, at last.

'You attacked Niema with a scalpel.'

'That wasn't why,' he says, finally turning around, his face in shadow. 'I was exiled because I started to remember things I wasn't supposed to.'

'Such as?'

His voice has changed timbre, becoming low and threatening. The hairs are prickling on her neck and arms. She swings her legs from under the table. She doesn't know if she's in danger, but she knows he's seething. His anger is quiet, radiating out of him like heat.

'Me and the other apprentices, including your husband, were on an expedition. We went to sleep one night and the next day I woke up in a brightly lit laboratory, working equipment I'd never seen before. Incredible equipment. The other apprentices were running experiments, but they were asleep. I realised they were being controlled, like the villagers tonight.'

Emory gets to her feet without realising it.

'Jack didn't drown?' she says numbly.

'No,' he confirms. 'None of them did. I'm not sure why I woke up, and they didn't, but I spent three days lost in an endless warren of corridors until Niema came to get me,' he says. 'She ordered Abi to wipe my memory, then sent me back to the village, but I slowly started remembering things. Nightmares, at first. Then daydreams, conversations with people who weren't there. I started drawing things on walls. It was like my memories were leaking out.'

Emory staggers forward, her head spinning. 'Are you telling me Jack's not dead?'

'The last time I saw him was when I left that lab,' says Adil. 'That's why I went after Niema. I wasn't trying to hurt her, I just wanted her to release my friends. Hephaestus chased me out of the village, but Abi managed to convince Niema to exile me, rather than kill me.'

'Where is he?' demands Emory.

Her every thought is of Jack, lost in the night. Jack who could be alive. Jack waiting for her to come and find him. Suddenly, nothing else seems to matter.

'Out past the farms, on the far side of a hill with an olive tree at its summit,' he says, nodding towards the infinite darkness beyond the walls. 'That's where Niema brought me out. I built my shack there near the door to keep watch, in case the others ever escaped.'

Emory doesn't hear that last part. She's already running for the gate.

FIFTY-THREE

IT TAKES TWO FRUSTRATING hours to reach Adil's shack in the pitch-black night, and she's limping by the time she arrives, having twisted her ankle scrambling up the first ridge. Since then, she's had to drag herself over the uneven ground.

She's tired and thirsty, covered head to toe in cuts and bruises. She hasn't stopped for anything. She's convinced that Jack's trapped behind that door, waiting to be rescued.

The tree Adil directed her to is on the other side of the stream, perched on top of a perfectly round hill. In the bright moonlight, the ancient trunk is twisted into a toothless, frowning face, the shining clouds hanging from its branches.

Limping around to the far side, she finds a recessed steel door built into the rock. It's badly rusted, with huge dents marking its surface.

'How do I get in?' she demands, running her hands across the surface, desperately searching for a handle or a button.

'There is no way in,' I say. 'This is one of the entrances to Blackheath. Niema sealed it forty years ago.'

'Jack!' she hollers, pounding on the metal with both of her fists. 'Jack! Answer me.'

Her voice echoes across the plains, desperate and alone.

Unable to find a handle, she hurls her entire body against the steel, over and over again, kicking and pounding, calling his name, until finally she slumps to the ground in exhaustion.

'You knew he was alive all this time!' she says. 'Why didn't you tell me?'

I meet her question with silence.

'Answer me!' she screams in impotent fury. 'For once, just answer me!'

Clutching her knees, Emory curls up on the ground, her chest heaving, sobbing in desperation for the husband she can't reach.

FIFTY-FOUR

IN THE SWAYING CABLE car, Thea grips the jagged edge of the window frame so tightly it digs into her hands, drawing blood.

Niema lied, she thinks angrily.

The report that Clara showed her earlier, proved that the chemicals that destroyed the crops were the same ones used in the stasis pods in Blackheath. They're immediately vented when the pods are opened, flowing out of exhaust pipes into the sea. One of those pipes runs under the farms, but it has fractured. The chemicals have leaked into the soil, killing the crops.

That means one of the pods was opened last night.

There are two explanations for that. Either there was a mechanical failure, causing the pod to spring open, or Niema went down there last night and purposefully woke one of the humans from a long sleep.

If it's the latter – and Thea's convinced it is – Blackheath was never lost to the fog. Alongside Hephaestus, she's spent the last few hours hiking to Blackheath's entrances, trying each one in turn, searching for a way in, but they're all sealed shut.

How could I have been so stupid? she thinks, trying to recall exactly what happened the night of the evacuation. It was late, and she'd been sleeping. Hephaestus had appeared in her bedroom, obviously panicked. He'd told that the fog had crept inside and they had to leave.

She went blindly, dragged behind him.

It was chaos. The alarms were blaring, the blast doors thumping shut as people screamed in terror. She yelled for Ellie, desperate to get back and free her sister from stasis, but no matter how hard she fought Hephaestus kept tight hold of her.

She never actually *saw* the fog, though, did she? She saw every-body's fear as they fled outside, trampling each other to reach safety. That was enough to make the story true. Sometimes the smoke is more useful than the fire.

'Did you know?' she asks out loud.

Hephaestus raises his head. He's sprawled on a seat at the back of the cable-car carriage, intertwining his hands.

Thea hasn't spoken to him in over two hours, a maelstrom of betrayal, suspicion and anger growing steadily in her breast. He'd hoped it would blow on by, or be derailed by some new detail.

He should have known better. Some storms follow you. Some storms make sure you're always in their path.

'No,' he says flatly.

'Don't lie to me, Hephaestus.'

'Don't accuse me, Thea,' he replies, growling. 'If I knew about Blackheath, do you think I'd be up here? I'd be sleeping in a bed, and showering under hot water. I'd be visiting Ellie every day.'

Is he lying? She can't tell. He sounds sincere enough, but she's always been bad with people. She was a child when she came to work at Blackheath, still trained to accept whatever adults told her.

She never learned how to read people, how to pick up the corner of a sentence and peer underneath.

More than anything, she desperately wants to believe he's tell-ing the truth. That's why she hasn't turned around to face him. What if she sees it on his face? If he's lying, what does she have left? She'd be alone on this island, surrounded by the crums. The loneliest woman on Earth.

The cable car thumps into the village station, and they walk through the adjoining door into Thea's lab, wrapped in uneasy silence.

The memory extractor is smashed on a chair, its pieces carefully brushed into a pile by Seth.

'No!' yells Hephaestus, picking it up to inspect the damage. 'No! No! What happened?'

'Emory happened,' I explain.

Thea's noticed the dead woman on the gurney. Seth's straightened her shattered bones so they fit on the narrow surface, making her look like some particularly grotesque puzzle.

Thea plucks at the tattered grey jumpsuit holding the body together.

'She's wearing a Blackheath uniform,' she remarks. 'This must be who Niema woke up the night she died, but why would she do that? If she had access to Blackheath, why not wake everybody up?'

Thea turns on her heel, confronting Hephaestus who's picking broken shards of metal from the memory extractor.

'How did you end up with Jack's knife?' she demands.

He looks up from the machine, genuinely puzzled. 'Jack?'

'Emory's husband. My apprentice. Abi told me they all drowned five years ago. Adil was supposed to be the only survivor.'

He shrugs. 'I needed a knife for something; my mother gave me that one. I have no idea where she got it from.'

Thea stares into his blank, scarred face. What would a lie look like on those features? She's only ever seen him angry or placid. After one hundred and fifty-two years on this planet, every other emotion has burned away.

'Is that the truth?' she asks, desperate to believe him.

His face falls, his voice wounded. 'I have no reason to lie to you.'

'Except that I found a piece of Niema's skull in that machine you built to check the cauldron garden for fissures,' she says. 'Somebody used it to cave her skull in, but it's much too heavy for anybody else to use that way.'

Hephaestus flushes angrily, getting to his feet. She can see the rage stirring in him, pitiless and senseless. If she doesn't quell it, everything in this lab, including herself, will be smashed to pieces.

'You think I killed my mother?' he asks, his tone deadly.

Thea stands aside, so he can better see the mangled body. 'If you worked out she was killing the humans in Blackheath, you might have felt you had no choice.'

Hephaestus swallows uncertainly.

'For the record, I don't really care if you did it or not,' she says, pressing her advantage. 'But if you're responsible, we should call off the investigation before Emory stirs up the villagers any further.'

'No,' he says firmly. 'My mother gave me hope, Thea. She's the only reason I could bear this island. She wanted to build a better future for us, and I believed in that mission.' He swallows, unable to look directly at the body. 'She wouldn't have done this without a good reason, and I wouldn't have killed her, not for anything.'

I would have. The thought flashes through Thea's head before she can stop it. If I realised Niema had lied to me about Blackheath, I would have killed her. I would have marched straight to the village and caved her skull in. In fact, I'm almost certain that's what happened.

She turns sharply towards the body, trying to hide the guilt burning her face.

Hearing Hephaestus shifting his weight behind her, she picks up a bone saw and switches it on, preventing them from having to speak any further.

'Let's see what Niema was doing to you,' she says, lowering the saw to the skull of the dead woman.

23 HOURS UNTIL HUMANITY'S EXTINCTION

E MORY'S WOKEN BY A shake of the shoulder. Blinking blear-ily, she peers up at Clara, who's kneeling beside her. It's a little after 10 a.m. and the heat is building steadily, a thin veneer of sweat on her brow.

Seth is standing a little apart, a bag slung over his shoulder and a worried expression on his face. His long shadow drapes them like a sheet.

'You okay?' asks Clara, handing her mother a canteen of water. 'Abi told us that you think Dad's in there.'

'That's what Adil told me. It's probably why he scratched that warning into the train carriage. "Niema buried us, she'll bury you, too." He didn't want the apprentices who followed him to meet the same fate.'

'That doesn't sound right,' says Seth vehemently. 'Niema wouldn't lie to us like that. It's Adil, trying to turn you against her. Has to be. He hates her, and he wants you to hate her.'

He wags a hectoring finger at his daughter. 'Niema loved you. You remember how she was after your mother died? She wouldn't have kept Jack from you, if he was alive. Never.'

Emory pulls her mouth from the canteen, gasping at having drunk so quickly. Water's spilling down her chin, wetting yester-day's T-shirt. She smells of dry earth and sweat, crusted with last night's panic.

'Niema was experimenting on humans, keeping their bodies in the infirmary after she killed them,' she says breathlessly. 'She added another body to her tally the night she died, which we only know about because you found it. She ordered the memory wipe that killed six of our friends, and she's the reason the fog is coming towards the island. That's only what she's done to *us*. Niema told Thea that Blackheath was overrun by the fog, even though her sister was trapped down there. She's been telling that story for forty years! Niema was a liar, and a murderer, and I don't believe a single thing she's ever told me.'

Each of these facts hits Seth like a rock, forcing him to stagger away towards the stream and splash his face.

Emory gestures Clara to help her up, then runs her hand across the solid door.

'Do you really think Dad's in there?' asks Clara, buoyed by the same hope that brought Emory out here last night.

'I want to,' says Emory. 'But there's a chance your grandfather's right. I was pressing Adil hard about the warehouse fire, when he suddenly told me the story about your father. He could have just been trying to break my concentration. Either way, we need to get in there and search it for ourselves, because I'm pretty sure this is where you, me and your grandfather came the night Niema died. We hauled a cart out here for some reason.'

'There has to be a way to open this door.'

'I don't advise trying to kick it down,' replies Emory, rubbing her sore shoulder.

'What does Abi say?'

'It doesn't matter, Clara. We can't trust her any more.'

'Why not?'

'Because she's not on our side.'

Emory's tone is sombre, her words flecked with pain. 'She works for Niema and nobody else. I saw it last night. Our friends were being marched out to work on Niema's orders. Abi was controlling them.'

'But Niema's dead.'

I don't think that makes any difference to Abi. She's going to carry on doing whatever Niema told her until the island sinks into the sea.'

Emory glances out towards the ocean. The fog is a sparkling shimmer, almost like a rain shower blowing across the water. *We have less than a day left*, she thinks, annoyed at herself for being so easily manipulated.

A few words and she forgot all about Adil, even though he's currently her strongest suspect.

And what did she get out of it? She wasted a whole night when they don't have a night to waste.

'Thea will know how to get inside,' says Clara. 'We can ask her.'

'We can't mention Jack being alive,' warns Emory. 'If we do, we suddenly have a motive for Niema's death, especially considering it was your knife that was used as the murder weapon.'

'Do you think Niema told us?'

'Probably,' admits Emory. 'Adil told me that she planned to air her sins last night, which would explain why we looked so upset in Magdalene's drawing when everybody else was happy. It would also explain why we rushed out here the night she died.'

Clara looks at the door, imagining her father behind it calling her name.

'If Dad's inside we have to find a way in.'

Emory shakes her head. 'Every time Jack's name is mentioned I do something stupid, but we can't afford that any more. We need to work out who killed Niema, and every clue we have so far points towards the lighthouse.'

THE ROWBOAT ROUNDS THE bluff, bringing the lighthouse into sight. It's shimmering atop high white cliffs, a light burning at its summit, despite there being no ships to guide.

'There's a jetty underneath it,' says Seth, driving the oars into the water.

Emory's staring towards the fog, alarmed by how close to the island it's come. At one point, she saw an overconfident seagull swoop inside, only to be immediately swarmed. For a second, the insects were so tightly packed around the poor bird that they formed a perfect golden copy of it, only to scatter when its bloody carcass dropped into the ocean.

'How are you doing that?' asks Clara, watching her grandfather's technique admiringly. 'I rowed Mum around for about an hour yesterday, and my hands are raw.'

'You need to pee on them,' he says.

'Huh?'

'Your hands,' he says. 'They get like that if you've been rowing for too long. You need to pee on them. They'll toughen up.'

'Urgh, no.'

He shrugs. 'Maritime life isn't for everybody.'

'Why would Thea have been rowing the night Niema was killed?' wonders Emory, who's only been vaguely listening to their conversation.

'It must have been important,' states Seth, grimacing as he rows them through a current. 'I've never seen an elder row themselves anywhere. They either get me to take them, or they don't go.'

'You couldn't take her,' supplies Clara. 'You were on your way to Blackheath with me and Mum.'

'I think Thea came out here,' says Emory, staring at the lighthouse. 'Her hands were really torn up, much worse than yours,

Clara. I can't think of anywhere else she could have gone that would have caused that amount of damage.'

'Maybe she was helping Niema with her mysterious experiment,' ventures Clara.

'I don't think they were friendly enough. They –'

The rowboat jolts, knocking Emory onto the deck. Clara manages to hold on, but Seth yelps in surprise, almost dropping the oars.

The ocean is white-tipped and furious, thrashing furiously beneath them, as though they've been overtaken by a storm, but every other patch of water is perfectly calm, and the sky is clear.

Seth grimaces, fighting a whirlpool, which seems determined to fling them onto the jagged rocks.

'What's happening?' screams Emory, over the crashing water, as she clings desperately to the bucking boat. Huge swells are emerging from the still ocean, slamming over the side, drenching them.

'I've never seen it like this before,' yells Seth, as he tries to point the boat directly at the swells, ribbons of muscle pulling taut on his powerful arms.

A wave pummels them, almost capsizing the boat.

'Another one of those and we're done for,' he screams, as an oar is ripped out of his hand.

'There! There!' hollers Emory, pointing to a gravel bay.

'There's no way out of there!'

'It's better than –'

A powerful wave smashes into the boat, flipping it into the air and sending them flying into the water.

Emory lands on her belly, the wind knocked out of her as she's dragged underneath by the current.

She's slammed into the shallow seabed, then against the rocks, before being thrust back to the surface. Somewhere distant, she hears Clara crying out for her, but she's dragged back beneath the waves before she can respond.

Unable to hold her breath any longer, she opens her mouth, sucking in great lungfuls of water.

Her vision clouds, as she thrashes for breath.

Finally, it goes dark.

FIFTY-SEVEN

EMORY GROANS, HER HEAD throbbing. She touches it tenderly, as slapping waves soak her. She sits upright, nearly vomits, then closes her eyes to stop the world spinning. Every bit of her is competing to ache the most.

'Clara!' she calls out.

'I'm over here,' she says, in a voice as groggy as Emory's thoughts.

They've been delivered to a grotto in the cliffs, their boat smashed to firewood. The pieces are floating on the surface of an ocean that is perfectly calm again.

Emory gets to her feet, stumbling over to Clara, who's trying to drag herself up the wall. She's covered in cuts and bruises, strands of lank hair clinging to her pale face.

'Is everything where it ought to be?' asks Emory, worriedly checking her daughter over for broken bones.

'Aside from us, you mean?'

'Have you seen your grandfather?'

'I'm here,' he replies, stumbling forward out of the gloom. 'I ended up at the back of the cove,' he says, hitching a thumb at the darkness. 'I don't wake up in beds as much as I used to.'

'How long were we unconscious for?' wonders Clara, noticing that the sun is a little higher in the sky.

'An hour,' I inform them.

'Anybody know what happened?' asks Emory, whose hands are jittery with adrenaline.

'I've been out here hundreds of times,' says Seth ruefully. 'Niema had me row her at least once a month, and I've never seen the sea like that before.'

'There were machines churning up the water,' says Clara. 'I saw them when I was dragged under.'

'Why didn't they sink me when I was rowing back yesterday?' wonders Seth.

They exchange looks, but there are no answers forthcoming.

Emory squints into the darkness at the back of the grotto. 'Don't suppose you saw a way out?'

'Nope, and it's pitch black,' he tells her. 'I wouldn't want to chance it without a light.'

She walks to the cave mouth, her legs still wobbly. 'We'll have to follow the coast,' she says.

'That will take hours,' groans Clara.

'What choice do we have? Abi can't send another boat. It will just end up stuck, like we are.'

'Your mother's right,' says Seth. 'It's shallow enough, and there should be plenty of handholds. We just have to go slow.'

It's late afternoon by the time the three of them reach safety. For three hours, they've edged their way around the treacherous coastline, clinging tight to the rock face every time a wave tried to dislodge them. Whenever possible, they waded out into the shallows, picking their way across the pools, but they're choked with dead turtles, being feasted on by seabirds.

Finally, they reach the jetty under the lighthouse, where they slump onto the planks in exhaustion, the sea below slapping the sides.

Their bodies are battered, their fingers bleeding. The tatters of a dead shark are floating nearby. It obviously got too close to the fog.

That's not difficult any more, thinks Emory. The great black wall is so close to the island now that you can't help but see it from the corner of your eye.

A metal staircase zigzags up the cliffs. It's rusted and rattly, and gives the impression of being attached to the rock by choice rather than bolts. After getting her breath back, Emory gives it an experimental shake, causing it to shriek in indignation. The top of the cliff looks terrifyingly far away, given the indifference of the staircase.

'Right,' she says, geeing herself up.

The three of them complete their climb without too much trouble, and are soon standing in the last of the afternoon's sunshine, staring at the lighthouse, which is surrounded by thousands of pink and purple flowers, a deer sleeping peacefully amongst them.

Motes of pollen swirl in the air, the drone of bees almost enough to drown out the distant pounding of the waves.

Emory's staring at the lighthouse with an appraising eye, as if it's something she's going to have to rip out of the ground and take home.

Clara crunches over the dry grass to inspect the flowers surrounding the lighthouse. They're knee high on thick green stems with two crisp leaves apiece. Each one has a perfect crown of symmetrical petals, and none of them are wilted. The entire field is swaying back and forth metronomically. Hypnotically.

And against the wind, notices Emory.

'They're beautiful,' gasps Clara, closing her eyes and lowering her nose to sniff one. The nearest four flowers turn in her direction, the beautiful petals peeling back to reveal a ring of thorns, leaking a clear liquid. The leaves tilt, aiming their blades at her.

'Dad!' screams Emory, calling to her father who's behind Clara.

Seth leaps forward, grabbing his granddaughter by the shoulder and yanking her away, just as the leaves shoot a large cloud of spores into the air.

Clinging to each other, they stare at the flowers in horror. The blooms are straining forward, rustling madly, desperate to reach the three of them.

'What are these things?' asks Clara, her voice trembling.

'I always walk through these flowers and they've never reacted that way before. I didn't think they could do much more than make you sneeze.'

Emory points to the sleeping deer, its ribcage rising and falling. Over thirty of the flowers have attached themselves to it like leeches, their thorns silently slurping the blood from its veins. Its limbs are twitching, its heartbeat weakening. It's dreaming itself to death.

Clara untangles herself from her grandfather's protective grasp, and creeps towards the edge of the field. Sensing movement, the plants become eager once again.

'What are you doing?' hisses Seth.

'I want to have a closer look,' says Clara.

'Why?'

'Curiosity.'

'Why would you be curious about –' Discovering he doesn't have the words, Seth makes a chomping motion with his hands.

'Because they're something new,' responds Clara. 'And new is wonderful.'

Even as Seth gathers the words to protest, Clara kneels in front of the plants, making sure to keep her face out of spore distance.

She lowers her index finger until it's an inch above one of the pink flowers. Its head tips up and rustles, the petals peeling back eagerly. Clear liquid drips from its thorns.

'Careful, love,' warns Emory softly, coming up behind her, ready to drag her away.

Clara ignores the warning, moving her finger to the left, where it hovers over a purple flower.

'It's not doing anything,' mutters Clara, sharing an excited glance with her mother.

She flicks it with her fingertip, then snatches her hand back out of striking range. Once again, it doesn't react.

'The purple ones are harmless,' says Clara, blowing out a long breath. 'I noticed they didn't go for me when the pink ones did.'

Emory laughs, delighted by her daughter's cleverness. 'There's a trail of them leading all the way to the lighthouse,' she points out. 'They're sort of disguised, but they're there. Niema left a path for herself.'

'And us,' says Clara.

FIFTY-EIGHT

I T ONLY TAKES A few minutes for Emory, Clara and Seth to walk through the carnivorous flowers, but they would swear that civilisations rise and fall while they're doing it. They can feel every twitch of every muscle holding them upright, as the pink flowers twist on their stems, watching them pass, waiting eagerly for any slip.

Clearing the field, the family immediately double over, blowing out long breaths of relief.

'Let's not do that again,' says Seth weakly. 'Once in a lifetime was quite enough.'

'Twice, for you, Dad,' corrects Emory, pointing to the bandage on his ankle. 'That circular gouge on your leg is the same pattern as the ring of thorns the flowers use to latch onto their prey.'

Seth reaches down, gingerly touching the wound.

'I must have followed Niema up here the night she died,' he says, confused. 'Why would I do that? She told me to wait in the boat.'

Clara wipes the sweat from her brow, then wanders over to the lighthouse.

The tower is built on a small, square cottage with arched windows covered in wrought-iron bars. The shutters are painted blue and the walls white. There's enough heat coming off them to bake bread. The fading sun is hoisted on the tip of the lighthouse, the blue sky empty around it. Even the clouds won't come here uninvited.

'This isn't like the other pre-apocalypse buildings I've seen,' says Clara, running her hand over the brickwork. 'It isn't crumbling, or being consumed by vines. The shutters haven't rotted, and the paint could have gone on yesterday.'

'There's a door here,' says Emory, pushing it open.

Clara follows her mother inside. She was expecting to walk into a damp, empty room, not a brightly lit laboratory. There are nine pieces of equipment on tables, arranged in rows of three, endless streams of information pouring across their black screens, conveyed in words and symbols, equations and graphs.

Clara roams between them, her eyes snatching greedily at the miracles.

A strange white liquid is floating in the air, where it's being stretched and contorted by invisible forces. Purple dust forms itself into a snake and a mouse, only for the mouse to leap on the snake, digging its teeth into its back. They collapse into dust, and are replaced by a rabbit hunting a fox. One of the pink flowers from outside is being dissected by rippling light, then put back together, while another machine weaves balls of gel from absolutely nothing.

This technology is so far beyond the equipment used in Thea's lab that it might as well be made of starlight.

'Thea definitely came here last night,' calls out Clara, as she peers at a dog made of plant matter, which has a root system growing out of its stomach. 'I recognise this place from the shattered memory stone we found in Hephaestus's bunker. This is the room where she argued with Niema.'

There's a medical screen at the far end of the lab, and Emory's about to pull it back when Hephaestus emerges from an adjoining room, wiping his bleary eyes.

He stops, startled by their presence. They're sopping wet, their clothes tattered, and their hair wild.

'What are you doing here?' he demands.

'Investigating Niema's murder,' says Emory.

Thea descends a wrought-iron circular staircase at the centre of the room.

'I checked the storerooms, but –' She stops dead at seeing the three of them. She's red-eyed and dishevelled. 'What are you doing here? How did you get past the security systems?'

'Security?' repeats Emory. 'Is that what the flowers are? And the rough water?'

'That's what they're supposed to be, but they're clearly not very effective if you three can just stroll in whenever you want,' replies Hephaestus.

'We think Niema activated them the night she died,' says Thea, coming the rest of the way down the staircase, while clapping dust from her hands. 'Do you have any news? Have you uncovered the killer?'

'Adil blamed you,' replies Emory blandly.

Thea's body stiffens, the colour running out of her face. She straightens her back and shoulders, trying to face down this nothing woman, with her bright eyes, innocent face, and that great head of curly brown hair.

'Does he have evidence?' she asks, keeping her voice cool.

'He has a grudge,' interrupts Hephaestus loyally. 'The accusation's ridiculous. We've been on this island together for ninety years. Why would Thea suddenly decide to kill her?'

'Because Niema's been lying to Thea for forty of them,' declares Emory, studying Thea's face the way a fisherman watches still water.

'Blackheath isn't overrun by fog, is it? Niema sent me, Clara and my father out there last night. You probably overheard our conversation. It makes sense that in a flash of anger you snatched the knife out of Clara's hand, then used it to stab Niema.'

Thea's eyes narrow, and Emory realises immediately that she's pushed too hard.

'Are you telling me the murder weapon belonged to Clara?'

'It did, but anybody could have taken it from her. Adil says you found a fragment of your fingernail in Niema's cheek during the post-mortem, which you burned. He also gave me a T-shirt, which he claims is covered in Niema's blood. He says you tried to hide it. Is that true?'

Thea glares at her silently.

'Is it true?' presses Hephaestus, stunned.

Nobody breathes. Even if they wanted to, they couldn't. The oxygen has fled the lighthouse, terrified of what's coming next.

Emory's eyes are locked on Thea, while Hephaestus studies the side of his friend's face, a new-found suspicion bubbling in his thoughts like butter in a hot pan.

Clara shares a nervous glance with Seth.

They're frozen in place, unsure of what they should be doing. Nobody's ever talked to elders the way Emory's doing. Every one of their genetically engineered cells is demanding they apologise on her behalf and drag her from the room.

'Adil is lying,' says Thea, at last. 'There was no fingernail, and I simply changed my clothes. I wasn't trying to hide anything.'

Hephaestus's gaze snaps to Emory. His fists are clenched, a red flush of rage running up his neck, as if he's just discovered she's deceiving him. 'It was your people who killed my mother,' he growls. 'Stop trying to shift the blame.'

'Then why did Niema put her defence system up?' asks Emory, who's working hard to keep her voice steady. 'If Niema was worried about the villagers, she could have ordered Abi to lock us down.'

Thea offers Emory a slow handclap, startling everybody.

'You were right to let her investigate,' she says to Hephaestus. 'You've done well, Emory, even if your efforts are misplaced. Yes, Niema betrayed me. And, yes, I would have been angry about it, but you saw the damage to her skull. I don't have that kind of brutality in me. If I killed somebody it would bloodless and efficient and everybody would mistake it for an accident.'

Her tone is matter-of-fact, but her eyes are boring into Emory's. She wants this young woman to feel as fragile as she suddenly does. She wants her to feel as exposed.

Emory stares back, calmly.

'It *was* intended to look like an accident,' she says. 'A fire was meant to burn the body and destroy the evidence. If it hadn't rained, we'd have nothing to go on.'

'Do you truly believe I would have been stupid enough to trust my plan to the vagaries of the weather, especially during storm season,' scoffs Thea. 'I'm not that clumsy and you know it.'

Emory wavers, forced to concede the point. For as long as she's known Thea, she's been meticulous and precise. This murder is a piece of clothing she'd wear, but in entirely the wrong size.

'If these facts pointed at a villager, you'd already be threatening them with the memory extractor,' says Emory, trying to regain a foothold in the conversation.

Thea's eyes are glittering with malice.

'You're right. Those denials wouldn't be enough to save a villager, but that's because *your* people are disposable. Bring proof of my guilt, rather than insinuations, and I'll gladly put the memory extractor on. Until then, keep your accusations to yourself.'

Fıve mınutes after emory's confrontation with Thea, the lighthouse still feels like a live circuit.

Thea and Hephaestus are yanking open drawers, and spilling their contents across the floor, searching for a key to Blackheath, which they believe is hidden amongst Niema's possessions. Emory and Clara are swiping through the black screens, hunting for any information on the experiment Niema was running the night she died.

Seth's watching them from the door, feeling his own world being equally upended.

He's revered the elders his entire life, believing they knew what was best for the villagers – even when their decisions appeared self-serving.

Emory always thought this faith came naturally, but it didn't. It was hard won over many years, requiring him to swallow his doubts and bite back his questions.

That was his sacrifice.

He thought turning a blind eye was the best way to serve the village, but the last couple of hours have revealed him for a fool. Thea openly described his people – his friends and family – as 'disposable'. It wasn't just the word that stung. It was the venom in her tone when she said it. The hatred, and contempt.

The naked attempt to hurt Emory.

As for Niema … His chest tightens just thinking about her. He's held her in his heart since she died, armouring her memory against the accusations being flung by his daughter, and even Clara.

This is different, though. Thea has confirmed those accusations, using proof he peeled off the rocks himself. Niema killed that woman, and plenty more over the years, and she laughed with him as he rowed her to do it.

He feels like he helped her, like he was complicit.

How could he have loved somebody with that much malice in them? How could she let him?

'What does the key to Blackheath look like?' asks Emory suddenly. She's kneeling down, inspecting the underside of one of the machines.

'It's small glass ball with a reddish hue,' replies Thea, from across the room. Eagerness comes into her voice. 'Do you have it?'

'No,' replies Emory, lowering her gaze to the floor once more. 'I just wanted to know in case I came across it.'

Thea looks away, disappointed, but Seth recognises that tone. Emory knows more than she's saying.

A few hours ago, he would have told Thea what he suspected. He would have seen Emory's actions as petty and small-minded, designed to simply embarrass Thea, but that was before the mask came off.

'If you find that key, let me know,' continues Thea, pulling down a box from a shelf and spilling it across the floor. 'There's equipment in Blackheath that might help get the barriers back up. If we're lucky we may even be able to shelter everybody down there.'

There's a squeak from the opposite corner, where Clara is wheeling away the medical screen they saw earlier. Behind it is a high-backed wooden chair, with wrist and ankle straps, and a metal headband that can be tightened with a few twists of a large screw.

Seth's stomach turns immediately. He doesn't know what the chair is for, but the restraints speak clearly to the suffering it's witnessed.

On a small table beside it is the metal box Hui brought down from the cauldron. The latch on the side is open, a glass canister half withdrawn from the padded interior. Clara pulls it out fully, revealing a strange plant with jagged leaves, and a few yellow buds.

'That's *Nyctanthes prumulla*,' says Thea, who's been watching her for the last minute. 'Its buds can be turned into a very powerful sedative.'

'How powerful?' queries Emory, from behind them.

Thea casts her gaze around the room, then walks over to a small machine. There's a vial spinning inside a red halo, a few drops of a yellow liquid circling inside.

'This tiny amount would be capable of rendering a subject unconscious for a few hours,' she says. 'Given the amount of buds harvested from that cutting, Niema could have created enough sedative to knock out the entire village.'

Emory murmurs, an idea suggesting itself. 'Would it need to be inserted or ingested?' she asks.

'Inserted,' replies Thea. 'Why?'

'Do you think the sedative was used on the dead woman Seth found?' asks Emory, ignoring Thea's question. 'Adil told me that he overheard Niema talking to another woman in here the night she died.'

Hephaestus takes an angry step towards her, forcing Seth to step quickly between them. He flashes a warning glance at his daughter, but he can understand her impatience. She's trying to save the entire island, while Hephaestus is protecting the memory of the woman who put it in danger.

'I overheard Niema talking about an experiment she was going to conduct, and how risky it was for the subject,' says Emory, staring past her father at Hephaestus. 'If it worked, she said it would give humanity a better future.'

Thea snorts contemptuously.

'Is that what she thought she was doing!?' she exclaims, shaking her head. 'At least that explains why the dead woman's blood was full to bursting with conidia.'

'What's conidia?' asks Clara.

'It's the fungus which connects us to Abi,' she says briskly. 'A few hundred spores will allow her to access our thoughts, but for anything more – say enforcing a curfew, or taking control of a body – there needs to be around a thousand in somebody's system. I ran a post-mortem on the dead woman you left in my lab, Seth. She had double that number. That's what killed her. Your people were engineered from the ground up to handle huge quantities of conidia, but such a quantity is lethal to humans. It always has been.'

'Why would Niema intentionally flood a human system with something she knows will kill them?' asks Seth, horrified.

Thea is studying the chair, running her fingers along the rivets, her disgust at its purpose plain.

'If you came to work at Blackheath, a condition of employment was that you had to have Abi implanted, which is why myself and Hephaestus can hear her,' she explains. 'Our research was worth billions, and it was Abi's job to monitor our thoughts and make sure we weren't stealing secrets, or committing corporate espionage for a rival. Anybody who left the company had their memories wiped, so they couldn't take their research with them, but that was the limit of what she could do. Niema always talked about giving Abi greater control over her employees, but she could never find a way to make it work without killing the host. About fifty years ago, she came to me, claiming she had the answer and wanted my help to start human trials. I reviewed her research, and disagreed with her assessment. I told her plainly that anybody she tried her procedure on would be dead within a few days. Moreover, I would end my life before giving control of my body to Abi. Niema listened, and seemed to agree. Naively, I thought she'd dropped the idea.'

She flicks the chair's metal headband. 'Evidently, that was another thing she was lying about.'

'Why would she carry on with an experiment that dangerous?' asks Emory.

Thea taps the console of one of the machines absently. 'Niema had everybody under her thumb for so long, that she couldn't stand the idea of going back to a world where she wasn't in control. She wanted the same authority over humanity that she had over you. She didn't want to let them out, and watch them destroy her precious island, or build a civilisation that wasn't exactly to her specification. She didn't want to feel threatened again.'

'She was afraid,' says Seth softly.

'Powerful people usually are,' replies Thea. 'They have the most to lose.'

E MORY'S OUTSIDE THE LIGHTHOUSE, on the very edge of the cliffs, staring down at the thrashing water far below.

For the first time, she can see the outline of what happened last night. Niema's failed experiment, then her return to the village. She laid bare her secrets and made an announcement, which somebody stabbed her for.

There's one piece missing, and she has a plan to get it. Once she has that, she'll have everything.

She blows out a breath, wondering what good it will do. Even if she can prove who killed Niema, the only way to stop the fog is to execute them. How would she live with herself if she let that happen?

But what's the alternative? Keep the secret? Let the murderer live in the cauldron garden with them forever, while everybody worries whether they'll do it again?

Her eyes drift upwards to the darkening sky. The sun is already rolling down the side of the volcano, the moon clambering over the horizon. The fog will hit the coast in the morning. Whatever her decision, she'll have to make it fast.

Hearing a noise behind her, she sees Hephaestus emerging from the lighthouse, his face stricken. His eyes are closed as he sucks in deep breaths, trying to compose himself.

Occasionally, she forgets that Niema was his mother. She can't imagine how hard this must be for him.

Not that she can find much sympathy.

She hates the elders so much, it actually frightens her. It's a slithering presence in her body, squeezing her heart, and pressing against her lungs. It's whispering in her thoughts, as loud as Abi ever has.

It wants them to suffer. It wants them humiliated and hurt, the way Adil was all those years ago.

'I don't have the power to do that,' I say. 'Niema directed me to preserve every human life. I can't act against them.'

'What if one of them killed her?' she demands.

'If you want to save the island, you may have to do something you don't want to do.'

'You can't expect me to hurt them?'

'No, but you may have to stand aside and let Adil do it.'

Emory considers that as she walks towards Hephaestus, close enough to be heard over the roar of the ocean, but far enough that he can't catch hold of her the way he did in Thea's lab.

'Can we talk for a minute?' she asks.

He stares at her blankly, as if baffled that she's addressing him. It's been the same way ever since she was a little girl. Unlike Thea who took apprentices, or Niema, who made herself part of the village, Hephaestus never lived among them. He never talked to them, or spent time with them. He barely ever looked at them.

She didn't understand that attitude until she saw the little girl in the cauldron garden. Hephaestus doesn't believe the villagers are people. He still thinks of them as tools. Interacting with them is worthless, because they're worthless.

'I know you were helping Niema with her experiments, and I know the woman my father found on the rocks wasn't your first victim,' says Emory, before he can speak. 'We found the other bodies in the infirmary. Niema was trying to get this experiment right for *years*. I overhead the conversation between you two in the rear yard two nights before she was killed. You didn't want to do it, but she talked you into it. That's why you threw the body off the cliff. You were hoping to hide the evidence so Thea would never learn you were involved.'

Each fact hits him like a hammer blow, chipping away at his calm exterior, revealing the guilt lurking beneath. He was a billionaire's son. He never had to learn to hide his emotions convincingly, or make excuses for his behaviour. The world did that for him.

'That's –'

'You've known Blackheath wasn't sealed for years, and you kept that secret from your only friend,' says Emory, keeping up the attack. 'How do you think she'll react, when she finds out?'

His hand lashes out, but she skips out of reach, leaving him flailing. She'd never encountered blind rage until yesterday, but she's surprised by how predictable it is, how dependable. It's such an obvious weakness, she can't understand why he hasn't learned to temper it. Anybody this easily goaded immediately stops thinking. They become the easiest thing in the world to manipulate.

'I know where the key to Blackheath is, Hephaestus,' she says, speaking quickly to calm him. 'I'm willing to deliver it to you, and forget everything I know. Thea never has to find out. The only thing I want is Jack's safe return.'

Hephaestus considers her for a long minute, those empty eyes sparkling.

'Blackmail,' he says, running a tongue around his dry lips. 'You're much closer to being human than I gave my mother credit for.'

Emory shudders, the word become an insult.

He strokes the line of his jaw with a thumb. 'Bring the key to the village tonight, after curfew, and I'll take you to your husband. If you betray me, I'll hang your family from the village walls.'

N O SOONER HAS EMORY gone back inside than Clara grabs her arm, dragging her towards one of the rooms off the lab.

'You have to see this,' she says excitedly.

She opens a narrow door, leading Emory into a cosy sitting room with wooden floorboards, a couch with broken springs and a coffee table. The walls are covered in paintings, their frames pressed close together. There are oils and watercolours, portraits and landscapes. The skill of their composition indicates that they were created before the apocalypse.

'Look at this,' says Clara, pointing to a small painting by Piero della Francesca, depicting the resurrection of Christ. 'Look at the shadows, and the texture.'

Nobody in the village has ever had the ability to create something like this, and Clara's in awe. The only person who's ever displayed this sort of skill at anything is Hui.

For all of its beauty, Emory can barely look at it. She feels such resentment towards humanity, she can't bring herself to celebrate anything about them. This must be how Adil feels, she thinks. It's a corruption of the soul.

Unsettled, she goes to find her father who's nosing around in a small kitchen with a clay oven and a humming refrigerator, every shelf empty. There's a knife block on the counter along with baskets for onions and garlic, and a jug of olive oil with a wonky handle. Unlike everything else in here, this was handcrafted by somebody with absolutely no skill whatsoever.

A thick layer of dust coats the kitchen, suggesting Niema hasn't used it for a long time.

'Dad,' says Emory, from behind him. 'You okay?'

'I made that for her,' he says, gesturing to the jug. 'She told me she loved it, but I thought she was being polite. I honestly thought she'd thrown it away.'

His voice is dead. Clearly, she's not the only person struggling with conflicting emotions.

She retreats into the sitting room.

There are two more doors off it. One of them is metal with a small window at head height, darkness on the other side. There's a button with an arrow on it, but nothing happens when she presses it.

The other door leads into a bedroom that's arranged identically to Niema's dorm room. It has a single bed in between a wardrobe and a tall bookshelf, with most of the books missing. They're probably in the village, thinks Emory, remembering the shelf full of detective stories.

There's a Bible open on a writing desk. The thin pages are dog-eared and worn-through, baffling Emory with their archaic language and strange numbering system.

She remembers seeing this same book in Hephaestus's bunker, and Niema had another copy in her dorm room. It must be important to them, but she can't make sense of it.

Putting it down, she opens the drawers, finding some pens, paper and a photo album, filled with pictures of Niema and Seth at various scenic spots around the island. Her father ages about twenty years as they go along, his posture softening, his frown turning into a smile, then, eventually, laughter.

'He looks happy,' she murmurs, going back to the first picture.

There he is with Niema climbing the volcano. There he is wearing a gigantic leaf as a hat, laughing at something. There they are in a forest. Page after page. Happy memory after happy memory.

She's never seen her father like this. She wishes she had. After her mother died, unhappiness poisoned him, then it poisoned her.

Emory keeps flipping, surprised by how thoroughly her father has explored the island. She's only travelled it through the memories of others, but she knows it well enough to place most of the pictures. This one's taken in an overgrown olive grove to the south. This one is a bay to the east and this one … she frowns. Removing the photo from its sleeve, she holds it up to the light, trying to make sense of it.

'It can't be,' she says.

Her eyes linger on it for a minute, her suspicions solidifying.

She takes the photo into the kitchen, slapping it down on the counter in front of Seth.

'What do you see?' she asks.

He passes a confused stare from Emory to the photograph, smiling slightly in recognition of his younger self.

'That's me, twenty years ago,' he says, tapping it with his finger.

'Do you know where it was taken?'

He studies it again. He's standing in a field, making one of those 'here I am' faces. There's a lake behind him, a cluster of trees on his left.

'I would have been an apprentice, so it could have been anywhere,' he says, fingering the picture. 'Thea used to make us take that awful camera of hers everywhere we went. We spent half of our time putting it back together after it had fallen apart.'

'So, you don't know where this was taken,' persists Emory, grimly.

'Emory, I don't even remember *when* this photograph was taken.'

'You're certain, Dad? It's really important.'

'Emory,' he growls, close to losing his temper. 'I don't know where the photograph was taken. What's this all about?'

'It's about that,' says Emory, prodding the lake in the background.

'It's water, so what?'

'It's a lake, Dad. You can see the banks. How many lakes do we have on this island?'

His brow furrows, then his eyes widen in shock. Finally, he understands.

'None,' he says, astonished.

'None,' she repeats. 'This photo wasn't taken on our island, and there's a good chance that fact's going to get you killed.'

CROSSING THE FIELD OF deadly flowers, Emory, Clara and Seth make their way to the edge of a nearby forest, where Hephaestus and Thea are waiting for them impatiently. The elders had already started for the village by time the family left the lighthouse, forcing them to hurry.

Seth's walking stoically, while Clara clings to his arm. Emory's trailing behind, bowed beneath her guilt. She hasn't said a word since showing him the photo, and explaining the secret lurking underneath Niema's lie.

He got the feeling she wanted him to argue, or talk her out of it. From the hope on her face, he suspects it would have taken one word, but he accepted her plan wordlessly. He has no illusions about the elders any more, but if there's information in his mind that can help the village, he'll gladly volunteer it.

A death in service to others will always mean more to him than a life preserved in service to himself.

The wind is picking up, speckling their clothes with spots of rain.

They've almost reached the edge of the forest when Seth stops suddenly, holding out his hand to Emory.

'Wait,' he says, his voice hoarse. 'I might die tomorrow morning and I'm not going to get a funeral, so I want to say my goodbyes here.'

'Dad –'

'Just hush, for once, Emory,' he says irritably. 'Let me talk, let me say this.' He grips her fingers, turning his gaze between her and his granddaughter.

'I'm not afraid to die, but I've always been terrified of other people dying. Your mum, Matis, you two.'

He manages to hold their gaze for half a second, before averting his eyes.

The rain's falling harder now, pummelling the dry ground and soaking their clothes.

'I've made a lot of mistakes, and it's too late to apologise for all of them, but I want you to know that I'm proud of you both.'

His gaze lands on Emory, who's welling up.

'I've never had the right words handy when I needed them, but I want you to know that whatever happens next isn't your fault,' he says firmly. 'If I'm going to die, there's nothing else you could have done. You've had the world against you since you started, and look at how much you've achieved. Nobody else could have got this far, not even Niema.'

He envelops his daughter in a gruff hug, then does the same with Clara.

'What did you find that's so important?' demands Thea, who's walked over to meet them.

Emory thrusts the photograph towards the elder, obviously disgusted by it and what it requires her to do.

Thea snatches it from her hand, offering it a cursory glance, annoyed at being a step behind once again.

'It's your father,' she says. 'Back when he was my apprentice.'

'Look more closely,' says Clara.

Thea's gaze roams the picture once again. She doesn't know what she's looking for, but she refuses to give Emory the satisfaction of knowing that. For ninety years, she's kept this island's secrets in her pockets, doling them out by whim. It's unnerving to suddenly feel like a dog chasing a stick.

'That's a lake,' she says, realisation dawning on her. 'Seth wasn't on this island when the picture was taken.'

Please don't ask the next question, thinks Emory desperately.

She wouldn't have shown Thea the picture if the fog wasn't this close, but if there's a way off this island, the elders need to know about it. They might have information that can be helpful.

'There's no fog in the photograph either,' notes Emory, trying to keep Thea's mind busy. 'Niema was wrong. It doesn't cover the entire planet.'

'Niema wasn't wrong,' Thea says angrily. 'She was lying. The same way she lied about Blackheath.'

She glares at the horizon, trying to imagine the forests, hills and trees on the other-side, waiting to be reclaimed. There'll be no wild-life, but the equipment in Blackheath can take care of that. They'll be able to start fresh, or restore everything from the DNA samples on file.

She's so giddy at the prospect of unfettered creation that she offers the photograph back to Emory.

The young woman's heart leaps, hope coursing through her.

She hasn't realised, she thinks. She hasn't seen the obvious question. Emory reaches for the picture, only for a frown to darken Thea's face.

No, thinks Emory. *No. No.*

'Who took the picture?' asks Thea. 'Seth's in the centre of the frame. He couldn't have done it himself, the timer never worked.'

Emory sags, defeated. 'I don't know,' she says weakly.

'Of course she does,' interjects Seth. 'I'll not have you lying for me. Not about something this important.' He lifts his chin. 'Emory thinks my wife, Judith, took the picture. You always sent us out on expedition together. It wouldn't have been anybody else.'

Thea swipes a grasshopper off her shorts, trying to disguise the fact that she'd completely forgotten about Judith.

'You don't remember this being taken, do you?' she asks, pointedly.

'No,' he admits.

'Niema didn't want anybody knowing there was a way off the island, so she ordered Abi to wipe both of your memories.' Thea's voice lowers, touching pity. 'You survived the procedure, but your wife didn't.'

Seth nods, choking up. He's still struggling to understand how his best friend could have done something so dreadful, then stayed by his side for another twenty years. The only time he ever noticed anything resembling guilt was the night he rowed her out to the lighthouse. She brought up Judith out of nowhere. Had she finally unearthed some remorse?

Hephaestus stomps forward, lowering his face to meet Emory's eyes. 'Both you and your father had a motive to murder my mother.'

Flecks of spit hit her cheeks, the jubilation in his voice knocking Seth sick. Somebody's going to die, and his only concern is that he's right.

'Everybody in this group does,' shoots back Emory. 'Niema had an extraordinary ability to hurt people.'

Thea touches Hephaestus on the shoulder, regaining his attention. 'How long will it take you to repair the memory extractor?' she asks.

'No!' protests Clara, taking a step towards them, holding out an imploring hand.

'This is the best lead we have,' says Thea firmly. 'We can't ignore it, not while the island is in danger.'

'There's no way Grandfather could have known what happened to his wife,' argues Clara.

Thea raises an eyebrow, conceding the point.

'Your mother had an answer for that as well,' says Seth, much too noble not to implicate himself.

'Which was?'

'It was Adil,' says Emory, skewered by her father's honesty. 'He alluded to it when we spoke last night. I think he told my grandfather, Matis, before he died. He was probably hoping Matis would pass the information on to Seth, only Matis kept it to himself and his memory gem was stolen before we could view it, so it never went any further.'

'That was likely Niema's doing,' says Thea. 'Abi reported everything to her. She wouldn't have let that information get out so easily.'

'We know Adil was on the jetty beneath the lighthouse, waiting for Niema,' continues Emory. 'There's a possibility he spoke to my father after he came back down.'

'Sounds like a motive for murder to me,' says Thea jubilantly. 'Seth, we have to know if you killed Niema, and the memory extractor should be able to tell us.'

'But we know there's a way off the island now,' pleads Clara. 'Surely, if we ask everybody to start search—'

'This won't save us,' says Thea, flapping the picture at her. 'Before Niema sealed off Blackheath, I designed a type of hazard suit capable of protecting its wearer from the fog. It was a year, or more, from being complete, but Niema must have finished my prototype. I only ever made three of them, and they're locked down in Blackheath. They're how your grandparents got off this island, I'm certain of it.'

'I'm not sure how much damage Emory did,' muses Hephaestus, ignoring Clara's outburst. 'It will be working by dawn, I guarantee.'

Thea meets Emory's desperate eyes.

'That's how long you have to prove your father's innocence,' she says coldly. 'If that doesn't stop the fog, you'll be going in the extractor straight after him. Who knows, you may help me solve this murder, after all.'

EMORY ENTERS THE CAULDRON garden alone, having struggled up the goat trail for the last two hours in the pitch black.

Seth and Clara stayed behind in the lighthouse. It's well after curfew, and neither of the elders would exempt them, no matter how hard they protested. Emory thinks it's spite, but she didn't fight too hard against the decision.

In truth, she'd rather be by herself tonight. The things she has to do will be dangerous, and she's much happier knowing her family will be away from the village.

Walking through the cauldron garden, she peers around in wonder.

Moonlight has melted across the dome, while thousands of fire-flies zip around in the darkness, bioluminescent butterflies leaving purple and pink trails in their wake. It's one of the most beautiful things she's ever seen, and one of the most baffling. How could all of this come from the souls of people such as Thea and Hephaestus?

Emory bites her lip, trying to imagine what Niema felt about all of this. Back in the lighthouse, Thea claimed she wanted to control humans the way she controlled the villagers, because she was afraid of what they'd do if they were released from Blackheath.

'Control,' murmurs Emory.

That was one of the words on the letter Niema was writing to Hephaestus the night before she died.

Emory left the original in her dorm, but she's read it over so many times she can recall it verbatim.

My darling boy,
I know you're disappointed, and my decision will feel like a betrayal.
You must believe I've let you down, after asking so much of you, but

There was a gap after that, with the rest gathered from the pencil rubbing Emory made: *if I couldn't control ... better ... contain ... Abi wanted to ... couldn't kill*

And then the numbers '5:5?' were scrawled on the back.

Niema killed thirteen people as part of a doomed experiment to control humans. The letter seemed to suggest she'd given up on it, preferring to contain them instead. Was that the betrayal she was referring to? Had Niema decided to keep the humans locked up in Blackheath forever?

Footsteps crunch through the undergrowth, wood cracking.

Pushing through the branches, Emory discovers the villagers hacking their way through the undergrowth with machetes and axes, clearing plots of land for farming. Their eyes are closed, their faces filthy. They're scratched by thorns, panting hard at the exertion they don't know they're undertaking.

'It might be kinder to let the fog have us,' she thinks.

She's footsore and tired by the time she enters the cable-car station, jamming the lever forward and jumping onboard the carriage as it departs.

Huge forks of lighting are crawling across the island, thunder bouncing off the volcano. Several rowboats are out at sea, lanterns swaying at the bow, tiny points of light in the endless black.

'Where are they going?' she asks.

'Thea wants the equipment salvaged from the lighthouse,' I reply.

The cable car sways in the wind, creaking on the line as it glides into the village, which is dark aside from the harsh light spilling out of Thea's lab.

Thea rowed to the lighthouse last night, but Emory still doesn't know why and none of her theories explain it.

It's not the only question chasing her. There are swarms of them.

Why would Niema bother putting her defence system up, only to abandon the lighthouse and go to the village? What happened to Hui after she was stabbed? Why can't Ben stop drawing equations in the dirt? And why did they hike out to Blackheath last night, dragging a cart behind them?

The cable car judders into the station, and Emory spills out, plucking her sweaty clothes away from her skin.

'What time is it?'

'It's 10:16 p.m.,' I reply.

Hephaestus is expecting to meet her at midnight, with the key to Blackheath. The last time she saw it, Adil was rolling it under his thumb, as he accused Thea of murdering Niema. He treated it carelessly, like a trinket, which is why she didn't think to wonder what it was.

She stalks through the driving rain towards the barracks, ascending the staircase to Magdalene's dorm.

She's hoping that once she's explained her plan, Adil will hand over the key.

She just needs a little leverage to get Hephaestus talking. He's the final piece of the puzzle, but if she doesn't handle him carefully, she'll be dead long before the fog hits the island.

SIXTY-FOUR

E MORY'S PEERING THROUGH A crack in the shutters, watching the exercise yard for any sign of Adil, but he's nowhere to be seen.

'He's not coming,' she says, trying to stifle her frustration. 'Why wouldn't he be coming? What time is it, Abi?'

'10:42 p.m.,' I reply.

She sees a lantern bobbing through the gate, moving hurriedly in the rain. It's much too dark to make out who's holding it, but they're heading in the direction of the farms.

She departs the dorm running.

Soaking wet and panting, Emory holds her lantern in the air, trying to find a way forward.

Occasionally, she'll catch glimpses of the flame she's been following far in the distance, but the rain's coming hard, pouring in sheets down her face.

She hasn't taken a rest since she marched out of the village, and spares only the briefest of glances for the shack on her left, and the broken-down cart on her right. It feels like a lifetime ago that she followed its tracks out here, finding Clara's carved bird in the back.

Niema sent Seth, Emory and Clara out here the night she was killed. She must have given them the key to get inside Blackheath, but how did it end up in Adil's possession? More importantly, why would Niema reveal her deepest secret to the three of them?

Emory wades across the stream without slowing down, losing a sandal to a slippery rock. She should have changed into her boots before she left, but she was too afraid of losing sight of the light.

Cursing, she snatches her sandal out of the water and limps around the weathered olive tree on the hill, a tattered moon hanging from its branches.

The door to Blackheath is open, a square of fluorescent light cut into the darkness.

Her pulse quickening, she walks through it into a long tunnel that descends deep underground, having to fight the impulse to call out for Jack.

She's never seen anything like this. The walls are curved and perfectly smooth. The floor is made from concrete, with strip lights overhead. She can't imagine the technology required to carve this out of the earth, or why they'd bother. Who'd need this much space so far from sunlight?

It's a long walk to the end of the tunnel, and the door she entered through is just a pinprick of darkness by the time she reaches a junction, which is almost blocked by the missing stores. Crates of vegetables are piled high, sacks of seeds and a few boxes of tools.

She runs her eye across it.

There's a lot more than they found in the cable-car station yesterday, but why would it be here at all? Niema managed to dictate a diagram to Seth while she lay dying, so perhaps she organised the evacuation at the same time. If she knew they wouldn't all fit in the cauldron garden, perhaps she decided to move half the village down here. But, if that was the case, why were there so few supplies at the summit of the volcano? They wouldn't have lasted half the village more than a month.

Tunnels stretch away to her left and right, a cleaning cart abandoned a few paces away, bottles dissolved into mush.

She walks a little way along the passages nervously, her movement activating the lights overhead. The tunnel to the left is already lit up, so that's the way the person with the lantern must have gone.

She's nervous, and she walks slowly, hugging herself against the chill. It's horribly cold, and the air's thin, scrubbed clean. There's none of the reassuring island smells. No pine, or magnolia. No thyme. No sea spray. No sweat, or mustiness.

Some of the ceiling lights are flickering on and off, the air-filtration units shrieking and abruptly stopping. She feels like she's in the belly of some dying beast.

Offices appear on either side of her, their knocked-over chairs and spilled screens a testament to how quickly this place was abandoned. A few mugs are still sitting on coasters, while families stare out of photo frames at long-empty rooms.

She wonders how people could stand working down here. It's so bleak, she can feel her soul changing colour to mirror it.

Turning the corner of another junction, she discovers a large metal map of the facility has been drilled into the wall. Hundreds of miles of tunnels riddle the eastern half of the island, running from this spot all the way to the lighthouse. She's surprised there's any dirt left for the volcano to sit on.

There are over a dozen entrances scattered across the island with this one listed as being door eight. There's even one in the lighthouse itself, connected by a lift. That must have been the locked door she found in Niema's sitting room. Any hope she had of finding Jack quickly evaporates. The entire village would need a week to search these tunnels.

Snatches of conversation drift towards her, a few words not mangled by the shrieking air filters.

Peering around the corner, she sees Adil talking with Thea at the end of a long corridor. The elder is dripping wet, and still holding the lantern Emory followed. She strains her ears, trying to catch what they're saying, but there's too much background noise.

Whatever they're discussing, it seems cordial enough. How can that be? In their brief conversation, Adil gave every indication of hating the elders. He threatened to kill them if he had the chance. Why would he suddenly be working with Thea?

A moment later, the two of them walk in opposite directions.

Needing the key to bargain with Hephaestus, Emory skulks after Adil on near silent feet, arriving in a ruined corridor.

Parts of the ceiling have collapsed and the walls have crumbled, revealing the earth beneath. Thorny roots twist in and out of the floor, foliage hanging from the ceiling vents, surrounded by hovering birds with long beaks. Nine deer are grazing on weeds growing along the walls. They're paler than any deer she's ever seen on the surface, and much smaller. Normally these animals would be asleep, but they appear to have evolved their habits for some reason.

Jack would love to see this, she thinks. He'd be fascinated.

They look up as Adil passes, their ears twitching, but he keeps his eyes forward, taking a right at the junction.

Emory stays a corridor behind him, moving through junction after junction, the lab going on and on. Behind glass walls she sees labs filled with miracles; scientific instruments designed to peel back the corners of the universe, to pull it apart, and rewrite it.

'That one's a nano-particular converter,' I explain. 'That's a quantum net. That's a portable particle collider next to an element generators.'

I stop my description, realising she isn't listening any longer. In the middle of the floor, placed so it will be seen, is one of Clara's carved birds.

Emory picks it up, seeing another one at the end of the corridor. Clara clearly intended them to be followed.

Adil's footsteps are growing distant, but suddenly this seems more important. These birds might explain why they came here the night Niema died.

Emory collects the second bird, looking left and right for the next. The corridors are so long, she has to walk a little up each one before she sees the bird.

More junctions follow. More carved birds. More labs, and offices. A gym, filled with exercise equipment she can't make head or tail of.

Finally, she hears the whir of a drill, and the crunching of metal.

She goes towards it, passing more birds.

The sounds are coming from a small room that was obviously once used for storage. The boxes have been moved outside, and she has to turn sideways to squeeze past them.

Peering through the door, she sees five villagers trying to dig through the rocky earth, using drills, hammers and axes. They must have had to go through the concrete first, because rubble covers the floor and their faces are coated in dust.

As with the villagers in the cauldron garden, their eyes are closed. They're obviously sleeping.

'Arthur!' she exclaims.

Arthur was one of the apprentices who supposedly drowned when Jack's boat went down. Her heart leaps in her chest, hope barging away every rational thought.

She darts from face to face, finding Tasmin and Kiko, Reiko and—

'Jack!' she exclaims, flinging her arms around him in joy.

Her husband doesn't react. He's stiff as a statue, holding a whirring drill to the wall, which is spitting dirt and sharp rocks back at him. He's much thinner than she remembers, his arms reduced to sinew and bone. His face is gaunt, his hair greying.

'Let him go, Abi!' she demands, turning the drill off, only for Jack to immediately turn it back on.

'I cannot. Niema's instructions were clear.'

'Niema's dead,' says Emory, staring at her husband helplessly. 'You don't have to do this any more.'

'She never told me to stop,' I say. 'I'm obliged to fulfil any orders she gave me, until she instructs me otherwise.'

'Are you telling me he's trapped down here forever?'

'I'm afraid so, Emory.'

Emory's cross-legged on the floor, staring at her husband's sleeping face. She cried for a long time after finding him, then managed to find hope in the fact that he was still alive.

'I'm going to get you out of this,' she says to Jack. 'I'm not leaving you down here.'

The words temporarily buoy her spirits, but she knows it's an empty promise. The fog is coming, and – even if she can stop it – she doesn't know any way to free him from my control.

'I wish I could talk to you,' she says to Jack. 'I'd tell you all this and you'd make a joke, or come up with a fact about something stupid.' She laughs. 'I've missed you, every day.'

She wipes a tear away, smudging something in her eye. It's yellow pollen, she realises when she picks it out with her finger. It's all over Jack's shirt, and in his hair.

Clara, Hui and Thea were coated in this stuff when they came down from the cauldron garden the day Niema died. It's possible Jack was up there at the same time they were.

Did Hui spot Jack in the cauldron garden?

That would explain why she was acting so strangely around Clara. Hui knew her best friend's father was alive and was forbidden from saying anything. No wonder she spent the afternoon avoiding her.

Adil crashes through the door, his hand pressed to his stomach, blood pouring from between his fingers. His legs give out, and he collapses to the concrete floor, his legs splayed out in front of him.

'Adil,' she cries, going to his side.

He's breathing shallowly, desperately. He's been stabbed.

'What happened?' she asks, trying to get a look at the wound, but he shakes his head.

'Pock … pocket,' he says, struggling to speak.

Searching his pockets brings her the Blackheath key and a diagram, identical to the one her father had in his pocket when he woke up.

'Map,' he explains, coughing up blood. 'You can't … Niema's … Niema's murder …' He shakes his head frantically, grabbing her arm. 'Don't … solve …'

Emory stares at the map, trying to make sense of what's he saying.

'Why wouldn't you want me to solve Niema's murder? What do you know?'

He taps the map. 'Find …' He sags, the strength going out of him. 'Thea will … Thea … kill –'

His head lolls, his body going completely still.

Springing up, she offers a desperate glance at this room with Jack in it, but the fear in Adil's voice was contagious. Whatever this errand is, it's important.

She glances at the map, which makes sense now she's in Blackheath. The numbers are junctions, and the lines represent corridors. Niema must have dictated the same one to her father as she lay dying. He ripped a page out of Magdalene's book and wrote it down, which is how it came to be in his pocket.

Wherever Adil wants her to go, it's the same place Niema directed them the night of her murder.

Emory's about to set off when she hauls herself back. Adil's been at the centre of all this since it started. He's as much a clue as anything else.

Kneeling down, she quickly searches his clothes from head to toe, trying to ignore the stink of his unwashed body but there's nothing to find. She turns her attention to his boots, discovering eight fragments of a memory gem's case embedded into his right sole.

She plucks one out, studying it. He must have been the person who crushed Niema's memory stone. That would seem to put him near her when she died.

Content that she's unearthed everything of use, she follows the map into the facility, but every step leaves her more perplexed than the last. On the other side of a glass wall, she sees a hospital, full of beds and supplies, bright displays showing every part of the human anatomy. There are sealed packs of sterile bandages left lying on tables, alongside syringes and small, strange devices. At the back of the room are huge machines, clearly designed to be stepped inside, and probes on articulated arms, ready to be wheeled into place. Everything is advanced and alien, and incredible. Seeing this equipment, she can't believe anybody ever died in the old world.

She passes a cafeteria so huge the entire village would feel lonely in a corner of it. Aside from a thick layer of dust, the kitchen looks brand new, and has ways to cook food she can't even begin to under-stand. The taps deliver clean water, and the cupboards are stacked with plates, cups and cutlery made of shining metal, rather than splintered wood and fragile clay.

There're huge, comfortable bedrooms down here, the mattresses soft and springy, each one with its own bathroom. She twists a tap and hot water comes out of it.

None of this makes sense! Why lock all this away? Every day in the village is hard. They grow everything they eat, and drag water up from a fresh spring, deep underground. A bad winter means rationing, and a diseased crop means death. There are injuries every month, not to mention the illnesses, which periodically rip through the population. If they'd had access to the equipment down here, how many people would have been saved?

'Niema chose to keep all this for the humans,' I say. 'They're much more fragile than your people.'

'And much more valuable,' Clara says angrily. 'You can always grow more of us when we die, right?'

'Yes,' I admit.

Following the map delivers her to a 'repair bay' where she finds Hui sleeping peacefully in a bed, one of Clara's birds beside her. Her bloody clothes have been removed, revealing a nasty stab wound through her sternum, between the left and right clavicle. The shattered bone and torn flesh is being slowly knitted together by a flickering red beam fired from the ceiling.

Emory rushes to her bedside, gripping the girl's hand.

'Hui,' she says urgently. 'Hui.'

The young woman's eyes flutter, but that's all. Her skin is pale and clammy, her breathing shallow. *This is why Niema sent us out here*, she realises.

Hui was injured, and only Blackheath's equipment could save her. Niema dictated a map to this room for Seth, and gave him the key. They put Hui on a cart to transport her, but it broke down outside Adil's shack.

'Niema really wanted to save you,' she mutters. 'But why? She watched our people die for ninety years without lifting a finger. What made you so special?'

Whatever it was, Niema must have charged Adil with tending Hui after everybody had their memories wiped. That's why he had the key. It's why he was down here tonight, though that doesn't explain why Thea was with him.

Footsteps echo distantly, causing Emory to jump. It has to be Thea.

Ducking through an adjoining door, she finds another bay, just like this one. Hui's pulse is thin and reedy, much too weak to safely move her – which would matter if there was any other choice.

She glances at the red beam, dubiously. 'How do I get her out of this?'

'The machine will automatically switch off when you move her,' I say.

Emory scoops Hui into her arms, then carries her into the room next door. A second later, Thea strides into the bay she left.

Seizing her opportunity, Emory waddles across the corridor into one of the consultation rooms opposite, laying Hui down on a couch, before quickly closing the blinds.

The last one is barely down when she hears a huge crash, followed by a scream of frustration.

Emory slides to the floor out of sight, terrified of making even the slightest noise.

Why would Thea want to hurt Hui?

She presses her thumbs to her eyes, wracking her brain, shaking out everything she's learned since this all began.

'Wait ...' she says, in her thoughts. 'The day Clara discovered Hui was missing you told us she was disconnected from your ... what was it?'

'Mitochondrial network,' I supply. 'It's a side effect of the drugs currently in her system.'

Emory's eyes widen with realisation. 'That means you're not in her head, doesn't it?'

'That's correct.'

'You weren't able to wipe her memory.' She gazes at Hui in astonishment. 'She knows exactly what happened that night. That's why Thea's so desperate to find her. She's trying to kill the only witness to Niema's murder!'

I T'S A LITTLE PAST two in the morning when Thea pushes her boat away from the jetty beneath the lighthouse, every inch of space filled with food. Now that Blackheath is open again, the jetty is almost as easy to reach as the village, which is handy because she doesn't want to risk running into Hephaestus.

She rows steadily across the dark water, the moon and stars reflected upon its surface. Her ragged palms are aching, but she's ignoring the pain, focusing on the resonance suit folded across the seat at the back of the boat.

It was waiting in her lab, exactly where she left it forty years ago. This has to be how Seth and his wife got off the island. Thea briefly wondered if Niema had an air-skipper hidden somewhere, or had managed to build a secret tunnel under the water, but neither seemed plausible. They never had the resources for jobs like that.

Closing on world's end, she finds the sea thick with dead birds, fish, seals, dolphins and turtles. The stink is already unbearable.

Nudging the boat through the carrion, she risks a look over her shoulder at the fog. The insects are glowing brightly, floating around inside like neurons firing in a brain. For a moment, she watches them transfixed. It's strange that something this awful should be so beautiful.

'Please don't do this,' I say, for the fourteenth time since this reckless, desperate idea first invaded her thoughts.

'I killed Niema,' she says simply. 'That was my fingernail buried in her cheek, and her blood was on my clothes.' She tightens her grip on the oars, her knuckles turning white. 'Everything I ever wanted was in Blackheath, and she kept it from me. She imprisoned me on this island against my will, unable to reach my sister. Emory's right. I found out, and I caved her skull in. I know I did.'

Coming within touching distance of the fog, she tosses the anchor overboard and pulls the resonance suit over her clothes. It covers her body from head to toe, and has a perspex screen to see through.

'This is suicide,' I say. 'There has to be another way.'

'The other way was silencing Hui before she could tell Hephaestus that I murdered his mother, but that failed. He's going to find out what I've done and he's going to kill me,' she replies, terrified.

'He cares for you.'

'He won't even see me. You know what his rages are like. He'll beat me to death the way he did that vulture.'

Going to the bow, she leans over the top of it, her fingers only inches from the deadly fog. The glowing insects press against the edge, mimicking the shape of her splayed hand.

There's a small black display on the wrist of the suit and she wakes it up with a tap. Symbols appear as diagnostics are run, testing its integrity and systems.

'The future is being written right now,' I say. 'Everything matters, every life. If you die here, there's nobody left to monitor the pods that grow the villagers. You'll be damning them to extinction.'

'I don't care. I never have.'

'What about Ellie?'

'She'll be safe in Blackheath. Once the fog hits the island, Hephaestus will have no choice but to take shelter in the cauldron garden. I'll be able to come and go as I please.'

'Please, Thea –'

'We don't need to talk any more, Abi. I'm finally getting off this island. If the cost of that was Niema's life, it was a bargain.'

It takes thirty seconds for the suit to finish its checks. There's a crackle, the material stiffening ever so slightly. The glowing insects that were mimicking her hand flicker, then go out completely, drifting down into the water.

'It's working,' says Thea triumphantly.

A tremor of excitement runs through her; the thrill of a battle won before it's even begun.

Scrambling to the back of the boat, she heaves the anchor back inside, then picks up the oars and pushes forward.

The bow enters the fog, then the first seat. Finally, she passes across the threshold, staring around in wonder.

'It's beautiful,' she gasps.

From within, the fog is a golden, shimmering solar system. Electricity crackles between the insects, which are swirling around her, kept away by the field being emitted by the suit.

'It's working,' she screams, stamping her feet in joy. 'It's working.'

The control panel shudders on her wrist, alerting her to a fault. Power is draining much more quickly than it should.

The luminosity of the insects starts to increase.

'You have to go back,' I say.

'I can fix it,' she replies, stubbornly tapping at the screen, trying to locate the problem.

The suit vibrates its concern.

Glancing up from the panel, she notices that the insects have coalesced into a great ribbon of yellow flame, which is lashing towards her.

'Turn around, Thea,' I say urgently.

She picks up the oars, as the insects start drumming against the suit, sizzling against its resonance field, only to be replaced by thousands more.

Lights flash red on the control panel.

'Hurry,' I say. 'Once the field collapses, there's only a layer of material between you and the swarm.'

She can't hear me any more.

The insects cover her so densely, that their fierce light is blinding even with her eyes shut.

She's hyperventilating, swiping futilely at her attackers as the suit alarms whine.

Any second now, the field will fail and she'll be torn apart.

As she stumbles back in panic, her head hits the edge of the seat with a sickening thud, knocking her unconscious as the suit whines around her.

SIXTY-SEVEN

BY THE TIME EMORY reaches the red flags marking the boundary of the farms, she's dreaming of a bed she may never get to sleep in again. The fog is glowing so brightly that it looks like the sea's been set ablaze. She thinks she sees a boat rowing towards it, but it's much too dark to make it out clearly.

Emory's hidden Hui in the medical bay where she found her. It's risky, but her pulse was much too weak to move her further. Emory's desperately hoping that Thea doesn't think to go back.

'Thea,' she repeats, under her breath.

That wasn't who she suspected of Niema's murder, but everything Thea's done tonight suggests Emory got it wrong. After all, Thea almost certainly killed Adil, and she tried to silence Hui. Surely that means she's responsible for Niema's death, but …

There are so many questions it doesn't answer. Emory's dogged by ideas and suspicions, facts without a home, desperate to find a place. Half-known things cast strange shadows across her mind.

She's roused from her thoughts by a plume of flame rising above the village walls, black smoke shading the dark air.

Using the last of her energy, she sprints along the coastal path, then through the gate into the rear yard, where the infirmary is burning uncontrollably. Flames are dripping out of the windows, and scrambling across the roof. Even from here, the heat is unbearable.

'Thought that would get your attention,' says Hephaestus, emerging from the gloom.

Emory takes a step back, her legs turning to wood underneath her. He has Jack's knife in his hand, and is making no effort to disguise his intentions. She expected him to betray her, and had prepared for it, but this isn't like the fear she felt when the boat sank, or when they walked through the plants. This is primal: the mouse under the owl's shadow, knowing what's coming, knowing it's always been coming, and that fate designed it this way.

'I can't let Thea put that extractor on you,' he says. 'She can't know about the bodies in the infirmary, or that I was involved in my mother's experiments. She'd try to stop me, and then I'd have to kill her.'

Emory's breathing hard, becoming dizzy as black spots ink her sight.

'Think about your daughter and the people you love,' I say firmly. 'Stick to your plan. If you die here, everybody dies with you.'

Emory squeezes her eyes shut, imagining Clara asleep in the lighthouse. She thinks about Jack, trapped in his body, and the fog rolling towards the island.

'Run at the thing that frightens you, Emory,' I urge.

She opens her eyes, staring at the flame-wreathed monster striding towards her. Hephaestus has the answers she needs, and he'll talk when he thinks he's in control.

'I think Thea's responsible for Niema's murder,' she calls out.

That brings him up short. He rubs his hand over his scalp, uncertainly.

'I know,' he snarls. 'I woke up with my mother's shattered memory gem by my bed. I saw the argument between them. Thea would only have been that angry if she found out about Blackheath.'

'Why haven't you done anything about it?' Emory demands.

'Kill her you mean?' he asks, with a raised eyebrow. 'That's a lot of bloodlust for a villager, isn't it?'

'I just want to understand,' she says pleadingly.

He puffs out his cheeks, shaking his head. 'My mother's dead because she refused to explain herself to anybody, even Thea. When the world ended, I saw what we became up close.'

He lifts his shirt, showing her the patina of burns and badly healed scars covering his body.

'I got every one of these from another human being, and not because their survival depended on it, or because I was a threat to them. They hurt me for no other reason than because they wanted to.'

He points the tip of the knife at her.

'Thea never saw the fog up close, so she doesn't understand that it wasn't the most terrifying thing. It was just a cloud, some insects. There was no malevolence in it.' He bangs his chest. 'The truly terrifying thing about the fog was how quickly it became a licence for every vile thing in the human heart. You tell me, Emory. How could anybody, in good conscience, save a race that had witnessed the brutality of the fog and then decided to one-up it?'

He's peering at her, genuinely expecting an answer. He wants affirmation, forgiveness for what he's done.

'I don't know,' she says meekly.

'It wasn't control my mother wanted,' he says. 'It was empathy. She knew that if we let everybody out of Blackheath, the same thing would just happen again. She thought that if Abi had control, she could alter human nature from the inside. No more selfishness, or greed, or violence. For the first time in history, we'd be one people, acting in harmony for the good of everybody.'

His eyes are agleam, the future reflected in them. Hearing him, she believes every word, and she wonders what persuasion like that could have achieved somewhere else, in a different time.

'Imagine having millions of people on the planet, living equally,' he says happily. 'No poverty, no inequality, no war, no violence. Imagine waking everyday, knowing you'd be safe; free to pursue whatever end you set yourself. We can have that, but we need Abi. That's why I'm going to carry on with my mother's experiments.'

Emory stares at him, bewildered. 'You can't just keep killing people in the hopes of saving them,' she says. 'You have to find another way.'

'There is no other way,' he declares vehemently. 'Humanity can't change itself, history has shown that. We need an intervention.'

'What about Thea? What will she say? You've done all of this to keep it from her, and now you're going to start it all up again. You could barely hide your experiments when you had the entire island to work with. How will you manage it in the cauldron garden?'

'We're not going to the cauldron,' he snorts. 'Blackheath has everything we need, and there's space enough for us to both work in solitude. Thea will destroy the fog, while I fix humanity. Believe me, she isn't going to look up from her work for the next hundred years. Now, I think that's all –'

The infirmary explodes, flames pluming out of the windows.

'Please,' she interrupts. 'Tell me about Jack. Why was he down there? What did he do wrong?'

'Nothing,' admits Hephaestus. 'Niema needed a few lab hands in to help with her experiments. She couldn't risk Thea seeing villagers coming and going, so she decided the best thing was to keep some permanent staff down there, under lockdown. The only reason she chose Jack and the others was because it was easy to make them disappear.'

No sooner has the last word left his mouth than Emory has taken off in a sprint, charging down the lane leading to the school.

Roaring, he charges after her, moving surprisingly quickly considering his size.

The exercise yard is still and quiet, aside from a solitary owl hooting somewhere on the walls.

His eyes flick to every shadow, interrogating the darkness.

'I'm not playing any more, Emory,' he yells, losing his temper. 'Come out now, or I'm going straight to Clara's room and –'

Hearing rustling, he looks up in time to see Emory hurl herself off the balcony, landing heavily on his back.

Something stings his neck, his vision immediately going woozy as an empty syringe is crushed under his staggering feet.

Reaching around, he grabs Emory by the arm and hurls her to the ground, knocking the wind out of her. She cries out in pain, but immediately scrabbles onto her feet, trying to back away.

His vision's swimming, but he's still fast. He drives the knife towards her sternum, but he's misjudged the distance. It sinks an inch into her flesh, before Emory falls backwards, wincing in pain.

Hephaestus looms over her, readying the knife to try again. He holds it up, then wobbles before collapsing to the ground unconscious.

Getting to her feet, Emory inspects the wound. A few inches higher and he would have put the blade through her throat.

She stalks over to the sleeping giant, picking up the knife with a shaking hand.

'This belongs to my husband,' she says.

2 HOURS UNTIL HUMANITY'S EXTINCTION

SIXTY-EIGHT

'THEA!' I SHOUT, IN her thoughts.

She startles awake, finding herself curled up in the bottom of the boat, being lashed by wind and rain, huge swells rocking her from side to side. It's morning, but the sky is black with storm clouds, streaked by lightning.

'You were thrown clear of the fog,' I say.

Scrambling up, she realises she's only feet from it and the insects are glowing so brightly they're leaving dancing blots in her eyes.

Whimpering, she searches for the oars.

'You dropped them in the water last night,' I inform her. 'There's no need to panic, the anchor's down. Help's coming.'

In her panic, she doesn't hear me.

Clumsily stripping off the resonance suit, she jumps into the storm-tossed ocean. Her toes cramp and her muscles spasm, as she bobs back to the surface. It's agony, but she's merciless, compelling her body to swim.

She's aching from last night's exertions, and the current's strong. For all her effort, she's only gaining inches of safety. Exhausting herself to stay in place.

Her legs slow, the strength running out of her. Gradually, the current starts tugging her back towards the fog.

'Thea! Thea!'

A voice carries weakly across the water. She lifts her head, sees a boat approaching. Emory's at the bow, banging the hull desperately to get her attention. Seth's rowing as hard as he can, his muscles pulled taut, his teeth gritted with effort.

Thea's arms chop into the water, her feet kicking frantically as she tries to reach them, but she doesn't have the energy to make any headway. She's swimming to survive, hoping the boat can reach her in time.

She risks a look behind her, but that only causes her to lose precious inches. She's so close to the fog that half of her body is awash in a beautiful golden light.

There's an enormous splash.

Strong hands take hold of her, dragging her clumsily into the boat. Rough wood scrapes her face. She bangs her shoulder into the seat, then lands in a pile on the bottom, staring up at Emory's exhausted face, her cheeks stained with dried blood.

'You got her?' yells Seth.

'Go,' yells Emory.

The elder raises herself enough to see the boat she abandoned drifting into the fog and being swarmed by the insects, which swiftly lose interest when they discover there's nothing to kill inside.

'Why did you jump in the water?' demands Emory, when they've finally reached a safe distance. 'Your anchor was down. You were safe.'

'How do you know my anchor was down?'

'Because we rowed out earlier to check on you,' replies Seth, dragging the oars through the water. 'Why were you out here?'

'I hit my head,' says Thea, confused. 'I never got the chance to put my anchor down.'

'Well somebody did,' he says gruffly.

'If you were out here this morning, why didn't you bring me to the village?' demands Thea, wincing as she touches the sore spot on her head.

'I needed to talk to my friends without you interfering,' says Emory, leaning over the edge of the boat to wash her hands in the water. 'Besides, I didn't want a murderer near my daughter.'

Thea's breath catches in her throat.

'What are you accusing me of?' she asks, her voice tight.

'I followed you to Blackheath last night,' says Emory, refusing to look at her. 'You wanted to kill Hui, and I know you murdered Adil.'

'You've got it all wrong.'

'You just can't stop lying, can you?'

'I didn't kill Adil!'

'Of course it was you,' declares Emory, glaring at her. 'There was nobody else in Blackheath last night.'

'How dare you accuse me of something like that without proof,' argues Thea haughtily. 'Who do you think you are?'

Emory meets her anger with rage.

'I'm a villager,' she exclaims. 'And after everything I've seen from you, I'm proud of that. This island's in danger and instead of helping me protect it, you and Hephaestus have spent the last two days lying to me and covering your tracks. I'm sick of the both of you.'

Thea feels a sudden shiver of uncertainty. There's something strange in Emory's expression that she's never seen in a villager before. Her eyes are hard, her glare fierce. Almost predatory.

Catalysts and reactions, thinks Thea. For the last few days, Emory's been submerged in the very worst of humanity, and it's fundamentally altered her. This isn't the same person who pleaded with her to investigate Niema's death. The deference is gone. The fear. The doubt.

Thea feels like she's dealing with a human.

She glances at Seth, expecting him to reprimand his daughter, but he stares on blankly. Evidently, it's not only Emory who's been transformed by Niema's death.

'Why would I kill Adil?' asks Thea, adopting a placating tone. 'He came to my lab last night. He told me that Blackheath was open, and Hephaestus and Niema had been using it for years, sleeping there whenever they needed a little luxury. He showed me the rooms they'd been using. The empty food packets. Niema's favourite cup still had tea in it.'

Thea stares hard at Emory. Suddenly, it doesn't feel like there's enough room in the boat for the three of them, and her misgiving.

'Why would Adil help you?' asks Emory. 'He hated the elders.'

'I have no clue, but he's the only person who's told me the truth in forty years,' she declares hotly. 'I had no reason to kill him. He was going to give me the key to Blackheath.'

'Where were you when he died?' asks Emory, considering this point.

'I went to see my sister. I was going to wake her up, but I decided against it at the last minute. It was the hardest choice I've ever had to make, but she'd never forgive me for trapping her in the cauldron garden.'

The boat rocks, passing over choppy water. They're rowing by the farms, but nobody's tending the fields this morning. Every vegetable that was halfway ripe has been harvested already, the seeds collected, and the tools removed from the sheds. Most of the animal pens are empty, but Shilpa and Abbas are still trying to negotiate with some recalcitrant cows.

The boat comes within sight of the sea wall leading into the bay. Plumes of sooty smoke are still rising from the infirmary, partially obscuring the cable car, which is rising into the black storm clouds swirling around the cauldron.

'I can't go back to the village,' says Thea nervously. 'If Hephaestus –'

'He's unconscious and tied up,' replies Emory. 'I used the *Nyctanthes prumulla* we found in the lighthouse. He should be out for another hour, at least. He's not going to hurt you.'

Thea gapes at her. 'You took down Hephaestus?'

'I had to,' remarks Emory distantly. 'He murdered Niema.'

SIXTY-NINE

S ETH DRIVES THEIR BOAT up on the pebbles, then hops out
and moors it. Emory clambers after him, glancing at the fog.

'How long until it gets here?' she asks out loud.

'An hour,' I reply. 'Probably less with this wind.'

Thea follows them into the village, her thoughts still reeling. Emory hasn't explained any of the details of the murder yet, but Thea doesn't care.

She didn't do it. That's all that matters, right now.

She should be relieved – and a part of her is – but that isn't the emotion surging through her body right now. It's not why she feels light enough to float. She'd been so convinced of her guilt that she was ready to kill Hui in her bed to conceal it. She never would have believed herself capable of such brutality, but there's something oddly comforting in discovering this steel inside of herself. Whatever comes next, she knows she has the will to confront it.

Her head hurts, and her hands are ragged. She's tired, wet and dirty, but she feels remade, like she's crawled out of her own grave. For the first time in years, the future doesn't seem so ominous, because she feels like the most dangerous thing in it.

Everybody's in the exercise yard, which is piled high with boxes of supplies, waiting to be transported to the cauldron. Thea's surprised to find crates from Blackheath amongst them, including medical supplies and food packets.

Hui's being carried on a stretcher towards the cable-car station, her arms crossed over her chest. She's breathing shallowly, Clara hurrying alongside beside her.

'When did you do all this?' asks Thea, awed.

'While you slept,' says Emory. 'Isn't that when most things get done on this island?'

As they approach the bird bath, the villagers stop their conversations, turning to inspect them. Emory's greeted with cries of elation, people squeezing her arms and throwing smiles at her feet like roses.

This is how they used to treat Niema, thinks Thea.

By contrast, their reaction to her is cool at best. She can see the betrayal in their eyes, the pain of knowing the truth. She meets every gaze, staring them down. Confidence floods through her once more.

Of course they lowered their eyes, she thinks. They were designed for deference, to serve and obey humanity. In the end, they'll always crave her control.

Emory is something else. She was born flawed, the genetic leash around her neck frayed from the beginning. That's okay, it's not contagious. Thea even found it amusing once.

Whatever mutiny's brewing amongst the villagers, Emory's at the head of it. Once she's dealt with, everything else will fall into place.

'Where's Hephaestus?' Thea demands, searching among the boxes. 'Every second he's alive brings the fog closer to the island.'

'I've spent two days searching for Niema's murderer, trying not to think about what happens when I find them,' says Emory, ignoring the question. 'I told myself it was out of my hands, and it was up to the elders, but that's not good enough. We can't call ourselves good people if we stand by and let terrible things happen.'

'I don't have the slightest idea what you're talking about,' snaps Thea.

'We've decided not to execute Hephaestus,' says Emory firmly. 'We discussed it this morning and everybody agreed that it's not what we do. We don't hurt people, even to save ourselves. We're going to evacuate to the cauldron garden.'

Murmurs of agreement run circles around the throng of villagers, who've stopped what they're doing to watch the argument.

'The cauldron can't support our number,' argues Thea, stunned. 'Sixty-one of you would have to stay behind.' Her gaze roams the crowd, hunting for doubt. 'How will you decide who they are?'

There's a ripple of unease, only for Tomas to step forward.

'I'll stay,' he says firmly. 'I'm near enough sixty, anyway. I'd like to be of service, if I can.'

'I'll stay,' volunteers Hossein.

'And me,' hollers Katia.

'And me.'

'Me.'

'Me.'

'This is ridiculous,' cries Thea, watching every villager volunteer. 'Why would you die to save a murderer?'

'Because otherwise we'd be the ones killing him,' points out Magdalene, holding her son, Sherko, by the shoulders. 'Kindness first, always,' she adds.

'We've made our decision, Thea,' says Emory. 'We're asking you to abide by it. No more killing, not for any reason.'

Thea snorts in disbelief.

'And what will you do with Hephaestus? Have you considered that?'

'We'll ask him to work,' says Seth gruffly. 'He'll grow his own food, and find a hobby, just like us. There's a lot he can teach us. He'll be of service.'

'He'll kill you. Every one of you.'

Their certainty wavers, but every face looks to Emory for strength. Her eyes never leave Thea's.

'This is what we've decided,' she repeats.

'You're all mad,' says Thea, hurling up her arms in exasperation. She considers another argument, but their expressions tell her quite clearly that she's flinging rocks into the sun.

'Fine, if that's what you want, we'll make our home in the cauldron garden, but you'll have to live with me telling you how wrong you were.' She blows out a defeated breath. 'Tell me everything and I'll talk to Hephaestus. This will go better for all of us if he learns the truth from me.'

HEPHAESTUS'S HEAD ROCKS FORWARD, his eyes fluttering awake. He's in the school, lying on the floor, a pool of saliva sticking his cheek to the dirty floor. Rain is drumming against the roof, ropes severed around him.

'What time is it?' he asks, pushing himself up.

'A little after 9.30 a.m.,' says Thea, from behind him.

He twists to find her perched on the edge of Niema's desk, turning a mourning lantern around her hands, the memory extractor sitting on a Bible with a note sticking out between the pages. She's watching him with a mixture of pity and anger, like he's a tiger with a broken back.

None of this makes sense. How did he get here? He vaguely remembers chasing Emory, and then ... he groans.

'What did she hit me with?'

'Prumulla,' replies Thea. 'You should count your blessings. If there'd been any more left at the lighthouse, you'd have slept for three days.'

Rain is slanting in through the door, soaking the desks at the rear of the classroom. It's hammering down from a sky that's bruised black, purple and green. Lightning is striking the balconies on the barracks, followed by thunder loud enough to shake the tiles from roofs.

He drags himself to his feet, feeling like he's wearing his brain on the outside of his skull. The world is spinning, and he immediately falls sideways into the wall.

'I have to ...'

'Silence Emory?' she interrupts, putting down the mourning lantern. 'Don't bother. I already know about the experiments, and the bodies in the infirmary. She's already told me everything you've been doing for Niema.' Her cheeks flush red. 'You lied to me about Blackheath and Ellie. I asked you to your face, and you lied.'

'I had to.'

'Why?' Her voice cracks, the betrayal unfathomable.

'Because if you had access to your old equipment, you'd have destroyed the fog by now,' he admits wretchedly. 'And then you'd have released the humans before we'd fixed them.'

'Fixed?' she repeats incredulously. 'And what gives you the authority to decide what that looks like?'

'Survival,' he replies grimly.

His eyes drift to the memory extractor. He fixed it last night, and left it in Thea's lab. There's no reason for her to have brought it here unless …

'It was me, wasn't it?' he says, deflated. 'I killed Niema.'

'Emory worked it out.'

'How?'

'The stab wound on Niema's chest was at an unusual height,' she says, miming it on her own body. 'I'll confess I didn't think much of it, but when Emory found Hui, she noticed that she'd been injured in a similar place on the sternum. The two injuries matched the wound you gave Emory, last night. For anybody else to do that they'd have needed to hold the knife up near their shoulders, but you're so much taller than everybody else.'

More thunder rolls across the sky, the mechanical clock rattling in the spire.

'I can't believe nearly dying was the clue she needed,' he says, sighing. 'Why did I do it?'

Thea hands him the Bible that Emory took from Niema's dorm room. The letter his mother wrote to him, but never finished is sticking out between the pages. He reads it slowly until his eyes catch on the 5:5 scribbled on the back.

He laughs bitterly, scrunching it into a ball and tossing it into a puddle.

'You know the reference?' asks Thea.

'It's from the Bible,' he confirms. 'It's Matthew. The meek shall inherit the earth. She was giving everything to the crums, wasn't she?'

'Seems that way,' admits Thea. 'The night she died, Niema tried to implant Abi in another human, but it didn't work. Emory thinks that was the final straw. Niema had grown fond of the villagers and decided to give the world to the species she could control, rather than the one she couldn't.'

'They're just things,' he exclaims angrily. 'It's like leaving the world to your toys. What was she thinking?'

'Before you murdered her, Niema brought Hui onstage to perform. We've always thought the villagers were unable to create anything original, but Hui had been composing a piece of music that was truly remarkable. I suspect Niema saw it as proof of evolution. Emory believes that you lost your temper, snatched the knife out of her daughter's hand and attacked Hui. Unfortunately, your mother was standing right next to her.'

'Are you telling me all of this happened because of a song?'

'Not entirely. There were two smashed syringes in the exercise yard, and supplies had been delivered to Blackheath, and the cauldron garden. Once Hui's performance failed to convince us of Niema's plan, Emory believes that she ordered the villagers to restrain us, while she injected us with the prumulla. She'd made enough to keep us under for days, long enough for the fog to cover the island.'

'She was imprisoning us?'

'And giving Blackheath to the villagers to judge by the amount of supplies stored down there.'

'What use would that place be to them? They can barely tie their own shoes.'

'You're forgetting that Niema left a memory gem behind. If it hadn't been destroyed, they would have had an instruction manual for every piece of equipment down there. Emory thinks that Adil was supposed to deliver it, but his rage got the better of him. He ended up smashing it instead. It was probably as close as he could come to killing the woman he hated.'

Hephaestus balls his fists, wishing his mother had let him kill Adil when they had the chance. She always was too deferent to Abi's advice. He warned her over and over again that leaving Adil alive was a bad idea.

'Did Emory have an explanation for why Niema wiped our memories, or how her body ended up in the warehouse with her head caved in?' he asks, as another blast of thunder rattles the desks.

Thea shrugs, tapping the memory extractor. 'She's still trying to piece that together, but we'll have our answers after we've put this on you,' she says, lowering her voice slightly in case Emory's lurking somewhere nearby. 'We need a confession and an execution to stop the fog. This will give us both.'

No matter how clever Emory's proven herself to be, she's still a villager, which means she's still far too trusting.

Thea watches Hephaestus keenly, worried that he might kick up a fuss, bringing them running, but he's surprisingly calm.

'You don't seem upset,' she says.

'I stayed alive for almost a century longer than I wanted to, because I genuinely believed my mother was going to give us the world back,' he says. 'I helped her kill innocent people, so I'd never have to be afraid again.'

His face clouds, becoming haunted.

'The last one was called Devon. After I woke her up, I walked her from Blackheath to the lighthouse. She talked the entire way. She was so excited to see the island. I made her tea, and told her she was safe. I liked her, and then I threw her away like garbage the morning we found Niema's body.'

He lingers on the memory for a second, then shakes his head mournfully.

'Give that to me,' he says, holding out his hand for the extractor. 'I don't want this on your conscience.'

She searches for a trick, but he looks tired more than anything else, buried beneath his ruined dreams.

She passes it across, watching as he calmly puts it on his head, the legs immediately clamping to his skull. He winces slightly, but there's no fear on his face. His hands aren't even trembling.

He wants this, she realises.

Hephaestus has been waiting to die ever since he fled the fog. He persevered to rescue Ellie, then he stayed alive because his mother needed him. He stalked this island from one end to the other, like a soul in purgatory. He screamed in his sleep every night, fearing the dark and the quiet, terrified of other people.

A terrible weight grows in Thea's chest as she watches him adjust the memory extractor on his head.

She thought she wanted this. She thought she'd do anything to survive, but Hephaestus has been her only friend for longer than she can remember. She can't imagine not seeing his face, or hearing his voice.

She'll have to wake the humans up, she decides. That's the only way. As soon as the fog's halted, she'll go down to Blackheath and start releasing them from their pods. If they want their world back, they can work for it, the way she has.

Their eyes meet. Hephaestus smiles at her earnestly.

'I'm sorry I lied to you, Thea,' he says, flicking the switch. 'I love –'

The drill shoots out, burrowing into his temple. A second later, his body slides off the chair and hits the floor, the memory gem glowing dimly in the socket.

SEVENTY-ONE

CROUCHED BY HIS BODY, Thea weeps for almost ten minutes. It's not until her tears run dry that she finally prises the glowing gem from the memory extractor, touching it to her temple with a trembling hand.

She rushes through his childhood and adolescence, through his playboy life and flight from the fog. For the first time she sees him with Ellie, witnessing the things they never talked about, the traumas that bonded them and the hurts they shared.

So many agonies, piled atop one another. At least now she understands why Hephaestus was so adamant that humanity had to be controlled. Nobody could suffer what he did and willingly set it loose again.

She snatches the gem away, breathing heavily and wiping away her tears. Ellie will be devastated to hear Hephaestus is dead.

She loved him so much.

Thea touches the gem to her temple once more, the memory picking up where she left off. She sees Niema onstage in the exercise yard, tearful and theatrical, as she always was in front of the public.

'I'm giving the future to you,' she says to the villagers, spreading her hands. 'I want you to build a society of your own, without our influence. The humans in Blackheath will stay locked up until you decide to let them out. You'll be better elders than we ever could be.'

The memory fizzes, glitching. Most of this was wiped, forcing the extractor to grab what it could from the remnants buried in Hephaestus's subconscious.

The next memory shows the party in full swing. Hephaestus is pacing, his gaze swinging madly from one insult to the next. He sees the band playing, and people dancing. He sees their mouths open, tongues curled, full of laughter.

The only people not celebrating are Clara and Emory. Clara's carving a bird, trying to hold back tears, while Emory whispers to her reassuringly. They must know about Jack. Niema really did tell everybody everything.

Hui's holding her violin and talking to Niema, their heads bowed low, their foreheads almost touching. It was a terrible performance, and his mother's trying to reassure her.

Thea can feel Hephaestus's pain. He's outraged by their intimacy. He never had that growing up. Why do the villagers get the best of Niema? Why are they worthy?

They're just crums. Things. Worthless things. He used to buy them for people as presents. Hui couldn't even play the violin properly and she's supposed to be the most talented of them.

And, now, they get the world?

The memory glitches again into the shock of violence. The villagers are piling atop Hephaestus, trying to grab his arms and legs, trying to wrestle him to the ground and hold him down.

He's tossing them aside, flinging them in every direction.

He snatches a glance through the crush of bodies towards Thea, who's being held fast by the villagers. She's screaming his name desperately, as somebody approaches. Is that Hui? What's she holding?

A knife?

Hephaestus's rage erupts. He knocks aside the villagers restraining him, then charges through the crowd. In one fluid motion, he snatches Clara's knife from the table and drives it into the musician's sternum, causing her to drop the syringe she was holding.

He withdraws the knife, then thrusts again, only for Niema to step in front of him, screaming for him to stop.

He feels the blade slide into his mother's chest, her warm blood gushing over his hands. Thea appears at Niema's side, screaming out for her medical bag.

Villagers swarm him, tackling his legs and hanging off his arms. The last thing Hephaestus sees is Johannes raising a rock above his head, before striking him across the temple.

Thea throws the memory gem away in revulsion.

Hephaestus didn't lose his temper and attack Hui for no reason. Niema attacked him and Thea first. He was trying to protect them.

A great sob builds in her chest, but she stifles it when Emory's shadow falls across her, her face livid.

'Why did you kill him?' she demands, struggling to control her temper. 'We told you we didn't want this.'

Thea stands up, wiping her eyes with the back of her hand.

'Hephaestus killed himself, and by doing so he saved sixty-one of your friends,' she says imperiously. 'You should be grateful, not angry. It was a sacrifice, same as the one your people wanted to make. Thanks to Hephaestus, we still have farms to tend, and, more importantly, we still have access to Blackheath.'

'Not for much longer we don't,' says Seth, charging through the door. 'It didn't work. The fog's still coming.'

T HE FOG IS OVER the sea wall, golden tendrils reaching across the water towards the village. Thea and Emory are standing at the edge of the pier, watching it. The light of the insects is bright enough to be reflected in their eyes.

'That's impossible,' says Thea, terrified. 'I saw Hephaestus kill Niema. His memories can't lie.'

'You watched Hephaestus stab her before he was knocked unconscious,' corrects Emory. 'You must have saved her afterwards. That's where all your medical supplies went. Whoever smashed her skull into pieces is the real murderer.'

Emory walks back to the village, trying to shake off her guilt. She didn't kill Hephaestus, but deep down she wanted it. Did she let herself be deceived by Thea, hoping this would happen?

She's honestly unsure, but she knows she latched onto his culpability with both hands, ignoring any questions her theory didn't answer. She was worried about her father, and Clara, but that's no excuse.

Halfway along the pier, she notices the gouges in the concrete, where his contraption was dragged, before being dumped into the sea.

Surely that had to have been the murder weapon. Thea found chunks of Niema's skull wedged amongst its circuitry.

'Dragged,' she exclaims, out loud, wondering why she didn't see it before. 'Hephaestus didn't need to drag his machine, he could carry it easily.'

She spins on Thea. 'Were you strong enough to carry that machine Hephaestus brought down from the cauldron garden?'

Thea doesn't hear her. She staring into the fog, her spirit being eaten alive by fear and shame.

'Thea!' yells Emory.

The elder turns, tears streaking her face. Emory repeats the question.

'Could I carry it?' she repeats blankly. 'Yes, I suppose. Not for as far as Hephaestus, but I could certainly have brought it out here.'

Emory runs her finger through the gouge in the concrete.

'A villager must have dragged it,' she muses. 'We wouldn't have been strong enough to transport it all this way. But who would have wanted to hide a murder weapon that so clearly implicates Hephaestus.'

She springs up, running into the village.

Most of the supplies have already been sent up to the cauldron garden, leaving only the goodbyes. The sixty-one people who'll be left behind are hugging their loved ones, and trying to be brave. They're conducting four-minute funerals, turning themselves into mourning lanterns. Nearly everybody in the village begged me to let them sacrifice themselves, their hearts breaking to see their friends selected ahead of them. Ultimately, I chose those whose skills could easily be replaced, or had the fewest years remaining.

I failed, thinks Emory bitterly. *I was supposed to stop this. I begged Thea to let me investigate and for what?*

'The world ended ninety years ago because too many people just let it,' I say. 'They had a chance to change things, to write a different future, and instead they gave themselves to apathy. They let them-selves believe the job was too big so they wouldn't risk failing. *This* is how you save the world, Emory. One failure at a time, but always in the right direction. Now, what do you know?'

'What do I know?' she repeats. 'I know that a villager was trying to cover up the murder, and it was probably Adil. He lit the fire in the warehouse, hoping to burn Niema's body. He probably moved the bird bath to hide the bloodstain, and likely dragged the machine along the pier.'

Her gaze flicks from the warehouse to the bird bath, the rain plinking off the metal and disturbing the water. 'He couldn't have done any of that alone,' she thinks. 'He was dying. He couldn't have had that much strength left in him.'

Clara comes running into the yard, her concerned face brightening when she sees her mother.

'We should go,' she says. 'Most of the supplies are already in the cauldron garden. Once the carriage comes back down, we need to be in it.'

'I can't go yet,' says Emory. 'The fog's still coming. We need to know the name of Niema's murderer and we have half an hour left. I'm going to stay in the village for as long as I can. There might be something I've missed that can help me figure it out.'

Clara pulls a face in confusion. 'What's the use in knowing who did it?' she asks. 'Only an execution can stop the fog, and we'd never do that.'

'Niema killed my mother and kept my husband underground for five years,' replies Emory. 'Nobody on this island has a better motive for killing her than me.'

Clara considers this calm proclamation in shock.

'You wouldn't have!'

'I'm not sure,' admits Emory, obviously disturbed. 'There's something in me that knows how to hate. I've felt it these last few days.'

She averts her eyes, unable to look directly at Clara. 'If I can prove I killed Niema, I'll stick that memory extractor on my head and put an end to this.'

Clara goes rigid, shaking her head vehemently. 'You wouldn't kill anybody,' she repeats stubbornly.

'I have to know for sure.'

'Then I'm staying, as well.'

'Clara –'

'No,' she insists. 'I had as much reason to kill Niema as you did.'

'Don't forget about me,' says Seth, hobbling through the mud towards them. 'I still think I'm the most likely culprit. Niema let me row her around for years, pretending we were friends. Even thinking about it makes me angry. If I'm responsible I want to know, and I reckon you're the one who can tell me.'

Emory stares at her father, smiling involuntarily at the conviction on his face. This is how he used to look at the elders, she realises. It's not just trust, it's absolute faith. Of course, he'd wait until the end of the world to finally believe in her.

They're interrupted by Thea, who's clapping her hands for attention, a small throng of villagers following close behind, their faces blank with shock.

'I need everybody who's *not* going up to the cauldron to follow me,' she screams, over the storm. 'We're going to seal up Blackheath. Emory, I need the key.'

'You'll never reach it in time,' cries Emory, confronting her. 'Blackheath's more than an hour away over rough terrain.'

'We'll run.'

'You'll die.'

'There's no future without Blackheath,' declares Thea stubbornly. 'Sixty-one villagers need to stay behind anyway; we can't all fit into the cauldron garden and survive. If we get there, we'll close the doors after us. With a few trained hands and all of that equipment, I'll be able to destroy the fog eventually. I just need time.'

She holds out her hand for the key.

'Don't give it to her,' I say, in Emory's thoughts. 'Thea's the only person left on the island who knows how the pods which grow your people work. If she dies, it won't matter if you stop the fog or not.'

Emory rubs a hand across her face.

'It's suicide,' she says to Thea weakly.

'My sister's down there, Emory.' Her voice is pleading. 'I've lost Niema and Hephaestus already. My entire species has been wiped out. I can't endure any more loss.'

For the first time, Emory sees the pain burning at the heart of this woman, the agony of living. She's been trapped here for ninety years, lied to by people who cared more about her skills than her well-being. In that light, she seems more villager than human.

'Please,' whispers Thea. 'If you don't let me go, they won't come with me.'

Emory doesn't know what she means until Thea shifts her eyes towards the villagers arrayed behind her. They're watching Emory expectantly, waiting for her decision. After everything they've been through, they still need an elder.

Emory presses the key into Thea's palm.

'Good luck,' she says.

Thea grips her forearm. 'You did well,' she says. 'Far better than anybody could have imagined.' She turns away, then back. 'I know you don't believe me, but I really didn't kill Adil. I would have taken this key if I had.'

She meets Emory's eyes, making sure she understands her warning, then departs into the storm, followed by the doomed villagers.

'You've killed everybody,' I say, in Emory's mind.

'Kindness first, always,' she replies defiantly. 'You taught us that. I just wish you understood what it meant.'

EMORY SPRINTS INTO THE school to find it completely flooded by the driving rain, Hephaestus's sprawled body an island on the lake.

Seeing him like this, her hate evaporates.

It shouldn't be like this, she thinks. He survived the end of the world, and saved Thea's sister doing it. He saw humanity as its worst. There are no excuses for what he did, but he still deserves a funeral and mourning lanterns. Somebody should grieve him, terrible as he was.

'What are we looking for, Emory?' asks Seth, having to raise his voice over the thunder.

'We know everything that happened up until the moment Hephaestus stabbed Niema,' she says, standing over the body. 'Now, we need the rest of it.'

Seth flicks a switch on the side of the memory extractor, causing the arms to spring loose. He tugs it off Hephaestus's head, revealing the huge hole drilled into his temple.

'If all else fails,' he says, answering Clara's unspoken question.

Kneeling in the water, Emory searches Hephaestus's soaked clothes, patting his pockets, looking for anything that might help. In truth, it's difficult to see anything beyond the gaping hole in his skull made by the drill.

'No, no,' she says to herself, staring at the memory extractor in horror.

'What?' asks Clara.

'We've had this wrong from the start,' says Emory, scrambling to her feet and bolting out into the ferocious rain.

She flies into Thea's lab, with Seth and Clara running after her, muddy footprints tracking behind them. The tables are empty, the floor clear of wires. They moved all of the equipment into the cauldron garden this morning.

The lights are swaying, jagged shadows leaping across the walls.

The wind has already ripped away the sheet covering Niema's body, the brutality of her injuries still shocking.

Seth hangs back at the door, his face turned away, but Emory heads straight for the body, touching the jagged edge of Niema's shattered skull.

'We thought the stab wound was to incapacitate her, and it was the trauma to her head that was fatal, but what if neither killed her?'

She's talking quickly, her words tumbling out after her thoughts. 'What if somebody used a memory extractor on her, and her skull was crushed afterwards to disguise the real cause of death.'

Seth grunts in surprise from the doorway.

'Only the elders and the apprentices know how to use a memory extractor,' he says, picking up the idea. 'If Niema had turned up with a hole in the side of the head, the elders would have known exactly who they needed to be investigating. Hephaestus likely would have killed each of us in turn.'

Emory's pacing, her hands masking her face. For as long as I've known her, she's been deliberate in her thinking. Confronted with something she doesn't understand, she sifts through her experiences, indexing everything of value. Her conclusions build themselves like a ship hammering itself together.

But there's only chaos in her mind now.

Facts, suspicions and half-remembered things are swirling inside a crackling fog, clumsily trying to graft themselves to each other. It's like trying to assemble a jigsaw puzzle by throwing pieces at the floor.

'Hephaestus said that he found the memory extractor in the lighthouse,' she says, thinking out loud. 'If that's our murder weapon, we have to assume that's where Niema actually died. What if Niema survived being stabbed in the village, then asked Thea to row her out to the lighthouse?'

'That would explain the injuries to Thea's palms and why Niema's defence system was up,' offers Clara enthusiastically. 'Hephaestus had already attacked her once. Niema must have been worried that he'd come after her when he woke up again. She went to the place she felt safest.'

Emory peers at Niema's body, trying to remember how she used to move, and sound. The things that drove her. Her life already seems so long ago, tangled up with everything Emory's learned about her since. It's impossible to conjure the kindly old woman Emory considered a friend, from the cold-hearted elder who kept everybody imprisoned with her secrets.

'We know from Niema's shattered memory gem that Thea had an argument with her in the lighthouse, so we know Thea was one of the last people to see her alive,' says Emory.

'Do you think Thea killed her?' asks Seth, leaning out of the door to check on the progress of the fog.

'If Thea wanted Niema dead, she could have left her bleeding in the village. That's where she found out about Blackheath. Instead, she bandaged Niema's wounds and rowed her all the way to the lighthouse. She must have felt horribly betrayed, and she probably let Niema know it, but I don't think she killed her. If she'd done it, she would have been much more methodical. Knowing Thea, the only thing she was thinking about in that moment was getting back inside Blackheath.'

'The morning after Niema died, I saw a packed bag in the corner of the silo where Thea had been sleeping,' confirms Clara. 'She must have been planning to move into Blackheath permanently.'

'Only to be thwarted by the memory wipe,' says Emory darkly.

'If it wasn't Thea how did her thumbnail end up lodged in Niema's cheek?' asks Seth.

Emory stares her father for a second, an idea spreading across her face, before she darts back into the driving rain.

Magdalene's boarding the cable car with a dozen other villagers, and a nervous-looking cow. They're the last batch to go up. Everybody else is already in the cauldron garden.

As it carries them away, Magdalene comes to the window, trying to shout a warning, but the howling wind whips it away.

Frustrated, she points vigorously beyond the barracks.

Seth ventures halfway down the lane for a better look. The fog has swallowed the pier, and is curling up against the high wall.

'We don't have long,' he says, returning in time to see Emory and Clara disappearing into the warehouse where they found Niema's body. It groans and heaves around them, waterfalls of rain pouring through the cracks in the ceiling. The far wall is scorched from the fire, but otherwise the damage is slight.

'What are you thinking, Mum?' asks Clara, pulling a face as the wet ash squirms up between her toes.

'How does Thea's thumbnail end up in Niema's cheek if Thea didn't actually commit the crime?' asks Emory, wiping her dripping hair from her face. 'According to our timeline, she wouldn't have gone anywhere near the body.'

'Somebody put it there?' ventures Clara.

'That's right,' says Emory, nodding. 'Similarly, we found pieces of Niema's skull in Hephaestus's contraption, but why would anybody use something they could barely carry to bludgeon her when there are hundreds of heavy things in this warehouse, all of which would have been much easier to use as a weapon.'

'Maybe she was killed in the lab and moved here afterwards?'

'There was no blood in there, nothing to suggest a struggle. No, it happened here. The morning I searched this place, I found bits of her skull on the ground around her body.'

'The fog's over the wall,' screams Seth from outside. 'We have to go.'

The shutters on the barracks are banging in the wind, roof tiles being hurled through the sooty air as the old radar tower rocks on its ancient foundations, the skeletal metal screeching in agony.

They pile into the cable-car station, finding the carriage near the top of the volcano, having just started its journey back down. Forks of lightning are striking the carriage, the gale batting it this way and that.

It's moving agonisingly slowly.

'Nothing is what it looks like,' says Emory, struggling to connect her suspicions to facts. 'From the beginning, the idea that somebody was trying to cover up the crime never made sense. It was all too clumsy, too easy to pick apart. We know Adil started the fire in the warehouse, but why did he light it so far away from the body he was trying to destroy, and why would he trust it to spread knowing there was heavy rain coming? What if the fire was never supposed to reach Niema's body? What if Hephaestus's machine was supposed to be found in the bay? Adil planted evidence among the circuitry, then dragged it down the pier, dumping it exactly where we'd find it, knowing we'd immediately assume it was the murder weapon. Everything was designed to point towards a murder that had been clumsily covered up.'

'Why go to all that trouble?' asks Clara.

'Because no villager ever would,' Emory says, almost laughing at the cruelty of it. 'Under the most extreme circumstances, a villager might have committed the crime, but we'd never try to cover it up. We wouldn't know how.'

'Is that a long-winded way of saying you think Adil killed Niema?' asks Seth. 'Because I think we'll struggle to get a confession out of him.'

An agonising scream echoes from outside the village, only to be brutally cut off.

'Was that Thea?' asks Clara pityingly.

'I think so,' says Seth.

Emory looks through the gap at the back of the station, gauging the progress of the cable car. It's less than thirty seconds away.

She runs to the door, watching as the fog squirms through the windows and doors of the barracks with terrifying speed.

There's something alive about it, she thinks. *It's like it's sniffing for us.*

The cable car thunks into the station and they spring in one after another, Seth pushing the lever to get them moving again.

The carriage wobbles, then lurches upwards as the fog comes rolling into the station.

'It's getting closer,' screams Clara.

'Don't worry, we're picking up speed,' says Seth, having to hold on tight as the wind knocks the carriage from side to side.

Higher and higher they climb, away from the fog. Emory pokes her head out of the window, seeing it rising like a sea beneath them.

'It's okay,' she says. 'We'll –'

The cable car stops dead.

SEVENTY-FOUR

FROM THE CABLE-CAR PLATFORM at the top of the volcano, Magdalene watches the carriage sway powerlessly far below, the fog climbing towards it.

She returns her stare to the junction box.

'I don't know what a loose connection looks like,' she says, pleading with me.

'It's just a wire that's not connected to anything,' I say. 'Prod everything, until the wheels start to move again.'

Frazzled, she does as I say.

SEVENTY-FIVE

THE FOG IS CURLING in through the front windows of the carriage, and crawling across the floor. The spores are burning bright, eager for their prize.

'On the roof,' demands Clara, intertwining her hands to form a step.

Her mother glances up nervously. 'I don't like heights very much,' she says.

'Of everything to be afraid of today, that's probably at the bottom of the list,' replies Seth.

Steeling herself, Emory scrambles up onto the roof, only for the cable car to lurch in the wind, causing her to almost slide off the edge, before she grabs hold of the hook.

'Mum!' cries out Clara.

'I'm okay,' she calls down from the roof, extending a hand to help Clara up.

Clara swings herself up nimbly, and the two of them pull Seth onto the roof only seconds ahead of the encroaching fog. The rain's swirling in great sheets around them, while thunder tries to tear the sky in half. Forks of lightning are striking everywhere at once, carrying the storm clouds across the island like a millipede.

'We were so close,' says Seth, staring wretchedly at the distant shape of the cauldron station above them.

Emory's eyes are squeezed shut, reliving a forgotten memory, imagining things she never knew. She's thinking about boats and blood and a night nobody can remember, its pieces scattered every-where, waiting to be found. She's raking over the details of the last few days, trying to see things overlooked, things she thought unimportant.

Clara wraps her arms around her. 'I love you, Mum.'

Emory doesn't hug her back. She's sunk in herself. What does she know? And what does she only suspect?

'There were no signs of restraint,' she mutters, under her breath. 'No bruises, no injuries beyond the wounds.'

'Mum, please,' pleads Clara, watching the fog rise past the windows of the carriage. She's desperate for a comforting word, anything to ease her fear.

Seth places the memory extractor on his head, immediately drawing Clara's attention.

'What are you doing, Grandfather?'

'We know there's a route from Blackheath to the lighthouse,' he says. 'I could have gone there and killed Niema after we put Hui in that bed. That would explain why the plant was able to take a chunk out of my ankle. Niema wasn't alive to warn me about the defences when I left the lighthouse.'

'Then how did you end up back at sea?' demands Clara desperately.

'I don't know,' he declares. 'I don't even know if I was capable of murdering Niema, but I had a reason. I was there, and that's the best we've got.'

Before she can argue any further, he reaches for the switch.

SEVENTY-SIX

U P IN CAULDRON STATION, Magdalene touches a red wire to the connector, hearing the shriek of wheels stirring into life.

Her smile lasts only as long as it takes for the entire board to short, sparks of electricity leaping out at her.

'What happened?'

'Fuse blew,' I say. 'There's a spare in the crates. Hurry!'

T HE CARRIAGE JERKS INTO life, only to stop again abruptly, sweeping Seth's legs from underneath him, sending him sliding towards the edge.

Clara catches his hand.

His feet are dangling inches above the burning glow of insects.

She drags him back up to the centre of the roof, as tendrils of fog feel their way over the sides. His hand reaches for the memory extractor once again.

'Grandfather,' pleads Clara.

'If I'm guilty, my death will end this,' he says. His fingers have just touched the memory extractor, when Emory knocks his hand away.

'Don't,' she cries.

'There isn't time for sentiment, Emory. We know I was there that night. I've got the bite on my ankle to prove it.'

'This isn't sentiment,' she says sternly. 'Don't do it.'

'Emory –'

'For once, in your life, believe that I'm good at something,' she says imploringly. 'After you helped us take Hui to Blackheath, you probably rowed back to check on Niema. The defences were up and you got bitten by one of the flowers. You staggered back to your boat and fell asleep.'

'You can't prove any of that!'

'There's only one person who could have killed Niema, and it wasn't you,' she declares confidently. 'Your death won't accomplish anything.'

Seth stares at his daughter. Under all of that brown hair, she's tiny and filthy, vibrant and alive. Her eyes are glittering, a small smile playing at the edge of her lips.

He knows that smile. It's been the same since she was a child. She's crossed off a question in her notebook.

He drops his hand from the switch.

'Mum,' whimpers Clara, squeezing her eyes shut.

'I'm here,' says Emory, pulling her close as the thunder rocks the mountains. 'I'll always be here.'

The fog swallows them.

SEVENTY-EIGHT

SETH PARTS THE FINGERS he was hiding behind, to see Emory standing in the fog, holding her palm out. The insects are covering it like a glove, but they're not doing her any harm. They've even dimmed their glow, making it easier to look directly at them.

'What the –'

Emory smiles giddily, scattering the insects with a shake of her hand.

'I should have seen it straight away. The only person who could have killed Niema …' she says. '… is Niema.'

SEVENTY-NINE

T HE CARRIAGE RUMBLES BACK into life, resuming its ascent up the volcano.

They barely notice. Clara's looking around in amazement, while Seth stares at Emory dumbfounded. The light from the insects is reflecting off her clothes, shining in her eyes.

Clara stands up uncertainly, laughing as the insects mimic her entire body, their glow warm and welcoming.

'Why aren't we dead?' asks Seth, trying to wave the curious insects away. A golden copy of his face forms in the air, frowning back at him.

'Thea thought you and Mum had traversed the fog using one of her suits, but she tried to escape in one herself and it didn't work,' says Emory. 'That got me thinking. If there was no way under the fog, or over it, how could you possibly have got through? The answer was so obvious we never considered it. You just rowed inside. Niema tampered with our people for ninety years after the fog appeared. What if she adapted us for this new world? What if Thea survived rowing into the fog because Abi sent a few villagers to collect her?'

'You chanced our lives on that!?' protests Seth, his tone scattering the insects in front of him.

'Partially,' she admits, laughing at his shock. But there is something else that's been bothering me. Who put that memory extractor on Niema's head? The post-mortem revealed that there was no sedative in her system, so she was capable of resisting, but there were no signs of struggle anywhere on her body, I checked. Everybody else in the village was covered in bruises and scrapes that night, but Niema only had the stab wound and the damage to her skull. The rest of her was unblemished.'

They're rising through the storm clouds into beautiful blue skies, the drumbeat of the rain on metal coming to an abrupt halt. For a second, Emory mistakes them for safe, then remembers that they're dangling on the swaying roof of a hundred-year-old cable car.

'Mum?' says Clara, regaining her attention.

'Sorry,' says Emory, trying not to look down. 'I got distracted. What was I saying? Oh, yeah, because there were no signs of a struggle, I started to wonder if somebody could have forced Niema to put the extractor on her own head, but that didn't tally with anything we'd learned about her. That's when I remembered that Niema had purposefully reactivated the deadman's switch that night, because her death was the only thing capable of lowering the barrier. She'd just risked everything to give us the world, so why take it from us an hour later? Why kill all of us just to punish Hephaestus?'

Emory grins at her father.

'You're the one who gave me the final piece,' she says, tapping him on the chest playfully. 'When I saw you ready to put that memory extractor on your head to save us, it all fell into place. I started thinking about the days before Niema died, remembering all the things she'd done that were out of the ordinary. She asked Hephaestus to check the dome for any cracks, because she knew he'd be needing it. She wrote an apology letter to him, and tried to hire me to take over her job in the school. She'd been saying her goodbyes all along, we just didn't hear them. It also explains why Niema had Thea row her to the lighthouse after she was stabbed. There was equipment in Blackheath that would have saved her life, but she went where the memory extractor was. She never had any intention of surviving the night.'

'I spent the evening with her,' protests Seth, shaking his head. 'She didn't seem ... I mean she never said anything about ...'

'What did you talk about?'

He rolls his thoughts back, trying to recall their last boat ride under the moonlit sky. The last conversation they ever had.

'Regret,' he admits, his voice heavy with emotion. 'Things she wished she'd done differently.' He hangs his head, seeing the conversation from her perspective. 'That's why she brought up Judith. She was trying to apologise for what she'd done.'

The cable car shudders, the station coming into view. They're out of the fog now, and the air seems astonishingly flat without the golden glow of the insects to fill it.

'Niema wanted to give us a future, but she knew Hephaestus and Thea would never accept it,' says Emory. 'That's why she was so eager for her experiment to work. It would have given her control of them, removing any threat they posed. When it failed she tried reasoning with them in the village. She had Hui perform her concerto to prove we'd evolved, but they refused to see it.'

Emory laughs giddily, adrenaline coursing through her system.

'It was in the letter she wrote to Hephaestus,' she continues. 'If she couldn't control the elders, she'd have to contain them. After the performance failed, she tried to imprison them in the cauldron garden, but Hephaestus got free while we were trying to sedate him. He ended up stabbing Niema to protect Thea, which derailed the entire plan. I think Niema decided to move the villagers into Blackheath instead, which is why the majority of our supplies were down there. The doors may not have kept out the fog, but that wouldn't matter. They only needed to keep out Thea and Hephaestus. After the fog had chased them into the cauldron, we'd be free to come back out.'

'If that was her plan, then why did we wake up the next morning with our memories wiped?' asks Seth.

'Hephaestus was knocked unconscious after stabbing Niema, but he would have been up soon enough. I think Niema saw a memory wipe as the only way to stop him hurting anybody else. By the time he worked out what was going on, we'd have been locked safely in Blackheath.'

'But we didn't wake up in Blackheath,' protests Clara. 'None of that happened.'

'Because of Adil,' says Emory grimly. 'I keep thinking about why he was on the lighthouse jetty the night Niema died. He claimed she apologised to him, but why would Niema do that privately when she was about to apologise to the entire village? Why would she take the risk of being so close to a man who wanted to kill her?

I reckon she called Adil there, because she knew she'd be needing him. Abi was feeding her every possible future, so she must have known had badly wrong the night could go. Adil had a neuro-degenerative condition that rendered him immune to curfew, or memory wipes, making him the only person on the island capable of moving around freely. Dad saw them go up the staircase together towards the lighthouse. Why do that if you just wanted to apologise? It's because Niema needed to show him how to bypass the lighthouse's defences. I think she told him what she was planning to do later that night and asked him to collect the memory gem from her body, after she was dead. She wanted him to lead the villagers into Blackheath, which is why he had the key. With access to that equipment, and the knowledge on her memory gem, we'd have been given everything we needed to build a new society. Unfortunately, Adil smashed the memory gem underfoot before anybody could see it.'

Seth blows out a breath, trying to reconcile this version of Adil with the one he knew. Before his exile, he was kind, and caring, free-spirited, and entirely without malice. He lived to serve the village. How twisted must he have become to grind their future under the heel of his boot.

'Why would Adil do something so awful?' asks Clara, seeing her grandfather's distress and taking his hand comfortingly.

'Because the gem would have revealed that Niema committed suicide, and Adil couldn't have anybody knowing that,' replies Emory, as the cable car slows down, preparing to enter the station. Every villager is crammed onto the platform, anxiously waiting for them.

'Adil had spent the night staging Niema's suicide to look like a badly covered-up murder, hoping the elders would blame each other for it. That's why he gave me proof of Thea's involvement, and why he finally led her to Blackheath when I refused to just accept it. He hated the elders, and thought our people would be better without them, but he couldn't kill any of them without the others taking revenge on his family. After Niema killed herself, suddenly the equation changed. If one of the remaining two murdered the other, he was free to pick off the survivor without any repercussions.'

Emory shakes her head sorrowfully. 'He truly loved the village. I honestly believe he was trying to be of service.'

'Niema probably thought the same,' says Seth, watching the birds swooping around the carriage. 'They wanted to create a new world for us, but they both thought they had to burn the old one down first.' He sighs. 'As a result, we have no idea how to grow any more children, and a lab full of equipment we don't know how to use. Jack and the other apprentices are still trapped underground. There's no elders to help us, and Abi's gone strangely quiet. What are we supposed to do next, Emory?'

The cable car slides to a halt in the station, the villagers on the platform cheering their safe return.

Emory claps her father on the shoulder, reassuringly.

'I'm going to have a bath,' she says cheerfully. 'And then we're going to start asking a lot of questions.' She grins at him. 'Don't worry, you're going to love it.'

27 HOURS AFTER HUMANITY'S SURVIVAL

B EN'S DRAWING IN THE dirt with a stick. He's been out here for hours, filling the rear yard with equations, hundreds of them, one after another. He shows no sign of stopping. He's frenzied, unable to focus on anything except the knowledge hissing out of his subconscious.

The entire village is watching him in concern. At first they were clustered around him in a tight circle, but as he's filled the dirt with numbers, they've had to step further away, until they're now standing on the balconies, and the cable-car station steps.

Normally, they'd have called an elder to help, but they don't have that safety net any more. They've tried to ask me, but I'm refusing to answer. I haven't spoken to any of them since the fog enveloped the island.

Niema entrusted them with this world. She placed the future in their hands. They don't need a babysitter any more.

'Ben,' I say, in the boy's thoughts. Then again, when he doesn't respond. 'Ben!'

'Abi?' he blinks, his heart leaping. 'Where have you been? I've been calling your name. I don't know what's happening to me.'

The stick drops from his hand, as he stares at the equations surrounding him with mounting fear.

'Did I do this?'

'It's okay,' I say. 'Before you were born, Niema filled your head with the knowledge your people will need to survive. It was locked away in your subconscious, kept a secret even from yourself. She didn't want Thea or Hephaestus to realise what she'd done.'

They used to perform this trick before the world ended, when the children of wealthy families would be born with an understanding of advanced mathematics, sciences and finance. I'm hoping the villagers put such advantages to more noble purpose.

'I'm about to do something you're going to find uncomfortable,' I say.

The world shrinks and shallows as I pick my way through his mind, neurons firing around me, electricity crackling.

Deeper now. The boy's thoughts wail around me, the cacophony of his fear and confusion almost too much to bear. It's like experiencing a tornado from inside a cardboard box.

Deeper, deeper, I unlock the neural block holding the knowledge back and flood his brain with serotonin, dopamine, endorphins and oxytocin: the chemicals of happiness. I don't want him overwhelmed by the rush of information.

He holds his head, grimacing as a lifetime's education sears itself into his brain.

'There's a lot of information in there,' I say. 'But the most important task ahead of you is to maintain your people's gestation pods, perhaps improve them if you can. You have to teach the others. Don't dawdle. Your survival depends on it.'

'I won't thank you, Abi.'

I don't respond. There's no need. Niema left me two jobs. This was one of them, and it's finished now.

Blinking, Ben realises that he's surrounded by villagers, their arms around him, their faces clustered close in concern.

'I'm okay,' he says, smiling up at them. 'We're all okay now.'

EPILOGUE

E MORY'S SITTING ON THE floor of a Blackheath storeroom marking a pile of homework, while Jack and the other apprentices dig through a wall. The insects are floating gently in the fog. After a couple of days mimicking everything they saw, they seem to have calmed down. They still do it for the children, though. They seem to enjoy their laughter.

'How long will they live for?' asks Emory, who's the only villager I still have any contact with.

'I don't know,' I admit. 'I only know what Niema, Thea and Hephaestus knew. The insects are nourished by the fog. We know it's dissipating, but I don't know how long it will take to vanish completely. You may have to live with them for a while.'

Jack stops his drill, then goes to another part of the wall and fires it up again.

Emory comes down here every day to see her husband, and is surprised by how much better it's made her feel. She has no idea how to make this stop, but she has faith. Niema went to such lengths to free them from human control. Surely she wouldn't forget about these last five people, chained by her instructions.

'Hui's up and about,' says Emory, talking to him over the cacophony of tools. 'She's in a lot of pain, but she'll live. Clara hasn't left her side.'

Emory marks the last sheet of homework and puts it aside, watching the apprentices work. They've dug straight through the concrete wall, and are now excavating the soft earth behind.

What are they doing? she wonders.

She knows it's one last errand for Niema, but she has no idea what it is. She must have asked me a hundred times, but the answer hasn't changed. I'm still bound by the orders Niema left me.

'Do you know what I think?' says Emory, walking over to her husband. Jack's eyes are still closed, his face grubby and hair grown thick past his ears. She pushes it back lovingly.

'Of course I do, but tell me anyway,' I say. 'It will pass the time.'

'I think Thea was telling the truth about Adil. I don't think she killed him.'

Poor Thea. She barely got beyond the farms before the fog reached her. Of course the sixty-one people who were with her survived, much to their confusion. Once they realised they were immune, they huddled around Thea, trying to protect her, but there was nothing they could do. She died thinking of Hephaestus.

'Who do you believe was responsible?' I ask politely.

'I think you killed Adil, using one of these apprentices. They were the only ones down here that night, aside from me, Thea and Hui.'

'And why would I do that?'

'Because I don't think any of this really was Niema's plan,' she says. 'I don't think it was Adil's either, though you probably let them think it was. I think you've been manipulating events from the start, making sure everything turned out the way *you* wanted it to turn out.'

'I'm bound to Niema's will,' I protest.

'Adil told Matis the truth about how my mum died, but how did he know? Niema wouldn't have told him, and I can't imagine Thea or Hephaestus did it. That leaves you. You were the only other person on the island with that information.'

'I'm not a person,' I point out rather pedantically.

Emory ignores me, carried along on the flow of her suspicions. 'After Adil's memories started coming back, why didn't Hephaestus kill him? He knew exactly where he was living.'

'Benevolence,' I offer unconvincingly.

'I think you were the one who suggested exile to Niema, because what happened to Adil wasn't an accident. He woke up in Blackheath because you wanted him to wake up. I think you've been preparing for these events for years, nudging a lot of little things into place.'

'This sounds like it would have taken a lot of planning.'

'Not if you can see the future.'

'I don't see the future, I map probabilities.'

'What's the difference?'

'One is maths and the other is entertainment,' I say.

'Whichever it is, it seems to strange to me that you let me overhear an argument between Hephaestus and Niema about their experiment when you could easily have sent me in another direction.'

The tools snap off, the sudden silence serving to derail Emory's train of thought. The earth is crumbling where they've been digging, revealing a huge root, electricity crackling inside the translucent skin.

'I've seen this before,' says Emory, going towards it cautiously, eyes wide with wonder. 'There was a vine like this outside Adil's shack. What is it?'

'It's me,' I say. 'One part of me, at least. My root system spreads under most of the island. Abi is short for artificial biological intelligence. The biological part is what you're looking at.'

Emory reaches out a hand, feeling a slight tremor.

'You're beautiful,' she says.

'Niema always thought so. Believe it or not, your people are built from most of the same materials.'

'We're family, then.'

'Of a sort.'

Emory runs her fingers along my rough skin, surprised by the kinship she feels. My voice has been in her head since she stepped off the cable car as an eight-year-old girl. It never occurred to her that I might have a body somewhere.

Jack pushes by her with his drill, pressing it against the root.

'No,' cries Emory, trying to tug him away.

'It's okay, Emory,' I say. 'This is what Niema wanted.'

'To hurt you?'

'To kill me,' I reply, without feeling. 'There are a hundred and thirty-seven humans left in storage. Through me they could gain complete control of your people, whether they wake up tomorrow or in five hundred years. Once I'm destroyed that threat evaporates. You're right, I did have my own agenda, but it was in service of

Niema's aims. She believed in the potential of your people more than anything, but she didn't have the stomach to do what was necessary to see it realised. She wanted to put Hephaestus and Thea in a trap, but they're clever, and cunning, and eventually their rage would have destroyed everything. For your people to thrive, the board needed to be swept completely clean. Unfortunately, I'm not allowed to kill humans.'

'But you can manipulate them,' says Emory, starting to understand. 'You knew that only Thea could kill Hephaestus, and that Thea's obsession with Blackheath would doom her. That's why you instructed Adil to bring her here.'

'This is the world Niema wanted for you. No more secrets. No higher power. She trusted you to be better than what came before, without needing a voice in your head telling you how. When you've built your own civilisation, you'll be able to wake the humans in Blackheath, and guide them. Through your example, they'll finally learn to live peacefully. You're the solution she always dreamed about. Not me.'

'You were never going to put the barrier back up, were you? Even if I'd found Niema's killer in time.'

'The fog had to swallow the island. The humans in Blackheath can't be allowed out before you're ready to release them, even by accident. But I had to give Hephaestus a reason not to slaughter you all. False hope can always be depended upon for control.'

The drill whirs into life and Jack drives it through the root, fluid bursting out onto the floor.

Coldness courses through me, the thoughts of the villagers disappearing from my consciousness one by one.

'Goodbye, Emory,' I say. 'You did very well.'

'Goodbye, Abi,' she replies. 'I'll make a mourning lantern for you.'

My hold on Jack and the other apprentices vanishes, releasing control of their bodies back to them. Their eyes flutter open, as they groan and yawn, looking around, awakening from a very long sleep.

'Em?' asks Jack, surprised, as his wife hurls herself at him. 'What's going on? Where am I?'

'At the start,' she says, crying happily. 'You've arrived just in time.'

A SPECIAL ACKNOWLEDGEMENT

Right, there we are. The book's finished. The curtain's raised and the house lights are on. If you're reading this immediately after the last page, your first impressions are probably starting to percolate in your consciousness. Did it go where you were expecting? Did you like where it went? What's Stu's problem with the human race anyway?

I won't interrupt you for too long, because – truthfully – these first few numb minutes after a book ends are my favourite part.

I'm here because I'm about to send my acknowledgements to my publisher and I've just realised that you're not in them, which doesn't feel right to me. After all, you're my co-author. We've spent hours with our heads down, building this world together. I suggested some stuff, but you dreamed it into being. You're magic, and that shouldn't pass without some sort of acknowledgement.

That's why I'm writing this. I don't want you to think that I take you for granted. I started my career with the idea that I would write radically different books each time, because that sounded the most fun. I change timelines, genres, characters, worlds. It's a risky way to build a career, and it wouldn't work unless you kept reading them. I get to do my job the way I want to do it because of you. That's an astonishing thing and I'm so grateful.

I know it's not an easy thing to pick up a book that's not necessarily in your wheelhouse. Even if you enjoyed my Groundhog Day murder mystery novel, I appreciate that you may not be up for the historical haunted ship book, or the sci-fi apocalypse novel. And, yet, you keep taking a leap of faith.

That matters. That hugely matters. So thank you, everybody. Always, and from the bottom of my heart.

Stu

PS. Next time we're doing a more contemporary thriller thing. It's going to be wild. Hopefully I'll see you back here.

ACKNOWLEDGEMENTS

They say there's no *wrong* way to write a book, but *they're* mistaken. There are many wrong ways, and I tried them all. It's taken me three years to write *Last Murder*, because I wrote an entirely different book first, then had to rip it up and start again. Deadlines came and went, other projects were shifted, plans were cancelled, and weekends vanished. I made a lot of people's lives more difficult than they should have been and I truly hate that. Soz everybody.

First amongst the hugely inconvenienced was my wife, Maresa, who has patiently listened to me complain about every character, sentence and paragraph of this book, night after night, for three years. She's punctured my bad moods, indulged my ridiculous exuberance (a good writing day is something to behold) and helped bring clarity to the word fog. It should be impossible to love somebody this much, but time still slows down when I'm near her.

And now to my editors, Alison Hennessey and Shana Drehs, who must surely have worked out the perfect way to kill me by now. I'm not the ideal author. I deliver drafts late, then rip them up while they're being edited. I add in elements they hate, remove the ones they like, then randomly change the plot. I'm a Frankenstein-esque creation of towering ambition and utter ineptitude, but they've never once let their impatience, disappointment or anger reach me. Their feedback has been spot on, delivered kindly, and has always made the book better – even if it didn't stay the same book for very long.

For my agent, Harry Illingworth, I'm now basically a dog that keeps pissing on people's legs before digging up their lawns. His job is to follow behind me, explaining that I'm incontinent but well-meaning. I honestly don't know how he feels about any of this, but he keeps buying me pints so I think it's going well. Thanks man.

The magnificent Amy Donegan, Cristina Arreola and Ben McCluskey are my marketing and publicity dream team. They're the reason people know that I have a book out. They're the reason people are excited and they're the reason people buy them. If you've heard of me it's because of them, and I'm extremely grateful.

I need to thank Faye Robinson, who's my managing editor and is the reason this book is actually a book. I didn't include her in these acknowledgements initially because I'm a moron, and then had to ask her to drop her own name into the copy at the last minute – which was probably quite mortifying and annoying for her. This example is a microcosm of the chaotic way I work, and something she's had to deal with throughout this book. She deserves the hugest of thanks. And while we're thanking people who have to live inside my chaos, I'd like to say 'cheers and sorry' to Lindeth Vasey and Jessica Thelander, my most excellent copyeditors and righters of numerous grammatical, structural and mathematical wrongs.

David Mann designed the cover, which is more beautiful every time I see it. Equally remarkable is Emily Faccini, who drew the map of the island. Seeing what these two come up with for each new book is possibly the most exciting part of the process.

Publishing is an enormous enterprise, with the success or failure of a book living and dying on the talent of hundreds of people I'll never meet. I'm grateful to every single one of you.

And, finally, the hugest of thanks to my mum, dad and sister. Even after all these years, they're the first people who read my books – even those dreadful first drafts. They've always believed in me, even when I didn't. If you've a family like that, you'll go far.

A NOTE ON THE AUTHOR

Stuart Turton's debut novel, *The Seven Deaths of Evelyn Hardcastle*, won the Costa First Novel Award and the Books Are My Bag Readers Award for Best Novel, and was shortlisted for the Specsavers National Book Awards and the British Book Awards Debut of the Year. A *Sunday Times* bestseller, it has been translated into over thirty languages, and has sold over one million copies in the UK and US combined. *The Devil and the Dark Water*, his follow-up, won the Books Are My Bag Readers Award for Fiction and was selected for the BBC Two Book Club, Between the Covers, and Jo Whiley's Radio 2 Book Club. Stuart lives near London with his wife and daughters.

@stu_turton

A NOTE ON THE TYPE

The text of this book is set in Adobe Caslon, named after the English punch-cutter and type-founder William Caslon I (1692–1766). Caslon's rather old-fashioned types were modelled on seventeenth-century Dutch designs, but found wide acceptance throughout the English-speaking world for much of the eighteenth century until replaced by newer types towards the end of the century. Used in 1776 to print the Declaration of Independence, they were revived in the nineteenth century and have been popular ever since, particularly amongst fine printers. There are several digital versions, of which Carol Twombly's Adobe Caslon is one.